THE DARK MOMENT

THE MACMILLAN COMPANY
NEW YORK · BOSTON · CHICAGO
DALLAS · ATLANTA · SAN FRANCISCO

The Dark Moment

by ANN BRIDGE, pseud.
Mary Dolling (Sanders) o'malley

NEW YORK : THE MACMILLAN COMPANY : 1952

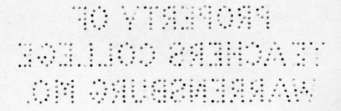

Acknowledgements

THE AUTHOR desires to express her indebtedness and grateful
thanks to the following:

To the Foreign Office, the Admiralty, the War Office, and
the Royal United Services Institution for questions answered
and information supplied; to the officials of the Turkish Foreign Office for assistance and facilities afforded; to *The Times*
newspaper for permission to copy and reprint the wording of
their communiqués; to the Vali of Kastamonu and the Kaimakam of Inebolu for assistance in researches and transport, and
generous help and hospitality; and to the very many friends,
acquaintances, and even strangers, Turkish and otherwise,
without whose detailed personal recollections, so freely and
patiently given, of the Sultan's regime, the War of Independence, and Mustafa Kemal Atatürk this book could not have
been written.

Finally an immense debt is, self-evidently, owed to *The
Aftermath*, the last volume of the Rt. Hon. Winston S.
Churchill's *The World Crisis*, which remains an indispensable
guide through the tangle and confusion of Turkish history from
1914 to 1923.

Note on Pronunciation

IN the modern romanised Turkish spelling introduced by
Mustafa Kemal Atatürk the pronunciation of the Turkish
words most frequently used in this book is as follows:

yali	*pronounced*	yallöh (as in the German *schön*)
dadi	*pronounced*	dadöh (as in the German *schön*)
çarşaf	*pronounced*	charshaf
Eski-şehir	*pronounced*	Eskishehir

In Turkish the i ending *yali* and *dadi* is undotted, but for
convenience it is printed normally here.

The modification sign over a vowel is pronounced approxi-
mately as in German—e.g. in Nilüfer the ü corresponds to the
German *süss*, in Kiösk to the German *schön*.

Part One

Chapter One

"FANNY! Fann*eee*! Where are you?"

No answer. The small dark girl, whose print frock was both torn and dirty, pushed her dusty hair back from her hot forehead with a narrow dirty little hand, and stood listening.

"Fanny!" she called again, with a sharp note of impatience in her voice.

"Come and find me!" another voice called, from far away.

"No. I'm tired. It is too hot for *cache-cache*. I shall sit down"—and she did so.

"Oh, you are slack!"

"I desire to be slack. In hot weather it is nice to be slack. Come out, dji-djim!"—this in a rather coaxing tone.

"Oh very well, lazy!" There was a rather prolonged pause. At last— "I can't get down," the voice called.

"Why not?"

"I'm stuck. Come and help."

Reluctantly, Féridé rose. "Where are you?"

"In the big cedar."

The small girl climbed uphill for some distance till she reached a large cedar, some of whose branches grew out almost from the root. Fanny had scrambled up one of these to where, about twelve feet above the ground, some disease had caused a sort of bush of short dense growth— from this her yellow head and fair flushed pink face stuck out like a big flower. Féridé burst out laughing.

"Oh, la Canaria in its nest! You look so funny."

"It isn't funny—I can't get down."

"But you got up."

"I know—but I can't get down alone."

"What can I do, then?"

"You might fetch Zeynel."

"Oh, it's so far to go down. And he will be so cross to come right up here."

"Then fetch Uncle."

"Your Uncle is with Baba—I can't go to him; you know that."

After some argument Fanny forced the reluctant Féridé to climb a

· 3 ·

few feet up the sloping branch and lie along it, clasping it tightly; Fanny then lowered herself till she could get her feet on her companion's head, and then on her shoulder—scrabbling and sliding, they came to the ground together in a heap.

"Well, that was a silly place to hide," Féridé observed frankly, as they picked themselves up. "I couldn't have found you, ever. And oh, how you have torn your frock!"

"So I have. I am a sight!"

She was. Her face was flushed and dirty, her yellow hair full of dust and pine-needles, her frock quite as dirty as Féridé's, and more torn.

The two little girls were playing up in the koru, the rough wild sort of park, on a steep tilt, which extends uphill behind so many yalis, its big conifers rising out of a tangle of bushes and shrubby aromatic herbs. Paths, considerably overgrown, wound through it—Zeynel, the gardener, didn't bother much about the koru; here and there stone seats stood beside them, or rocks jutted out, on which small green or brown lizards warmed themselves in the hot June sun. Fanny and Féridé moved out from under the cedar to an open slope, where they could see the waters of the Bosphorus gleaming blue below them between the dark shapes of the trees, with a low line of hills opposite; away to their right they could just catch sight of Scutari, the minarets of its fragile beautiful mosque standing up like ivory needles, faintly stained with grey; more in front the white mass of the Palace of Beylerbey, half-hidden in trees, and then the blue sweep of the Bosphorus curving away north-eastward. The scent of thyme—from bushy plants far larger than the creeping thyme of England—was strong in their nostrils, in the hot afternoon sun. Fanny pulled a grass, and chewed it reflectively.

"I do like it here," she said. "It is much nicer than at Madame Kaftanoglou's. Féridé, I think you are a very lucky person.'"

"Do you? Tell me why."

"Because you live in such a lovely place, and because your Grandmother is so frightfully nice—I think she's one of the nicest, most *distinguée* people in the world." (Fanny was, as usual, speaking Turkish, but she used the French word for distinguished.) "And I think the Pasha is wonderful, though I am a little afraid of him."

"I see no reason for being afraid of Baba," said Féridé—"though I agree with you about Niné. But Fanny, before you envy me too much, remember Mademoiselle Marthe! She is *not* so amusing. And Dil Feripé!"

Fanny laughed.

"Poor old dears! They aren't too bad!" She glanced at her watch. "O'ı Féridé, it's getting late! Uncle Henry may be ready. Come on down."

The two children sprang up and scrambled downhill till they came to one of the paved paths, and ran down it; it ended at a narrow iron footbridge, spanning a cutting through which the road from Péra passed up towards Therapia; by means of the footbridge the inhabitants of the yali could reach the koru in privacy, without setting foot on the road itself. As they reached it, Féridé checked with a dismal cry—"My çarşaf! Oh, *where* did I leave it?"

"You had it on as we went up," said Fanny.

"Yes, but I took it off when we began to play. Oh, *where* have I left it, horrible thing?—I tore it, anyhow," she added, with a comical half-vindictive expression on her small face. "But I must find it"—and she began to retrace her steps up the stone-paved path.

"Oh, Féridé, *need* you go back? Can't you send Zeynel to look for it?"

"Chérie, really you are stupid! That would never do. And I can't go in without it—I am over thirteen now, you know." There was a slight note of importance about the last words.

"Oh all right," said Fanny, reluctantly. As they toiled up the path again—"I must say that's a thing I don't envy you, all this bother with çarşafs," she pursued. "It was much nicer last year, when you didn't have to wear one."

"Oh well, everyone has to do it," said Féridé resignedly. "Now—it was about here we began." Her grey eyes roved about.

"There it is," said Fanny—"under that bush." She stooped in, and drew out the shapeless-looking piece of black veiling. "Goodness, you *have* torn it! What will Dil Feripé say?"

They ran down to the bridge again. Some fifty yards beyond its further end a flight of stone steps led steeply down to the house and garden. This last was a long strip between the hill and the sea, shaded by huge magnolias with solid grey trunks and glossy leaves, and slighter Judas-trees; a marble balustrade extended along the water's edge, with marble seats beside it; lawns and sanded path wound and spread between groups of shrubs and beds brilliant with flowers, and at the end furthest from the house water from a fountain with carved marble panels fell into a pool surrounded by a curb of damp-stained stone. This was the harem-lik garden, belonging to the women's or private portion of the house—harem merely means "private"; the steep stony cliff clothed with bushes and creepers, where the hill had been cut away to make space for house and garden alike, screened it completely from the road running through the cutting below the footbridge, and a high wall behind the house on the landward side cut it off from the garden of the selamlik, or public portion, where men were received.

The yali itself was vast, stretching along the water-front for over 150 yards; like all yalis of a respectable age it was built of wood which, unpainted, in the course of a hundred years had taken on the most delicate tones of silvery-grey—the graceful windows with their baroque pediments, the arched loggias and balconies, gained an unimaginable charm from the combination of this exquisite colour and fragile substance with the architectural forms usually associated with the white solidity of stone. For externally there was nothing oriental about the house, no pointed arches or Moorish doorways—it was pure European 18th century building, translated, so to speak, into wood; the one specifically Turkish thing about it was the brick-built hammam or bath-house, topped with little domes, embedded in the great wooden structure. Within, however, the place was rather un-European: a big central hall, running right through the house from the embankment on the water in front (with steps to alight from a boat) to a door giving onto the garden at the back; rooms all round, and a broad graceful staircase rising from the hall to the next floor, where the same arrangement of rooms was repeated—a passage led from the hall to the adjoining selamlik.

This, however, was so to speak the bare bones of a yali, the simplest single unit; in larger houses the unit of central hall, surrounding rooms, and staircase was often repeated once or even twice, with combinations and permutations—in the case of Féridé's enormous family house it was repeated three times, with the variation that at the opposite end to the haremlik garden the great hall ran parallel with the water-front, instead of at right angles to it, and opened on a stone-paved space from which a short drive led up through the selamlik garden to a gate in a high wall, giving onto the main road, which here emerged from the cutting.

From the top of the steps the two small girls could look down on all this. Up by the gate, overshadowed by one of a group of immense plane-trees which filled the end of the selamlik garden and overhung the water, stood a small gate-house with a stone seat beside the door—the abode of the door-keeper; the door-keeper himself, an oldish man, was busily engaged in doling out water, drop by drop, from a delicate copper jug with a long slender spout to some cactuses in pots which stood on the seat. He was, like most of his kind, an Albanian Moslem, magnificently dressed in baggy blue trousers over coarse white woollen stockings, a blue waistcoat or tunic with floating sleeves and richly embroidered in gold folded high across his chest, and bound in round the waist by a flamingly vivid scarf of striped Damascus silk. He wore the usual fez on his head.

"Someone must be here," said Féridé, observing him—"Mahmud Agha has his best scarf on."

"Uncle is here."

"Yes, but he doesn't put on that scarf for your Uncle—he comes so often. Do let us see who it is."

They ran along a narrow path on the cliff edge above the house to where a second flight of steps led down into the selamlik garden: from the top of these they commanded a view of the front door. Sure enough, on the cobbled space in front of it a large shiny car was drawn up; by it stood a tall footman in a neat chauffeur's uniform.

"Oh, that's Javid Bey's car!" Féridé exclaimed. "I know that tall kavass —he's called Ibrahim."

"How do you know?"

"Mahmud Agha told me."

Fanny knew all about Javid Bey, pillar of the Committee of Union and Progress, and now, in the summer of 1914, Minister of Finance.

"What do you suppose he's come about?" she asked.

"Oh, he often comes to see Baba," said Féridé. "He likes to hear his views. Many people wish to hear his views."

Fanny realised quite well that Féridé's father, Murad Zadé Asaf Pasha, was a person of some importance; he had governed a big vilayet, and even since his retirement occupied a certain position. But any speculations on the Finance Minister's visit were cut short by a voice which they now heard, faint but imperative, raised from the other garden. "Féridé! Fanny!"

"There she is!" Féridé exclaimed. "Come on—we must meet it!" She was still flapping the torn çarşaf in her hand, but as they ran back to the other steps she flung it carelessly and unskilfully over her small dark head and person.

At the bottom of the steps a curious figure awaited them among the flower-beds. Dil Feripé was a short, thin, angular woman, with a withered and rather yellow face; she had been nurse to Féridé's mother, and was now getting old. She wore a long skirt down to her ankles and a sub-fusc alpaca jacket, so long and so loose as to be almost a tunic, over a blouse with a high neck—the whole producing a very old-fashioned and even Victorian effect; but—incongruously enough above the Victorian ensemble—a voile scarf draped her head, and across her face below the eyes hung a short piece of pale muslin, the peçe. As the little girls approached her, she let out a shrill torrent of dismay, in the tones of an agitated pea-hen.

"But Féridé! Oh, what a shameless girl, showing your hair! You may burn in Hell for this!"

"There is no one to see but you and Fanny, Dadi," Féridé protested.

"Torn, too!" Dil Feripé grumbled on, as she adjusted the çarşaf with a skilful hand. "Oh, what would your poor Mother say!"

Since Féridé had never known her mother, who had died when she was born, she could hardly reply to this—purely rhetorical—question. They crossed the garden, the dadi still grumbling at their lateness and the state of their frocks, and passed round the end of the house and along a narrow marble terrace between the silver-grey façade and the sea. This was an approach which never failed to entrance Fanny; she had been coming along it for four summers, but it never lost its romantic charm. The central portion of the house was built right out over the water in an immense formal bow—another peculiarity of this particular yali; in the angle between the bow and the main frontage was a door by which they now entered the great cool central hall, with its panelled painted ceiling and painted doors all round. At the further end rose a broad graceful staircase, which in two right-angled bends reached the floor above; up this Féridé now bounded, followed by Fanny, regardless of the poor dadi's shrill shrieks of protest at their dirty and disordered appearance. The staircase emerged at the top onto a hall—it was more than a landing—duplicating the one below, and faintly lit by a curtained window over the stairs; here chairs, and carved and inlaid tables with bulging legs, stood about between sofas against the walls covered in brilliant fabrics; doors led off it on three sides. Féridé flew to one at the end opposite the stairs—as she flung it open, light poured in from the room beyond.

This room, the salon and principal sitting-room of the haremlik, filled the great bow which formed the centre of the yali's façade; its three large windows gave onto the narrow blue of the Bosphorus and the wide blue of the sky above. Across the western window carved perforated wooden shutters were drawn together, excluding the sun, save for small brilliant paillettes of light which fell through the tiny lozenge-shaped openings onto the floor beneath—the other two were unshielded. By the eastern one an old lady sat on a low sofa, working at a piece of embroidery— on a small inlaid table beside her were silks, scissors, and a new French book. Féridé darted across to her, and flung her arms round her neck in an eager hug.

"Niné, we are so late! I am very sorry. I apologise."

The old lady kissed the child gently, then held her away at arm's length.

"Dji-djim! But look at your dress!" Then, seeing Fanny, who had followed more soberly—"Et Fanny! Bonjour, my child."

Fanny had lived long enough in Turkey to know how to behave properly to elderly ladies. She took this one's hand, kissed it, and then laid it lightly against her—rather dirty—forehead.

"Bonjour, Réfiyé Hanim," she said. "I ask your pardon that we are late. It was my fault."

Féridé, who had pulled off her çarşaf and flung it on a chair, began to pour out an explanation.

• 8 •

"We were playing *cache-cache,* and Fanny was up a tree, and couldn't come down—"

"Ah," Réfiyé Hanim interposed quietly, "that explains the state of your dresses—and your hair! But my children, it is time for tea—I think you had better go and make yourselves presentable."

At this point Dil Feripé, whom they had completely outdistanced on the stairs, appeared and lifted up her voice.

"Hanim Effendi, what are we to do with this Féridé? Look at her dress!—her face! And worst of all, when I found them, she had her çarşaf half off, her hair plainly visible! Ah, what would her dear, her excellent Mother have said, to see a child of hers thus?"

Réfiyé Hanim was a woman of great powers, and those powers expressed themselves largely in an immense calm, coupled with an immense benevolence. (She also possessed, but seldom showed, a strong sense of the amusing.) She now raised one hand a very little way—it was the slightest of gestures, but it silenced Dil Feripé.

"Where were you playing *cache-cache?*" she asked Féridé.

"Up in the koru. And Fanny climbed a tree—and her head stuck out —and she looked like the canary she is, in a bush!"—Féridé bubbled out, in a burst of giggling. "But it took a long time to get her down, and then—"

"Yes. Very well. Now, Dil Feripé, take them both to Féridé's room, and change their dresses and make them clean, and then we will have tea." There was an unmatched combination of benevolence and command in her tone. Féridé however lingered to kiss her grandmother once more—when another elderly woman, almost as Victorian in her dress as Dil Feripé, but with no veil of any sort on her iron-grey head, came in. At the sight of Fanny and Feridé, she in turn held up her hands, and burst into horrified exclamations in rapid French.

"Oh, ces enfants! Oh, les petites étourdies!"

"Dil Feripé will take them to get tidy," said Réfiyé Hanim quietly, also in French. "Assez, assez, Féridé—run along with Fanny." As they went off—"Come and sit down, Mademoiselle Marthe," she said pleasantly.

The sofa on which Réfiyé Hanim sat was really a divan, filling the shallow angle between the window and the inner wall, and continuing along under the window itself; there was a similar one in the opposite corner, below the shuttered window which looked towards the west— they were built against the wall, broad, low, gracefully shaped and curved, and upholstered in satiny stripes of prune and gold brocade, with cushions heaped up in the corners: typically Turkish furnishings, and deliciously comfortable. Mademoiselle Marthe did not, however, **sit** on the divan, large as it was; that, and the table by it, constituted the special corner of the mistress of the house, her own undisputed place. The Frenchwoman drew a small white-and-gold Louis Quinze chair up to the little inlaid table, and sat down.

And in the Pasha's house, be it noted, Louis Quinze really meant Louis Quinze. That monarch had presented a complete set of drawing-room furniture—chairs and settees, elegant and fragile, their curves painted in cream and gold, their backs and seats upholstered in sea-green brocade—to the Sultan of his day; but Queen Victoria having subsequently presented a later Sultan with a drawing-room suite characteristic of her reign, the French King's gift had been turned out to make room for it, and became the perquisite of Réfiyé Hanim's father, who had been a Court Chamberlain at the time. The presence of all this French furniture made the big salon at the yali a curious mixture of the oriental and the European. The ceiling, with shallow diamond-shaped panelling painted sea-green, was purely oriental, but the floor, covered in the centre by a huge Savonnerie carpet in pale creams and pinks and blues was purely European, so was the grand piano in one corner; but there were Kayseri rugs under the windows in the bow, and here and there, among the faded French elegance of the furniture, stood those small tables inlaid in mother-of-pearl or pale wood, like the one in Réfiyé Hanim's corner, while more of the maroon and gold divans stretched along the walls between the panelled sea-green doors. The most obviously oriental thing about the room was in fact the walls themselves. They displayed no pictures: instead there were delicate examples of calligraphy, on small square panels richly framed—of gilding on dark wood, or darkly painted on pale or golden grounds—and, where the space between the doors allowed, rich silken embroideries stretched out in oblongs of exquisite colour, texture, and design. Light, fragile, somehow uncertain in its general effect, it was nevertheless an unusually beautiful room, and one that could be seen nowhere but in Istanbul or along the shores of the Bosphorus—where for centuries East and West have, whatever Kipling may have said, met.

Mademoiselle Marthe, then, seated on her little French chair beside the small Turkish table, entered on a pleasantly confidential talk with her employer. She was on the best of terms with Réfiyé Hanim, for whom she had a deep respect. She had come to Turkey thirty years before as governess to Féridé's mother, and apart from a few brief holidays she had lived there ever since, in only the two families: as governess to her first pupil's young sisters for some years, and then to that pupil's own daughter—now married—and to the motherless Féridé. She was completely at home in her foreign surroundings, and had adjusted herself admirably to the Turkish way of life, much of which had her entire approval—*mariages de convenance* and keeping young girls well under one's eye had always seemed to her thoroughly desirable objects, and if she thought the veil possibly an exaggerated means of achieving them, she kept her thoughts to herself. Féridé's mother she had dearly loved, and her desire now to bring the child up as that mother would have wished was as ardent, if more intelligent, as Dil Feripé's own. Old Marthe Chanrion was, for her generation, a fine scholar, with a passion for classical French literature, and a strong sense of elegance, in life as in prose; she had found elegance of life among the Turkish upper classes, and appreciated it. She was by no means a silly woman, in spite of her twitterings over dirty faces and torn frocks—these were just part of the stock-in-trade, as she conceived it, of a high-class French governess in good families. Rather surprisingly, she had learned to speak Turkish really well, a thing which Réfiyé Hanim appreciated very much—so many "Françaises," however cultivated in their own tongue, never reached the point of being able to do more than talk like children or servants in that of their pupils. Also they were often "difficiles" in the household—a bore at meals, hyper-sensitive about their position, and, above all, at odds with the dadis; whereas Mdlle Marthe, partly by her her own force of character, partly, no doubt, owing to her excellent command of the language, had made and maintained for herself an acceptable, and accepted, position. These were valuable qualities, and rightly valued by Réfiyé Hanim.

"Grand Dieu, what had they been doing to get in such a state?" the Frenchwoman now asked.

"Playing hide-and-seek up in the koru—I have not heard all the details yet, but no doubt I shall," said Réfiyé Hanim, with a quiet smile.

"Sans doute! She is very wild, this little Fanny; like all English girls, du reste"—with a suitable sigh.

"Yes, and she makes Féridé wild too—but she is a charming girl, all the same," replied Réfiyé Hanim, who believed in answering the unspoken as well as the spoken word.

"Oh Madame, there you are very right, if I may say so," said Mdlle Marthe seriously. "She *does* make Féridé wild, certainly; but there are worse things than wildness! Companionship is good for Féridé, and this is a wholesome one; there is no silly talk, or gossiping, or whispering, with the little Canaria."

Fanny Pierce's yellow head, rather beaky little nose, darting bright glance and swift movements, as well as her constant bubble of chatter, had earned her the nick-name of "The Canary" in the Pasha's household when she first appeared in it four years before; it was in fact the Pasha himself who had called her so originally. And while Mdlle Marthe and Réfiyé Hanim talked in the salon, the Canary and her small friend were being tidied up in Féridé's room. From the hall at the head of the stairs doors opened right and left onto two broad passages, from which a succession of lesser rooms at the back of the house opened out —Féridé's was along the left-hand corridor, between Dil Feripé's and Mdlle Marthe's. It was a pretty little room, gaily done up in blue and white cretonnes; cool, and rather dark, since it gave onto that bushy cliff only a few feet away; the window was closely curtained in muslin. Here Dil Feripé, now assisted by two kalfas, aged attendants as old and as Victorian-looking as herself, was washing, brushing, and combing the two girls with a flow of rather comminatory comment. Fanny, accustomed to doing all these things for herself—whether at school, or in her Uncle's house at Oxford or, as at present, in Madame Kaftanoglou's pension—thought all this elaborate waiting-on very amusing; but she was quite used to it, and submitted cheerfully to being cleaned, arranged, and dressed in a clean print frock of Féridé's. It was rather too long for her; though she was a year older than her friend, she was—as she was to remain—small, whereas Féridé's legs were already as lanky as a young colt's. At last their appearance satisfied the three old women, and they returned to the salon, followed by their attendants. Réfiyé Hanim asked Dil Feripé to tell the servants to bring tea, and then put away her work and slowly rose.

"Where do we have tea today, Niné?" Féridé asked.

"On the east balcony, my child; there will not be sun there."

On either side of the great projecting bow in the centre of the house were two long deep balconies or loggias, with arches supported on slender pillars rising from a balustrade on the seaward side; to reach the eastern one from the salon the party had to pass through the dining-room, a long low apartment where the light filtered in, dim and subdued, through the French windows from the curved arches of the loggia beyond. Living in a climate of blinding sunshine, Turks generally prefer a dim light in their rooms, and half-closed shutters or lowered jalousies are the rule; Réfiyé Hanim's habit of sitting in the full light in the salon was quite exceptional, and her son sometimes remonstrated gently with her about it—she never argued with him, and would tell one of the kalfas to close the shutters—but next day she would be found again sitting in her corner with her book or her embroidery, in the full light.

Out on the balcony they took their places at two small tables—took the places, that is, that Réfiyé Hanim, with a certain gentle formality, indicated to each. Standing as she did so, she was an imposing figure—in the long straight tunic-like coat of *écru* brocade, fresh and impeccable, that she always wore, over some lacy thing of which the folds appeared at her throat. Fanny had never seen her in anything else, and wondered sometimes how many of them she possessed, so fresh and uncreased they always were! A piece of cream tulle was lightly arranged over her hair, which still had hardly a thread of silver in it; her skin, despite some wrinkles, was clear and fine, and her brows drew down above her eyes with a look of concentration that was strangely repeated in her grandchild's small fresh face. She summoned Fanny to a chair on one side of her, Féridé to one on the other; Mdlle Marthe sat opposite, and the kalfas, joined by two more, drew up to a second table.

Fanny loved having tea on the balcony. At the further end a sort of grotto of rocks had been constructed, where water fell musically into a miniature pool; ferns smothered this grotto, green creepers climbed the rocks and twined themselves round the nearest pillars of the loggia; below, the unpredictable currents of the Bosphorus sent small waves slapping against the embankment in front of the house, so that to those who sat there, water spoke with two voices at once; the silvery curve of the carven Roman arches framed pictures of blue water, blue sky, and the low gentle outline of the hills of Chamlidja between the two. It was, Fanny always felt, a magical place—and the magic was somehow not lessened by the delicious pastries, the sweet cakes rich with nuts and honey, and the jams—grape jam, fig jam, rose-leaf jam—which one consumed there, sipping water to relieve the almost unbearable sweetness of these exotic conserves.

Today, however, her tea was cut rather short—a maid-servant appeared to say that the Doctor Effendi was ready to leave, and was waiting. Fanny sprang up, with her usual impetuosity—thanked Réfiyé Hanim, kissing her hand as before, and said goodbye formally to Mdlle Marthe and all five old maids.

"Your hat, Fanny—do not forget your hat," said Mdlle Marthe.

"Oh no—thank you. I left it in Féridé's room; may I go and get it?" she asked her hostess.

"Certainly, my child."

Féridé, like all the others, had risen to say goodbye.

"May I go with Fanny to get her hat, Niné?"

"Yes, run—but come back at once."

The two girls ran off together.

"Shall you come tomorrow?" Féridé asked.

"If Uncle brings me. I do not know what his plans are."

"Oh, do come! I hope you will come. It is so *very* nice when you are here," exclaimed Féridé, kissing her warmly.

"I love coming," said Fanny truly. "Goodbye, dji-djim."

"And today we did not sing! I have a new song that Ahmet has taught me, that you must learn."

"A folk-song?"

"Yes. Oh, why must you go?"

· 13 ·

"I must—you know I must. Remain with God"—and Fanny ran out. The maid was waiting on the landing to escort her downstairs, but with a nod of thanks Fanny ran down alone. She knew her way perfectly— through a door at the foot of the stairs out into a covered way at the back of the house; this was much quicker than being escorted by the maid through the whole series of corridors, rooms, and lobbies which circumnavigated the male part of the dwelling, leading at last to a door giving onto the taşlik, the paved court at the main entrance—and she hated to keep her uncle waiting. But when she reached the open air she found that she need not have hurried. The Pasha and her uncle were walking up and down beside the balustraded sea-wall, deep in conversation, passing from the shadow of the great plane-trees at the further end into the shadow of the magnolias near the house, Dr. Pierce's panama and the Pasha's red fez both catching the light as they crossed the patch of sunlight between the two. The Finance Minister's car had gone. Fanny hesitated to disturb them, but she wanted her uncle to know that she was there; so she crossed to the sea-wall, when they were at the further end, and sat on the parapet swinging her feet. As they approached her, still deep in talk, she could hear what they said.

"My dear Pasha, of course I understand your fear of Russia—we should fear her, if we lived where you live," her uncle was saying. They noticed her then, and came to a halt a few paces from where she sat. "But I don't trust the Germans any more than the Russians, you know," Dr. Pierce went on. "I think His Excellency is biased—their military competence has dazzled him. But military skill isn't the only thing; morals count, even in politics."

"Ah, morals! The English always talk about morals!"

"We find it so practical to have them," said Dr. Pierce drily. "All this talk about perfidious Albion is really only an expression of envy at the way the English seem to make morality pay!"

The Pasha laughed, rather unwillingly—then he brushed morality aside. "You see that His Excellency is anxious, and no wonder. No one knows when this thing will begin."

"I expect His Excellency has some idea," said Dr. Pierce, even more drily. "Unless his dear friends want it, it need never begin at all."

"But do you know when *they* will be ready? One was promised for this month, and the other a little later. Everything hinges on that, for us—once we have them, we are safe. You see that I speak in confidence," said the Pasha, who had now forgotten Fanny's presence—there was no mistaking the urgency of his tone. "And you have no conception how our people pinched and scraped—the poorest!—to raise the money for them," he ended, almost wistfully.

• 14 •

"My dear Pasha, I have a very good idea! You forget that I was here in 1911 and 1912, when the subscriptions were open," said Dr. Pierce. "But seriously, how should I know anything about that matter? I don't move in Government circles, or ship-building circles either. Oxford is totally ignorant of such things!"

Again the Pasha gave his courteous, half-unwilling little laugh. "Ah well," he said. He now noticed Fanny, and went over to her; she sprang down off the wall at his approach.

"Eh, la Canaria! And what mischief have you been up to?" he asked, addressing her in French.

"I climbed a tree and tore my frock, Excellency."

"Oh—well—that is a form of amusement like another, I suppose," he said, turning again to Dr. Pierce, with a smile. "Come again, soon," he said, taking his friend's arm affectionately; "I have something new to show you—a lovely piece of Izzet's work, that my dealer in Broussa sent me only yesterday; but with that unexpected visit from the Minister, I lacked the opportunity to show it to you."

"Izzet's, eh?" said Dr. Pierce, "I should like to see that."

"Well, come and do so! Tomorrow I am occupied, but do come the day after."

"Thank you, Pasha—I will."

"And bring this little person, this yellow bird," said the Pasha, patting Fanny's head. "To tear more dresses with Féridé, eh?"

"No, Excellency, I hope not—but I want to learn Ahmet's new folk-song."

"Oh, so Ahmet has a new folk-song! You see, my friend, you are turning all my family into students of folk-lore, as well as myself," said the Pasha to Dr. Pierce, smiling. He was a tallish man, very spare, with a dark, severe, rather sombre face, and altogether the air of one much accustomed to command; when he smiled, however, the severe expression changed into one of great charm. He walked with his guests the short distance to the gate, talking now of Turkish popular poetry; Dr. Pierce slipped a tip into the hand of the gloriously dressed Mahmud Agha, who had finished watering his cactuses, and stood in a respectful attitude holding open one wing of the door; with a final farewell the Englishman and Fanny passed out, and the high door closed behind them.

Out in the road Dr. Pierce looked at his watch.

"Half-past six," he said. "We shall just miss the next ferryboat. Are you tired, or shall we walk?"

"Oh, let's walk! I'm not a bit tired."

"We might pick up a carriage," said Dr. Pierce, glancing up and down the road.

"No, let's walk. It's not hot any more."

Dr. Pierce often felt (as well he might) that if a bachelor had suddenly to be left with a child on his hands, to bring up as best he could, he himself was in luck to be left with one as sensible, as healthy, and as accommodating as his niece. A child who was delicate or stupid, or fretful or exacting would have been a terrible trial—in fact impossible. But Fanny was always well, never tired, and seemed to manage her own side of her small life excellently: from the outset, if she needed such things as dresses, clothes, or shoes, she asked him for the money she thought she would require at the beginning of term, and made her purchases with the help of one or other of her schoolmistresses; in the holidays, she mended her own things fairly neatly, or caused someone else to mend them if they were beyond her powers—these last two summers she had even taken to darning his socks and sewing buttons on his shirts. He always took her away from school when it suited him to start for Turkey, i.e., for the whole of the long vacation, despite the protests of the authorities—these he ignored, and Fanny was delighted. She kept herself amused—how, he didn't exactly know—during the many hours of each day when he was at work; he knew that she diligently practised writing the Turkish script, at which she had become sufficiently accomplished even to do some transcribing for him now and then, and he heard her tinkling away sometimes on the indifferent piano at the pension; she borrowed books in French from Féridé, too. However she did it, she always seemed to be occupied and contented, and when he was not at work she was a very pleasant little companion—one could talk quite rationally to her.

As they walked along the road now, under the shadow of the plane-trees—"What is this new song of Ahmet's?" he asked.

"I haven't heard it yet, Uncle—Féridé only told me that he'd got one just as I was leaving."

"I wonder where he got it," Dr. Pierce speculated.

"At the Military College, I expect—he said last time that there are some cadets there from the Eastern provinces now, and he hoped to get some new songs and tales from them."

"He's a good boy, Ahmet," said Dr. Pierce. "It seems a pity he should be a soldier, with his brains."

"Don't soldiers need brains?"

"Well, not so much as scholars, and a different sort," said Dr. Pierce, with a faint grin. "I always wonder why the Pasha, who's got so much taste for scholarship, should want to make a soldier of a boy like that."

"He didn't—he wanted him to be a diplomat, only Ahmet insisted on being a soldier," said Fanny promptly.

"And how do you know that?"

"Well, partly Féridé told me; partly I heard Réfiyé Hanim and Mdlle Marthe talking about it two years ago, when it was being settled; and partly, Ahmet said so himself."

"Well, that's pretty categorical," said the Doctor, again with that grin. He thought, not for the first time, how much more close and intimate Fanny's knowledge of the Pasha's family life was than his own. As men, they had been friends for years, freely discussing matters of scholarship, and sometimes of politics, but Fanny had twiddled her way, in all simplicity, into the very heart of this Turkish household.

"Uncle, what did Murad Zadé Asaf Pasha mean when he asked you when 'they' would be ready?" Fanny asked presently.

"When what?" Dr. Pierce said absently—he had been thinking about Ahmet and his father, and wasn't paying attention.

"He asked you when two things would be ready, that he said the poor people had subscribed for," said Fanny, with her usual accuracy; "he said one had been promised for this month, and one for later on."

The Doctor's brow darkened.

"Oh, that," he said, almost irritably. "That fellow Enver will ruin this nation before he's done—he and his German ideas!"

"But what are 'they'?" Fanny persisted.

"'They' are two battleships that we are building for the Turks," said Dr. Pierce—Fanny thought that he said it rather grimly.

Chapter Two

WHEN Fanny had gone, and tea was over at the yali, Réfiyé Hanim went down to walk in the big garden with the fountain, which was allocated to the haremlik, the "private" side of the house. Féridé accompanied her; it was an understood thing—well understood, that is to say, by Mdlle Marthe—that the reading of Racine or Mme de Sévigné which normally filled the time between the *gouter* and the evening meal should wait on the old lady's pleasure in her grandchild's company. They walked together along the sanded paths, the old woman and the very young girl, whose attentive eyebrows were so alike, Réfiyé Hanim noting the progress of the flowers bedded out by Zeynel, and of the shrubs which she herself had caused to be planted more than sixty years before, and commenting on them aloud.

Presently—"Niné," Féridé said, as they sat down on one of the marble seats close to the little lapping waves, "Javid Bey came to see Baba this afternoon—did you know?"

"No, I did not. I thought Fanny's Uncle was there. How do you know that?"

"Because as we came down from the koru we could see Mahmud wearing his best scarf, so we went to look; and there was the car, and that big kavass of Javid Bey's, Ibrahim—I knew him at once."

"You did not go down into the garden of the selamlik, Féridé?"

"Oh, certainly not, Niné—only to the top of the steps; one can see from there."

"So," said the old lady, thoughtfully. Her thoughts were on the inevitability, in feminine life, of this gossiping curiosity about all contacts with the outside world; and also on the possible reasons for the Finance Minister's call on her son. Féridé had told Fanny, airily, that Ministers often came to see her father, "to hear his views"—but Réfiyé Hanim knew that these visits usually coincided with happenings of some sort. After a while—"Let us go in," she said; "you must have your reading with Mdlle Marthe."

They entered, crossed the hall, and started to mount the stairs, but after a couple of steps the old lady stopped, her hand against the wall. "Go up and ask Mdlle Marthe to come to me for a moment—here," she said.

Féridé sprang away; Réfiyé Hanim stood still, and pressed her other hand to her breast—then very slowly and carefully she turned round, went down the two steps again, and seated herself on an inlaid chair. She was sitting there, her hand still at her heart, when Mdlle Marthe came down.

"My good Marthe, bring me my drops."

Mdlle Marthe's old face was full of concern.

"It is the heart again, Madame?"

"Yes—but nothing unusual. Only I will have my drops, I think, before I go upstairs." "Do not mention it," she added, as the Frenchwoman hastened away.

In a few moments Mdlle Marthe was back again, with a small glass— Réfiyé Hanim drank the contents and sat quietly, while the other watched her with an anxious face. At last—"That is better," the old lady said. "Thank you. Let us go up."

"Are you able? Shall I not fetch Dil Feripé?"

"No, thank you—she would talk so much!" said Réfiyé Hanim, with a half-smile. "With your arm I can manage very well."

Slowly they ascended the stairs, and Mdlle Marthe steered her employer to her corner in the salon.

"My good Marthe, be so kind as to half-close the shutters."

Marthe did so. She knew why the shutters were to be closed; the Pasha usually came up about this time, and if the light was dim, he would notice nothing.

"It was very hot today," she said.

"Yes, it was. It is only the heat—that always affects me. Thank you, my friend. Go to Féridé now."

Soon after Mdlle Marthe had gone to join her pupil the Pasha came in, entering by the door from the dining-room, which served as a sort of neutral zone between the two parts of the house. He came up to his mother with a manner of great respect—bowed over her hand, kissed it, and asked, "How is your health, Ané?"

"By the goodness of God, I am very well, my son," the old lady replied. This was always his form of greeting, and her reply was invariably the same, even when, as now, she was not well at all. The Pasha drew up a chair and sat down near her; the room was becoming dim and shadowy, with the half-closed shutters; asking her permission, he lit a cigarette. They talked rather desultorily at first. Réfiyé Hanim wished to hear about Javid Bey's visit, but was too discreet to ask a question directly—however when the Pasha presently mentioned the Izzet piece she saw her chance of referring to at least one of his visitors, and asked if Dr. Pierce had admired it.

"He did not see it," the Pasha replied.

"No?"

"No. We were going through some transcriptions that he has received recently of some poems of old Fuyuli of Baghdad—most interesting; one or two were new to him, and to me. He will have to see the originals, of course, to be sure that they are genuine." He paused for some moments; she waited. "And then," he went on, "we were interrupted." He paused again, looking across the shadowy room.

"A pleasant interruption, I hope?" she asked.

He turned to her, and spoke in an altered tone.

"Javid Bey came."

"Oh, indeed." Now that the fact was admitted, discretion could be relaxed a little. "He had business to discuss? But what about Dr. Pierce?"

"He knows Dr. Pierce. And I am not *sure* that he had any specific matter to discuss. But I could see that he was anxious—and Ané, I am anxious too."

"Why, my son?"

The Pasha stretched his long thin legs out in front of him, and slowly lit a fresh cigarette. He seldom, from habit and tradition, talked politics with his mother; but when he did he could rely on the two ideal qualities in a listener—perfect sympathy, and complete discretion.

"This affair between Russia and Germany," he began, thoughtfully— "that is always the preoccupation. It *must* come—but when?" He blew out smoke, and the pale blue cloud, in the darkened room, seemed itself a question-mark.

"My son, you know my ignorance. But—should that concern *us*? My Father often said that it was England who always protected us from Russia. What have we to do with Germany's quarrels?"

The Pasha stirred in his chair.

"Ah, there you have it!" he said. "Formerly, yes, it was so. But seven years ago England made a Convention with Russia, and now we no longer know where we are—except that we have a frontier, of land and of water, with Russia a thousand miles long! That always remains. And so whoever is Russia's enemy is, potentially, our friend."

The old lady considered this. It agitated her a little; she put her hand up to her heart, automatically—and then put it down again.

"But if Russia and Germany went to war, should we be involved? If we were, could Germany protect us? And *would* she?"

The Pasha moved his hands.

"I wish I knew! That is what Dr. Pierce said, that one cannot trust the Germans. But you know what Enver Pasha is—he was trained there, and he believes in them. And von Wangenheim is very clever."

The old lady sat thinking, and then spoke again.

"But my son, are we committed in any way? And are they?"

The Pasha once more blew out one of those questioning clouds of smoke.

"Ané, this is entirely secret," he said. "Naturally Javid Bey did not touch on it today, in the Doctor's presence. But I have reason to believe that if Germany and Russia go to war, and Germany succeeds—which I think she undoubtedly would; there I agree with Enver Pasha—we have been promised a free hand in the Caucasus."

"And what would that involve?"

"That we could march in and take the territory up to the Caspian. After all, it is our people who live there—by race, by language."

"But are we *committed* to do this?"

"Ané, it would be right, I believe. After all, those lands are lived in by our own people—and you know what we have lost in this century already, of alien lands! So much in Europe—and Tripoli."

"And do you know when?" Réfiyé Hanim asked, slowly.

"No. Nor can we control that, as I see it. That is what makes me anxious. For us it would be fatal to be involved in a war with Russia until we have command of the Black Sea, and we shall not have that till England delivers to us the *Reshadieh* and the other."

"What are they?" Réfiyé Hanim asked. (It was exactly the same question that Fanny had put, a little earlier, to Dr. Pierce.)

"The two battleships, that are being built for us in England. The *Reshadieh* is promised for this month."

"This month! May Allah in his goodness preserve us! And can Enver Pasha persuade the Germans to wait till we have *both* these ships before they start their war?"

"Ah, Ané—as usual you see the crux! That is just what I do not know."

At about the time that this conversation was taking place at the yali Dr. Pierce and Fanny arrived at their boarding-house; they had after all met a carriage on the road, and taken it. Madame Kaftanoglou's establishment was a modest and inexpensive place of the pension type. It stood between the road and the sea, one of a row of tall structures of the same fragile wooden baroque as the Pasha's house, but without a garden; Dr. Pierce and Fanny had rooms in front, looking out over the water; Fanny's had a loggiaed balcony that was a miniature edition of the one at the yali, and it was here that she spent most of her time. From it she could watch the whole life of the Bosphorus going on: the ferries going up to Therapia or down towards Istanbul, the big steamers that came in from the Black Sea, out of sight round the bend beyond Büyük-dere; the caïques with their curved prows and huge sails, painted in light blues and greens, shooting across to Beykos on the opposite shore, or loading and unloading on the embankment just above. And at all hours of the day, what she could never be tired of watching, the Levantine Shearwaters, the "Lost Souls," skimming to and fro across the water, barely a foot above the surface—a black flock when their backs were towards you, a flock of gleaming silvery shapes when they turned in unison and showed their white under-sides.

As always on returning to the pension, Fanny at once made her way to the balcony, to see what was going on among all these objects so familiar to her—remembering that it would soon be supper-time she went in again, changed her shoes, washed her hands, and still drying them on the towel went out to watch a caïque which was struggling up against the current towards Büyükdere. At that moment her uncle joined her, a bundle of papers in his hand.

"Fanny, was it tomorrow the Pasha said we were to go again?"

"No, the day after."

"Oh—well, we can't go then, either," Dr. Pierce said, sitting down on one of the two shabby wicker chairs with which the balcony was furnished.

"Why not, Uncle?" Fanny asked, but without allowing any of her disappointment to creep into her voice.

"I've had a whole heap of stuff come in, from Broussa—it will all have to be gone through, and I expect some of it must be copied. It's at least three days' work."

"I can copy some for you, can't I?"

"I expect you can—that will be a good thing."

"And you must write to the Pasha—and I can put in a note for Féridé."

"Yes. We'll do that tonight, and send them first thing." But he sat without moving, looking out at the quiet view—at Beykos opposite, a little town of dark weather-stained wooden houses with white staring windows, like eyes, lying in a glen among trees, its mosque a white pearl, with a white minaret pointing up among the black pointed shapes of cypresses.

"There's another thing, Fanny," Dr. Pierce went on.

"Yes, Uncle?"

"You know those transcriptions that came the day before yesterday?"

"The Fuzuli ones from Erzerum?" Fanny was, as usual, completely *au fait* with her uncle's work.

"Yes, I showed them to the Pasha today. Two or three of them are quite new to him—so they are to me. If they're genuine, they're rather important. But it's impossible to tell if they are genuine without seeing the originals."

Fanny flung her towel through the open door.

"Oh, how lovely! So shall we go to Erzerum? I've always wanted to go to those Eastern vilayets. How do we go?—steamer to Trebizond, then on?"

"Steady, steady!" Dr. Pierce said. "I don't know if I can take you, Fanny. I shall have to telegraph to this man anyhow, and see if he will let me see the originals—and I must find out about steamers to Trebizond. And the travelling will be pretty rough. I think it might be best if you stayed here—it's not a cheap journey, either," he added. "Should you be all right here alone, for ten days or so, do you think? You're over fourteen now."

Fanny swallowed a little.

"Oh yes, of course I shall be *quite* all right," she said. "Only it would be *so* lovely to see Trebizond and Erzerum—if it weren't too expensive. I really wouldn't be any trouble—at least I'd try not to be."

Dr. Pierce ruffled up his hair.

"No, Fanny, I don't think you'd better come this time," he said at length. "You'll be a good girl about it, I know."

Down in the house a bell tinkled out, rather dismally.

"That'll be supper," said Dr. Pierce. "You all ready? Come on, then."

At supper they learned that their landlady's son was driving in to Péra that evening; accordingly they went upstairs the moment the meal was over, and wrote their notes quickly, for him to drop at the yali on his way. Fanny was sorry at this need for haste—she took a pride in writing to Féridé in Turkish, but she could not do that with any great speed as yet, so she scribbled a few lines in French—"Not tomorrow, nor the day after, nor the day after that—what a long time! But on the fourth day, my *joujou*, I shall be with you." And then, like the good child she was, she settled down under the lamp at the big table in her uncle's room to do some copying for him, her yellow head bent over the work, her little beaky nose almost touching the paper—poking her tongue out, now and then, as she concentrated on a particularly difficult character.

The replies to their notes came next day. The Pasha would be delighted to see Dr. Pierce on Thursday, and politely regretted the postponement. Féridé wrote in Turkish, and at greater length.

"My two eyes! How sad is this! And Dil Feripé was making the maids hurry with washing and mending your frock, to have it ready for tomorrow. Anyhow it will await you when you do come. Come soon, dji-djim; I miss you very much. Let the hours hasten.

"Excuse me—I must stop; Niné wants me. I embrace you every day!

Féridé."

Meanwhile Dr. Pierce had ascertained by telephone that there was a boat for Trebizond on the Friday, and had sent a messenger to take his ticket. He and Fanny worked hard, at opposite ends of the big table which he had bought himself three or four years ago and installed in the pension, since the rather gim-crack furniture provided was useless for his purpose. He had an interview with the Greek woman, who willingly undertook to look after Fanny while he was away. "Ten days at most," he told her. He had urged his correspondent in Erzerum by telegram to come down and meet him at Trebizond, to shorten his absence.

At last, on Thursday, they arrived again at the Pasha's. Fanny sped off to the haremlik, while Dr. Pierce was ushered into the selamlik proper. The main apartment in this was an enormous room with a stone pavement, on the ground floor, with a double staircase rising at the further end to a landing above with closed doors leading to other parts of the house; a small fountain played in the centre. Handsome but rather uncomfortable highbacked chairs stood formally round the walls; slightly more comfortable ones were grouped round tables which stood here and there about the room. Into one of these Dr. Pierce sank gratefully; it had been hot walking up from the ferry, and this great stonefloored room, with its tinkling fountain and the subdued light from the windows on either side of the entrance door, was deliciously cool. After a moment or two the Pasha entered from a door behind the staircase; coffee, that indispensable preliminary to conversation in Turkey, was at once brought. Dr. Pierce apologised for postponing his call, and explained the reason—"A whole batch of stuff came up from a friend of mine at Broussa, and I had to go through it all, and transcribe what I needed, as I am going away; I don't like leaving that sort of thing about."

"You are going away?" the Pasha asked, surprised.

"Oh, only to Trebizond, to see those Fuzuli originals—if they are originals. I telegraphed to Mirza Ali Temel at Erzerum, and he has agreed to bring them down to the coast for me to see, to save time. I ought to be back in ten days. But that is why I had to deal with the things from Broussa immediately."

"Is there much of interest?" his host enquired.

"More so to me than to you!" Dr. Pierce said, smiling at his friend. "You are very polite about my folk-lore researches, Pasha, but I know you think them hardly worthy of serious attention."

"No, on the contrary, I think them certainly of interest, but I am a little surprised that a scholar of your eminence should give so much time to something that is—well, purely popular."

"Well, I'll let you into a secret," said Dr. Pierce. "Up till this year they have been just a side-line; in England, you know, folk-lore and folk-songs have been a matter of interest for a long time, so it was natural that I should be interested in such examples as I came across here. And then I became fascinated, I admit—surely I've told you this—by their relationship to classical poetry: the same allusiveness, the same symbolism, the same nostalgic element, in both. So I collected what I could, for my own amusement. But last winter, at home, I met a very intelligent publisher at one of our College dinners; we got onto the subject of folk-lore, and I mentioned that Turkish folk-lore was peculiarly fascinating—he was interested, and asked if I could let him see some examples in translation. So in the Christmas holidays Fanny and I set to work—I was too busy to tackle it in term time, and alone—and ran off quite a bunch of translations."

"Your *Niece* made translations?"

"Oh yes—Fanny's quite up to that, with simple stuff," said Dr. Pierce breezily. "I check them over, of course."

"What a remarkable girl that is!" said the Pasha. "Making translations for publishers—extraordinary!"

"Oh, they weren't difficult," said Dr. Pierce—to his scholar's mind there was nothing odd about a fourteen-year-old girl translating simple folk-tales from the Turkish. "But when we'd got them typed I sent them to this man, and he was delighted; he wants a lot more, and then he will publish a book of them."

"Now what about that Izzet piece?" Dr. Pierce went on. "I should so much like to see that."

"Ah yes—it is in my study. Will you come and look at it?"

They rose—the man-servant who stood all the time in attendance at the far side of the room opened one of two doors at the further end, and bowed as they went out. They passed through several smaller rooms, all opening out of one another, and entered the study. This was under the salon, in the bow, and was built right out over the water, but it was a much more oriental room than the one above. The low ceiling, rather heavily panelled in an elaborate diaper pattern, was painted all over in geometric designs in bright reds and blues and umbers; divans covered in thick woolen stuffs, equally brilliant, and vivid with small sharp designs, ran round the wall. But the chief ornaments were a large number of framed specimens of calligraphy, square or oblong; their curious sweeps and curves, combined with the profusion of patterns on the divans and ceiling made the whole room almost prick the eye with shapes and colours. The only modern—or European—things in it were the Pasha's writing-desk and chair, a chaise-longue by one window, and a large table standing near another. Telling the man-servant to open the shutters, the Pasha opened a drawer in his desk, and drew forth his treasure. Dr. Pierce took it and held it to the light; held it near him, held it away, with all the motions of expertise.

"Beautiful! I've never seen a better specimen of his."

While the two men stood together, examining and pointing out special merits and perfections to one another, perfectly content, Fanny and Féridé, upstairs, tucked up on a divan under the window of a smaller room beyond the salon were chattering away to their hearts' content.

"But what was this work that took you so long?"

"Oh, a great many pieces that came in from Broussa, from a friend of Uncle's, who collects for him."

"Folk-lore pieces? Are they good?" There was no politeness about Féridé's interest in folk-lore—her little friend had thoroughly infected her with her own enthusiasm.

"Some were—two were delicious. But you see," Fanny went on, "the man wanted them back, and as Uncle is going away, he had to finish them first."

"Going away? When? Where to? *You* go also?"

"No, I *don't!* Oh and dji-djim, I *did* so want to! You mustn't mind that I did—it is only for about ten days. But he is going to Trebizond, and perhaps even to Erzerum, if this Mirza Something doesn't come down to Trebizond with the things. And I've never been on the Black Sea, and I've always wanted to see Trebizond, and above all Erzerum."

This was an enthusiasm that Féridé did not share. To Turks under the Ottoman Empire there was Istanbul, where all life, culture, and interest were centred; there were the yalis up the Bosphorus for summer, and perhaps the vineyard houses out in the hills behind Chamlidja; there were picnics and excursions to beauty-spots, or to springs where the water was of a special deliciousness. But exploration of remote parts of the country as such had little or no appeal.

"Well, my sweet-meat, I am sorry for you, if you wanted to go. But what shall you do while your Uncle is away?"

"Oh, I shall stay at the pension."

Féridé was shocked.

"Stay there alone? But you have no maid, no dadi! No, Fanny, this you *cannot* do."

"Oh, I don't mind. I'm alone a lot of the time anyhow. Only I shan't be able to come here—that's the pity."

Féridé's small face took on an expression of concentrated resolution; she spoke with decision.

"Come here is exactly what you *will* do! You will stay here with us. No, you need not argue—you would like it, I should love it, Niné would wish it. I shall settle it with her now, this instant." She sprang off the divan. "I shall have you *here*, with me, for ten whole days!" And she ran off into the salon.

"Niné," she exclaimed, pouring out her words in a rush, "here is a plan! Fanny's Uncle has to go away to Trebizond, for ten days or more, and he cannot take this poor Fanny. But how can she stay alone at the pension? I want her to come here—I should be so *very* happy to have her. May she come? Oh, I am sure you will say yes, Niné-djim," she said coaxingly.

"When does Dr. Pierce go?" Réfiyé Hanim asked.

"Tomorrow! So we must settle it now."

"And does he agree?"

"He does not know—I have only just heard of it. But if you say yes he *will* agree, and so will Baba."

This was indisputably true; Réfiyé Hanim fondled the child's head.

"Very well, my child; it shall be so, if her Uncle agrees. It will be pleasant for you."

"Niné, thank you *very* much." She gave her a hug. "I shall tell her!" —and she flew into the next room.

"There! I said so! It is all arranged. Oh, how glad I am!"

"We shall just have to ask Uncle, though I'm sure he'll be pleased," said Fanny.

"Niné will arrange that," said Féridé. And in fact Réfiyé Hanim had already left the salon and gone to her boudoir to write a note.

A moment later the door opened, and a tall young man in uniform put his head round it. Féridé flung herself at him.

"Ahmet, oh Ahmet! How nice."

"Where is everyone, small mouse? There is nobody in the salon," Ahmet said, kissing his little sister affectionately.

"Niné was there a moment ago. My Father is . . ."

"In his study, looking at pieces of calligraphy with the Doctor—this I saw as I came, and left the savants to their learning!" Ahmet said.

Then he caught sight of Fanny, and greeted her rather politely and formally. He was a good-looking creature of about 23, with Féridé's grey eyes, but with a good deal less character and decision in his face.

"But I have brought Fuad with me," he went on.

"Oh, how nice. Where is he?" Fuad was a very favourite cousin, a little younger than Ahmet—as children they had been more or less brought up together, he, Ahmet, and Etamine.

"Here I am! May I come in?" called a merry voice, and Fuad too stepped through from the salon. He was a short, round-faced, cheerful creature, very dark.

"You know Fanny, don't you?" said Féridé.

"Of course I know Mdlle Fanny! How-do-you doh?" he said in English.

"Oh, and *now*, Ahmet, you can sing Fanny the new song! She wants so much to hear it!"

"It is not a *new* song—it is one of the very old ones, I believe. But of course I will sing it for Fanny. Let us go into the other room—a friend of mine called Orhan has made an accompaniment for the piano for it."

"Orhan? Who is Orhan?"

"As I say, a friend of mine, at the College. He is musical, and when I sang him the air, he composed this setting. *C'est un beau type*," Ahmet said.

"And you have brought it? Oh, come then!"

As they went into the salon by one door, Réfiyé Hanim entered by the other; Ahmet went up, bowed and kissed her hand, and enquired after her health. The business of greetings was always rather formal and protracted.

"And now," Ahmet said when they were over, and Fuad had also kissed the old lady's hand, "this little tyrant Féridé wishes me to sing a song for la Canaria to hear. You permit it?"

"But of course. I should like to hear it myself."

Ahmet spun the music-stool down to a height suited to his tall figure, placed a sheet of music-paper on the rack, and began to play some long slow chords—then he lifted up his voice in the song:

> I launched my falcon in flight
> From the one fortress to the other fortress—
> But waking alone in the night
> I found the darkness full of tears.

Réfiyé Hanim listened with attention. Ahmet played a few bars of the accompaniment, and then repeated the song—his voice was a light baritone, very true and sweet; the air was hauntingly sad. "Ah," the old woman murmured at the end, as if to herself—"That is so altogether true!"

Féridé pounced on this.

"Why, Niné?"

"The two fortresses must be the two here on the Bosphorus, Anadol Hissar and Rumeli Hissar, I suppose," Fuad put in.

"Yes, certainly," said Réfiyé Hanim; "the Anatolian fortress and the other, one in Asia and one in Europe."

"Yes—yes, I see. But then why does he weep for the falcon? It is not far across the Bosphorus," Féridé persisted. "Does it not come back?"

"No," said Réfiyé Hanim with finality—"it does not come back."

"Niné, you mean something, and I do not know what you mean! At least, I do not know what the song means, to you."

"I have heard it before, long ago," said the old lady, pensively. "Ah child, the falcon is the heart—the heart that flies out of its own country.

The song is about the bitterness of love for the stranger—for the heart, like the falcon, does not come back."

Fanny listened in silence. It is the greatest possible mistake to suppose that young girls of fourteen or fifteen are not susceptible to those emotions which move the human heart later in life. On the contrary, in a curious selfless, almost sexless, half-dreaming fashion they are perhaps more subtly and more acutely aware of them than they will ever be again, especially when they are expressed in poetry or music. Fanny Pierce, sitting in the mixed and uncertain beauty of that sea-green room at the yali, with its strange fusion of Europe and the Orient, was moved deeply by the song, and by Réfiyé Hanim's interpretation of it. She, English as she was, knew and loved Turkey; Turkish literature and the wistful allusive Turkish forms of expression were beautiful and familiar to her; her Turkish friends, Réfiyé Hanim and Féridé particularly, were inexpressibly dear—with a quality of firmness and grace in their lives and personalities which she failed, often, to find among the little English friends whom she perforce acquired at her rather second-rate school. And at that moment a curious foreboding brushed her with its wing. Was *her* heart, in its love for the stranger, a bird that would not return? She glanced round the room—at Réfiyé Hanim in her corner, erect, calm; at Féridé with her delicate ardent face; at Ahmet still at the piano, so tall and slim and fine, his hands roving gently over the keys, still filling the room with the air of the song—and wondered: would she ever again, anywhere, find anything to equal this?

They went on then to other songs, more familiar: Féridé, in her clear little pipe, sang French children's songs taught her by Mdlle Marthe; Ahmet sang the sad minor melodies of Debussy and Hahn; Fanny, who was never shy, sang some English folk-songs. Dr. Pierce and the Pasha, in the study below, heard them and smiled.

At length Dr. Pierce glanced at his watch.

"Pasha, I must go. I have to pack, and arrange everything. Could you send for Fanny?"

"Yes, of course." The waiting servant was given a message.

"I must send a note to thank Réfiyé Hanim too—it is very good of her to have the child. It is really a weight off my mind."

"It will be a pleasure for us all," said the Pasha. "And what a strong clear voice she has, your Canary!"

The note was written, and given to the servant, who escorted them out through the rooms into the musical coolness of the stone-floored room, the "sofa"; they passed on into the garden—Fanny was already there.

"Well, la Canaria, so you are coming to be our cage-bird for a while," said the Pasha.

"Yes, Excellency—I am glad. It is so very kind of you and of Réfiyé Hanim. And Uncle, it is all settled, and Mdlle Marthe will come to fetch me tomorrow afternoon."

"Oh, how very kind!" said Dr. Pierce.

When they had gone, the Pasha went upstairs to the salon and greeted his mother, his son, and his nephew—then Féridé flew at him. "Oh, Baba-djim, how lovely that we shall have Fanny to stay! How glad I am that Dr. Pierce must go to Erzerum!"

"Erzerum! He is only going to Trebizond," said the Pasha—he sounded somehow startled.

"Oh well, one or the other! If the man doesn't bring the manuscripts down to Trebizond, he will go to Erzerum, Fanny says," said Féridé airily.

"So." He said no more, and presently carried the two young men off to his study for a talk before the evening meal.

"My Father, the College is full of talk of war," Ahmet said after a time. "Do you hear anything of it?"

"War of what nature?" the Pasha asked, non-committally.

"But with Russia! The *on dit* is that Germany and Russia will fight, and that we shall come in on Germany's side, and have a smack at *ces sales Russes*," said Ahmet, with considerable relish. His father said nothing. "But I hear," the young man went on thoughtfully, "that Colonel Mustafa Kemal is against it."

"And who is Colonel Mustafa Kemal, may I ask?" enquired the Pasha, who was in fact quite familiar with the name, and did not approve of that turbulent young officer.

"Oh, my Father, you must have heard of him! He is one of the most brilliant men in the Army. He is Military Attaché in Sofia now. He came to the College once—he is wonderful! If there *is* a war, I shall try to be on his staff!"

"And why is this paragon against going to war with Russia?" the Pasha asked.

"Because he says—this I was told in great confidence by a friend who is in contact with him—that if Turkey allows herself to be dragged into this war, whoever wins, the Ottoman Empire will be finished," said Ahmet solemnly.

"You young men know a lot," said the Pasha sarcastically. But he felt a little chill of discomfort, all the same.

Chapter Three

THE days of Dr. Pierce's absence sped happily for Fanny and Féridé. They were together all day long, from the moment of tiptoeing barefoot into one another's rooms on waking in the morning, to chatter in bed, till they crept again along the passage to wish one another a last good-night. In the big cool house, in the flower-bright, sun-splashed, shady garden, or up in the deserted wild beauty of the koru, they were to-gether—together they read French, or wrote compositions in that tongue with Mdlle Marthe, together they sang at the piano. In the salon, before dinner, they watched with secret smiles of amusement the old kalfos come in and fuss about, chivvying the maid-servants to tidy up the room before the Pasha's advent—having carefully changed them-selves into more elegant evening versions of the lacy blouses and those long tunic-like coats, and richer veils for their heads, with an aged and pathetic coquetterie.

It was not to be expected that Fanny and Féridé, at their age, should fully recognise the pathos of the position of these so-called "aunts." They represented a curious institution, now practically extinct; they were generally old maids, and vaguely related to the family; somehow or other they got taken into a rich household of distant connections, where they either fulfilled rather undefined functions, or acted definitely as Nannies to the children through one or more generations. Outside such a household their lives would have been of small compass—poor, without interest, despised and miserable; once installed in one, they enjoyed not only material comfort but a position in the world, and a passionate, life-giving interest in all the intimate concerns of the whole family. There were marriages to be arranged, all too often with their conniv-ance; babies were born, and they then exercised a delicious tyranny (usually quite unwarranted by personal experience) over the daily des-tinies of mother and child.

But marriages were *the* preoccupation, and in the Pasha's household, at this moment, there existed the delightful problem of settling Ahmet with a wife. He was twenty-three, so of more than marriageable age; he was handsome, he belonged to an ancient family, and would inherit wealth. From the "aunts'" point of view, something should be done at once.

Now in Turkey in those days there was no such thing as "boy meets girl"—it was the one thing that neither boy nor girl ever did. Officially a man never set eyes on his wife until the wedding-day. Marriages were "arranged," and the old women loved to have a hand in the arranging.

Three days after Fanny's arrival at the Pasha's, a delightful creature called Nilüfer came to spend the day. She was a remote cousin, whose family lived during the summer in a yali on the further side of the Bosphorus, near that deliciously-named place The Sweet Waters of Asia, from which she came across in a very smart private caïque. She was about sixteen, slender and very lovely, with immense velvety-soft eyes under high delicate brows that had none of the concentration of Féridé's—a gentle thing, dreamy, almost languid, rather silent and rather shy; in her very fashionable French clothes, with her slow graceful movements, she was the greatest possible contrast to Fanny and Féridé, a fact that was frequently pointed out, to Féridé's disadvantage, by Mdlle Marthe and Dil Feripé. Nilüfer for her part was very fond of Féridé; Fanny she regarded almost with awe, as one might a strange little animal from another continent. Nilüfer was too old to join in such childish ploys as hide-and-seek in the koru, but she played and sang, and on that particular day she was introduced to the Falcon song, and at once sang it, playing her own accompaniment with accomplished grace.

The possibility of making a marriage between this beautiful girl and Ahmet had of course occurred to both families; Réfiyé Hanim had discussed it with the Pasha and, discreetly, with Mdlle Marthe. But they had decided to make no move for the moment, till Ahmet should have finished at the College and Nilüfer should be seventeen; time enough then, Réfiyé Hanim considered. Naturally Ahmet and Nilüfer knew all about one another, but equally naturally they had never met face to face. However on this particular occasion one of the "aunts," Sitaré by name, a very old woman with a mole on the side of her nose, perhaps stirred up by the romantic song, perhaps by the aspect of the girl in the first flush of her beauty, could no longer control her match-making propensities. After the song she spoke of Ahmet, and how beautifully he sang it, how splendid he now looked; and later, seizing her chance when Nilüfer had gone to Féridé's room to tidy up, she slipped in, full of mystery, and showed her a photograph of Ahmet in all the glory of his cadet's uniform: the braided double-breasted tunic almost to the knee, the fez, the white-gloved hands resting on the sword—and insinuated, not very subtly, that this would indeed be a young man to marry. Féridé, with her usual impetuosity, dashed in in search of something while this was going on, and at once realised what old Sitaré was up to; she said nothing at the time, but carried Nilüfer off to the balcony to have tea. But later, when her cousin had gone, and she and her grandmother were taking their evening stroll in the garden she said —"Niné, is something being arranged about Nilüfer and Ahmet?"

"Certainly not—not yet; she is still too young," said Réfiyé Hanim, much surprised. "What put that idea into your head?"

"Oh, I saw Sitaré showing her his photograph, and I thought that must mean that a marriage was being arranged," said Féridé, who was quite familiar with these matters.

"No—it is not. And do you not talk of it—to anyone," said the old lady firmly, but without losing her accustomed calm. She went on to speak about the flowers. But she was secretly very much annoyed. Sitaré was the oldest, the silliest, and the most irresponsible of the "aunts"; she had done very wrong; photographs should never be shown till an actual betrothal was in question. After dinner she must be spoken to.

But Réfiyé Hanim did not after all speak to Sitaré that night. On that same Monday afternoon at the end of June Ahmet had come to see his father; they sat together in the Pasha's study, conversing with urbane enjoyment, when Osman, the servant who went daily to Bebek to fetch the afternoon paper brought it in: the *Tercümani Hakikat*. The Pasha bade him put it on the table. The man cleared his throat. "Pasham [My Pasha] there is news."

"Oh, is there? Let us see," said Ahmet lazily, stretching out his hand for the paper; he glanced at it, casually, and read that the Archduke Franz Ferdinand, the heir to the Austrian throne, had been assassinated the previous day at Sarajevo.

"My Father! Look at this!" he exclaimed, and handed the paper over.

The Pasha read it, and frowned.

"What does this mean?" the young man asked.

The Pasha continued to frown. "At the moment, it means an assassination," he said. "But what it *may* mean, God the All Powerful alone knows."

Later the two men went upstairs to dinner; by mutual agreement they said nothing of the news either in the salon, among the flowers, the chiffon-veiled heads and lacy blouses of that feminine world, or while the whole family sat at the long table in the dim richness of the dining-room, waited on by the tall Circassian maids, eating the abundant and delicious Turkish food: the hot vegetables cooked in butter, the cold vegetables served with oil, the pilaf, the mountains of fresh salad. Sitaré, the rather gaga old thing, recounted that Nilüfer had been there, and started some coy remarks—only to be suppressed with the utmost elegance by Réfiyé Hanim. After coffee on the balcony Ahmet had to leave; the Pasha gave his mother his arm in to the salon, Mdlle Marthe and the rest faded out, and Fanny and Féridé, obedient to something almost imperceptible in the atmosphere, took themselves off too. Then Asaf Murad Zadé told his mother the news.

She asked the question that Ahmet had asked—"My son, what does this mean?"

Gloomily, he gave her much the same reply—"Ané, I don't know."

For some days it seemed to mean nothing very much. Life flowed on at the yali. On July the 8th the Pasha received a telegram from Dr. Pierce—"Much regret delayed here unavoidably but Fanny can return pension at any time." It was sent from Erzerum.

The Pasha showed it to his mother. Féridé was there, and danced about. "Oh, lovely! Let me see it with my own eyes, Baba-djim!" She took it from her father. "Oh, but she *can* stay, can't she? Why should she go to that horrid pension? I *want* her."

"Of course she can stay, if your Grandmother agrees," said the Pasha.

"Then I shall go and tell her. Niné *does* agree, don't you, Niné-djim?" But at the door, across the wide space of the Savonnerie carpet, she turned back.

"You see the Doctor *did* go to Erzerum, Baba-djim," Féridé said, and ran out.

When she had gone—"He can't have heard," the Pasha murmured, half to himself.

"About the assassination?" Réfiyé Hanim asked.

"Yes, about the assassination. It may precipitate matters."

But because she had been thinking so much about the sort of matters that the Archduke's murder might precipitate, Réfiyé Hanim forgot all about her intended rebuke to Sitaré.

In fact Dr. Pierce, though he sent the telegram from Erzerum, had gone further. The egregious Mirza Ali Temel had not come down to Trebizond according to promise, so the Doctor took horses and rode up to Erzerum; this was slightly quicker than by carriage, especially over the Kop Pass. There he spent a day or so in examining the manuscripts; but there he also heard that a man at Kars, away to the east in Trans-Caucasian Russia, had other scripts, of the deepest interest. So of course he went on after them. Like all prudent people in those days, he never went to Turkey without a Russian visa on his passport—and in those blessed faraway days, let it be remembered, it was only for Turkey and Russia that European travellers required passports at all.

Dr. Pierce had been coming to Turkey for close on twenty years, and spoke the language as fluently as his own; in his pursuit of the songs and tales and proverbs of the people he made a practice of conversing with all sorts and conditions of men, and could adapt his idiom to theirs; and partly with a view to getting their confidence, on his journeys in the interior he usually travelled in a fez, so that his foreign status was not immediately noticeable. Officials in towns who saw his papers of course always knew that he was an Englishman; but in casual contacts on the road or in hans (roadside inns) he frequently passed for a Turk, a thing he found very convenient. It was the custom in those days for travellers going the same way to journey in convoy, and to beguile their time in conversation. On his road eastwards from Erzerum, to Hasan Kale and on to the Russian frontier post at Karaurgan, where he would pick up the light railway to Kars, Dr. Pierce again decided to ride; the weather was hot, but he did not mind that, and Selim, the teamster he had engaged at Trebizond, rather unexpectedly agreed to make the further trip, and at a reasonable price—moreover he was fussing a little about Fanny, and wanted to save all the time he could.

His little troop, on the very first day, found itself joining forces with a much larger one—that of six Turks, very decent, substantial sort of men, mounted on good beasts; he asked no questions, but took them for merchants. Selim, however, with the inquisitive free-masonry of his kind, soon found out, and told his master, where they came from— from Istanbul, on the boat before the Doctor's own. But almost at once Dr. Pierce was struck by something slightly odd about their behaviour. The usual thing when a party of travellers arrived at a han was for them all to go in and eat together. His new companions didn't do this —at least all of them did not. Two or three might, but the others went off by themselves; sometimes to another han, if there were two. Then he noticed that in almost every village they passed through, three or four farmers or well-to-do peasants were hanging about, apparently waiting for his merchant friends, and one or more would dismount and talk with them; constantly he saw them make notes in small books, and money changed hands. But there was something a little odd, a little secretive, about the way it was done—and if they were merchants, they carried no samples; moreover they seemed to be buying, not selling, for it was they who handed over the money.

"Selim," Dr. Pierce asked his teamster at last, "who are these men? And what do they buy?"

"Effendim, it is my belief that they buy grain."

"For what purpose?"

"Effendim, I do not know."

Dr. Pierce was puzzled. Beyond Erzerum seemed a remote place to be buying grain for Istanbul—the cost of transport would be immense; there were grain-lands much nearer the capital, and lying along the Taurus Railway. H'm—it was rather peculiar.

Some distance short of Karaurgan, lying in its gloomy glen, the six men left the main highway and took a side road; they bade Dr. Pierce a hearty farewell. He expected it to be a final one. He crossed the frontier with only the normal amount of delay and inquisition that attended all dealings with Russia, but his hopes of going on by the light railway to Kars were dashed—a landslide had blocked it a few days before. He had to get fresh animals and another teamster, all of which took time; late as it was, he set out that same evening—the days were long, and he rode on to a small han which he only reached after dark, indeed so late that they had to knock the landlord up. He slept in the usual small wooden-floored upstairs room; as always, the animals were housed immediately below in a vast stable, and he was disturbed at an early hour by the stampings and snortings attendant on a party's setting out. Looking out of his small square window, to his immense surprise he saw the six merchants again all ready for the road, standing bargaining—one can never mistake the gestures of Turks at a bargain—with some farmers in the early sunlight, immediately beneath. As before, they made notes in little books, and then handed over money—but now, as the Doctor could actually see with his own eyes, *Russian* money.

Now this was really extraordinary. And how had they sneaked across the frontier, and why? Dr. Pierce, casual as he usually was about everything but matters of scholarship, felt that he must find out what was going on. In this part of the Russian Empire (as the Pasha had told Réfiyé Hanim on the evening of Javid Bey's visit) the bulk of the population was Turkish by race and language, and it would be easy enough for Turkish merchants to do deals with the local farmers. But *why*, he asked himself as he dressed in his little cubicle, should Turks from Istanbul be buying grain in Trans-Caucasian Russia? And thereupon the Doctor, that most improbable person for such activities, determined to do a little detective work. He overhauled the men again before nightfall, and they eventually rode into Kars together; he made a point of putting up at the same inn. But postponing his pursuit of the scripts, next day he hung on the heels of his fellow-travellers, marked down the men with whom they conversed, and later contrived to get into conversation with some of them himself. Turks are all past masters at the art of withholding information, but he thought these men in Kars unusually reticent, almost nervous. However eventually he got hold of one very old man (who suffered from a tremendous stammer), lured him to a café, and at last persuaded him to talk. "We shall hold the grain," the old fellow stammered, leaning his turbaned head confidentially across the table, "till our troops come. Then they will eat it—they will be sure of bread."

Dr. Pierce was startled nearly out of his wits. "And when," he asked the old man, "will our troops be coming here?"

The old man looked infinitely sly, and jerked a gnarled thumb meaningfully over his shoulder, eastwards. "When we begin to deal with *them!*" he muttered, and broke into an aged cackling laugh.

Dr. Pierce was greatly disturbed. If *this* year's harvest was being bought up, and for that purpose, it meant something very grave indeed. The Pasha's urgent enquiries about the two Turkish battleships building in the Tyne flashed into his mind. No wonder they wanted them ready quickly! But he could hardly believe his stammering old acquaintance —and yet he seemed too old and too silly to invent such a lie. The Doctor now went with all speed to seek out the Kars manuscripts, only to find, as so often happens in the Near East, that it was all a false alarm—they had been removed from Kars to Sivas some time before. Normally he would have been exasperated—now he was almost relieved. If there *was* any truth in this story, the sooner he was back on the right side of the frontier the better. The railway being still impassable, he returned on horseback to Erzerum, where for the first time on his journey he took the trouble to look at a paper, and learned of the assassination of the Archduke. Still, Serbia and Austria!—what on earth had they to do with Turkey and Russia? None the less, he made rapid stages down to Trebizond, where he caught a boat that was on the point of sailing; on July the 17th she entered the Bosphorus.

As the ship steamed down between those familiar shores a particular worry rose up in the Doctor's mind, prompted by the sight of the burntout ruins of the British Summer Embassy at Therapia, among its beautiful trees. Ought he to go and tell someone about this grain business? Dr. Pierce did not much frequent Embassy circles, and what little he knew of them he did not greatly care for; there always seemed to be a great many very smart clever young men, who intimidated him— if he were to go now with this story they would, he feared, snub him. But as the boat swept on down the narrow blue waters, past the tall grey frontage of Madame Kaftanoglou's, past the vast lovely façade of the Pasha's yali, he realised that he ought to go. Very well, better get it over; and on landing at Istanbul he took a ferry straight back to Therapia, where the Chancery still carried on in another building during the summer months.

It all happened, at first, as he had expected, only worse. He was still wearing the fez in which he usually travelled, not his old Panama, so the first kavass that he encountered at the door—splendid in his long blue coat, brass buttons, and sword slung from a belt of gold braid—took him for a Turk, and was not very civil to him. (A lamentable habit, this, of indigenous Embassy employees to their co-nationals, and one by no means confined to British diplomatic establishments.) Dr. Pierce, provoked beyond endurance, lambasted the man in his own tongue, though in a low voice, with a wealth of invective that astonished him; then he started to speak English. Now the head kavass appeared, faultlessly polite, and asked in excellent English whom he wished to see? Any member of the staff, said Dr. Pierce, bringing out a card. He was led into a small featureless waiting-room; a pause ensued. (In those days Embassy waiting-rooms did not, as they do now, flower like parterres with the literary productions of the British Council—there was one very old copy of the *Illustrated London News* and two still older copies of *Punch*.) Finally a young man of the sort Dr. Pierce so rightly dreaded appeared, holding his card, and asked, in tones of neutral politeness, in what way he could be of service to him?

Dr. Pierce, nervous anyhow, and upset by his encounter with the kavass, made rather a bad job of his recital. He had just come back from Erzerum and Kars, he began. "Oh yes?" said the young man— who had only arrived in Istanbul a few weeks before, and did not yet carry the map of Asia Minor in his head; he had only a very vague idea of where Erzerum was, and had never heard of Kars. Dr. Pierce struggled on: there was a lot of grain-buying going on up there—by Turks, he said, with considerable emphasis; Turks were buying grain in Kars! "Ah yes," said the young man; "an early harvest this year, I suppose?" He was still thinking in terms of the late harvests of Northern Europe.

"No, it's a normal season," said Dr. Pierce shortly, beginning to think the young man must be half-witted—"But the point is, the buyers aren't taking it out—it's being *held* there." And he fixed the young man with an emphatic eye.

"Oh really?" said the young man, who had no idea what ought to happen to Turkish grain when bought, but saw no point in mentioning it—"And who is holding it?"

"The peasants and farmers," said Dr. Pierce, "but . . ."

The door opened at this point, and a second young man put his head in. "Oh Wilmington, there you are. The Counsellor wants you—when you're free," he added politely, with a glance at Dr. Pierce.

Mr. Wilmington said "Right," and turned to Dr. Pierce again; he was beginning in his turn to think that his visitor was possibly a little mad—Embassies drew lunatics as with a magnet—and he saw a chance of escape. "If it's about grain, I think you should see the Commercial Attaché," he said firmly. "I'll see if he's free. One moment"—and with that he picked up Dr. Pierce's card and went out. On his way to the Counsellor's room he poked his head in at a door—the Commercial Attaché was there. "I say, there's an old boy in the waiting-room who seems rather potty; he wants to talk about grain. Can you cope? Marchmont wants me—" and he flipped the card onto the table. The other took it up. "Dr. Henry Pierce," he read. "Why, it's old Pierce!" he said—"*He's* not potty, except about scripts." "Well, he never mentioned scripts—he's talking about people buying grain at a place called Arse or Carse," said young Wilmington. "I say, *could* you cope? Marchmont's waiting." He fled.

The Commercial Attaché went to the waiting-room, where Dr. Pierce was fretting, and wishing he hadn't come—pure waste of time!

"How do you do? My name is Hepburn. I'm delighted to meet you," said a man of reasonable age, coming in and holding out his hand. "Won't you come to my room?—more comfortable there."

In Mr. Hepburn's room Dr. Pierce indeed found everything much more comfortable. He was given a cigarette, and in this soothing atmosphere told his story clearly enough. Mr. Hepburn listened with attention, putting a sensible question now and then; at the end—"I think the M.A. ought to hear this," he said—"Would you mind? I'll just fetch him." He too went along the passage and poked his head in at a door. "Bill, could you come to my room for a second?" As the Military Attaché rose and went with him—"I've got old Dr. Pierce in there; he's just come back from Kars," Hepburn said.

"Kars, eh? How on earth did he get in?"

"He says he always comes with a Russian visa, just in case." He opened the door. "Dr. Pierce, here is Colonel Scott. It would be very kind if you would tell him what you've told me."

Dr. Pierce did so; the Colonel also listened attentively. "Ah, Lonsdale wired that report from Trebizond on Tuesday," he said thoughtfully; "but this fills it out nicely." He questioned Dr. Pierce, closely but reasonably: it was in Kars that the old man had told him the reason for holding the grain? None of the others had said so? Ah no, they wouldn't talk. There was some buying done *before* the frontier?—from Erzerum onwards? And after? All the way to Kars?

"Yes, well that looks plain enough," he said at the end to Hepburn. "I think H.E."—he checked himself. "Thank you very much, Sir," he said to Dr. Pierce. "It was very good of you to come to us, and your information is most useful. Where are you staying, by the way?" Dr. Pierce gave the address of the pension, and Hepburn saw him out, between the now bowing kavasses.

The next week passed quietly. Fanny and Dr. Pierce returned to the pension, but paid constant visits to the yali, where the Pasha and the Doctor pored over and discussed the Fuzuli texts—but the latter refrained from saying anything about his journey to Kars even to Fanny, let alone to his host. He felt vaguely uneasy—there was a sense of disquiet in the air, or so it seemed to him.

Exactly a week after his return, on July the 24th, a Saturday, Fanny pressed to be taken to the yali. Ahmet and Fuad were coming, she said, and had promised to take her and Féridé out in Ahmet's boat. In spite of a vague feeling of reluctance, Dr. Pierce agreed. As they went in at the gate a car, with a very smart footman beside the chauffeur, swept up the drive, going out—Dr. Pierce, stepping hastily aside, hardly looked at it, but—"That was Javid Bey," Fanny observed.

"You don't know Javid Bey."

"No, but that was his man, Ibrahim—I know *him."*

Ahmet and Fuad were already in the salon when Fanny ran upstairs, and with Féridé they went off to the boat. This was kept in the caïque-hané, a long dark narrow boat-house behind the fountain at the far end of the haremlik garden; to reach it one had to squeeze round the end of the screen of marble panels, from spouts in which the fountain played, into a sort of passage under the bushy cliff. Order and civilisation ended here; this was where Zeynel, the gardener, kept his rubbish; dead branches, heaps of leaves, piles of faggots for the sweet peas, odds and ends of old iron encumbered it; a narrow path under the high wall separating the Pasha's domain from the next yali led to a door at the landward end of the boat-house. Two of the caikdji, or boatmen, awaited them there, in their baggy white trousers and velvet waistcoats; they got in and set off.

In the selamlik Dr. Pierce found his friend abstracted; there was a certain constraint in his manner. They studied the variants in the new Fuzuli texts, but half-heartedly. Presently Osman, the servant, as before brought in the *Tercümani Hakikat*—and as before the Pasha told him to put it down. "Oh, could I just glance at it for a moment?" said Dr. Pierce—"I was too busy this morning." He opened it, and read of the Austrian ultimatum to Serbia.

Dr. Pierce's jaw dropped. "Pasha, look at this!" he said. Unwillingly —uninterestedly, he thought—the Pasha took up the paper. And the idea struck the Doctor with inescapable force—It isn't news to him! Javid Bey told him! But he himself was shocked. The crudity, the savagery of the terms were unbelievable. "The Serbs can't accept that," he said. "That means war."

"If the Austrian Empire and Serbia go to war, Serbia will go down," said the Pasha—he spoke almost coldly.

"Yes, but will Russia *see* Serbia go down?" Dr. Pierce asked. And then he remembered those decent substantial men, those pleasant companions of the road, buying grain all the way from Erzerum to Kars, just a fortnight ago—and he said no more. He was relieved when the caïque returned, and he could collect Fanny and take his leave.

(What Dr. Pierce did not know—what not even his acquaintances at the Embassy knew till later—was that on that Saturday, when they had passed Javid Bey's car in the Pasha's drive, the Ottoman Government had started negotiations with the German Government for a Treaty of Alliance, a Treaty which was signed in secret on August the 2nd. That, as well as the Austrian ultimatum, the Pasha might well have learned that day from Javid Bey.)

But before August the 2nd other things had happened. The sky grew darker and darker all that week. Dr. Pierce felt almost awkward about going to the yali, but the Pasha continued to invite him, and even seemed to wish to discuss the political situation—it occurred presently to the Doctor that his host was "sounding him out" on England's probable attitude. "After all," he said more than once, sitting in his fez, elegant and calm, in his study sipping coffee—"whatever happens, there is no reason whatever for either of *our* countries to be mixed up in this." Dr. Pierce, again thinking of the grain-buyers, found it hard to make a very hearty response.

On Saturday, August the 1st, the Doctor was there again. Mirza Ali Temel had sought out and sent down from Erzerum three more Fuzuli scripts, and for the first time for many days the two old friends were happily and whole-heartedly concentrated on them, bending over the big table in the bow window, the centre shutters thrown back, when Ahmet hurried in, brandishing the afternoon paper.

"My Father! Look at this! It is monstrous!" He was all in disorder.

"You know Dr. Pierce?" said the Pasha, in calm reproof.

"Oh yes—indeed. How do you do?" The young man gave the coldest of formal bows. "But—excuse us one moment," to the Doctor— "My Father, this is a *terrible* thing!" He thrust the paper into the Pasha's hands.

There were two sets of banner headlines in it. Germany had declared war on Russia; and England was holding the *Reshadieh*, the first of the battleships built for Turkey. She was ready, the Turkish crew of 500 was on a transport in the Tyne waiting to take over, and the English would not let her go, had placed guards on board! It was to this item that Ahmet pointed, with a shaking finger.

The Pasha read it, incredulously. "But it isn't possible," he said, slowly. "Not England!" He held the paper out to Dr. Pierce; the lines flashed to the eye. The Doctor's discomfort was acute.

"But they are *paid for*," the Pasha said, still slowly, unbelievingly.

"Then be sure of this, Pasha; every penny will be paid back," said Dr. Pierce, stoutly.

"But *why*? Why do this thing?"

"Why do you want them in such a hurry?" the Doctor countered. "If we go to war with Germany, we may want them pretty badly ourselves."

"But why should you?"

"Why should *you* go to war with Russia? The Germans aren't your allies."

The Pasha's face changed, and Dr. Pierce saw it. "By Jove, Wangenheim *has* dragged them in—or will," he said to himself. "Oh Lord, what a mess!"

"You know our difficulties with Russia," the Pasha was saying slowly.

"Yes, my old friend. And you know who has generally bailed Turkey out of them in the past!" He went up to the other. "I am most terribly sorry—you know that," he said. He could not say more—his old friend had not been frank with him, he felt sure; it was an unhappy moment. He gathered up his papers, put them in his shabby old case, and as soon as Fanny could be found, took his leave.

Things moved fast after that. On the Monday, two days later, came, first, the news that England had mobilised the Fleet, and in the evening that the German army had entered Luxembourg. Then events came like an avalanche—and as an avalanche fills some smiling alpine valley with the distant roar of destruction, bringing dread to the hearts of all who hear the sound, so did the rumour of these events, so far away, penetrate to the sunny shores of the Bosphorus, and send dread into hearts there. One after another came Germany's ultimatum to Belgium, England's ultimatum to Germany—telling the Germans that, as a guarantor of Belgian neutrality, England would go to war if it was violated. The Pasha heard this last piece of news with an incredulity that was shared by half Europe—and then remembered the Doctor's words in the garden about England and morals, before he went to Erzerum. But it was appalling. The Pasha knew definitely, now, that his government had signed a secret Treaty of Alliance with Germany, only last Saturday; war between England and Turkey could only be a matter of time, unless the Germans accepted the English ultimatum— and they would never do that! He paced the stone floor of the "sofa," that Tuesday afternoon, to and fro, to and fro—down past the little fountain with its silly tinkle towards the door that gave onto the garden, back past the fountain to the door leading to his study. The English ultimatum was to expire at midnight; he kept looking at his watch. Different thoughts jostled one another in his head, claiming attention.

One recurred, with the persistence of the water falling into the fountain—the recollection of Colonel Mustafa Kemal's ominous words, as reported by Ahmet a month before: that if Turkey allowed herself to be dragged into the conflict, whoever won, she was doomed. He tried to brush it aside. This business of losing the two ships, though; that was disastrous—must the whole Caucasian plan founder for lack of them? Worse—what was now to stop the Russian fleet from coming down the Bosphorus and bombarding Istanbul? Oh, had Enver Pasha really been wise?

The thought of the ships brought another, more personal concern into his mind. Public anger was rising over them—would rise higher when England and Germany were really at war, as seemed inevitable. The Pasha thought of his old friend, so scholarly, so unworldly, there at the pension—with his small niece, the bright little Canary, Féridé's dearest, most beloved companion. Things might become very disagreeable for them—they ought to go. They ought to go as soon as possible. He went through to his study and wrote a note to Dr. Pierce, asking him to come, if he could, next day to discuss some points which had occurred to him in connection with the scripts.

Touched and pleased, after their last gloomy conversation, the Doctor went. The papers that morning had brought the news that England and Germany were at war, and this troubled him—he would be glad to see a friend. They sat again in that room, so staccato with colour and pattern, and talked of Fuzuli. But at one point the Pasha asked, casually, when Dr. Pierce thought of leaving? The overland route, by the Simplon Orient Express, was of course closed to English travellers, since Germany and Austria stood together; and with France, England and Germany at war, sea-passages through the Mediterranean might become difficult. "You should, I think, perhaps reflect on this," the Pasha said.

From a Turk, as Dr. Pierce instantly recognised, this was a hint so direct as hardly to be a hint at all. He thanked his host, and said that he would certainly reflect on the matter. And next morning he hastened in to the city to book passages home. To his dismay he found crowds at the steamship offices, all bent upon the same errand—English tourists, who thought it would all be over in six weeks, but anyhow they had better get home; and a large number of French. He was there half the day, but at last he secured a single cabin—(he could sleep on the floor) on a small ship which was sailing on August the 12th. Everything earlier was booked up.

On his return, tired out, to the pension, he sent a note to the Pasha, thanking him for his views on the scripts—at the end, quite casually, he mentioned that he found himself obliged to leave, and stated the date of their departure, and the boat on which they were to sail.

Fanny and Féridé also exchanged sad little notes—"Oh, my Two Eyes, when shall I see you again?" Féridé wrote. But the feeling about the two requisitioned battleships was now so strong that Dr. Pierce turned a deaf ear to Fanny's imploring requests for a farewell visit to the yali—it would hardly be suitable, he said.

The Pasha had half expected a visit, suitable or not, and was sad that none was proposed, though he guessed the feeling that prevented the Doctor from suggesting one; Féridé's little face, sulky and miserable, made him wish to get Fanny there once more, too. Those ships!—what distress they were causing. But later that week the Pasha suddenly became a degree less concerned about the non-delivery of the *Reshadieh*. Javid Bey paid another of his calls, and the Pasha learned, under seal of secrecy, the heartening, the wonderful news that the *Goeben*, the crack German battle-cruiser, and also the light cruiser *Breslau* (which were both in the Mediterranean) had been ordered to proceed to Istanbul. This was news indeed! Once in the Sea of Marmara, the capital could be protected from any Russian raid; the *Goeben* in particular could outsteam and outshoot anything the Russians had in the Black Sea. But would they get there?—or would the British Mediterranean Fleet intercept them before they entered the narrow waters of the Dardanelles?

The Pasha's anxiety was intense. This was a secret so deadly that he could share it with no one, and he paced up and down under the magnolias and plane-trees in the selamlik garden—wondering, wondering, hardly daring to hope. So much, so much depended on whether those two ships arrived!

.   .   .   .   .   .

Dr. Pierce and Fanny sailed at about 3:30 on August the 12th. In Turkey, at the departure of any ship from any port, the quay is always occupied by a howling mob, seven-tenths of which are not only not travelling, but have no sort of business on board. Through such a mob they struggled towards the gangway, Dr. Pierce for comfort's sake wearing his fez—only his height made him conspicuous. Fanny, clutching a bag and trying to keep their porter in view, presently noticed two Turkish women not far off amid the throng, who seemed also to be edging towards the gangway; densely veiled in their long black çarşafs, their heads merely round black knobs above the floating drapery, they were, like all Turkish women in public places, totally unidentifiable. Slowly they made their way nearer, the taller forcing her way between other bodies with unusual energy, till at last they found a place at Fanny's side.

"Dji-djim!" said a soft voice. "Shsh! Don't say my name. But I had to see you again."

"Who's with you?" Fanny whispered, through the veils.

"Dil Feripé—I *made* her come! Niné, even, doesn't know. Oh, I shall pay for this!"

Fanny realised what Féridé had done—the wicked, the impossible! She hugged her through the veiling. "Little angel, how good of you! Oh, I am so glad," she whispered.

"And you will come again, and stay with me; and love me and be happy, as we have been? *Whatever* happens?"

"Yes, *whatever* happens," Fanny said.

The crowd surged forward towards the gangway; Fanny moved with it; the two black knobs above black draperies fell behind. Turning her head, she saw them—Féridé in front, making their way against the human stream, away from the boat, towards the town.

Their boat—Italian, with a crew largely composed of Maltese—was not very comfortable; the food was indifferent, their single cabin small and rather stuffy. Dr. Pierce insisted that he would sleep on the floor, from which Fanny's young supple bones would not have suffered in the least; he stayed on deck till the last possible moment, as they chugged down the Sea of Marmara—Fanny was already asleep when he finally lay down. He woke just before sunrise; stretching himself stiffly, he decided to take a turn on deck, and went up and forward to the bows.

They were just approaching the Narrows. On his right, in Europe, rose low pale hills, darkly speckled with scrub; to his left lay flatter sandy shores, beyond which, far far away, the enormous blue bulk of Olympus-in-Asia stood up into a sky faintly flushed with pink. But Dr. Pierce hardly looked at the view, lovely as it was in the cool half-light; his attention was arrested by something else. From the narrow waters ahead of him two grey shapes were emerging, slowly, majestically; the leading one so vast that its great superstructure seemed to dwarf those low scrub-covered hills. Dr. Pierce gazed in astonishment. They were two enormous men-of-war! But men-of-war were not allowed through the Dardanelles, he thought with astonishment. A bell rang sharply below; the *Martelli* altered course slightly, and the two great vessels passed by on his left hand, their wash making a line of white along both shores.

"Tedeschi!" said a deck-hand in a striped jersey, with an unshaven chin, coming up to the rail beside him. Dr. Pierce continued to gaze; they couldn't possibly be German ships. But the deck-hand was right—though Dr. Pierce only learned it later, he was watching the *Goeben* and *Breslau* entering Turkish waters.

Part Two

Chapter Four

ON A sunny morning half-way through September, 1918, Réfiyé Hanim was sitting in her corner in the salon rolling bandages with her old hands; Dil Feripé and two of the other old women stood in front of her, each holding out, as best she could, an immense bed-spread of prune-coloured velvet embroidered in gold thread. They were of different shades, one more red, one more purple; Réfiyé Hanim looked at them with her head on one side.

"I think that one," she said, indicating the one held by Dil Feripé— "but we had better ask Féridé Hanim. Dil Feripé, show me the prayer-mat, too."

The dadi laid the bed-spread over a chair, and picked up a much smaller square of velvet embroidered to match; Réfiyé Hanim took it on her lap and examined it critically, lining and all, to see if it was in good condition.

"Yes, that will do. Put it over there, Dil Feripé; put them together."

Réfiyé Hanim was engaged in the delightful task of going through the household treasures stored up by her for years to fit out her darling Féridé on her marriage. For Féridé was going to marry Ahmet's friend Orhan, him who had composed the accompaniment to the Falcon song four years before; the wedding was to take place in a fortnight. The great painted chests had been opened, and maids and dadis were coming and going with armfuls of things; the Louis Quinze chairs and settees had almost disappeared under a sea of linens and fine muslins and embroideries. What Réfiyé Hanim was choosing at this moment was the bedroom set: the great bed-spread for the bed, always of velvet embroidered in metal thread, and the small prayer-mat to match, on which the husband knelt to say his prayers—most of all the ceremonial prayer on his wedding night.

"Put those two near it," she went on to the other two old women; "then the child can choose. Now, let me see the towels."

"The best, Hanim Effendi, or the ordinary ones?"

"The ordinary ones first."

The "ordinary" towels would have struck most Europeans as almost too beautiful to use. The hand-spun thread was woven in a very loose open texture, not much heavier than muslin; the ends were embroidered solidly eight or nine inches deep in silks in pale colours. Réfiyé Hanim looked them over swiftly and expertly, counted out five or six dozen, and told the "aunt" to let the maids take them to the room where Féridé's things were being assembled. "Now the others."

As for the best towels, which were now produced, they were astonishing. Rather narrow strips, as much as five feet long, of the same muslin-fine material were so thickly embroidered with gold thread that the original stuff was hardly visible; in the centre was a very small patch of regular "Turkish towelling," but very silky and fine. There were not so many of these, and Réfiyé Hanim looked them over with more care; she counted out a dozen, and they too were taken away—such towels were of course only used for very honoured guests, or on ceremonial occasions.

Other things followed: diaphanous muslin bed-spreads; tablecloths, some small, more vast, richly embroidered in brilliantly coloured silks—over these the old lady lingered a little doubtfully. "I wish Féridé were here," she said.

"They should be back soon, Hanim Effendi. Madame Hélène is always very slow over her fittings," said Dil Feripé consolingly. "But Féridé is sure to be pleased with whatever the Hanim Effendi chooses—she does not care much about such things."

"She will when she has a house of her own!" said Réfiyé Hanim. "I hope Mdlle Marthe will see that Madame Hélène makes that *tailleur* fit properly, and that the skirt is long enough. Ah, these shortages of everything, with this war! No English cloth for *tailleurs!* And no other is so good. The child will not have the trousseau she should have had." She sighed, and turned again to her task. At length—"Very well—those, and those. Let Ayshé take them away." Steps were heard in the hall outside—"Wait! Perhaps it is she," said the old lady.

But it was not. The sea-green panelled door opened a little, and a lovely face looked round it. "Niné, may I come in? Do I disturb you?"

"No—come in, Nilüfer my child," said Réfiyé Hanim warmly. "*Comment ça va?*" she asked, as the young woman came up and kissed her.

Nilüfer was now her grand-daughter-in-law. Ahmet had married her two years before, in the middle of the war—poor old Sitaré, the silly "aunt," had lived to see that vicarious ambition realised, though she did not long survive it; she died the following year. Ahmet had realised an ambition too—in 1916 he had been taken onto the staff of his idol Mustafa Kemal, when the latter re-captured Bitlis and Mus from the Russians. And by now Mustafa Kemal was Mustafa Kemal Pasha, a renowned General of Brigade, commanding the Seventh Army on the Palestine front. Orhan was on the Thracian front, but both young men were completely devoted to the commander, and Ahmet was even on terms of friendship with him.

And Nilüfer was living in the yali. This was an unusual arrangement. A house had actually been bought for her and Ahmet, but since he was always at the front, and she a great favourite with Réfiyé Hanim and the Pasha, an apartment had been organised for her in the vast house, in one of those curious re-duplications which were characteristic of old and important yalis. Féridé and Orhan were to live in another portion, at least while the war lasted; but in Féridé's case the arrangement was much more typical of the patriarchal fashion obtaining in wealthy Turkish families—a son-in-law who was approved of and liked (as Orhan was) was quite often fitted in, with the beloved daughter, under the vast family roof-tree.

"Oh, what lovely things!" Nilüfer said now, looking at the table-cloths, and greeting the old women with familiar kindness.

"Yes—these are old things of mine; one can get nothing new! I was looking them out for Féridé."

"Where is she, Niné?"

"Gone with Marthe to a fitting, so I am trying to choose some of these things for her ménage without her—just look at the room!"

Nilüfer took her at her word, and wandered about, picking up one object after another and exclaiming at their beauty, as well she might. Here was a wrought-silver ewer and basin for washing one's hands, and with it a small silver bowl shaped like a lotus, with opened petals filling the centre—most exquisite of soapdishes; there a high slender fluted silver sherbet jug, a complicated heap of gilt fruit and leaves forming its lid. And high-heeled and high-soled sandals, enamelled in black on silver, to wear in the bath-house—nahlins, more for ornament than for use; and embroideries without end—mats, doyleys, covers for toilet-tables. The room was like Aladdin's cave.

"Niné, what riches! Really, she is lucky," Nilüfer said, handling the various beautiful things lovingly.

"She cares little for them as yet, as Dil Feripé there was saying," said Réfiyé Hanim smiling; "she is not like you, my child. For her it is all the war, and Kemal Pasha!"

Nilüfer returned to her. "Yes, Niné, that is true. She saw him once, you know—last year, at a concert, and she has always retained the impression. She thought him wonderful—blonde, and so young! And his eyes!—she cannot get over his eyes; like spears of ice, she said. They all talk about his eyes—Orhan, Ahmet, all of them."

"Have you heard from Ahmet?" Réfiyé Hanim asked. She was really not greatly interested in Kemal Pasha's eyes.

"Yes—today. He will be here on the 28th, for the wedding—Kemal Pasha is giving him leave, of course. When does Orhan come?"

"About three days before—for the Nikia, and so forth." (The Nikia was the marriage contract, often signed as much as a couple of months in advance; there was also a document signed by the bridegroom, undertaking to pay a very considerable sum of money in the event of a divorce. But in war-time all these arrangements had to be telescoped together, as it were.)

The last four years had laid a light hand on Réfiyé Hanim; as she sat talking to her grand-daughter-in-law in her accustomed corner, rolling bandages from strips of muslin in a huge basket by her side, there was little visible change from the Réfiyé Hanim of four years ago. (In fact, time does make little difference to people in the eighties.) Her laces, her long *écru* coat, were as crisp and impeccable as ever. Nor had the "aunts," who went on bringing piles of linen and embroideries for approval, and carrying them away again, changed much; they were mostly in their eighties too, or nearly.

A resonant merry voice was suddenly heard on the big hall-like landing outside; the door was flung open, and Féridé came running in.

"Niné, my very dearest! I am so late! To fit with Madame Hélène is a torture! Nilüfer, chérie!" She pulled off her long black çarşaf, revealing a cool summer silk frock, and kissed them both.

"Where is Mdlle Marthe?" asked Réfiyé Hanim.

"Gone to her room to rest—she is worn out, and no wonder!" The girl looked around the salon, and began to laugh. "Niné-djim, but are we in a bazaar?"

Time had changed the two girls more than the old lady, but it had not altered the fundamental differences between them. Both were now elegant young women, wearing smart French-made dresses, their hair fashionably arranged, their shoes the last word in frivolous and expensive perfection. But Nilüfer was still languid, almost clinging, softly slow in voice and movement; Féridé was now taller than ever, and her childish impetuosity had developed into a swift decisiveness of mind and manner, very noticeable in those tranquil feminine surroundings—her eyebrows were even more expressive of concentration than of yore.

Réfiyé Hanim laughed at her last sally.

"My bonbon, we were looking out things for you—but I had to begin. Look—there are the three coverlets and prayer-rugs; those you *must* choose. I think the centre one."

Féridé cast a swift eye over them.

"Yes, certainly; that prune-brown tone is much the loveliest. Darling Niné, thank you ten thousand times! You are far too good to me."

There were a few more choices to be made and decisions to be taken, which were all pushed through by Féridé with a remarkable combination of speed, affection, and gratitude; no one's feelings were hurt, but the business was somehow completed in an uncommonly short time, and the white-and-gold furniture re-emerged from under the sea of fabrics which had drowned it. Then she sat down between her grand-mother and Nilüfer.

"Now, Niné dearest, that that is all settled—and how can I ever thank you enough!—do tell us what my Father said about the dancers. Are we to have them?"

Réfiyé Hanim looked slightly distressed.

"Your Father thinks better not."

"Oh Niné-djim, *why?* They were so fascinating at Nilüfer's wedding."

"That was two years ago, my child. Since then the losses, the suffering, have increased so greatly; it would be ostentatious, in bad taste, to have too much display, your Father thinks."

"Oh Niné! And do *you* think so, too? I am sure you do not," the spoilt child of the house exclaimed, pouting.

"Yes, I agree with your Father," said Réfiyé Hanim quietly. "But everything else will be the same—the receptions, and your Father's dinner in the selamlik, and the sheep to be slaughtered and roasted for the populace—to give them a proper meal, for once, when they come to wish you well on your marriage day."

Féridé tapped on the floor with her pretty foot, a little impatiently: roasted sheep for the populace seemed rather dull to her by comparison with the hired dancers who had so delighted her at her brother's wedding. She was only seventeen—her vexation was natural enough. Réfiyé Hanim watched her regretfully. Not for worlds would she have mentioned that in fact the wedding reception itself would cost a great deal, and that the Pasha had at first been tempted to veto the traditional feast to the poor people of the district, on grounds of expense. She had got round that by saying that she would pay for it herself; and she had sold—by discreet means—some of her jewels to have the money at hand for the purpose.

While Féridé was still tapping mutinously with her foot on the floor, her hands occupied in rolling a bandage from Réfiyé Hanim's basket, the Pasha himself walked in. On him also four years had wrought little change. Tall, spare, well-dressed, only different from any European father in the red fez that he wore on his head above his neat suit, he greeted his mother, his daughter and his daughter-in-law, and sat down. (To have appeared before them bare-headed, without the fez, would have been a grave discourtesy.)

"And what are the ladies of my household about?" he asked pleasantly. Féridé sprang up, and went over to him.

"Oh Baba-djim, we speak of the dancers! Niné tells me that you do not wish me to have them and I do desire to, *so* much!"

Asaf Pasha frowned. He hated not to give this youngest child of his, his worshipped toy and treasure, whatever she wanted, but his sense of rectitude was immovable.

"No, my child," he said. "It would be impossible; wrong. When the nation is in suffering, in danger, it is no time for such things. The reception of course there must be; that goes without saying. But music, dancers—no."

There was a little silence. Then Féridé sprang up again and went over to her Father, who had risen from his chair. "Baba-djim, if it is really for our country, I say nothing more." The Pasha kissed her on the forehead, and went out, looking gloomy.

He had good reasons for his gloom. The early successes of Turkish arms against the Entente in 1915 and 1916 had not been sustained. The entry of America into the war in 1917 had been a tremendous shock to all Germany's allies, and latterly General Maude in Mesopotamia, and Allenby in Palestine, had been hitting the Turkish troops—under German command—hard. North of the Aegean the Bulgarians were now retreating before the Entente forces based on Salonika; if this advance could not be checked, Istanbul itself, the capital, would be menaced. As he returned to his study and sat down before his writing-table the Pasha recalled, unwillingly, what Ahmet—in that very room four years before—had quoted as Mustafa Kemal's dictum: that if Turkey went into the war, whoever won, the Ottoman Empire would go down. The Pasha, through his official contacts, knew all about the many differences that Kemal Pasha had had throughout the war with the Higher Command, Turkish and German alike: and the trouble was that whether he advised an attack or a retirement, in the long run the fellow always proved to have been right! Everyone knew how by an unauthorised attack at Anafartalar (as the Turks called Suvla) he had saved the day and precipitated the retirement of the British from the Dardanelles Peninsula. But now things looked black, very black. His little Féridé, his cherished and beloved child—what circumstances in which to get her married! Right and dignity, however, must be adhered to, whatever happened.

The next fortnight was a busy one for the women of the household. Féridé and Orhan were to occupy that part of the house beyond the central portion where she had hitherto lived with Réfiyé Hanim; this was of course already furnished, but the supplies of household linen and so on, chosen and given by Réfiyé Hanim, must be placed there, and the rooms arranged—all of which had to be done with a certain formality. The wedding-presents, too, had to be set out in what would be in future Féridé's own main salon; chief among these was the dinner-service in Saxe porcelain, without which no upper-class Turkish bride was ever allowed to set up house, and always given by some near relation. Since new Saxe dinner-services could not be brought from Dresden to Turkey in 1918, Réfiyé Hanim had given her own. Then there was a lot of silver, mostly of the hand-wrought and florid indigenous sort; and, since Féridé was Murad Zadé Asaf Pasha's daughter, some fine framed specimens of calligraphy. But silver was the standard gift.

Dil Feripé, however, was dissatisfied about one thing. In her youth, and among the circles from which she came, it had always been obligatory for the affianced bridegroom to bring one gift in particular, as an earnest both of his love and of his substance—a pair of very broad stiff bracelets of gold, or of silver filigree washed with gold, and a belt of fine plaited silver wire, also gold-washed, and as supple to fold as cloth, with a heavy gold buckle. With these objects Orhan, away at the front, had failed to provide her darling, and she was greatly upset. She grumbled about it to Réfiyé Hanim.

"My good Dil Feripé, he has sent the emerald ring and bracelet," the old lady said pleasantly.

"But the other! He should have sent that too."

"Well, there is the war now; everything is otherwise. How can he find such things at the front? Do not fret; there is nothing we can do."

But there was something that Dil Feripé could do—and she did it. As a girl a match had been arranged for her, and her betrothed had brought the correct, the customary gift; he had been killed in an accident a day or so before the marriage, and she had remained single. But she still had the belt and the two bracelets, her own wedding gift, the nearest she had ever come to marriage; these she now brought forth from their hiding-place, and presented them, rather mysteriously, to Féridé. The girl, busy and hurried, undid the wrappings hastily—when she saw what was in them she flung her arms round the dadi's neck, tears in her eyes.

"Oh Dadi, how good you are to me! Oh, worthless that I am, to have tormented you so, all these years!"

Dil Feripé, by now herself in tears, muttered—"Oh, light of my eyes! —my little sweet-meat, my jewel!—these you *should* have! Orhan Bey would, I am confident, have made you this gift rightly, but for this terrible war. Oh, may Allah be merciful! But since he could not, you shall not lack the gift that a bride should have. My poor Hassan!—he bought them at Broussa. He was a man of Broussa; there we should have lived, had he not died! They say it is a beautiful place, with many mulberry-trees, and much beautiful silk." And the poor old woman, overcome by these memories of a past full of youth and hope, wept unrestrainedly.

In the days of the Ottoman Empire a Turkish wedding was normally both a splendid and a protracted affair. The actual marriage, performed by the Imam, took place on the first day, attended by close relatives only; on the following day there was a tremendous reception, or rather two tremendous receptions, one for men and the other for the women. In the course of the proceedings the local people from round about were allowed at some point to come in—the gatekeeper admitted and welcomed them at the appropriate time, they were fed on a splendid scale, and then proceeded to admire the presents and see the bride in all the splendour of her (always French) wedding-dress, and of her new quarters—in particular they loved to inspect the bridal bedroom.

But what with war conditions, Orhan's very short leave, and the Pasha's scruples, it had been decided to cram all the ceremonies into a single day, so as to give the young people as long a spell of peace afterwards as possible. The honeymoon was not really a Turkish institution; newly-married couples retired on their wedding night to the house and rooms in which they hoped and expected to live and bring up their families—a very calm and dignified idea. (Can we say that hurrying off to the unaffectionate anonymity of strange hotels, at such a moment, is really a great improvement?)

Orhan duly arrived on the 25th of September. He stayed with his family, who had a yali near Scutari, but came over next day to pay his respects and to settle the final arrangements. He saw the Pasha first, and then was taken up to Réfiyé Hanim. Dil Feripé was hanging about, and when he left the salon she detained him in the big upper hall outside.

"Just one moment—please to come in here," she said mysteriously, and opening a door ushered him into a small pretty sitting-room; as he turned to ask her what she wanted, he saw the door silently closing behind her. There was no one in the room. A little puzzled, Orhan glanced about him curiously. He was taller than Ahmet, and slighter still—a willow-wand of a young man, with the ash-blond hair, light blue eyes, prominent cheek-bones and jutting hawk-like nose of many Anatolians; there was both vision and resolution in his face, fresh and youthful as it still was, and he had a curiously engaging open expression, as he stood looking round that small empty room. His visits to the haremlik at the

Pasha's, since the war, had been as frequent as the exigencies of military service allowed; but that was not very frequent, and they had been strictly confined to the salon. Why had the old dadi pushed him in here, he wondered.

From behind a door, ajar at the far side of the room, which he had not noticed at first, came a soft laugh. "Orhan, is it you?" said a low voice.

He sprang to the half-open door.

"Féridé, is it you?"

"Shsh! Yes." Peering through the opening he saw in the rather dim light a slender figure in a light silk frock, with a very elegant çarşaf of the same material covering her head and coming down to the elbows; a pale chiffon peçe hid the face, but above it two brilliant grey eyes gleamed under dark concentrated brows. It was all he could see, that and a slender hand with long narrow fingers, very white, which held the door.

"What is the news?" she asked at once, eagerly.

"Bad!" he said, plunged back from his happy eagerness into gloom by the question. "We keep on retreating—all the fight seems to have gone out of the Bulgars. And in the South it is worse; they say there has been a big attack down there—some say an actual break-through."

"Oh Orhan!—Ahmet!"

"Ahmet will be all right—he's on the staff. But this Allenby is a devil of a general, and has splendid troops; and there is a fiend—or a genius—called Lawrence who has stirred up all the Arabs, like a Mullah proclaiming a Holy War! And you know these unspeakable Germans direct everything, and over-ride our people, in their wooden-headed way." He sighed, an angry sigh.

"But will they not listen to *him*? He is down there now."

"No, indeed they will not! He always said it was absurd to attempt to recapture Baghdad; I hear he wrote direct to the Grand Vizier and the Minister of War about it, but they paid no heed. He resigned over that, you know."

"No!"

"Yes. Of course they had to put him back. But it all sounds very bad at this moment."

"It is terrible," Féridé said. "What will happen?"

"Ah, who knows? Ahmet writes wretchedly—we are all discouraged." He stopped, and recollected himself. "My two eyes, now it is only two days!"

"Yes." A single, satisfying word, softly and warmly spoken.

"And are you glad?"

"Yes, I am very glad."

The outer door opened and Dil Feripé's old head, çarşafed and peçe'd, was thrust in.

"Féridé, you must go to the Hanim Effendi. Come with me, if you please, Orhan Bey."

"Wait!" Férdié's voice was imperious. "When does Ahmet come?"

"Tomorrow, he said."

And so the interview terminated. It was not a typical one; but the circumstances were exceptional, and in fact Féridé was rather exceptional too. It was not every Turkish bride, even in 1918, who would have spent so much of an interview with her lover, illicitly contrived by a dadi, in discussing military affairs.

.   .   .   .

The wedding ceremonies began on the morning of September the 28th with the Nikia, the marriage contract. Besides the Pasha and Orhan's father there was the Imam, picturesque in a long black robe and spotless white turban; two witnesses for the bridegroom, Orhan, and one for the bride. She herself was not actually in the room—her representative went through into a smaller room where she waited with her attendants; asked her consent, obtained it, and returned and affixed his signature to the contract on her behalf; Orhan's representatives did the like for him. The Mihir, the document by which the bridegroom undertook to pay a certain lump sum in the event of a divorce taking place, had been signed when Orhan came over a couple of days previously—so the actual wedding-day was not clouded by this gloomy though practical proceeding.

The legal formalities being over, there was a light luncheon, eaten rather hastily, for the family part of the ceremonial was still to come. For this all the nearest relations, men and women alike, assembled in the "sofa," the big stone-floored room with the fountain—where in the past Dr. Pierce had so often taken coffee and discussed poetry with the Pasha. The women stood a little apart, all in rich and very fashionable dresses, but with that curious adjunct of the short çarşaf in the same material, covering their heads and coming down to their elbows, and the pale silken peçes masking their faces except for the eyes—somehow these made them look like a static ballet of a fashion-parade, turned into ghosts. The men, wearing the fez, stood in another group, in which uniforms predominated. The bridegroom was not present at this stage of the proceedings—nor most strangely, was Ahmet, who should have been there for the Nikia in the morning too; there were a few subdued whisperings among the group of women, but no one could explain his absence. Now came the ceremony of the Koltuk, symbolic of the bride's chastity: very calm, very dignified, rather sombre. An elderly Aunt took Féridé by the hand and led her up to her Father; she kissed him dutifully. He then took a rich scarf, and made the gesture of knotting it about her waist; the oriental, rather barbaric thing looked strange enough on her shimmering modern lamé dress—after a tiny pause another woman removed it and took it away. Very formally, according to age, Féridé then went round the group of male relations, lightly embracing each in turn; then crossed to the group of women relatives, and kissed them warmly. This was the farewell to the family, and most of the women were in tears; only Réfiyé Hanim—who cared more than any of them—remained magnificently controlled.

After the ceremony of farewell came the bestowal of gifts, for which this was the traditionally appropriate moment. From a leather and white satin case Murad Zadé Asaf Pasha, first, drew out a superb string of pearls, which Nilüfer clasped round Féridé's neck—rather disarranging her çarşaf in so doing. Réfiyé Hanim gave an exquisite collarette of diamonds. Then it became a shower: diamond, emerald, and sapphire brooches were pinned all over the bosom of the lamé dress, bracelets and rings pushed on or fastened over the white kid gloves; more necklaces were piled round that slender neck. Smiling, laughing, kissing, Féridé accepted and thanked for this wealth of presents.

Now there was a little confusion. The correct procedure at this juncture was for the men to retire into the selamlik to receive the guests who had not been asked to the Koltuk, while a man of the family brought in the bridegroom, who would then escort his bride into their own quarters, where she in her turn would presently receive her guests. The proper person to do this was of course Ahmet—but where *was* Ahmet? On this day of all days? The Pasha, a rigid formalist, led the men off to his study through one of the twin doors under the two staircases; Réfiyé Hanim summoned Fuad, the young cousin, who was in full uniform, to her, and despatched him through the other door to fetch Orhan, who throughout the ceremony of the Koltuk and the present-giving had been waiting in an empty room, smoking innumerable cigarettes, and walking up and down in understandable agitation. The cousin led him through into the "sofa," where Féridé was presented to him—officially, for the first time. He saluted her gravely, then gave her his arm, and led her up the right-hand staircase, her train shimmering behind her as they went. On and on, through one room after another, till at last they reached their own apartments, full of flowers and presents—full already, moreover, of women guests, who had not attended the family function downstairs, and who so far had only been received by the servants and Mahmud Agha, who had greeted them one and all with much emotion; they now greeted the young couple with little cries of "Bonheur!" and "Lifelong Happiness!" Greeting in return, it was now Féridé who knew where to stop—on the big settee in what would in future be her own boudoir, next to their bedroom. Here someone, knowing the rules, closed the door after them, and for about five minutes they were left in peace—Féridé still veiled in her peçe, but together, and alone. Rather overcome, Orhan took her hand; she pressed it in return. But at first they were silent, a little embarrassed, and just sat, holding hands.

"What a lovely room," Orhan said then, looking at the delicately panelled ceiling, on which were paintings of an almost Persian freshness and fineness.

"Yes—it was done for my great-grandmother. But Orhan, where is Ahmet? What *can* have happened to him?"

"I cannot imagine. He was to have come up on last night's train."

"Could he be wounded?"

"Oh no, I do not think so." Orhan was embarrassed—he knew that the Turkish army in Palestine was in full retreat, and he was anxious himself. "Do not torment yourself, my bride," he said. "Something must have delayed him."

There was a tap on the door, and Nilüfer slipped in—a married woman of two years' standing, she knew the correct formalities.

"Orhan, my brother, the time is up. You should go to the selamlik to greet your guests."

He rose, and bowing, asked his wife's permission to leave her; then he went out—the two young women could hear through the half-open door the little gale of gay feminine greetings that saluted him as he passed through the outer room.

"My bijou, before they come in, let me take off *some* of these things," said Nilüfer, beginning to unpin one or two of the brooches that loaded the breast of Féridé's dress.

"Oh yes, do—I look like the counter in a jeweller's shop!" Féridé muttered, laughing, standing up and glancing at herself in a French gilt mirror. "*Ah*, and these rings are so tight over my gloves! And the bracelets so heavy." She began to pull them off herself, and put them on a small table which had been placed ready for the purpose. But when Nilüfer began to unfasten some of the necklaces—"*Not* that of Pederim! [my father] and not that of Niné!" said Féridé quickly.

"No, no," Nilüfer said soothingly—"but look, sweet-meat, do sit a moment; you are so tall, I can't reach! That's better. And don't throw those bracelets down like that—arrange them properly," she murmured in a low tone; "people will want to look at them."

Indeed, before the process was complete, the throng of gaily-dressed ladies came surging in from next door, of course unveiled, since this was now a women's gathering; kissing, congratulating, admiring—admiring Féridé's dress, her pretty suite of rooms, her tableful of jewellery. Dil Feripé came too, and let out her familiar pea-hen screech of disapproval at sight of the table—there was no cloth on it! She went pattering off in haste, and returned with a piece of Broussa cut velvet, on which she re-arranged all the glittering gifts in accordance with her own taste, scolding Nilüfer the while for not having sent for the cloth, and Féridé for having taken off too many of the brooches. This did not in the least discompose the guests, who had dadi's of their own; they stood about and shifted through the three rooms, talking and laughing—Féridé however kept her correct place, on or near the big settee; Dil Feripé saw to that.

Then one of the "aunts" came in to say that the populace had arrived. And in accordance with that pretty and gracious tradition, in they came, mostly in black from head to foot, long black çarşafs moulding their heads to black spheres, and covering everything but their eyes; among the bright dresses they looked like a flock of crows in an aviary full of birds of Paradise. Work-worn hands reached out from under the voluminous dark draperies to take the bride's hand, kiss it, and lay it to their cheeks—and then to point at and finger, very discreetly, the beautiful things all about. Most of all they wanted to see the bridal chamber and the bridal bed; they stood in there in crowds, admiring that vast velvet and gold coverlet on the bed itself, and the prayer-mat spread ready in the corner, while a couple of kalfas stood by, pointing out their beauties, themselves full of vicarious pride and happiness. Another marriage; hope for another family of children—this was the source of their very sane and human joy and satisfaction, and the black-clad women of the district shared it with them.

The populace presently took their departure, still exclaiming over the splendours they had seen, still wishing the bride long life. Those great things in human existence, custom and good manners—which, strictly observed, make life so smooth and pleasant—prescribed the duration of their stay, and they knew the rules and adhered to them. The black crows, happy and chattering, again mingled for a moment or two with the birds of Paradise, as they passed out and down the stairs to be regaled with roast mutton. "May they have many children, and strong!" said the goodwives of the neighbourhood as they took their leave.

Upstairs, more conversation—during these happy moments, the war seemed forgotten. Except for Ahmet. There was a great deal of whispering and speculation about Ahmet's absence; the ladies who had been present at the Koltuk ceremony mentioned it to their friends upstairs, and set the tide of wonder flowing. Meanwhile maids clad in silk walked in, carrying huge silver trays laden with sherbet in silver cups, followed by others bearing trays—also silver—of ices. (One might have been at the court of King Solomon.) The "aunts" fussed about, Dil Feripé whispering to Nilüfer and Féridé that the sherbets should have come much sooner.

At last, in a sort of pause before supper, Nilüfer shepherded the guests out of the boudoir and left the bride to enjoy a few moments' peace and quiet. Dil Feripé and a maid helped her to re-arrange her hair and face, as she sat for the first time before her new dressing-table, covered with her new silver and crystal toilet set, her new blond tortoise-shell brushes and combs and power-boxes. Then she went out into her boudoir, threw back the shutters, and sitting on the divan under the open window, breathing the evening air, she watched the calm beauty of the light over shore and water and the low hills of Chamlidja beyond. She was married!—and life spread out before her, to be lived in these lovely rooms that were now *hers*, with her husband, in intimacy and love, and yet within daily, hourly reach of her Father and Réfiyé Hanim. What could be more perfect? The seventeen-year-old bride sighed with happiness—and then sighed again, differently. "My little Fanny, my Canaria! I wish *she* were here today. I wonder where she is, and what she is doing," said Féridé.

The supper which followed the reception was not, for the women at any rate, a formal meal at all; in fact it was all rather elegantly haphazard. Not only in the great dim dining-room and Réfiyé Hanim's salon, but through all the rooms of the haremlik and in Féridé's suite, servants in bright silken dresses came bearing big circular trays which they set down on the innumerable small tables scattered about, and the women sat round them in small groups to eat. But however informal the serving, a Turkish wedding-feast in those days was always a notable thing. There were certain dishes, principally sweet ones, such as the Turks love, which always appeared at weddings—special jellies and creams, thick with honey, ices, and towards the end "zerdé," a concoction of rice, sugar, and saffron, which traditionally was never served save at marriages.

Down in the selamlik, however, the men ate more formally; an immense dining-table, presided over by the Pasha, was set out in a large room, with smaller tables round it for the younger and less important guests; and there rows and circles of red fezzes bent over the groaning and abundant boards. Into the midst of this festivity there came limping a young officer. Apologising, he approached the Pasha—"A message from the Ministry of War," he murmured, very low. The Pasha excused himself, rose, and stepped aside; the young man handed him a paper, which he read—they spoke for a moment or two; Orhan, also with apologies, left his place and joined them. The young officer, bowing and saluting, then left; Orhan returned to his place, his face grave. The Pasha, standing in his, addressed the company, who had fallen silent at this unexpected intrusion.

"I have just received a telegram from my son Ahmet, explaining why he cannot be with us today," he said. "He is very sorry; he apologises"— and he sat down.

"Orhan, what *is* it? Did you see it? What did it say?" Fuad, the young cousin, asked urgently, in a low tone.

"Yes, I saw it. It said that there was 'activity' down in Palestine, and that leave was cancelled," Orhan replied, equally low.

"That was Hassan Bey, wasn't it?" Fuad asked.

"Yes. As you know, since he was wounded at Anafartalar he is in the Ministry of War—and he brought out the telegram. But Fuad— don't talk about it, Asaf Pasha doesn't seem to have noticed it—but the telegram is dated the 23rd."

"No! But today is the 28th! And why did it go to the War Office, and not to the Pasha direct?"

"Because Kemal Pasha countersigned it—he is always kind, and he is very fond of Ahmet. But as to the delay, there must be great confusion down there. We must not tell Nilüfer, but Hassan says there has been a tremendous English attack, really a breakthrough; our troops are re-treating on Damascus—headlong!"

"How frightful! Was he sure?"

"Perfectly sure. And my dear Fuad, there is worse than that."

"What can be worse?"

"The Bulgarians have signed a separate Armistice with the Entente."

"It's not possible!"

"I tell you it has happened. Hassan heard it in the Ministry. May Allah destroy them! They have been half-hearted these weeks past— but to run out now, and without a word to us!"

"But this is shocking!—appalling!" Fuad stopped, almost speechless. "What is to prevent the Entente troops, now, from coming *here?*"

"Well, *we* have little enough up in Thrace to hold them with," said Orhan bitterly. "We have relied on those wretched Bulgarians so largely —we had to."

At this point the Pasha made a move from the table, and all the men rose. The muttered colloquy between Fuad and Orhan had not passed unnoticed, and there were whisperings from ear to ear; released from their places, several of the younger men came over to join them, and heard the evil tidings.

"Ah, if they had only listened to *him!*" said one young officer. "He said from the beginning that it would be fatal for us to go into this war—and when has Mustafa Kemal Pasha been mistaken?"

Meanwhile the older men had gathered round the Pasha, and listened to the bad news with grave faces. Presently he summoned a servant with a gesture, and despatched him on some errand—a few minutes later Mdlle Marthe entered the room. (As a foreigner and a Christian, she could come and go freely between the men's and women's quarters.) Grey-headed, dignified, calm, she stood while the Pasha spoke to his guests. "You will excuse my absence for a few minutes—I must bring my son's message to my daughter." Amid courteous murmurs of acquiescence he left the room, followed by the Frenchwoman.

But once they entered the haremlik she preceded him—into room after room she went, scattering the unveiled female guests with the words "The Pasha is coming." He waited in an anteroom for a few moments while she cleared Féridé's own suite, and then passed through to his daughter's boudoir, between the chairs thrust aside in haste and the abandoned tables of delicacies, to where she stood before the great settee, awaiting him.

"My Father, is it news of Ahmet? Oh, not bad news!" she said, clasping her long hands. Such a visit, at such a moment, was so unprecedented that she was trembling with anxiety.

"Of Ahmet himself the news is not bad, no," he said, and handed her the telegram—she scanned it rapidly. "Ah, my dear brother!—he sends me his love," she exclaimed; then she read it again, and like a hawk pounced on the date. "But my Father, this was sent *five days ago!*"

"Was it? Let me see," her father said, taking it from her again.

"Why such a delay? Something must be gravely amiss," she said. "And 'activity,' 'all leave cancelled'! What can it mean?" She glanced quickly at him; his face spoke of disaster. "My Father, there is more than this—I see that you know it. Please to tell me."

He told her the shattering news of the Bulgarian Armistice. She considered it, with thoughtful eyebrows. "Does Niné know?" she asked then.

"No. Please convey the news to her, and also about your brother. Now I must rejoin my guests; farewell for the present, my child. This is a sad wedding-day for you—not what I could have wished."

How much sadder it was to become neither of them knew then—but at his words she flung her arms round her father's neck.

"Baba-djim, but for Ahmet's absence, and now this terrible news, it has been a wonderful fête! I thank you for it."

Féridé said nothing of what she had learned, except that Ahmet was delayed, till just at the close, when the ladies were muffling themselves in their cloaks and çarşafs for departure; then she murmured the disastrous tidings in the ears of some of the younger ones. And when they had all gone, she told Nilüfer and Réfiyé Hanim. The old woman listened with a shocked face; at last she said—"Send Dil Feripé to me. I am a little tired; I think, dji-djim, that I will go to bed." But as she moved away on the old creature's arm, Féridé heard her murmur— "Notre pauvre pays!"

When she had gone to bed Féridé and Nilüfer withdrew to Féridé's rooms, and sat disconsolately eating sweets from one of the innumerable boxes that had come as presents. This was the bridal night, and there were still ceremonies to be gone through: the bridegroom should hand to the bride the yüsgürumlük, the gift made for the privilege of seeing her unveiled face; and then should see it, when he removed her veil. And he must make—kneeling on that velvet mat embroidered with gold thread—the ceremonial prayer to ask a blessing on his marriage. But so far there was no sign of any bridegroom! The two young women talked in low voices, discussing the news, huddled together on a divan— picking nervously at the bonbons, and equally nervously, now and again, breaking into giggles as they recalled this or that odd incident during the day's events.

The men, meanwhile, had been holding a gloomy discussion about both the reported break-through and the Bulgarian Armistice down in the selamlik, over innumerable tiny cups of coffee. Eventually most of them left; the Pasha and one or two old cronies moved to his study. Orhan and Fuad started to follow them, mechanically, but at the study door Fuad paused. "My dear Orhan—your wife. Should you not go up and see her? Mon Dieu, what a wedding for her!"

"Yes—indeed. Of course I will. But—Seigneur Dieu, do you know that I am not sure that I know the way!"

"No wonder—this house is like Versailles!" Fuad said, laughing. "I know it—I was here so much as a child, when Féridé Hanim's mother was alive. But I have no business up there!"

"Ah, nonsense. What does that matter, at a time like this? Take me up, like a good fellow. She will be so anxious, and poor Nilüfer too, I don't doubt."

They made their way upstairs. In the outer room they encountered Dil Feripé, hanging about, clucking like an anxious hen; at sight of them she began to scold. It was late, the bride was tired—and she was abandoned! Where was the yüsgürumlük? Why did not Orhan Bey give it, and let her prepare the child for bed? Dil Feripé had known Fuad since he was born, and Orhan was now a son of the house, so she scolded away, freely and impartially. Affectionately, firmly, Fuad brushed her aside. "Wait, aunt! Just five minutes! We have matters to speak of."

"Has he the gift?" the old woman persisted.

"Yes, yes!—he has it. There! Now, leave us in peace, my good aunt."

He pushed Orhan before him into the boudoir, and closed the door gently after him on the fussing devoted old creature.

They found the two young women still sitting forlornly on the divan. Féridé sprang up, flashing like a sword in her silver dress, and went to them. "At last! But now, please to tell us all about it. What does it involve? Can we not fight on without them? The Germans are not yielding, are they? And how bad is it really, down in the South?"

The young men, sitting down, proceeded to explain what it involved. Practically speaking, it left the land route to Istanbul through Thrace open, except for the rather scanty Turkish forces up there—so Fuad explained. Orhan took him up on the strength of these forces, and the two officers argued it between them, while the girls listened in growing dismay. Dil Feripé kept poking her head in at the door and being chivvied away by Fuad, with a—"Wait, Aunt! a little patience, in Allah's name!"—then he would turn to renew the discussion. These interruptions introduced an element of the absurd into what was anyhow the strangest of scenes, for that place and that time. One thing struck Orhan particularly, about this bride of his of whom he knew so little at first hand—how swiftly she grasped, and how remorselessly her question pursued the crucial, the vital points: What would the Germans do? Would they hold on? What were they doing in the South? To that, neither of the young men knew the answer. The news from France, now the main theatre of war, was not good; the German stroke against Amiens in the spring had failed of its main objective, and now their forces were being slowly pressed back against the Hindenburg Line. The outlook was gloomy whichever way one turned.

But when they began to discuss Hassan's rumour about the Palestine front, Nilüfer's nerves gave way. Tired, anxious, overwrought, she burst into tears. At once the others were all concern: Fuad, glancing at his watch, saw the incredible lateness of the hour, and fled; Féridé led Nilüfer off to her own rooms, comforting her as best she could, and handed her over to her maid, who was waiting for her. Then she returned to her new suite—and now, at last, Dil Feripé, still waiting, came into her own. She hurried in, all tender bustle; brushed Orhan aside, and led her darling into the bedroom, where she undressed her, brushed her thick hair, and robed her for the night, putting a rich dressing-gown of Broussa silk over her nightdress. Then she summoned poor Orhan, who had gone off to his dressing-room—a little embarrassed, but still wondering chiefly what was really going on in the South. He came in slowly; Dil Feripé went out. The two young people stood for a few moments in silence, looking at one another. And then there came a light tap on the door. This was unbelievable—Orhan and

Féridé stared at each other in silent astonishment. "It must be Dil Feripé again!—what can be the matter?" said Féridé, and went to the door. To her immense astonishment, Fuad stood there, with Dil Feripé beside him.

"Féridé—Féridé Hanim, I beseech you to pardon me!—but I must speak with Orhan." He had a piece of paper in his hand.

"With Orhan? Now? But about what?"

Orhan, hearing his name, came out, also in his dressing-gown—they all stood together in the boudoir.

"A military messenger has just brought that," said Fuad, handing Orhan the paper. "I stayed a little talking with Mahmud Agha at the gate, and the messenger came while I was there. The paper was only folded, and I took the great liberty of reading it, hoping that it could wait till tomorrow—but it will not wait."

Orhan unfolded the paper, whose colour and texture were all too familiar—then checked himself. "Will you permit me?" he asked Féridé.

"Of course! Read it quickly! What is it?" With a brother in the army for more than three years, Féridé also was familiar with the appearance of such missives.

"'Urgent. Rejoin your unit immediately.'" Orhan read out slowly.

"But you were given leave for a week . . ." Féridé began; then checked herself. "Yes—I see. It is this new development." She turned away, twisting her narrow hands together.

"But can this mean now?—tonight?" Orhan asked Fuad, in bewilderment.

"The messenger says that everyone on leave is going back tonight—there is a special train." Fuad looked distressed and embarrassed.

"Then I must go. I shall have to see your Father, and take leave of him, and explain," he said, turning to Féridé. "Will he be awake? And—mon Dieu—how shall I find him?"

"I will go and tell him," said Fuad. "I know the way. I will come back here for you."

"Very well—thank you, mon ami." As Fuad left he turned again to Féridé. "Oh, my bride, my darling!"

"It has to be!" she said—she had recovered herself now.

"There is one thing still," the young man said. He went back into the bedroom, Féridé following, and kneeling down on the gold and velvet mat, he made his ceremonial prayer, asking for a blessing on their marriage. Féridé, standing by the empty bed, prayed too, silently. When he rose, he took her in his arms. "Sometime, oh light of my eyes!" he said, and went away to dress. He did not come back; she heard his swift abrupt movements in the next room—packing, and snapping his valise to—and then the sharp closing of his door, and his footsteps crossing the boudoir. She sank down then on the edge of the bed, and sat very still; she felt cold.

What was that? The door from the boudoir was opening. What now? she thought, springing up.

The door opened further, and Dil Feripé sidled in. "Oh my lamb, my jewel!—and he has had to go to the war!" The old woman wrapped her beloved child in her arms, rocking her to and fro—then she took off the gorgeous dressing-gown, thrust her into bed, and tucked her up, as she had done so many many times. "Allah be merciful!" murmured the dadi as she turned out the lights, and tiptoed away.

It was only next morning that they found the yüsgürumlük, the gift for the sight of the bride's face, lying, ungiven and forgotten, on a chair in the boudoir.

Chapter Five

Fuad called a couple of days later to see Féridé. He had been badly wounded some months before, and on his recovery was considered unfit for active service and given a job at Haidar Pasha—but now he had been re-called, he told her, to the Southern front. Since she was now a married woman, at least in status, and he a first cousin and an *intime* of the family, this visit was quite in order; but Féridé felt a little strange nevertheless, receiving him in her own salon, and alone, instead of in Réfiyé Hanim's presiding presence.

But Fuad had not merely come to say goodbye. He wished, he said, to tell her about Orhan's farewell interview with her father, and proceeded to do so.

"Asaf Pasha was in his dressing-room in his *robe-de-chambre*," Fuad began, "smoking a narghilé—you know how he does, sometimes, when he has been busy, or agitated. I told him what had happened. 'But naturally he must go,' he said; and then—oh *ma chère cousine*, I wish you had seen his face—he got up, rather stiffly, as he does now, and went and stood looking at some of those verses in calligraphy on the wall—you know he has them even in his dressing-room—and began to mutter to himself. He spoke low, but I heard what he said. 'My poor child!' first; and then he stood up suddenly very straight, in his long robe, and looked—oh, like a prophet!—and said very clearly and firmly: 'It appears that Turkish women must be heroes now, as well as Turkish men.' I never heard him say such a thing, and in such a manner, before!"

"My *dear* Father! Well, and then?" Féridé asked.

"Then I went to fetch Orhan. I met him here, with his valise in his hand," said Fuad. "He had been very quick. We went down together. The Pasha had gone to his study—imagine, he must have lighted the candles himself!—but he was still in his dressing-gown. He said to Orhan—'I hear you have your orders.' 'Yes, Excellency,' Orhan said, and drew the paper from his pocket, and held it out. Asaf Pasha took it, and read it, and handed it back, and said—'Well, for a soldier, immediately means immediately. Farewell, my son,' And that was all."

The next weeks were very strange to Féridé. They would have been strange enough if Orhan had been opposite her when she sat down to meals in her new dining-room; to sit alone was almost incredible. All her life she had been lapped round with companionship and love; escorted by Mdlle Marthe or an "aunt" for every excursion outside the house, and even in the garden usually accompanied by some elder, except when Nilüfer or Fanny was with her. Fanny had brought an unwonted breath of freedom and independence into her life, as no one else had done; and now, in her new solitude, her thoughts turned often to her Canary, her little yellow-haired friend, whom she had not seen or heard of for four long years. But she would not break her isolation, and return to her grandmother's table; some curious instinct forbade that. Réfiyé Hanim had fitted her out with a staff of servants, and soberly she ordered her meals and ate them in that astonished solitude, after the chatter of Mdlle Marthe and the old women rattling in her ears all her life till now; she dealt with her little household, she must learn, it was all practice; and one day Orhan would come back, and she would be ready for him.

But she did often slip through the endless rooms of the great house to sit with Niné and roll bandages, and hear the latest news that the Pasha had brought back from his Club, the Cercle de l'Orient; or she would seek out Nilüfer, who always drooped and flagged, like a broken lily, in Ahmet's absence, and rouse her up to come and walk in the garden or the koru, to get some air. The weather was growing chilly, as it does on the Bosphorus in October; cold winds blew down from the Black Sea, tearing the small pink and yellow leaves off the bushes on the cliff and up in the koru, and whirling them high in the air, and heaping up the tough rounded leaves of the Judas-trees under the marble seats in the garden, or sending them out in scuds over the water, to join the leaf-like flights of the "Lost Souls."

"Oh, it is so sad, autumn," Nilüfer would say, leaning on the balustrade and watching the doomed leaves flying out over the rushing strait after the haunted birds.

It was of course high time that they should have moved back to Péra, into the konak, the great town house. But with the general situation so uncertain, the Pasha had decided to keep his household at the vali for the moment. In 1918 Istanbul was even more largely built of wood than it is today, and the effect of a possible bombardment on that wooden city, with streets so narrow that fire-engines could hardly get along them, was too ghastly to contemplate. The great Fire Tower, its crenellated top rising high above the steep slope of buildings, whence watch is kept for outbreaks, is to this day a constant reminder of that peril, even in peace-time—and no one who has watched a fire, after dark, over by the Galata quarter, the flames leaping as high as the dome of Hagia Sofia, is ever likely to forget the horror of the sight.

So they stayed—and the great braziers of bright brass, the mangals, a metre wide and wrought like huge open lotus-flowers were brought in and set on the floor in the salon, the dining-room (because Réfiyé Hanim was so chilly nowadays) and the Pasha's study; filled with red-hot charcoal they glowed away for hours, giving out a surprising heat, and the women of the household tended more and more to gather round them, together in the pleasant warmth, and discuss the news in lowered tones.

It was never good news, now. It got steadily worse. Quite soon after Féridé's wedding the tidings of the retreat in the Levant—first to Damascus, then on to Aleppo, abandoning the whole of Syria, began to filter through. The Pasha alone realised how much of a rout that retreat actually was; but on the map—and Féridé had a map, and studied it—the names spoke for themselves. He and Réfiyé Hanim and Féridé combined to keep the facts from Nilüfer as far as possible—she was not a person who studied maps. It was only very much later that they learned how skilfully Kemal Pasha had carried through that retreat, and saved the bulk of his army, and some of the panic-stricken Fourth as well; riding constantly, not in safety at the head of his columns, but at the tail with the stragglers, cheering them on by his presence, and by that blunt exchange of talk with the humblest conditions of men which, all his life, was one of his greatest pleasures as well as one of the main secrets of his political strength.

And then the telegram came to say that Ahmet was a prisoner, captured by the English at that disastrous crossing of the Jordan, when the rearguard of the Seventh Army was taken by surprise and caught more or less en bloc. It came to the Pasha, and he went straight up with it to Réfiyé Hanim. She saw the paper in his hand, and her own crept to her heart—the kalfas, who had risen at his entrance, at some almost imperceptible gesture of his scurried out, but Mdlle Marthe, rising too, went and stood beside her old employer.

"No, Ané," he said at once: "it is not the worst. Really it is good news. He is a prisoner."

"Not among the Arabs?" Réfiyé Hanim knew something about the Arabs.

"No, by God's mercy—he was taken by the English."

"Ah, God be thanked and praised for that!" She, always so erect, for once leant back against her cushions; Mdlle Marthe's eyebrows enquired, silently, whether she wanted her drops—she was very white. She made a faint gesture of negation.

"Tell me, my son," she said then. He told her what he knew, which was little beside the bare facts: Ahmet was a prisoner, in English hands, taken at the Jordan crossing. Like her grand-daughter-in-law, Réfiyé Hanim did not study maps, nor had she any very clear idea of the timing of the campaign—it never occurred to her that Ahmet had actually been a prisoner for three or four days at the time of Féridé's marriage. "Ah, thank God that he is in English hands," she said again, when the Pasha finished. "I am sure they treat their prisoners well." But then she turned to the practical aspect. "Does Nilüfer know?"

"No, Ané. I came at once to you."

"Féridé must tell her," said the old lady, with decision; "she is the person who will do it best. My good Marthe, send someone to ask Féridé to come here, if you please."

Féridé, graceful, tall and elegant in one of her warm autumn trousseau frocks, came hurrying in. To this daughter of his, the Pasha merely handed the telegram without a word; no precautions, no managements, were necessary with her—he realised that.

She ran to her grandmother, knelt at her feet, and embraced her. "Oh Niné, how good God is! He is safe!"

"Yes, my jewel—he is; you are right," said the old lady, kissing and fondling her as if she were still the small wild child who used to lose and tear her çarşaf.

"And Nilüfer? Does she know?"

"No, not yet," said the Pasha.

"But she must know at once! It is really for her, such *good* news."

"We thought you could tell her best," said the Pasha.

"Oh, I will, I will—at once. May I have this?" She took the telegram, and hastened away.

Here Mdlle Marthe put in her word.

"Mais quelle merveille, cette enfant!" she ejaculated.

"Yes—there are few like Féridé," Réfiyé Hanim replied. "She owes you much, my dear Marthe," she added.

Féridé had some trouble to persuade her sister-in-law that the news was really so good. "But *when* will he return, when?" Nilüfer kept saying, disconsolately.

"Chérie, at least he *will* return—prisoners are always safe," Féridé encouraged her. She spent most of her time for the next few days with the lovely unhappy creature, trying to cheer her up.

In spite of all the bad news which preceded it, the Armistice of Mudros, when it was announced, came like a thunderclap to the Turkish people. Féridé always remembered how she first heard the news, because she was in the hammam, having a bath and washing her hair. A bath in Turkey under the old régime was, like so many other things in life, rather an elaborate performance. The interior of the hammam consisted of several rooms, walled and floored with marble: in one the bather left her garments, and then, wearing a more modest version of those nahlins, or sandal-clogs, went on into another where hot and cold water fell from spouts into marble basins, and washed. If it was the hair, that was washed first—anything up to seven times—and then bound up in a turban on the head. Next the body was washed, also several times. But there was no comfortable plunge into a steaming tub; the temperature in the bathing-room was of course kept high on purpose, but one stood on the marble floor and scrubbed and scrubbed, over and over again, while a maid or dadiv dipped up water in a hammered silver bowl from a hot spout and dashed it over one's body to fall all over the marble floor and drain away, at last, through small holes or gratings. (Turks are inclined to think that to lie and soak in a bath in the same soapy water into which you have just scrubbed off all your dirt is an extremely unpleasant and unhygienic proceeding—as it well may be; in any case even today every public bathroom in quite modern Turkish hotels is provided with an enamel bowl for the water-dashing process, and the westerner, European or American, who goes to take a bath is liable to find the floor a swamp as a result.) After this vertical scrubbing and splashing, one got into a bathrobe of Turkish towelling and retired into yet another room to dry off and, probably, to be rubbed and lightly massaged by some personal attendant.

Féridé had finished with her hair, but had only scrubbed herself twice, and was preparing for a third effort, when Dil Feripé came pattering into the hammam—where Féridé was concerned she had no reserves or inhibitions at all.

"News! Wonderful news!" she screeched. "The war is at an end. Oh, Allah be praised! Now, my jewel, you can really be married! Orhan Bey is sure to return at once." (Dil Feripé did not know much about the process of demobilisation.)

"How do you know this?" Féridé asked incredulously, soap in hand.

"Osman brought the paper, and saw it, and passed on the word."

Féridé flung on her bath-robe, and hurried into the drying-room; she sat on a couch while the maid rubbed her down, but today there was no resting, no massage. She dressed hastily, went up and put something more respectable over her damp hair, and went at once to the salon.

"Niné, have you heard? Is it true? How has it been arranged?"

"I have only heard what the dadis know from the servants. Allah grant that it is true!"

Féridé fidgeted about impatiently.

"Oh, I wish my Father would come! I wish we had a paper of our own—how convenient that would be!"

"I see no need for such a thing," said Réfiyé Hanim, calmly; the old maids looked faintly shocked at the mere suggestion.

At that moment the Pasha walked in, the paper in his hand. He seemed greatly concerned, but did not omit his usual greeting—"I trust, Ané, that your health is good?" And—"By the goodness of God, my son, I am very well," the old lady replied. Then he greeted his daughter—"I trust, my child, that you also are well?" Féridé, as a married woman, now received more formal courtesies than before.

"Very well, I thank you, my Father," she replied, living up to her new position—but then her fine married manners broke down. "Oh Baba-djim," she cried, reverting to her childish form of address, "is it true? Is it *good* news? Oh, do please tell us all about it!"

The Pasha sat down slowly in a small chair by the brazier, his long thin legs stuck out in front of him. Suddenly he looked very old, Féridé thought. "It is true," he replied slowly, "but it is by no means good. I can hardly credit that our Government can have agreed to such terms."

"What are the terms, my son?" Réfiyé Hanim asked.

The Pasha unfolded the paper.

"We are to open the Dardanelles and Bosphorus to Entente men-of-war, and give them free access to the Black Sea," he said, obviously giving a résumé as he read; 'we are to hand over our whole Navy, and any other warships now in our waters—and in addition, should they require it, we are to place our mercantile marine at their disposition.'"

"Mais c'est incroyable!" Réfiyé Hanim murmured.

"That is not all," said the Pasha, with indescribable bitterness in his tone. "We are to demobilise the Army immediately—well, ça se comprend; but in addition we are to hand over to the Entente all our troops now in the Caucasus, in the Hedjaz, in Irak and the Yemen, and in Syria."

"But that means Fuad!" Féridé interjected. "Will he become a prisoner of war?"

"He will if these terms are actually carried out. But—" most unexpectedly a tiny smile crept round the Pasha's grim mouth—"I have an idea that that hero of Ahmet's may somehow arrange that very few of our troops are still in Syria by the time the Armistice terms are put into execution."

"Baba, are you coming round to approve of Mustafa Kemal Pasha? No!" Féridé exclaimed.

"He is skilful and resourceful, one must admit that," the Pasha said, judgematically. "God grant that he uses his powers now! I understand he is to have a new command, of all the Yilderim Armies, as from tomorrow. But do not speak of this."

"Is there any more, my son?" Réfiyé Hanim asked, her eyes on the paper.

"Oh yes," he replied, once again bitter. "They are to take over the tunnels of the Taurus Railway, to have free use of our ports and railways for their transport, and to control all our wireless and cable stations."

"But—our railways, the tunnels, our cable stations!—and to pass through to the Black Sea! If all that is the case, we—we are not independent any more!" Féridé burst out, her grey eyes wide.

"No, we are not," said the Pasha, more bitterly than ever. "A beaten nation is not usually left with much independence."

"But have *we* really been beaten? The Germans have so taken things into their own hands—" For once Féridé's voice faltered.

"Yes, my child, we have; avouons-le," said the Pasha. "By this Allenby —and of course this strange devil of a Lawrence has helped, he and his Bedouins."

Réfiyé Hanim put down the bandage she had been rolling; it looked as if bandages would no longer be necessary.

"Well, at least we have been beaten by the English," she said. "Not by the French, or these barbarous Russians or Bulgarians. The English are 'gentlemen'—(she used the English word)—and they will treat us well. My Father always said that we could trust the English; that they had often helped us, and were our best friends. He saw much of them—he liked them."

Poor Réfiyé Hanim, and many beside her, were to suffer a sad disappointment. What she did not reckon on was that in the 1914-18 War England had allies, and that with her vast commitments, and the urgent desire for demobilisation, she might now have to delegate certain tasks to those allies. Once the war was really ended she handed over a good deal of the business connected with Turkey to her allies the French. But at the moment there was a general crumpling-up of all those nations on whose side Turkey had entered the war. On November the 3rd came the news that the Emperor Charles of Austria had fled to Switzerland; then that the Kaiser had abdicated and fled to Holland; there were rumours of mutiny in the German Fleet; finally, on November the 11th, the Armistice between Germany and the Entente Powers was announced. Two days later an Anglo-French fleet came steaming up the Marmara, and cast anchor off Istanbul.

The Pasha, who had gone into the Club to pick up the latest news, saw them. He heard that they were there, and went down to the water-front by Dolmabatché to look at them. There they lay, the great wicked-looking ships, made grotesque by the uncouth camouflaged designs along their sides, their gun-turrets and super-structures profiled against that wonderful outline of rounded domes and pointed minarets, above Seraglio Point, that is like nothing else in the world. The Pasha stood and stared at them, almost incredulous, bitterness and humiliation filling his heart. So an American might feel who should see a Japanese fleet off Hoboken, or an Englishman at the sight of German destroyers lying in the Thames within revolver-shot of the Tower of London. The wonderful Narrows of the Dardanelles, guarded by those tremendous fortifications, from which all attacks had been beaten off, should have kept these waters, at least, inviolable—now they might as well never have existed; that hideous loss of life, the decimation of the Turkish Army, had been all in vain. As he climbed slowly up the hill again to his carriage, the Pasha remembered the last time he had seen foreign warships arrive in the Marmara: four years ago, when he had looked with satisfaction on the *Goeben* and *Breslau*, lying where these others now lay. Had that really been such a good thing, after all? At the time he had only thought how magnificently they replaced the *Reshadieh* and the *Sultan Osman*, which the perfidious English had retained for their own use; he had watched them, some weeks later, steaming up the Bosphorus to the Black Sea for their cruel raid on Sevastopol and Novorossisk. Then, that also had seemed natural enough—but now? Was that one reason why the Armistice terms were so terribly severe? Had the Germans, Enver Pasha's dear friends, just used Turkey for their own purposes? Had it really been so wise to refuse the guarantee of the absolute integrity of all Turkey's dominions, offered her at the outbreak of war by her old friends Britain and France and—under their pressure—even by Russia, merely as the price of maintaining her neutrality? If that offer had been accepted, this at least he would not have seen, he thought, as through a gap in the wooden houses he chanced once more to catch sight of those alien iron-clads, riding the blue waters below.

A strong current was setting down the Bosphorus, while a fresh wind blew up the Marmara from the west; where the two met, around the Entente fleet, they created a jobble of little short waves with white curling crests. This is a familiar sight from the heights of Ayaz Pasha, under these conditions, and there came, irrelevantly, into the Pasha's mind at that moment the recollection of one day during that summer of 1914, when his friend Dr. Pierce had been with him, talking about his book on Turkish folk-lore. He had meant to tell him the charming local saying about those small curly white waves: "The Captain Pasha is driving his lambs to pasture." But for some reason he hadn't done so—ah, Osman had brought in the paper, with the news of the Austrian ultimatum to Serbia. Sighing, the Pasha turned away from the sight of the Captain Pasha's lambs gambolling round the French and English fleet, and walked on. Those had been happier days! His good friend Pierce, to whose annual summer visits he had so much looked forward—he hadn't seen him, heard of him, for four years! And the little Canary, with her loud clear voice, whom Féridé had loved so much—little monster, Féridé, dragging her poor old dadi down into the crowds on the quay to say goodbye to her friend! Whoever heard of such a thing! But Féridé was not like other girls—she never had been; a smile, half pride, half fondness, gathered round the Pasha's rather grim old mouth. Lost in the happier past, he got into his carriage—the coachman had to call out "Pasham!" (My Pasha!) to him, or he would have walked by it, unseeing—and drove home.

·   ·   ·   ·   ·   ·

Dr. Pierce heard the news of the arrival of the Allied fleets off Istanbul on that very day. Not, as one might have expected, in the scholastic calm of a semi-militarised Oxford, but in Syria. He had in fact spent most of the war in the Middle East. During that struggle the British Intelligence Service mobilised expert knowledge as never before: the Aegean Islands were full of archaeologists disguised as sponge-gatherers or lemon-buyers, the Levant of academic fig-sellers or vendors of sweet-meats. A lot of them sat in Cairo, others in Beirut, as well. Dr. Pierce did, for some time; but when Allenby's advance in Palestine began—began with that fantastic mustering of cavalry, infantry, and field artillery in the shelter of the orange-groves near Jaffa, the men heating their food on "Tommy's Cookers" so that no smoke from fires should give their presence away to prying German air-craft—he was attached to those divisions as an interpreter in Turkish. It was with them that he heard the terms of the Mudros Armistice—and he heard them with mixed feelings. As an Englishman he could not but feel that Turkey, whose wilful, disingenuous, and needless entry into the war on the wrong side he had always deplored, had got what was coming to her; but he loved the Turks, and he could not forget his friends among them. "My God, what will poor old Murad Zadé say to this?" was his first reaction to the news of the Mudros Armistice; and then he scowled. "That Enver, with his medals and his German friends! —I always said he would do them no good." But he was still terribly sorry for the decent Turks, like the Pasha, or even poor Javid Bey, a very decent fellow. Moreover, he found moments in which to wonder what Kemal Pasha, whom young Ahmet had always been raving about, would say to all this? That retreat of his had been an astonishing performance, and he had given a bloody nose to the Indian troops at Haritan, too.

One of Dr. Pierce's tasks—he was called "Major Pierce" in the Army

—was the interviewing of the more important prisoners. He sat behind a small table, wearing the khaki uniform in which he somehow contrived always to look shabbily academic, never in the least military, and questioned them in their own tongue. Turkish prisoners had a thoroughly English habit of tough silence under examination, but the Doctor, from his long familiarity with the country and the people, got better results than most. Owing to the exceptional swiftness of Mustafa Kemal's retreat—the British troops lost touch for some days—there was a certain time-lag in the examination process, and it was nearly a week after the Bulgarian Armistice that a young officer came to him one morning and said—"I say, Sir, we've got a Staff officer here. He doesn't seem much inclined to chat, so we haven't bothered to try to break him open—thought we'd leave him to you. May I bring him along?"

"Yes, do, by all means," said Dr. Pierce, who was as unmilitary in speech as in appearance.

"Right, Sir. He looks such a nice chap," the young officer added, presumably infected by Dr. Pierce's naturalness, as he departed. And a few minutes later he returned, accompanied by Ahmet.

For a moment the two men stared at one another across the little table, Ahmet standing stiffly at attention; then Dr. Pierce got up and went over to him, and wrung him by the hand.

"Ahmet!—my dear fellow! How glad I am to see you! How is your Father? And Réfiyé Hanim? Still alive? Oh, excellent—wonderful old lady! She must be, what—over eighty now, isn't she?" He turned to the young officer, whose eyes were expanding at all this—"Shearer, send for another chair, or stool or something, there's a good fellow; Ahmet Bey is a very old friend—we have a lot to talk about." Captain Shearer produced a seat for Ahmet, and then went off—to tell a crony that "the old Doc" and the Staff officer seemed to be "terrifically thick—practically blood-brothers."

After making Ahmet sit down, which wasn't easy, and giving him a cigarette, the Doctor went on with his very unprofessional questions.

"And Féridé—how is she? She must be nearly grown up now."

"Féridé was married last week—on the 28th."

"Married? Good God! Who to?"

"A very dear friend of mine called Orhan." Ahmet was still a little stiff.

"He in this show?"

"No—he is up in Thrace."

"Little Féridé! Well, I wish her every happiness. Ah dear me—married! *How* jealous Fanny will be of me, seeing you like this."

Ahmet asked how Fanny was.

"Very well. She's a V.A.D. now—a sort of military nurse, you know.

She was wretched those last three years at school—the war on, and not able to help or do a thing! Terribly frustrated. But she loves this— seems to spend most of her time scrubbing floors, but she doesn't mind; she's in on the job."

"Your women are wonderful," said Ahmet, less stiffly, with a little sigh.

"And you, my dear Ahmet—are you married yet?"

"Oh yes."

"Do I know her?"

"Do you remember Nilüfer, who came sometimes to the yali?—a distant relation. Miss Fanny knew her, I know."

"Oh, ah, yes—I've heard Fanny talk of her. Plays and sings very well, doesn't she?"

"*Passablement,* yes," said Ahmet modestly.

"Well, I congratulate you—and her too!" Ahmet thanked him, a little stiff again, as Turks used to be when their wife was spoken of.

"And your Father? How is he? All this must be very worrying for him," said the Doctor nicely. "Does he know about you?"

"I hope so—I am not sure. I expect Kemal Pasha would find means to send word. He countersigned my telegram to say that I could not come to Féridé's wedding, when this 'push' began."

"Ah, you missed that, of course. What a pity!" said the Doctor. "Well, well—I must write and tell Fanny all this; how pleased she will be. I tell you, she has fretted no end because she couldn't get letters through to Féridé, or hear from her. And now, my dear boy," Dr. Pierce went on—"you and I have got some business to do, so we'd better get down to it, eh?" And they got down to it.

That evening he wrote and told Fanny all about it; and Fanny wrote back urging him to send Féridé a wedding-present. The Armistice of Mudros had been signed by that time, and—"Why don't you go home via Istanbul, and see them all?" Fanny wrote. But Dr. Pierce couldn't do that; and in due course he was put on a very uncomfortable troop-ship, and sent home from Alexandria.

. . . . . .

Ten days after the Pasha had stood and watched the Allied Fleet off Istanbul, and thought of his old friend, Turkish public feeling suffered a fresh humiliation when Franchet d'Esperey, the French Commander of the Allied troops, marched into the capital with full military ceremonial. Perhaps it was really necessary or salutary—certainly it aroused intense bitterness. This display the Pasha did not see himself, but he heard all about it from those who had, and reported it to his mother, sitting by the brazier in the salon. "But why the French, grand Dieu?"

the old lady exclaimed. *"They* did not vanquish us. Why not the English?" Her son could not answer her.

These distresses, Réfiyé Hanim's concern at them, and other reasons caused Murad Zadé Asaf to linger on at the yali, even now that there was no longer any fear of a bombardment. There his family was out of sight and sound of the foreign troops swarming in the city, the women of his household safe from molestation by the soldiers in the streets—English soldiers, French soldiers, Italian soldiers, and worst of all the Senegalese, with their black scarred faces and their cruel insolent smiles—out of sight of the watching warships, all the outward and visible signs of total and calamitous defeat, disruption, and despair.

There were other signs of all this, not so outward nor so visible, but well known to the Pasha. "The Young Turk" Cabinet was finished with—Enver, Talaat and Jemal were gone, Javid Bey, who had so often visited him, was in hiding; both in the new Cabinet and in small groups outside it, men were fumbling and arguing helplessly for a solution, or rather, for some sort of basis for the future—*any* future. That the Ottoman Empire was really doomed, that Mustafa Kemal's prophecy had come true, was not yet fully clear to all. Men will always hope—and anyhow a nation must live. Could not something be saved from the wreck? What the new Sultan, Vahdeddin, and his immediate advisers sought to save was their own position; there were others, honest men—like the Pasha himself—who wished to save their country, but could not be certain how to do it. Turn to the Americans? President Wilson had already published his Fourteen Points, emphasising the principle of nationality and "self-determination"; there might be a possibility there. Or try the English, Turkey's old friends and protectors?— reliable people really, *Reshadieh* or no *Reshadieh*. Or the French?— also in the past good friends to Turkey, in spite of Franchet d'Esperey's recent tactless demonstration, and his abominable black troops. But there was no certainty, no decision, above all no action. Few nations, proud and naturally courageous, can ever have passed through a more wretched and demoralising experience.

Into the middle of this confusion and uncertainty Orhan returned home. At last Féridé had her young husband with her, and began to live as a wife—with a deep and abounding joy and satisfaction. It was still strange, her own ménage, her new independence, but now with a new and deeper strangeness, and an intense personal happiness. But their happiness, hers and Orhan's, was purely personal. The young man was in a state of deep concern over his country's situation, and profoundly depressed. He and Fuad—who had not been made prisoner; the Pasha's guess as to Kemal's resourcefulness had been well-founded— discussed it for hours, sitting, as a rule, in her little salon. They went out a great deal, too. They seldom said where they were going, but Féridé soon came to know—either to the small house at Shishli in which Kemal Pasha had taken up his residence on his return from the Syrian front, about a month after Mudros, or to groups of like-minded young men in their own homes. The youthful wife used to wait up, anxiously, alone or with Nilüfer, for her husband's return from these outings, which usually took place at night—the Allied agents were active everywhere, and Kemal Pasha was suspect. Fuad and Orhan were constantly together; their uniforms had been laid away, since the Turkish Army was now demobilised; going about in neat Western suits, they were an unaccustomed sight to Féridé and Nilüfer, after four years of war.

The Pasha, too, had some inkling of where they went, and whenever he could he lured them into his study and involved them in discussions on policy, hoping to learn what they were up to, or at least what they thought. Like so many of his generation, he at once admired and distrusted Kemal Pasha—he had won a signal victory at Anafartalar, he had kept the English out of Alexandretta; but he was a firebrand, a rebel born, always at odds with his superiors, Turkish and German alike —things must be done *his* way, or he simply resigned. Everyone knew— everyone in the Pasha's circles, that is—that he had been to see the Sultan, and almost everyone had expected him to be given a post in the Cabinet, probably as Minister for War. But nothing had come of it, and now he was sulking at Shishli, like Achilles in his tent—and there were some very queer goings on in that tent, if all one heard were true!

But it was hard to draw Fuad and Orhan. Both had in full measure the Turkish capacity for talking a great deal and saying absolutely nothing, which is partly what makes of that nation such excellent diplomatists. Moreover they knew perfectly well how divided the Pasha's attitude was to Mustafa Kemel—and theirs was *not* divided; it was single-hearted, clear, and concrete. If in war he had done what no one else could do, so he would do in this ruinous semi-peace, given the chance. Their young eyes saw far more clearly than the Pasha's experienced ones the degree to which indecision and despair had taken hold on official and political circles; for his were to a great extent blinded by the long years, covering his whole life-time, of habitual procrastination, habitual corruption, in the Ottoman Empire. Personally incorruptible, corruption and fainéantise did not shock Murad Zadé Asaf Pasha as they shocked his nephew and son-in-law, because they had always been part of his scheme of things. And while the young men cursed the Sultan Vahdeddin in their hearts for his weakness and self-seeking, the old man felt, they knew, that the Sultanate itself was sacred, inviolable. Their faith and belief was not in the Sultanate, but in the Turkish people; all this fawning on foreign powers for the right to live a subservient existence was utterly repugnant to them. The Americans, the English, the French!—it was the Turks who mattered, the Turkish nation, its dignity and its self-respect. There came a very unpleasant moment, during that long winter of their discontent, when Orhan, after a prolonged discussion of the situation with the Pasha and Fuad, burst out—"Excellency, if it is a case of choosing between the Turkish people and the Sultanate, I choose the Turkish people."

The Pasha was profoundly shocked.

"That is no way to speak," he said gravely; then his anger mounted. "These are the ideas of your new friends, I suppose. But I am unwilling to have such things said in my house."

Orhan, equally angry, rose, bowed respectfully, and left the room. He hastened up to his own suite, where, too much disturbed to contain himself, he said to Féridé—"We must leave; we must go to a house of our own, or to my Father's house."

Startled, dismayed, she asked him why?— he told her. When, still furious, he had gone out again—she could guess where!—she went down to the big salon to see her grandmother.

She had no need to open this difficult subject. The Pasha had been there before her, and Réfiyé Hanim knew all about it. She too was deeply shocked at the bare idea of any alternative to the Sultanate, or disloyalty to it—such a thing was unthinkable. But she was a woman, and put peace in her family above politics; somehow or other, by her intervention, it was all patched up, smoothed over, and Orhan and Féridé stayed where they were.

The winter dragged wretchedly on. Ahmet was exchanged in March, and returned home, to join Orhan and Fuad in their nocturnal visits to Shishli or, later, to the Péra Palace. The Peace Conference, which opened in Paris in January 1919, did nothing to resolve the problems which beset the minds of responsible Turks—problems of Armenians, Georgians, Daghastanis, Russians; in fact it merely bedevilled them. When the Conference opened the areas where these racial difficulties were most crucial had one stabilising element, and one only—the British occupying troops; but as the weeks and months passed, these were gradually withdrawn. Swift decisions, by those who had the power to take them, were essential—and they were not taken. President Wilson, new to the problems of the Old World, high-minded but uninformed, proud of America's position as "the only disinterested Power" in the Near East, suggested what everyone with any local knowledge realised could only be fatal—an International Commission of Inquiry into Turkish questions, which had for its object, at least in part, to convince the world that they had sought "the most scientific basis of settlement." This in regions where disputes were being settled, *ad hoc* and locally, by rifle-fire! The unfortunate idealist from another hemisphere was thinking in terms of an educated electorate; the realities were very different. (The greatest historian of this period rightly referred later to the dangers of "a peripatetic Commission of Inquiry making a roving progress in search of truth through all the powder-magazines of the Middle East, with a note book in one hand and a lighted cigarette in the other.")

Events did not wait on the experts. Movements of insurrection, local, tribal, broke out all through Anatolia during that spring. The situation was becoming dangerous. And since those who had had the power to control these districts delayed to use it, indeed were busily employed in withdrawing the forces of control, the Ottoman Government, decrepit as it was, was forced into action. In May 1919 it sent that turbulent and difficult creature Mustafa Kemal Pasha to Anatolia, as Inspector of the Third Army, the Turkish forces on the spot. He left by boat for Samsun on the 16th of May.

The Ottoman Government little guessed that in signing the order for this appointment they were in fact signing their own death-warrant.

Part Three

Chapter Six

THERE was not much publicity given at the time of Kemal Pasha's departure for Anatolia; even had there been, it would have been swamped by the outcry and public fury aroused by an event which took place the very day before. Under the guns of Allied ships, the Greeks landed in Smyrna on May the 15th, 1919.

Smyrna was one of those exasperating cities, like Danzig and Jerusalem, on which at least two nations had fairly valid claims. It had been Greek (as Jerusalem had been Jewish) from time immemorial; from long before the day when St. John the Divine, the author of the Apocalypse, writing in Greek, addressed his famous message "unto the seven churches which are in Asia; unto Ephesus, and unto Smyrna, and unto Pergamos, and unto Thyatira, and unto Sardis, and unto Philadelphia, and unto Laodicea." But then, six hundred years or more before the twentieth century dawned the Turks had overrun all Asia Minor, including the cities of the seven churches, and thenceforward Turk and Greek had lived side by side in Smyrna, the Greeks, as was their wont, trading and prospering, the Turks taxing them, and prospering likewise. It was, indubitably, part of the modern Turkish homeland of Anatolia; it had, indubitably, a large Greek population. The Turks had not treated the Greeks overwell, and Turkey was, apparently, breaking up. In any case the Peace Conference in Paris, busy with other matters nearer home, urged by M. Venizelo, led by President Wilson and Lloyd George, agreed—despite the protests of the British Army and Foreign Office—to this Greek adventure. They, too, did not realise that a nation would arise, like the Phoenix, from the ashes of the villages in the hinterland which the Greeks so blithely set about burning that May.

At the end of the first week in June Ahmet suddenly left the yali. He told poor Nilüfer, briefly, and at the last moment, that he had to make a journey; that he loved her, and would write to her—and then made good his escape. He took an even briefer farewell of Réfiyé Hanim.

"But where do you go? Is it for long?" his grandmother asked tranquilly.

"Very dear Niné, do not ask me for how long, for I do not know; and do not ask me where, for I am unwilling to say." He gave her a slanting smile out of his grey eyes. She smiled back at him, oldly, wisely. "May God's mercy protect you every step of the way," she said. He kissed her—this time on her old cheek, not on her fragile blue-veined hand—and went. And of his poor father the Pasha, dreading argument—even his few weeks of imprisonment had rather weakened Ahmet's nerve—he took no farewell at all.

But he told Féridé all about it. "I am going to him. It seems there is work to do—much work. The people must be aroused; the soldiers called back to the colours. Oh, it is hard for them!—just back on their farms, after four years away. But if we are ever to be a nation again, they must come back—and be co-ordinated, become a fighting force, not carry on their foolish, wasteful feuds. This is a thing I believe I can do—and he thinks so too."

"Where is he now?" Féridé asked.

"At Amasya. It was hopeless at Samsun—the English Intelligence Officers always prying and interfering! But of course I shall be all over the place." He embraced her—without stooping, as he did to Nilüfer; they were both so tall. "Goodbye, my dear sister. Watch over Orhan! What he has to do is really more dangerous, with all these *sacrés* foreign troops and agents about." And he went away.

Orhan of course knew all about it, and spoke to Féridé as openly as her brother had done.

"Ah, I wish I could go too. It will be tricky work, and so interesting. Kemal Pasha will have to get the senior officers on his side, as well as Kiazim Kara Bekir, and the Valis and Kaimakams also; and many of them are old men, linked all their lives to the régime—and in the Army there is still prejudice against him."

Féridé asked who Kiazim Kara Bekir was?

"The Corps Commander of the Eastern Army Corps. It is only a skeleton, that Corps—really just the *cadre*; and it is supposed to be occupied in handing over its arms to the Entente, or seeing that others do so!" Orhan laughed, a little gay laugh; his blue eyes twinkled delightfully. "I expect he will soon stop *that!*" He looked pleased, secret. "But even if the arms do get into the Allied dumps, they may get out again!" His laugh was as clear as a young boy's. But then he looked grave.

"My heart, you must not tell your Father anything of Ahmet. He is too much in touch with the Cabinet, and the Court—all these feeble creatures, young and old!"

"He does not know?" Féridé was really startled.

"No—Ahmet did not even bid him adieu."

"But—he will ask!"

"Then you must not answer. It will be better not even to say *where* he is gone."

Féridé frowned. "This will be difficult."

"My dearest one, you have wits—God the All Powerful had seen to that! Use them."

Féridé had to use her wits quite soon. Within three days of Ahmet's departure the Pasha became aware of his absence, and began to worry and ask questions. Nilüfer, beautiful and gentle, knew nothing—"My Father, he said he would write—but so far I have not heard." And remembering how at the same time her young husband had said that he loved her, her immense beautiful eyes filled with tears. Asaf Pasha knew that she was speaking the truth. But it was all most strange—to go, and not take leave of his own father! He tried his mother next—she had a marvellous way of knowing what went on; whether it was because her calm benevolence invited confidences, or that her watchful old eyes missed nothing, he did not know—perhaps, as he sometimes told her, with his grim charming smile, she had the gift of divination! But Réfiyé Hanim, apparently, knew nothing either. "My son, he told me that he was making a journey, and did not know how long he should be absent."

"But where to, this journey?" the Pasha fretted.

"My son, he did not say." (The old lady omitted to mention that Ahmet had told her that he did not *wish* to say where he was going.)

Thwarted—with a faint sense, which he often had with his mother, that he was being *ménagé*, treated almost as a child—the Pasha next tackled his son-in-law. There he fully expected to draw a blank, and he did. These young fellows all stuck together! "Effendim, I cannot say," was all he got out of Orhan, very firmly and politely said; not wishing to provoke another breach in the family peace, which was so repugnant to all his ideas of rightness and dignity, the old gentleman left it at that with the handsome stubborn young man, who stood there before him, so slim and graceful and well-bred. But when Orhan was out, he took occasion to visit his daughter. This was a thing he enjoyed doing anyhow; it gave him immense pleasure to sit with her in her own apartments, where she received him with such an eager happy graciousness, offering him cigarettes, bonbons, setting his chair just right, sending for coffee. *Très grande dame*, she was nowadays, his little Féridé!

"So Ahmet has gone away," the Pasha began conversationally, leaning back in his chair, his thin legs as usual stuck out in front of him, and gazing at the lovely Persian-patterned painted ceiling, where faint gilding brought out the colours—his grandmother's ceiling. He brought his eyes down, and looked intently at his daughter as he asked—"Did you see him before he went?"

"Yes, my Father."

"So. And did he tell you where he was going?"

Féridé looked him straight in the eyes. "Yes, my Father," she said again.

"And where has he gone?"

She rose and went to him with the utmost gentleness.

"My dear, my good Father, I beseech you not to ask me that."

"And why not?"

'Because I cannot tell you."

"My daughter, I *desire* you to tell me," the Pasha said, stiffening. He had already been slightly suspicious when he came to her, but this attitude in his own child—his wild, but loving and biddable child—affronted him strangely, and made him more suspicious than ever.

"My Father, I cannot tell you until my husband gives me permission. At present he forbids it," Féridé replied now.

The Pasha rose, and walked up and down the small beautiful room. So this was what it meant, to marry off one's darling daughter, the light of one's eyes, the treasure of the heart! Oh, it was so correct! She was perfectly right. The Pasha was a good and religious Mahometan; he knew the duties of a wife to her husband. But it is sharp, when the husband—younger than one's own son—usurps the position that has been one's own, as father, for so many years. On that head, however, there was nothing that he could say; she was doing her duty. But it was the first occasion of an open clash of wills between them, and the pain of it was astonishingly keen. In his pain, his irritation broke out; he stopped in front of her and said—

"Ah, it will be some idea, some plan, of this famous Mustafa Kemal Pasha's, I don't doubt. You are all besotted about him!"

"We believe he wishes to serve our country," Féridé said, as calm as her grandmother.

"And do others not wish to?"

"My Father, *you* do; you have served it," she said, gently now. "Let me offer you some more coffee."

She closed that conversation. She, his little child, closed it in his face!—perfectly, gracefully, sitting in her own boudoir, entirely mistress of the situation. Angry and upset as he was, Asaf Pasha could not withhold a grudging admiration, tinged with pride.

The Pasha learned fairly soon what was going on, and realised presently that of course Ahmet was mixed up in it. Mustafa Kemal lost no time when he reached Anatolia. Nine days after he landed at Samsun

he circularised all Military Commandants and Civil Governors, calling
on them to promote more vigorous nationalist demonstrations in favour
of independence—which was not quite what the Ottoman Government
had intended when they sent him there. By the third week in June he
was summoning a Congress of Delegates to meet at Sivas in September,
for the express purpose of considering the best means of promoting Turkish independence. Early in July he went to Erzerum to await the
opening of a similar Congress there—in this case from the Eastern Provinces; and while there he sent out, in the Sultan's name, an order to all
Military Commanders to cease surrendering arms to the Allies. Foresee-
ing what the reaction of the Government in Istanbul must be to such a
step, which was an open and flagrant flouting of the terms of the Mudros Armistice, a few days later he sent in his resignation both from his
new post of Inspector, and of his commission in the army. "I am pro-
moted," he told his entourage, with a grim smile, "from being an Ottoman General to being a Turkish private!" (Ahmet heard him.)

But this was by no means all. There were at that time two Turkish
Army Corps—much reduced, but still existent—in Anatolia: that in the
East commanded by sturdy old Kiazim Kara Bekir, of whom Orhan had
spoken to Féridé, the other in the West, based on Ankara, commanded
by Ali Fuad. Kemal Pasha persuaded both these commanders to come
to see him at Amasya, and there succeeded in convincing them that there
was a hope for Turkish independence after all—Sultan or no Sultan,
Armistice or no Armistice—if they could reassemble their respective
Corps and keep them in being. But that was vital; force would be
needed, and force must exist. It was no easy task to convince them; they
were old soldiers, loyal servants of the Sultanate all their lives. And
where were the arms to come from? Mustafa Kemal whispered in their
ears of the groups all over the country, headed by young officers loyal
to him, who were raiding the arms dumps night after night, and hiding
away safely what they took. (That was in fact Orhan's task, which
Ahmet had told Féridé was more dangerous than his own—which was
true.)

Somehow he did succeed in convincing them; persuasion was always
one of his great strengths. They returned to their bases pledged to reorganise their armies, and bring them up to strength. Ahmet, and others
like him, set about rousing the country—riding from village to village,
sleeping where they could; hot, wet, tired, dirty, sometimes hungry.
As Ahmet had foreseen, it was not always easy at first to persuade the
peasants, after four years with the colours, to leave their homes and
farms, their women and their families, and go back to the army again.
There was great discouragement; they had been beaten, and they knew
it; the country was exhausted and poor; a sullen resignation had set in.

Without the barbed and envenomed provocation of the outrageous Italian swoop on Adalia, and the insane, the criminal folly of the Peace Conference in allowing the Greeks to land at Smyrna, the task of young men like Ahmet might have proved an impossible one. But facts were their best, their unanswerable argument. The natural courage and pride of the Turkish people rose in them afresh as they heard of burnings and massacres, and of the occupation of their own soil, not by the conquering English, but by two nations whom they had long been wont to despise.

Moreover there was another element, one which nations and the rulers of nations overlook at their peril—the factor of moral sanctions. The Turks are a religious people; right and wrong mean much to them. Fairly beaten in a war which many of them felt they had had no just cause for entering at all, and subsequently treated with justice, they might, in their weariness, have remained quiescent. Instead they were treated by the Peace Conference with harshness and contempt— so much so that after Smyrna and Adalia Justice, in Winston Churchill's immortal phrase, had changed camps, and now sat, a refugee in rags, beside the bivouac fires of the poor men who would not accept injustice, and were trekking back from their homes and their livelihoods to the centres where, once again, they would take up arms to defend their country. There were endless stories, true ones, which Ahmet told later to Orhan and Féridé, of sergeants and corporals rounding up the men in their villages, drilling them for a week or so, and then marching them off to Erzerum or Ankara to re-enlist; there were the prisoners of war, released by the English and sent home from Istanbul, who were met as they got off the train (in their decent new clothes provided by the Ottoman Government) and told to fall in and march to the local headquarters, without so much as greeting their wives and families—and who went, with a good heart, without a murmur. Courage, devotion, self-sacrifice—these are great things; if ever a people displayed them, in their darkest hour, the Turkish people displayed them then.

This courage and devotion of a whole nation is a simple thing, always; the political manifestations of it are, inevitably, far less simple and clear. From the political angle the whole early period of the revolt in Anatolia was tremendously confused—a welter of meetings and Conferences and Committees with long names. These gave concrete form, which in the modern world is necessary, to the practical reality. But in this welter a few things stood out. The first was the adhesion to Mustafa Kemal of the two Corps Commanders; the second was the Congress of Erzerum, which opened on July the 3rd, and sat for a fortnight; the third was the Congress of Sivas in September.

One of the things which made the Erzerum Congress important was that it gave Mustafa Kemal some sort of recognisable status. When it opened, apart from the prestige of his military record and his tremendous personality, he had none. The Ottoman Government, usually so tardy in action, promptly deprived him of his army rank and his Inspectorate alike—he was, as he himself had said, a Turkish private; but a private in an army which had no official existence! The Congress made him its President—but as it only lasted a fortnight, that was insufficient. However it brought into being a permanent body, "The Action Committee for the Defence of National Rights," and of that too Mustafa Kemal was elected President. The title may sound pompous, but the reality it represented was far from pompous: the reality was those little groups of poor, war-weary, ragged men marching away from their homes to fight again, led by youths like Ahmet.

The Congress of Sivas, which took place in September, was even bigger and more important than that of Erzerum. Delegates came to it from all parts of the country, even—secretly and by stealth—from European Turkey. It called itself by an even longer name—The Association for the Defence of the Rights of Anatolia and Roumelia." (Roumelia was Turkey in Europe.) But like its predecessor it called into being a smaller, permanent body, the "Representative Committee," and this became henceforward the acting Government of the new Turkey. Kemal Pasha saw to it that all was done decently and in order, and as constitutionally as was possible to what was technically still a rebel organisation. Principles were set out, as they had been two months earlier at Erzerum: "The Country is one whole, and no parts of it can or shall be detached from it"; "The Nation will resist unanimously any foreign intervention or occupation, even should the Ottoman Government disappear"; "National Forces will go into action, and the National Will shall exert its sovereignty"; "There can be no question of accepting a mandate or a protectorate." And the day after the Congress closed Mustafa Kemal telegraphed to Istanbul, breaking off all relations with the Ottoman Government.

These were a new sort of words from a defeated nation which was supposed to be waiting submissively on the conquerors' will, and being parcelled out in the meantime; somehow they resounded. They resounded in Paris, where the statesmen lifted their heads in irritation at this interruption of their more important labours—was not that Commission of President Wilson's going to "settle" about Turkey? They resounded even in Oxford, where his friends asked Dr. Pierce, over their port in the Common Room, who in the world this fellow Kemal was? They resounded most of all in Istanbul, where they rang like a tocsin or a knell, according to one's point of view.

The Pasha really did not know which he thought. Smyrna and Adalia had angered him as much as the rest of the nation—it was all monstrous, insupportable. But surely the Government were the proper people to take steps, not a wild fellow from Salonika, who never had obeyed orders? And what language was this to address to members of the Government, such as Mustafa Kemal had used?—"You are nothing but cowards and criminals; you cabal with our enemies to betray the nation. You are incapable, I know, of recognising the force of will of your own nation. . . . But do not forget that that nation will remember your responsibilities, when she comes to pronounce sentence on the infamies that you are committing." Surely no one had ever written thus to high officials before—they might have had them strangled or poisoned, but to talk like that, no!

The whole summer was tense at the yali, and the autumn became tenser still. The Pasha suspected that Orhan was in some way helping Mustafa Kemal's movement, or at least that his constant and unexplained absences from the house were connected with the activities in Anatolia. The rebel government there was giving its own orders, and getting them obeyed; more and more of the country was coming under its control—by the end of September the authority of the Sultan's government hardly extended further than the actual littoral of the Bosphorus and the Sea of Marmara. The Allied officials were constantly making angry representations to the Ottoman authorities that arms and ammunition were not being handed in in conformity with the terms of Mudros—not only so, but officers and men sent to collect them were frequently beaten up and even imprisoned, while the existing dumps were being steadily depleted by daring raids, night after night. The few who were caught doing this were savagely punished. But if the Pasha guessed that his son-in-law might be among those who were running these particular risks, he said nothing—not even to his mother; nor did he ask any questions, either of her or of Féridé. Indeed after his one experience of questioning Féridé about Ahmet, he had no desire to try again.

But he did talk, both to his mother and his daughter, about the state of affairs in Anatolia; bitterly to Réfiyé Hanim, rather more restrainedly in Féridé's presence. In spite of his restraint, there were sometimes awkward moments. One day he quoted, with indignation, the "cowards and criminals" telegram: "That is no way to address the government of one's Sovereign," he said.

"But my Father, if it is true? If the nation *is* being betrayed?" Féridé said, her grey eyes flashing. "Does not the nation come before Adil Bey?" (Adil Bey was the Minister of the Interior, to whom the savage telegram had actually been sent.)

"My daughter, there are certain loyalties which should be observed," the Pasha said. "Mustafa Kemal has not observed them."

"It is, I suppose, a question of where the greater loyalty is due—to one's country, or to the Sublime Porte," Féridé said, now looking modestly at the floor.

The Pasha rose and walked about, irritably.

"My daughter, you do not perhaps fully understand these matters."

"My Father, you are almost certainly right."

It was all very uncomfortable, in spite of the elaborate courtesy on both sides.

Féridé was having to learn discretion, not a thing which came easily to her. She had never been told, in so many words, what her husband was really doing; the hint thrown out to her by Ahmet when he left was the nearest she had come to it. But she guessed. She could not fail to. In the spring, before either Ahmet's or Kemal Pasha's departure, Orhan had often enough come home in the small hours, but he had come back neat and clean, as one who returns from a party with friends; now he came with clothes torn and dirty, and though he always bathed before joining her, his nails were broken, and oily grime, that soap and water could not remove, clung in the skin of his hands. He slept, too, like a dog after a day's hunting, like a dead thing. In the mornings, when he had had his coffee, without a word she used to bring a pot of cream and her manicure things, massage the dirt out of his hands, and tidy up his nails; he would smile at her with unutterable fondness, but never said a word—only sometimes he attempted a caress. "No, Orhan!—put your hand down! I do not want all this cream on my hair, je vous remercie bien!" And he would laugh like the boy he really was still.

She was very careful, too, never to go down to the salon to sit with Réfiyé Hanim on the nights when he was out, when it would certainly have been realised that she was alone. She would dearly have liked to go, for those evenings were very long and lonely, and she had not been brought up to loneliness. And the solitary evenings became more and more frequent as the autumn wore on—Orhan never spent more than one night at a time at the yali. What Féridé did not know was that he now never slept two nights running under any one roof. The gang which he and one or two friends organised was one of the most audacious and successful units in the dump-robbing racket; he was suspected, and under constant observation both by the Allied agents and the Ottoman police.

A thing that Féridé could not prevent—and it worried her that she could not prevent it—was Dil Feripé's constantly popping up to see her on those solitary evenings. She would come sidling through the door, sit down, and pour out a long stream of gossip about the small events and doings of the day, the household, the servants and their virtues or misdeeds. Mahmud Agha's grandson had come to live with him, his mother being dead—"Yes, indeed; the Hanim Effendi (this was Réfiyé Hanim) said he should come; the air would be good for him, and he can be useful to the Agha." Féridé, really glad of someone to talk to, asked how old Mahmud's grandson was? "Eight, nine, ten!— what do I know? Very small, but a bright, a sharp little boy!" But oddly enough the old dadi, nowadays, never commented on Orhan's absence, as she had done earlier; Féridé did not know whether to be relieved or worried by this. Had she, so to speak, given Orhan up as a bad job, or did she too guess? Anxiously, Féridé spoke to Orhan about his dirty clothes; and after that, at her suggestion, he took to keeping a dirty suit in the caïque-hané at the end of the garden, changing when he went out, and changing back into a tidy one on his return. And again he said nothing, only gave her a deep smile, and a long kiss.

By day, though, Féridé often went down and sat with her grandmother. A couple of months after their marriage it would have been normal for a young couple, living as they did under the family roof, to begin attending the family meals, and to some extent sharing the family life; since Ahmet's departure Nilüfer did so. But it had been tacitly accepted that Orhan and Féridé had not done this—with the complicated and difficult relations obtaining between them and the Pasha, it was obviously much better that they should not. With Réfiyé Hanim, however, Féridé felt no sense of strain; in her constant anxiety she found immense relief merely from sitting in the old woman's presence, and sheltering, as it were, under the strong wings of her calm, her wisdom, her goodness. They were always happy together, those two—Féridé often thought it rather wonderful that they were still so happy and at ease, for Réfiyé Hanim's ideas were generally speaking those of her son, the Pasha, on all the subjects which divided him from Orhan and her, Féridé; the girl divined dimly that love was what worked the miracle, and created such peace around the old woman who stood half-way between the points of view of her much-loved son and her worshipped grandchild.

And she divined aright. Réfiyé Hanim loved Ahmet dearly, and was fond of Nilüfer—but her heart was Féridé's. In Orhan she discerned the promise of great things, and, in any case, she accepted completely the necessity for his wife's unquestioning loyalty to him. It was a long time now since, at her suggestion, he had called her Niné. She asked no questions, and though she received confidences, she did not make many to Féridé, save on trivial matters.

A few days after the changing of Orhan's clothes had been organised, Réfiyé Hanim said casually to Féridé, as they sat together one morning, "I have decided to send Dil Feripé over to Chamlidja for a time."

"To the vine-house? Why, Niné? Is not the grape-gathering nearly over?"

"Yes, but there is the drying of the grapes, and of the late plums, and the digging and so on. Silan is getting old, and I think he may be careless. It is better that Dil Feripé should be there."

Many wealthy Turkish families in Istanbul had vineyards outside the city, up in the hills behind Scutari, where the small sweet grapes were grown that supplied their vast households, the surplus being sold, and where the vine-leaves, earlier in the year, were salted in brine, to wrap round the small pieces of meat before they were stewed, or grilled over red-hot charcoal. Aubergines were grown there, and gourds and tomatoes; such places were really small farms. But besides the farmer's dwelling there was usually a little house where the owner could go and stay for a few days, he or anyone whom he might send to supervise operations; it was quite common for one of the kalfas to go out and superintend the salting down of the vine-leaves. And for some reason, these little dwellings were called "the vine-house" or "the house in the vine." They were simple places, generally with whitewashed walls, a tiled roof, a sitting-room in which one also ate, and two or three bedrooms; they were almost completely inaccessible, as a rule, to any wheeled vehicle, and could only be reached on foot, or on horse- or mule-back—the produce came down in panniers to the main road or the ferry.

Féridé was a little surprised that Réfiyé Hanim should send poor old Dil Feripé to the vine-house so late in the season—and if it come to age, she was not so much younger than Silan! But she was still very active— and anyhow age was not one of the questions one raised with Niné! The thought just flashed across her mind that her grandmother, who had a way of knowing everything, might share her concern at the old dadi's so often coming up to her rooms at night, when Orhan was not there, and might be sending her away to prevent her from chattering unwisely, and even dangerously. So she merely said that she thought it a very good idea, and then asked about Mahmud Agha's little grandson.

In fact Réfiyé Hanim was sending the dadi to Chamlidja because she recognised danger to Orhan—but it was not merely the danger of careless chatter which Féridé had suspected. The previous day the Pasha had come to her in a state of great concern, scattering with a glance the old kalfas huddled round the brazier, like hens huddling in shelter on a day of east wind. When they had gone—

"Ané, there is trouble about Orhan," he said, sitting down.

"What trouble, my son?"

"It is known, or believed, that he is one of those who go and steal arms from the places where, under that accursed Treaty, we leave them in the care of the English; more, that he is a leader, an organiser, of those who do this!"

Réfiyé Hanim had guessed months ago that Orhan was doing this very thing—but all she said was:

"How did you learn this, my son?"

"Ané, a good friend told me, when I was in the Club, yesterday. He told me out of friendship. But the boy is in danger—great danger. He is watched: by our police, and by these miserable Allied agents. At any moment they may come here—*here*, to my house!"—said the Pasha, outraged at the very idea—"to seek for him, to apprehend him! And consider the penalties. They are terrible. He must be stopped. Think of Féridé—of our child."

"My son, you are right," said the old lady. "Something must be done." She knew that it would be impossible to stop Orhan doing what he did, but did not say so. She had foreseen this; which was why she had imported the Mahmud Agha's grandson—small boys of nine or ten could run about, unquestioned, even in the feminine parts of a Turkish household—they were like mice or ferrets.

"But what, Ané? You know what that boy is, neither to bind nor to hold! And Féridé is as bad."

"My son, shall I see what I can do?"

"Yes, Ané; do what you can. You might bring Féridé to see reason, and she may ménager him, perhaps. But there is no time to be lost."

What Réfiyé Hanim did was first to arrange to send Dil Feripé and an old servant to Chamlidja—that meant there would be a comfortable hide-out for Orhan on the far side of the Bosphorus, in the safety of the remote little "house in the vine." She had a talk to Mahmud, and ordained that old Zeynel should sleep, for the present, in a small hutch-like room behind the doorkeeper's lodge; she had a talk to Zeynel himself. Ahmet's rowboat had been laid up for the winter; she made the faithful grumbling old man put it down in the water again, moored in the caïque-hané ready for use.

As for the tiny Ali, Mahmud Agha's little grandson, the old lady made a great pet of him; he was forever in the house, trotting all over the place; several times he pattered up with some message or other to Féridé's suite, so that presently he could find his way alone perfectly. And now, at night, last thing, Mdlle Marthe always slipped downstairs and unlocked and unbolted the door near the foot of the staircase which gave onto that covered passage at the back of the house, by which Fanny used to run in and out when her uncle brought her over from the pension. Having seen to all this, calm as ever, Réfiyé Hanim sat in her corner and waited, warming herself at the great brazier; it was late October now, and the weather was getting chilly.

She had not to wait very long. Murad Zadé Asaf Pasha's position had kept the Ottoman agents off for a long time, but one night, the last week in October, it happened.

Orhan was at home that night—for the first time for nearly a week. He and Féridé had come down and taken coffee with Réfiyé Hanim and the Pasha in the salon, and then went back to their rooms—dog-tired, as usual, Orhan suggested going early to bed, and was instantly asleep. Féridé lay beside him, but wakeful; propped on one elbow she watched, in the dim glow of the small night-lamp, his fair head on the pillow. How young he looked, asleep, almost a child!—all the sword-like intensity of his waking face gone. Their bedroom was at the back, looking onto the bushy cliff, and immediately behind the adjoining boudoir, which overlooked the water. Did she hear voices?—Féridé thought suddenly, as she lay there. Softly she got up and crept to the window, opened it, and listened. Yes, away to her right there were certainly voices, raised by the Agha's lodge, and then the sound of feet coming down the drive towards the taşlik and the front door. She glanced at her watch—it was after eleven, an improbable hour for guests to arrive. Hesitating, she turned back towards the bed, where her husband still lay in that deep childish slumber—and at that moment there came a soft, mouselike scrabbling at the door into the boudoir, and then a small urgent voice—"Orhan Bey! Orhan Bey!"

Féridé went to the door and opened it, her heart beating violently—there stood Little Ali, rather out of breath, his eyes as bright as a mouse's eyes.

"I have a message for Orhan Bey, Hanim Effendi."

"What is it?"

"That visitors have come for him, my Grandfather said. He said to tell him at once, at once—visitors!"

Féridé guessed immediately. "Thank you, Little Ali," she said quietly —"run back now." Then she paused. "Wait—how did you come?"

"By the big passage without the house, Hanim Effendi."

"Very well. Go down to that passage, and wait there; and when none will see you, return to your Grandfather's house."

"Yes, Hanim Effendi. So he said I should do."

"Run then—" and closing the door after the child she turned to the bed. "Orhan, wake!" she said, shaking him by the shoulder.

He woke at once. He had the faculty of coming out of the depths of sleep into full wakefulness in one movement.

"Orhan, they have come—they are here! You must go."

Before she had finished speaking he was out of bed and into his dressing-room, and was pulling on his clothes. She followed him.

"Where shall you go?" she asked.

"To the caïque-hané, through the garden, and then row across to the other side."

"But where will you go then? And you cannot manage the boat alone."

"Zeynel will be there—and I shall go up to the vine-house. Oh, where in the name of perdition are my tennis-shoes?"

"Here"—she gave them to him—all sorts of doors were opening in her mind at once.

"Who brought word?" he asked, as he laced them up.

"Little Ali."

"Ah—so the side door is open! But where are they now, do you know?"

Even as he spoke there came a noise of doors opening and shutting below, far away in the great house. Orhan stood listening, his head cocked intently, like a terrier's.

"If they are our people, they will go to your Father, decently, and ask permission, and that will give time; but if they are the others, no— they will be everywhere at once," he said. He went to the window, opened it noiselessly, looked out, and listened. "Blow out the light," he said very low; she did so. He stood, measuring the distance between the window-ledge and the face of the cliff.

"Orhan, you cannot! You cannot get a run at it!"

He turned with a stifled laugh. "Oh, dji-djim, who but you would think of that? Cover yourself, Light of my Eyes, and run down and see if the way is clear to the side door. Forgive me that I ask this of you."

Féridé flung on her dressing-gown and a scarf, and ran through her rooms and down the staircase which led up to the salon. At the bottom she paused—she could hear voices some way away, in the direction of the selamlik. She went on through a short lobby to the side door, and looked out—to right, to left. The covered passage had bare walls, with no obstructions; in either direction it ended, empty, showing a clear oblong against the faint star-shine without. Little Ali must have got home. She ran back, and upstairs; Orhan was in the upper hall.

"No one—the way is clear," she breathed.

"It is well. Farewell, my treasure, my jewel." He took her in his arms for a moment. "Lie in bed and feign sleep—God grant they do not search, but be ready," he whispered, and ran down the stairs without a sound.

Féridé went back to their room, and glanced about it in the dim glow of the night-lamp. The bed was disordered, and Orhan's slippers lay by the foot; she put them away, and straightened the sheets and the muslin coverlet. She took the lamp into the dressing-room—yes, there lay his pyjamas on the floor; these too she hid away in a drawer under the clean ones. All the time she was longing to go to the window, to listen—but she put all in order first; then, setting down the lamp by the bed, she stole into the boudoir, to the window, and opened it. There was, sure enough, the sound of oars, very faint above the dashing of the waves against the embankment; to her left a group of slender shafts of yellow light shone out over the darkened waters. She knew where they came from—through the pierced shutters of her Father's study.

Another sound, nearer, made her start—someone was crossing the drawing-room. Closing the window she darted back into her room, threw off her dressing-gown, and lay down in bed. Oh, just Heaven, she still had her scarf on! She pulled it off and kicked it down to the foot of the bed. "*In* the bed they surely will not look," she thought, and giggled a little, out of nervousness; then lay still and heard the thudding of her heart.

The door was opening. "Féridé?" said Mdlle Marthe's voice.

The girl half-turned in bed, stretching out an arm, as one who wakes from deep sleep. "Ahh?" she muttered; and then—"What is it? Who is there?" she said sleepily.

"It is I—Marthe." The Frenchwoman came in and closed the door; she wore a magenta flannel dressing-gown, and carried a small lamp, whose light gleamed on the curling-pins in her grey hair.

"Mais ma chère, what on earth do you want? Whatever time is it? Oh, mon Dieu, how sleepy I am!" Féridé now sat up in bed, stretched her arms, and gave an excellent imitation of a yawn.

"The agents have come; they are seeking Orhan. I came to prepare you."

"Well, it is no good their seeking here; he went out the moment after coffee," Féridé said, yawning again.

"My child, you had better rise—they are coming with your Father," the old governess said.

"Indeed I shall not rise! I am sleepy! If they wish to have the impoliteness to search my room, they can do it while I am in bed," said Féridé, and snuggled down again under the blankets.

Steps were heard outside—there came a knock on the door.

"Who is there?" Féridé called.

"It is I—your Father."

"My Father, I am in bed. But pray enter, if you desire to speak with me."

The Pasha opened the door a crack, and spoke through it.

"My daughter, there are persons here who desire speech with your husband."

"But he is not here. He left after dinner, as soon as we had taken coffee"—Féridé spoke loud and clearly. There was a murmur of voices outside, and then a strange voice, rather embarrassed, spoke through the door.

"Hanim Effendi, I regret it infinitely, but we have orders to search the house. If the Hanim Effendi would have the great goodness to rise, so that we may search the room."

"My Father, is this essential? It seems to me most strange."

"My daughter, it would be best."

"Then ask them to have the goodness to wait while I dress. Ma chère Marthe, please to close the door, and light some candles."

Taking her time, Féridé got up, put on her dressing-gown, and smothered herself in the black folds of her çarşaf; then she opened the door and followed by Marthe went out into the boudoir, where a group of men were standing, looking profoundly uncomfortable; the Pasha, in his dressing-gown and fez, sat in a chair, the picture of outraged dignity. He rose at her entrance. Ignoring them, Féridé addressed him—"I presume, my Father, that I can wait here while these personages do whatever they desire to do?"

One of the men, bowing deeply, made a number of apologies, to which Féridé only replied by an inclination of the head. "Do ask them, my Father, to complete their business quickly—I am tired and I am cold," she said.

Awkwardly, the men stepped into the bedroom; one of them asked some question about the dressing-room door.

"Oh ma chère Marthe, do show him the dressing-gown. My bedroom, boudoir, dining-room and salon he has already seen!" said Féridé impatiently. The Frenchwoman did as she was asked; after a few moments they all returned to the boudoir. The man who had spoken before, with more bows and more apologies, asked when she had last seen her husband?

"This evening, at dinner."

"And he left when?"

"When he had taken coffee, as I have said."

"He did not say where he was going?"

"No. He goes sometimes," said Féridé thoughtfully, "to the Café Luxembourg."

This was a rather smart haunt, much patronised by the more rakish young men in Istanbul, but practically never by such as Orhan or Ahmet. The man thanked her, and with more bows and more apologies, he and his colleagues got themselves out of the room, escorted by the Pasha. When they had gone, and Féridé, back in the bedroom, was taking off her çarşaf—"*Where* is he?" Mdlle Marthe whispered.

"Gone!" Féridé said.

"Who warned him?"

"Little Ali. Ah, Niné is a person!—she has had a hand in all this! I hope," said Féridé, snuggling down in bed again, "that when I am Niné's age, I shall be at least a little like her."

"My child, you will be *exactly* like her," said the Frenchwoman, kissing her ex-pupil warmly.

Chapter Seven

As EARLY as possible next morning Féridé went to see Réfiyé Hanim. She flung her arms round the old lady's neck and hugged her, as she had done when a child, crying—"Oh Niné, what things you have done for us!"

"Good-morning, my child," said the old lady calmly, but looking a little amused all the same—"I hope you slept well?"

"Niné-djim, I never knew you maligne before!" the girl exclaimed. "*Yes*, I thank you, my revered grand'mère; once my bedroom was no longer full of policemen, I slept very well indeed!"

Réfiyé Hanim laughed.

"Your Father said you were wonderful, and embarrassed them very much—as was most desirable," she said, taking up her embroidery.

"But Niné—ah, how sly you have been!—when did you arrange all this? And tell Orhan? Zeynel ready at the caïque-hané, and Little Ali to bring word! Now I see it all; poor Dil Feripé banished to the vine-house, too, just to look after Orhan! But you never told *me*."

Réfiyé Hanim sorted all this out, and answered after her own fashion.

"There was no need to tell you, my child. Orhan knew, and that sufficed."

"But—who told you what Orhan was doing?"

"I learned, naturally. And I concerted certain means to make his escape easy, with him."

"But *when*?"

"One day when he was with me. Your husband does me the honour of visiting me sometimes," said Réfiyé Hanim, with fine irony.

Féridé almost blinked.

"Niné, you are tremendous! No, I am not jealous! You did what I could not have done, or not half so well. Did you hear anything, last night?"

"Voices of course I heard, and at that hour I guessed what it must be. I rose from my bed, and prayed to God, and then I went to bed again," said Réfiyé Hanim.

Féridé jumped up and gave her another hug. Re-seating herself— "But there is *one* thing—how came it that the door into the outer passage was open, for Little Ali to come in by?" she asked. "It is always kept locked."

"Oh, for weeks past Marthe has gone down to unbolt that, when the servants have gone to bed," said the old lady.

The autumn dragged on. Orhan now only came to the house after dark, and usually by water. Féridé never knew when he was coming; she spent most of her evenings, wrapped in a fur coat, huddled up on the divan under the open window in the boudoir, waiting, straining her ears for the faint chocking noise that oars make in the rowlocks, or the grating sound of a boat's keel against stone—and if she heard these, sooner or later she would hear a low whistle, a few bars of the Falcon song. That was Orhan's signal, and she would run silently downstairs to let him in. But after that first visit of the police she went with Zeynel, at Orhan's orders, and had two stout iron *pitons* driven into the face of the cliff opposite his dressing-room window, and a rope stretched across between them, concealed among the bushes; from two more *pitons* at the top a loop of rope, similarly concealed, hung down.

These precautions were not wasted, for presently the English took to coming, a couple of officers and a posse of men—which was a very different matter from the Ottoman police. They stood in no awe of the Pasha and his position, and while perfectly courteous, they were very efficient, posting men all round the outside of the house. Twice Orhan made that formidable leap—with the rope to snatch at he managed it, crawled along the top, and slithered down the cliff-face to the caïque-hané; he got away, to lie *perdu* at Chamlidja. But the third time the English had put men at the boat-house too, and when, creeping through the bushes, he reached a point above it he heard their voices, and smelt their English cigarettes; crouching there he listened with amused admiration to an officer examining poor old Zeynel in surprisingly good Turkish. Zeynel kept his simple head, and baffled them entirely. Yes, he was an old man, and poor; the Pasha allowed him to sleep in the boat-house—the Pasha was a devout man, fearing God, and merciful to the poor, as those who worshipped Allah should be. Orhan, above in the darkness, could hardly control his laughter—the old fellow was being so completely himself. Tired of these pious maunderings, the English at last left the boat-house, but their tell-tale Virginia tobacco still hung on the air, and Orhan went up into the koru and spent the night under the very cedar in which Fanny had got stuck, five years before, curled up on the short dry scented needles.

The efforts to raise and arm the troops in Anatolia went on, and by November they began to bear fruit—in the South an attack was launched on the French at Maraş; behind Smyrna the English, alarmed at the hornets' nest which the Greek landing had stirred up and by the toll which the Turkish bands, regulars and irregulars alike, were taking of the Greek troops, sought to control both by fixing "The Milne Line," a sort of neutral zone which neither side should cross. In fact all the English experts with real knowledge, both in the War Office and the Foreign Office, had protested against the Smyrna landing, but in vain— the peace-makers in Paris, who were politicians, not experts, had taken their own way. Lord Curzon and Mr. Montague, speaking respectively from the Christian and the Mahometan points of view—England was then still the greatest Mahometan Power in the world—were arguing in London as to whether the Sultan, indeed any Turks at all, should be allowed to remain on the mainland of Europe, or whether they should be expelled "bag and baggage"—an argument which dragged on for some months. The one sane voice uplifted in Paris or London, among all these divided counsels, was that of Mr. Churchill, who pointed out that Turkey could no longer be held down and divided in pieces save by main force, and that England, at any rate, no longer possessed that force—he gave the exact figures of the disposable manpower. He was not heeded.

The Ottoman Government, for its part, sat at Istanbul, frequently changing Cabinets, continually saying "Yes" to the Allies and doing nothing or next to nothing, in the best traditional Turkish manner; this did not prevent them, towards the end of October 1919, from sending an olive-branch, borne by Salih Pasha, the Minister of Marine, to that now uncomfortably powerful and menacing rebel Mustafa Kemal at Amasya—which really constituted practically an official recognition of his position. After conversations lasting three days Salih Pasha took upon himself, in the name of his Government, to sign certain protocols, of which the most important was that the Government in Istanbul recognised that organisation with the long name, the "Association for the Defence of the Rights of Anatolia and Roumelia" as having a juridical status; and further undertook that no provinces with Turkish inhabitants should be ceded to any foreign Power, nor would any foreign mandate or protectorate be accepted for any part of Turkey. All this sounded magnificent—how the Ottoman Government interpreted these undertakings in actual fact appeared later. And so the unhappy year of 1919 drew to its close.

But before that year ended, something else happened—on December the 27th Mustafa Kemal entered Ankara, and took up his residence in a railway-coach in a siding at the station.

Ankara lies right up on the central plateau of Anatolia, 3000 feet above sea-level, among the pale, bare, rolling uplands out of which rise mountain ranges, cream-coloured from the gypsum in them. Here the resplendent burning sun and the savage Asiatic winds rule unchecked, untempered by the moisture which the sea brings; from the air one sees the huge promontory of Asia Minor as a vast beige relief-map, with a green ribbon running round its borders—along the Black Sea, along the Marmara, along the Mediterranean—the strip where the ocean-bred moisture brings fertility. Ankara is an ancient city, and has borne many variants of its present name. One can see that there was a Greek town there once, and then a Roman one, by the inscriptions and bas-reliefs built (usually upside down) into the walls of the mediaeval Turkish citadel whose irregular outline crowns one of the twin hills on which the town was mainly built; over one of the many gateways leading in through the walls there is an inscription in very archaic Turkish which begins: "That the Name of God may in all things be glorified," and then goes on to prescribe very exact regulations governing the sale of grain—it dates from the 13th or 14th century. By 1919 the town had spread out beyond the citadel walls, and some distance down the slopes below; there lay the swarming market, with its narrow streets, each devoted to some special form of merchandise; there were the larger schools, and a mosque or two. But the site of the modern town of Ankara was just a rather swampy plain, in the middle of which sat the railway-station, with an odd house or so beside it, linked by shining lines of rails to civilisation—on the north to Istanbul, fourteen hours away, on the south to Adana and Syria. This was Ankara's one life-line, the German-built "Baghdad Railway." A strange, utterly oriental, barbarous place Ankara was then, with no water-supply but wells and the muddy river winding below and behind the citadel hills, no electric light, and no made roads; up in the old town the steep narrow streets were paved with cobbles of an excruciating steepness and roughness, between which domestic slops seeped away or stagnated; the so-called "road" to the station was just a track, a sea of mud in winter, a wilderness of dust in summer.

Such was the city, later to become his capital, into which Mustafa Kemal came riding, with an escort of whom Ahmet made one, on that day at the end of December. Ankara in winter is piercingly cold—the winds from Central Asia tear across the plateau, screaming between the ranges, whistling among the houses, rasping the skin of any face exposed to them; but the sturdy Anatolians did not care. Backward, barbarous, simple they might be, but there were certain things they understood, as simple people will: their Fatherland had been, and still was, menaced by hated foreigners, infidels; and their liberator, their Warrior Prince, was coming to them. In their thousands, from miles around, they assembled to greet him. Turks as a nation have no idea of time, usually they are late for everything; on this occasion they were early—three days early. They did not worry, they waited—camping in the streets, killing sheep and roasting them in the open, sleeping under the walls of mosques for a little shelter, sleeping anywhere. They were all in gala dress, in their best—and gala dress on the Anatolian plateau, even today, is something to see. The women wore full flowered trousers in a deep cherry-red, with brightly-coloured quilted jackets above, and brilliant scarves over their heads and faces; the men's trousers were hitched up by equally brilliant scarves round the waist, and they wore bright jackets or thick sheep-skin coats, and fezzes or skull-caps wound round with gay striped turbans on their heads. They had brought banners and flags, they had brought musical instruments—and it was through these flower-bright crowds, loud with music, animated with banners, and yelling their heads off that Kemal Pasha rode along the route to the Station. Thence he went to the Bairam Mosque for prayer, the crowd waiting outside, and then to the large ugly building, at that time a college, where a few months later the National Assembly was to make its home; here he spoke to the populace from the balcony, wearing his thick fur-collared coat and the kalpak, the high cap of caracul. As they listened to his words the people wept for joy, seeing for the first time that extraordinary face, hearing that resonant, rather ugly, but unforgettable voice speaking words of reassurance and faith— faith in *them*. Then he went to his railway-coach, and settled down to work, hearing reports, giving orders, studying maps—and the peasants roasted some more sheep, and presently trailed home to their villages along the narrow rutted upland tracks, through the sticky whitish gypsum mud, which rose above their ankles. But a new epoch had dawned, and simple as they were, he had made them understand it.

·   ·   ·   ·   ·   ·

On New Year's Eve, late in the afternoon, a very bent, dirty old man came to the door of the yali; when Mahmud Agha opened to him, he asked to speak with Nilüfer Hanim. Mahmud Agha was as obstructive as door-keepers are meant to be, but the old man was persistent—he must speak with Nilüfer Hanim in person. So he was taken down to the taşlik, Nilüfer was sent for, and smothered in her çarşaf and fur coat she spoke with him. He put a letter into her hand—the address was printed in capitals, but when she opened it she saw Ahmet's writing. "How came you by this?" she asked the old man, trembling in her excitement—"Where do you come from?"

"From Scutari, Hanim Effendi."

"But who gave you this?"

"A man, Hanim Effendi—a seller of sweet-meats."

"A *young* man?"

"No, Hanim Effendi—an old man; old and poor, as I myself am."

There was no more to be got out of him; Nilüfer gave him some money, and sped upstairs with her treasure. Letters from Ahmet had been few and far between during these six, nearly seven months of their separation; in her own rooms she read it greedily. It was headed Ankara, and "Here we are, at last" Ahmet wrote triumphantly—"and here by Allah's goodness we shall stay, away from all the weakness and cowardice and corruption of our capital. It is rough and wild and strange, this place, and *not* comfortable; but the people are splendid. Had you but seen them today as we came in!" He went on to describe the arrival, and at the end wrote—"I hope that soon we may see O here; I have spoken about him, and *he* knows what he has been doing."

When she had read and re-read the letter, Nilüfer went and sought out Féridé, and read most of it to her. "Has Orhan said anything of going away?" she asked at the end.

"No. I have not seen him for ten days. You and I lead strange lives, for married women!" said Féridé ironically. Nilüfer looked sad, and the younger wife laughed and teased with her until she was cheerful again. But Ahmet's words made his sister more eager than ever to see her young husband, and that night she sat again on the divan under the window, waiting and listening. The cold air off the sea blew into the room with the Persian ceiling, chilling her in spite of her coat; the damp salty sea smell was in her nostrils, the small unceasing noise of the waves against the stone embankment dinned in her ears, till she felt that her ears could never hear anything but that. And then, out of the darkness, came a faint chock-chock, the sound of oars. Instantly Féridé was alive all over. Now the grating noise of wood on stone— and then the low sweet whistle of the familiar tune—"I launched my falcon in flight." She rushed downstairs, to the door into the covered passage; silently Orhan came to her side.

"Come in, my love—come up. Oh, how cold you are!" she said as he kissed her and took her hands.

"My treasure, my love, I cannot."

"Why not?" She pulled him into the lobby, and by the hanging lamp saw that he was very oddly dressed. This was not his familiar dirty, dump-raiding suit—he was wearing peasant's clothes, with thick hand-knitted white woollen socks pulled up over his rather baggy trousers, goat-skin moccasins on his feet, and a striped turban wound round his head over a very shabby faded fez.

"Orhan, what is this?" she asked, astonished. "Oh, how very funny you look!" She laughed softly. "But what does it mean?"

"I have had the word that I was waiting for, and I am going," he said.

"To Ankara?"

"Why do you say that?" he asked quickly.

"Nilüfer had a letter from Ahmet today—a dirty old man brought it," she said. "Oh Orhan, was it you? You are dirty enough!" Féridé said, bursting into uncontrollable laughter.

"No, it was not I. What did the letter say?"

"Oh, it was all about their arrival up there, and the people, and the enthusiasm. It must have been wonderful! But Ahmet said that *he* spoke of sending for you. Has he?"

"My dearest love, you know too much—you are like your Grandmother!" said Orhan, half-smiling. "Yes, it is there that I go. At last I shall work *with* him, as well as for him! But listen, my treasure, my darling one—we cannot be separated like this for long! As soon as I can arrange something, will you come to me?"

"But naturally—of course I will come. Oh, how wonderful that will be! Entirely together!"

They embraced—then Orhan slipped away into the shadows of the covered passage, and Féridé bolted the door. There was no need to leave it open any more. She hastened upstairs, and sat again by the window, listening for the sound of oars; she heard them for a little, then they were silenced in the splashing of the waves.

Part Four

Chapter Eight

In Istanbul the year 1920 opened in uncertainty and gloom. What was, in the event, to prove the last session of the Parliament of the Ottoman Empire, the Chamber of Deputies, met on January the 12th. They did do one quite important thing during this session—on January the 28th they adopted the "National Pact," a series of resolutions, in essence practically the same as those passed at Sivas and Erzerum the previous summer, but couched in milder language—as well they might be, since the deputies were deliberating under the guns of the Allied Fleets. Plebiscites were agreed to for areas where there were mixed populations, but the Pact stated firmly that all the conditions essential to an independence as complete as that of any other State must be assured to Turkey, unhampered by restrictions inconsistent with the status of a free nation. But, though it was plain enough, it was mildly said.

Mustafa Kemal had foreseen under what pressure the Chamber would meet, if it met at Istanbul, and as far back as the autumn he had urged the deputies to assemble in the freer air of Ankara, or failing this, at least to gather there first and decide on a line of action. But the pull of the ancient capital and the habit of traditional loyalties were too strong—besides, the Ottoman Government, naturally, bitterly opposed such an idea. So at Istanbul the Chamber met. But once again Kemal proved to be right—he had an extraordinary "nose" for political situations. The Allied representatives, made suspicious by what was going on, first demanded and obtained the resignations of the Minister of War and the Chief of the General Staff, and then proceeded to arrest the President of the Chamber himself.

These measures appeared to do little good. The Allies might squeeze the lemon in Istanbul, but up in his mountain fastness of Ankara, out of reach of their troops and guns, Mustafa Kemal continued to do as he chose, and so did his shabby troops in the wilds of Anatolia. On February the 11th, under Nationalist pressure, the French were forced to evacuate Maraş, down in the South; and whether pro-Kemal or not, the whole nation lifted up its heart in rejoicing at this first concrete sign of renewed strength. On the 27th the whole contents of the big dump of surrendered arms at Akbaş was seized by the insurgents, and carried off to Anatolia. This was too much. That was no way for a conquered country to behave. And the Allies, unable fully to realise that there were by now *two* Turkeys, one within their grasp and one outside it, decided to teach a sharp lesson at least to that part of the nation within their reach. On March the 16th they made a complete military occupation of Istanbul.

Troops had of course been in the city since Franchet d'Esperey marched in in triumph in the late autumn of 1918, but at least the Ottoman Government had continued to function. What now took place was quite different. The most powerful ships of the fleets were moved up towards the water-front, fresh troops were disembarked, and marching through the narrow streets, with their strange traffic of donkeys, street-vendors, and horse-drawn carts, they proceeded to occupy the Government offices themselves. Far away in Ankara, Orhan and others, furious, heard what was happening *as it happened*; for a plucky telegraph operator, Manastirli Hamdi by name, sat at his instrument in the Central Post Office and kept ticking out the news as it was brought to him; at the end there came a sudden silence, as when a sinking ship finally goes down—the foreign troops, occupying the building, had reached the room where he sat.

The news of this last affront quickly spread over Anatolia. The Nationalists already had their own paper, a daily, the *Hakimiyeti Milliyet*, or "National Sovereignty," whose first issue had appeared on January the 10th. It was a little two-sheet thing, brought out by an editor with one assistant, in a room literally no bigger than a billiard-table; the printing-press occupied part of the stables of a han next door. Its modest circulation of two to three thousand copies gave no idea of its importance; couriers, on the tough little Anatolian ponies, carried it at astonishing speed over the rough tracks to all main centres, and a single copy would furnish news—uncensored news—to hundreds of people. Copies were even smuggled down to Istanbul, and read there greedily, passing from hand to hand.

Those were bad days for the Pasha. When he first heard of Orhan's departure for Ankara he really did not know whether to be glad or sorry. He was disturbed at yet another member of his family being now openly committed to what he regarded as plain rebellion; on the other hand he could not but be relieved that his own household was no longer implicated. "At least" he said to Réfiyé Hanim, when she told him the news, "we shall have no more disturbances at night." He was distressed for Féridé—he would have entirely agreed with her remark to Nilüfer that they two led strange lives for married women. But Féridé, unlike her sister-in-law, did not wilt or droop; she seemed more buoyant than ever as she went about the house—not smiling, for in spite of her expansive nature she smiled rather rarely, just serenely assured.

But the events of March the 16th fairly crushed the old gentleman. He said, constantly, that it was all Mustafa Kemal's fault, which in a way it was; but even blaming the man he disapproved of could not diminish his own angry sense of humiliation—a feeling which all Turks shared—joined to an intense resentment and hatred against their conquerors. Sitting in his study, his fez on his head, smoking a narghilé to tranquillise himself, the poor old man was sometimes shaken with a spasm of reluctant envy for those two young ones, up in the mountains, out of sight and sound of the infidels who at present not only filled but controlled the capital which he adored. He rarely went to the Club now—usually he kept away; and cold as the yali was in winter, one was at least left in peace there. But they, those young men, were in a position to do something, to hit back. And they did—or at least their leader did. Two days after the occupation of the city the wretched Chamber, already shorn of its President, met for the last time as the Ottoman Legislature; and the very next day Mustafa Kemal announced by telegram to every province in Turkey that a "National Assembly" would shortly meet in Ankara, armed with "extraordinary"—i.e. over-riding—powers. There was, in fact, no stopping the man!

But this was not yet realised in England. At Christmas an Anglo-French Conference had met in London and roughed out the dream-like provisions of the Treaty of Sèvres; and all through that spring, in the College common-room at Oxford, his friends asked Dr. Pierce—"Who is this infernal fellow Kemal? and why can't he keep quiet?" Poor Dr. Pierce tried to explain about Smyrna and Adana, but his fellow dons were still thinking in terms of Byron and Missolonghi and Greek independence, and his words fell on deaf ears. Besides, they had a new name to conjure with—Venizelos, a remarkable man! At home in his little house in North Oxford Fanny, now released from the V.A.D.s and keeping house for him, questioned, fretted. "Oh, I do wish I were there! Ahmet used to talk about Mustafa Kemal—he really worshipped him. He wanted to be on his Staff."

"Well, he was, my dear; he was that when I saw him—I mean he had been, till he was taken prisoner."

"And this Orhan, whom Féridé has married—I *wish* I had seen him! He made the accompaniment to the Falcon Song." Homesick for everything Turkish, Fanny went to the piano, struck some chords, and softly sang the words.

"Oh, I can't get it right—the accompaniment, I mean. I wish I had got it from Féridé!—it was beautiful."

The Doctor listened, like his niece carried back by the words and melody to the country they both loved so much, now in such travail.

"I *wonder* what Féridé and Nilüfer—poor Nilüfer, she was so lovely, but rather droopy, I always thought—are doing," said Fanny, and took up her darning again.

At that very moment Féridé and Nilüfer were in anxious consultation—anxious, and immensely excited. The same dirty old man from Scutari who had brought Nilüfer her letter from Ahmet on New Year's Eve had appeared again at the yali that day, and this time he got past old Mahmud with less trouble; the door-keeper never forgot a face—it was his business to remember faces. As before, the old man insisted on seeing Nilüfer in person; but now he asked for Féridé Hanim too, for he brought two letters. When they had thanked the old creature, and given him his baksheesh, the two girls fled upstairs with their precious missives, and read them together. Both said much the same thing: each husband had succeeded in renting a furnished house in Ankara, and wished their young wives to come up and join them there forthwith. They were to take a steamer to Inebolu, a small port on the Black Sea coast—there was one sailing in about a week's time; and from thence drive to Ankara. "If possible, one of us will come down to meet you, but if not I think you will manage it," Orhan wrote. "Many will be travelling. Do not bring much luggage, there are no social occasions here—but bring warm clothes, and some *tea*." "Bring me six pairs of socks, and my grey flannel trousers," he added practically, as a PS. "And take a spirit-lamp and some alcohol and a sauce-pan, so that you can warm things up en route." And he gave a good many other, rather detailed, instructions about their proceedings.

"But do you think we *can* go?" Nilüfer had asked, at first, doubtfully. "What will your Father say?"

"I shall consult with Niné—she will know how best to arrange it," said Féridé; "but till I have done so, Nilüfer chérie, please do not speak of it *at all*—not to anyone."

"But I must tell Hatijé; she will need to be getting her things together, and taking farewell of her parents." Hatijé was Nilüfer's maid.

Féridé sat up very straight, her brows drawn down over her eyes in a manner that always rather intimidated her sister-in-law.

"But you cannot take Hatijé!"

"Why not, chérie?"

"Does Ahmet say you can?"

"No—no, of course not; but he knows I cannot be without Hatijé! Who would dress me and wash my stockings and see to my clothes and do my hair?" The gentle creature looked distressed. Féridé bent over and kissed her.

"My dearest, it will be all right, you will see. I shall help you—Orhan says our houses are close, close together! But we cannot take maids with us. See what Orhan says, here"—she fluttered the pages of her letter: "'There are two berths reserved for you on the boat. Take Osman or someone you can trust down to the quay, and when you get on board, ask for Ibrahim Bey, the Captain, and he will see to your places.' You see there is nothing about a berth for Hatijé," said Féridé with finality. "Did Ahmet not tell you about the two berths only?"

"No, he did not write of such things! He writes of seeing me again, and—and so on," said poor Nilüfer, looking very disconsolate.

"Oh, my brother! He is not very practical! Well, sweet-meat, we shall manage alone, you will see."

"I wish they could come and meet us here, and not at this place Ine—whatever it may be," said Nilüfer.

"Ah no—that would be out of the question," said Féridé, her eyebrows decisive again. "For them it would be dangerous. Now chérie, first *promise* me, solemnly, that you speak of this to no one, no one at all—and then we will look out your luggage."

Nilüfer gave the required promise, but there was trouble again over the luggage. She wanted to take two large cabin trunks, and all sorts of cases as well. These Féridé firmly vetoed—two suitcases each, and a parcel each, and a picnic-basket. Nilüfer was almost in tears.

"But it is impossible! We are going for months and months! We must take so *many* things."

"Did Ahmet not tell you to bring very little luggage?"

"No—he did not. He said"—she too drew her letter out again—"'Do not bring too much with you'—that is all. And for so long a séjour these trunks are *not* too much." The gentle creature looked almost mutinous.

Féridé took her by the arm and drew her down to sit on the low bed, covered with one of those splendid velvet-and-gold quilts.

"Listen, my dearest sister," she said gravely, "I think perhaps my brother has not fully explained matters to you. Did he not tell you that we must go in secret?"

"No. He said"—again she consulted the letter—"'as for the journey to Inebolu, Féridé knows about it.' Yes, I see he did say that," she said, looking up at her sister-in-law. "Well, tell me then, my sister," she added with a little sigh of acquiescence.

"Bien! We must go together in secret; you will tell Hatijé that we are only going to your Aunt at Kandilli, for a few days, so we shall need little luggage and no maid. And though we can wear our own clothes and our fur coats, we must cover them with *old* çarşafs, and wear old shoes."

"But why all this?"

"Because it is known where our husbands are, and with whom; and if we go openly, we might be stopped. And we must take some food to eat on the boat—but do not worry about that, I will see to it," said Féridé cheerfully.

"But is it not a boat on which food is served?" said Nilüfer in astonishment, thinking of the meals she had eaten as a child on board a boat going to Mudanya, when she was once taken to Broussa.

"I am not certain. Anyhow we will take some to make sure."

"How long on the boat, then?"

"I do not know exactly—about twenty-four hours, I think. Now, dji-djim, see, take these two cases, and put in *warm* things; and for what will not go in, I will bring you brown paper to make a parcel."

"But I cannot take a parcel! I should look like a peasant!"

Féridé burst out laughing.

"So you *are* to look, my precious one! And remember, not a word to anyone except that we go to Kandilli." She kissed her again, and hastened away.

She sought out Réfiyé Hanim at once. Their enterprise could not be carried through without the old lady's knowledge, and in any case, not for worlds would she have left without telling her Niné; moreover she wanted her advice as to how to deal with her father.

Réfiyé Hanim still always sat in her accustomed place by the window in the salon, still kept the shutters open and the great sea-green room flooded with light, still had her embroidery things beside her on the little inlaid table—only now, instead of the latest French novel or volume of memoirs there was some older book; it was a long time since new French books had been readily obtainable in Istanbul. People said that a few were beginning to come in again, but she hesitated to send Mdlle Marthe, who had always gone to buy her books in the past, in to Hachette's in the Grande Rue de Péra now to see what there was to be had, when the streets were full of foreign troops.

Féridé broke the news to her gently, but directly—Orhan and Ahmet, she said, had made arrangements for them, and had sent for them—and said no more. The old woman looked almost stricken for a moment; then she lifted her head.

"God's will must always be done," she said. "A wife's place is with her husband. Of course you must go."

"Oh Niné, I thank you!" The girl kissed her warmly. "You know that I am sad to leave you," she said.

"I know it, my child," said the old lady, fondling her hand.

"And now, dearest Niné, as always I want your advice. Orhan is urgent that we must go quite secretly; I gather that if we went openly, we might not only be stopped ourselves but put others in danger also."

"Very probable."

"Ahmet has not told Nilüfer this, and I have only told her of the risk of being stopped ourselves. Indeed, he seems to have told her very little, except of his love!" said Féridé, laughing.

"Ah, our Ahmet! From a child his head was always in the clouds! And perhaps he fears to alarm her," said the old lady. "Whom do you take with you, my child?"

"Alas, Niné, no one—we cannot. Only Osman, to put us on the boat. But it is only twenty-four hours, and either Orhan or Ahmet will meet us when we land."

Réfiyé Hanim looked troubled.

"I do not like the idea of your going alone," she said slowly. "You have never done such a thing. Could Osman not accompany you until you are met, at least?"

"Orhan says not, Niné. And we are saying that we go to Nilüfer's Aunt at Kandilli, for a few days only, and therefore have no need of Hatijé and Süreyya."

"You will miss them. Oh my child, are you sure that you can do this thing? No one to serve you, to help you, all the way? And will there be maids *there*?"

"Oh, surely, Niné dearest; they have taken houses for us, all furnished, Orhan says—and if there are houses, there must also be servants," said Féridé blithely. "I am confident that we can manage everything."

"You, perhaps—but Nilüfer? She has not your energy."

Féridé's face grew a little grave.

"Yes, for her it *will* be hard—much harder than for me. But I can look after her, for such a short time; I know I can." She paused, and an amused look came into her face. "Niné, I have just thought such a funny thing—how easy it would be if instead of cette pauvre chère Nilüfer, it were la Canaria who was coming with me! She would think nothing of such a journey. Do you remember how she was expecting to stay alone in that horrid pension, when her Uncle went away? She did not mind a bit, and she was only fourteen or fifteen."

"Dear little Fanny!" said the old lady, smiling. "But for the English, everything is entirely different."

"Ah, I wish she were near! I wish I could see her, or at least hear of her! I do miss her so much—*still*, do you know?" the girl said, turning her great grey eyes full onto her grandmother.

"We heard from Ahmet."

"Yes, but that was a year ago! By now she might be married, anything." She gave a tiny sigh. "But Niné, the most important thing of all we have not yet spoken of, and it is there that I especially need your advice."

The old lady looked keenly at her. "You mean your Father?" she said, slowly.

"*Yes!* How do we do about him? Oh, my poor Father!—this will make him so wretched. How I wish that he felt more in sympathy with Mustafa Kemal Pasha: then he would be less upset—I mean, he would *mind* our going away, but he would not feel obliged also to disapprove!"

Réfiyé Hanim smiled a little.

"That is too much to hope." She considered, her eyes on the blue sky and the blue water outside the low window—Féridé waited. At last—"My child, I think we had better not tell him," she said. "Say to him what you say to others, that you go to Kandilli for a few days. That will save much difficulty and trouble; and it is always as well to avoid difficulties and troubles when one can."

"Oh Niné, could we do it like that? I have so dreaded telling him! Usually I am not much afraid of anything," said Féridé frankly, "but of this I am. But *who* will tell him? At some point he must learn it."

"I shall tell him, when I think fit," said Réfiyé Hanim—and somehow there was majesty in the way she said it. "Now, my child, this is settled; so go with calmness and make your preparations. I assume that this sensible husband of yours has told you what things you need to take?"

"Yes—warm things, and simple; and for himself, tea and a pair of trousers!" said Féridé, laughing again. She was careful not to mention the limit of two suitcases each; that would have worried the old lady nearly as much as it did Nilüfer.

"That is well. Ah, he has a head, your Orhan! Well, send Osman to me nearer the time, and I will give him his orders. He is quite trustworthy," said the old lady.

As Féridé was about to leave the salon, the Pasha walked in. After greeting them both—"I have just had a visitor," he said.

"Of interest, my son?" Réfiyé Hanim asked.

"Certainly to Féridé."

"Baba, *who*? Oh, tell me," Féridé said, clasping her hands.

"Not your husband, my daughter—not anyone's husband, yet; moreover, no one you have ever met."

"Then why should I be interested? My Father, you are just teasing me," the girl protested.

"No, I am not," said the Pasha, seating himself and sticking out his long thin legs, characteristically, towards the brazier. "Ané, you permit?" and he lit a cigarette. "My visitor," he said deliberately, "was a young English officer."

"But my son, how extraordinary! Why should an English officer visit you?"

"And why should such a person interest me?" asked Féridé, looking haughty.

"He was most strangely dressed, moreover," the Pasha went on—his expression showed that he was enjoying himself. "He wore a little short skirt, very full, like an Albanian, all in squares of various colours, rather dark; and bare knees, and a very peculiar little purse or wallet hanging down over this skirt of his in front."

"Baba-djim, vous blaguez! Officers cannot dress so," Féridé said, incredulous.

"Scottish officers do, it seems," said the Pasha coolly.

"But why the interest to me? What do I care for Scottish costume?" Féridé asked.

"Because this young man is, so he says, the innamorato of Fanny Pierce," the Pasha replied.

Féridé jumped up. "Baba, is this true? Oh, *where* is he? Could I not look at him through a door?"

"No. He is gone. And who are you, my daughter, to peer through doors at enemy officers?"

"Fanny is *not* my enemy!—she is my dear, dear friend. And so her fiancé is a friend also."

"He is not her fiancé."

"But you said—"

"I said he was her innamorato," said the Pasha firmly. "He made this quite clear, in the strange way these English have: he desires to marry her, but as yet they are not affianced." (What Captain Grant, whose French was not superlative, had said, smiling, was—"Nous sortons en promenade," by which he had hoped to convey that indefinable English situation called "walking-out"; it conveyed little, of course, to Asaf Pasha.)

"Ah." Féridé sat down again, with a long sigh. "What is he like, my Father?"

"Very large—and very red."

"How do you mean, red?"

"*All* is red—his hair, his face, his hands, his huge wrists, and those naked knees of his," said the Pasha, with something very like a grin.

"Oh Baba! Is he ugly?"

"No, not at all—apart from this tendency to vermilion, he is rather handsome."

"And what is his name?"

The Pasha pulled a card out of his pocket, and handed it to Féridé. "Captain Alexander Grant, The Gordon Highlanders," was printed on it; and above was written in French and in a very neat, crabbed hand— "Mdlle Fanny Pierce greatly desires news of Féridé Hanim. I come on her behalf."

"Ah, she has not forgotten! And did you give him of my news, for Fanny?" Féridé asked eagerly.

"Seeing that he came from our little Canary, I did, enemy as he was," said the Pasha. "He said he should write her a long letter, and tell her all."

"And did you ask him of her? How is she?"

"Yes—knowing how devouring your curiosity would be, my child, I did ask many questions. She lives now with her Uncle at Oxford, and directs his household, but she continues her studies in Turkish, and now in Persian also."

"Fanny—she will be a blue-stocking! Did he say if she is pretty now?"

"My daughter, I could not ask him this!—and in any case he is certain to think so."

"But how curious this is—that he comes openly on her part, and yet they are not betrothed," said Réfiyé Hanim.

"Oh, in such matters, the customs of the English, of all nations, are past fathoming," said the Pasha.

"I *wish* I could write to her! Do you think he would send a letter for me?" Féridé asked.

"That is against the regulations, he said," replied her father. Féridé's face fell. "But he said also that he would do it, for you and for her," the old man added.

"Baba, you cruel tease! But we have not his address."

"Yes, I have it. Write your letter, my child, and give it to me. If this young man is willing to break the rules of his own country, I have no objection to his doing so—peu m'importe," said the Pasha. "But write in French, in order that it can be censored, this Grant said."

So, in the middle of all her preparations Féridé sat down and wrote a long letter to Fanny Pierce, describing the war, Ahmet's and Orhan's part in it, and, generally speaking, as much as one can put of six years of one's life into even a long letter, which this was. It was not wholly discreet—Captain Grant, who censored it himself, smiled at many parts of it, under his little clipped red moustache. But of her imminent departure for Anatolia Féridé said no word.

Chapter Nine

A FEW days later Osman, helped by a ragged and wild-looking porter and closely followed by Féridé and Nilüfer, carried their luggage on board the steamer. As they struggled towards the gangway Féridé remembered vividly the only other time she had ever worked her way through such a throng on the quayside—when she had dragged poor Dil Feripé down to take a last farewell of Fanny. When they got on board they sat on their luggage while Osman went to see about the cabin. The steamer was not very large, and not very clean; the deck was crowded, mostly with very shabby seedy-looking men, peasants or artisans, to judge by their appearance. Nilüfer and Féridé both wore very old coarse çarşafs, procured for them by Dil Feripé, which entirely covered their fur coats. Presently Osman returned and led them to their cabin, where he dumped down their cases on two bunks, one above the other.

The two young women looked about them, appalled. It was a cabin for four, but very small; two stout Armenian women already occupied it. "Mais c'est affreux!" Nilüfer whispered to Féridé, who was looking for somewhere to put down the picnic-basket.

"This is really the place, is it, Osman?" Féridé asked.

"Yes, Hanim Effendi, it is—I asked twice."

"Well, it is only for twenty-four hours," Féridé said to Nilüfer. She made Osman push as many of the suitcases as possible in under the bunks, and then went out into the passage to take farewell of him.

"Hanim Effendi, if you desire it, I will stay on board and accompany you—to my mind it would be better," said the faithful servant. "I do not like to leave you alone, in such circumstances, and among such people"—he looked about him with disapproval, in the crowded passage.

"Hush! Speak lower, Osman. It is not for long, and we have our food; we can remain here," the girl replied.

"In your cabin are these two unveiled infidels—shameless creatures! It is hardly fitting that the Hanim Effendi should pass even an hour in the company of such, in my opinion," said Osman, with a sort of respectful forthrightness—he had known his young mistress from her earliest childhood. Féridé laughed.

"Do not fret—all will be well," she said. A bell rang, or rather vibrated, all through the ship; in the distance a voice shouted. "There!—you must go. Goodbye, Osman."

"May Allah protect you on the way," Osman said, and made his way up on deck.

Féridé went back into the cabin, where Nilüfer sat on the edge of the lower bunk, in tears. "We are leaving—come up, my dearest, and let us watch," she said.

Up they went, and found a place at the rail, whence they watched the ship manoeuvring her way out into open water. It was a bright sunny day; the wonderful skyline of Istanbul, with the soaring domes of its mosques, the sharp needles of its minarets, the steep fall to the water of those slopes of dark wooden houses, their windows like white sightless eyes, lay brilliant in the pale sunshine. The steamer moved slowly over towards the lighthouse which is called Leander's Tower, preparatory to starting up the Bosphorus; when she reached the fairway, and started full steam ahead, a shot was fired across her bows. The engines stopped, and the ship came slowly to a halt; a launch from one of the Allied men-of-war bounced across the bright water towards her.

"Oh, what is it?" Nilüfer asked. Everyone about them was asking the same question.

For many hours that question remained unanswered. With a deep clanking of chains the anchors were let down, and there she stayed; across the water, beyond Scutari, Nilüfer could see the grey shape of her Father's own yali, and the sight again brought her too-ready tears. Féridé, more resilient, kept on making enquiries, and eventually learned that the Allied authorities were detaining the ship because they suspected the presence of arms on board; indeed some foreign officers were seen scrambling up the side; presently they departed again.

The passengers hoped that the ship would now be allowed to proceed, but not at all. They stayed there three days and three nights—within sight of home, and yet unable to reach it. Féridé was acutely anxious herself, and was aware of an intense anxiety pervading the massed passengers on the ship. She began to doubt, presently, if all these shabby men dressed as peasants and workmen were really what they seemed; she saw several of them run up and down the steps from deck to deck with a brisk lightness very unlike the heavy deliberate movements of peasants or labourers. On the second day, while poor Nilüfer remained in the cabin, Féridé, who had come up on deck for a little air, noticed a man who walked with a slight limp; as he turned in her direction, in spite of his shabby clothes she thought she recognised him as Orhan's friend Hassan Bey, the young man in the Ministry of War who had brought the telegram from Ahmet on her wedding-day—she had seen him once at a concert. Cautiously, she moved in his direction: it might not be correct behavior, but she was determined to speak to him and find out if he knew anything of what was going on. After all, this journey of hers and Nilüfer's was not exactly conventional! When she reached his side—"Is it not Hassan?" she said, very low; she was careful to omit the "Bey."

He started, and turned towards her—yes, it was certainly he.

"Who is it?" he asked, as low as she.

"The wife of Orhan," she whispered.

"No! What are you doing here?" he asked, very low. The press of people was so thick about them on the crowded deck that it was difficult not to be overheard.

"I go to join him."

"Do you indeed? How splendid—I honour you! Then we travel together. How do you go, by Samsun or Inebolu?"

"Inebolu. He, or Ahmet, comes to meet us there."

"Us? Who is with you?"

"Nilüfer, Ahmet's wife."

"No! I should not have thought her equal to this."

"Oh, on se tirera d'affaire," Féridé said, thoughtlessly breaking into French.

"Shsh! Do not speak that tongue! There may be agents anywhere."

"I am sorry; you are right. But tell me, when do we go on, do you know?"

"No one knows! Have you any food?" Hassan asked.

"Oh, so little! We brought enough for twenty-four hours, and luckily the servants put in a lot, for that time—but we have eaten it nearly all!" said Féridé truthfully. "And you?"

"I brought none, idiot that I was! I thought there would be food on board, and anyhow, for one day and a night, it was unimportant."

"But have you eaten?"

"Not a mouthful, since the day before yesterday."

"But this is frightful! Come down, and I will give you some chocolate, at least."

He followed her downstairs. In the cabin, where the two Armenian women lay moaning in their bunks, she brewed some tea on the floor— there was nowhere else to stand the spirit-lamp—and handed him out a cup, a slab of chocolate, and a piece of bread into the passage.

"Ah, that is wonderful!" he said when he had finished.

"Let me know if you hear anything," Féridé said.

"I will"—he glanced at the number over the cabin door before he limped away.

On the afternoon of the third day another steamer, slightly larger than the one they were on, steamed up alongside and cast anchor beside them; more Allied officers were seen coming on board. Féridé, hearing noises, was making her way up on deck to see what was going on, when on the stairs she encountered Hassan, a suitcase in his hand, coming down.

"What is happening now?" she asked.

"Hush! Come to your cabin, if you please, quickly."

They went together. At the door he said, in a hurried whisper—"If you would lend me one of your suitcases, and keep mine with you? Could you do this?"

"Yes—but why?"

"I am told that we are to be transferred to the other ship, and it is said that they may search our luggage—the men's, that is; probably you will not be questioned."

"Well?" Féridé was still puzzled.

"But this has my uniform in it!"

"Ah." She understood now. "Very well—wait." She went into the cabin and pulled out her second suitcase from under the bunk, passed it through the door, took in Hassan's, and stuffed it in in place of the other.

The transfer occupied the whole afternoon, and went on until well into the evening. Allied officers checked the passengers off one ship, and onto the other; Féridé saw a few pieces of luggage being examined, but she and Nilüfer were not troubled with any search. Their quarters on the second boat were even worse than the first—they were in a cabin for six, and they were hungrier than ever; the cabin was very stuffy, too. Neither of the girls attempted to undress, they lay down as they were; they had not washed properly since they left the yali. They ate their last bit of bread, but Féridé insisted on keeping what little chocolate they had left. "We may need it," she said. "Ah, do you remember those bonbons that we munched together, the night of my wedding? We could do with a box of them now." Nilüfer only sniffed despondently in reply.

But Féridé could not sleep; hunger and anxiety kept her awake. After some hours she could bear her hard bed and the snores of her companions no longer—very softly she swung herself down out of her bunk (she had given Nilüfer the lower one), put on her fur coat and her çarşaf, and stealing out once more went up on deck—to be confronted by a most extraordinary spectacle. The ship on which they had originally embarked was still, for some unexplained reason, anchored alongside, though the gangways had been removed; in the murky half-darkness of a cloudy night with little moon she could see that its coal-ports and rubbish ports, down near the water-line, were open—a faint

reddish light of lamps within glowed from them. And out of these illuminated openings bundles, tied with ropes, were continually pushed
forth, and hauled up with astonishing speed onto the deck of their new
vessel; the ropes were loosed and tossed back, some Rembrandtesque
figure within the open ports managed to catch them, when they were
attached to yet other bundles, and hauled up again. She moved
quietly towards the nearest group of men who were hauling up these
mysterious objects, which were obviously heavy, and yet were being put
down on the deck in strange silence; when she was near enough she saw
why—mattresses had been laid on the planking. And now she could
see what the bundles consisted of: the long narrow ones were rifles
lashed together, and the square wooden boxes could only be ammunition. Now and again something oval and slender came up in a sack,
was tipped out, and the sack flung back on the end of the rope—shells!
And all the while men, breathing hard, came and went, seizing on these
various things and carrying them away below decks.

A faint greyness was beginning to show in the sky, away up the Bosphorus. Presently from below a voice called up, very softly—"That is
the last." Out from the illuminated ports men came, twisted themselves
into the ropes, and were hauled up as the rifles had been. An officer
looked over from the bridge above—"Is everyone on board?" "Yes, all,"
came the cautious answer.

"Then we go—Allah be my witness that I shall be thankful to get out
of this!"

Bells rang, the winches groaned, the chains clanked; in the strengthening light up came the anchors, as the engines began to turn over.
Slowly, slowly, the ship moved away from her companion, away from
the winking light on Leander's Tower, away from the diamond chain
of lamps along the Galata Bridge, and the street lights in the town—the
lights of Istanbul! Ah, when would she see them again, the girl wondered. Now that they were fairly in motion it grew chilly, and she
drew her coat more tightly about her, as she leaned on the rail. Others
were coming to do the same, wiping their brows and pulling on their
jackets after their arduous night's work; she saw Hassan limp across to a
space near her and lean, gazing up and back at the beloved city. His
thoughts were the same as hers, she felt sure. She went over to him—
he turned as she approached. "Is it Féridé Hanim?" he asked.

"Yes. Was all well?"

"Very well. They opened my case—your case—and accused me of
stealing the things! But they did not care about thefts of women's clothing, and let me go!"

She laughed. "C'est très bien!"

"Are you not cold?" he asked. "Should you not go below?"

"In a moment. There are things I want to see," she answered. He nodded. "I understand—I also."

The light was strengthening all the time, though still grey and colourless; to their right—they were standing well forward—was the dim and rather formless outline of the Chamlidja hills, with the lights of Scutari and Kadikeui below them, wan in the increasing day; to their left familiar things came in sight now, as the ship breasted the current—the huge serrated outline of Rumeli Hissar, the Fortress in Europe, climbing from the sea right up the hill, and not far from its foot the long, delicate, silvergrey shape of the yali, with the dark smear of the koru stretching up the slopes behind. Within those carved baroque walls, Féridé thought, her Father and Niné slept—when would she see them, too, again? She looked resolutely ahead, where the narrow blue waters stretched away, leading to the vast spaces of the Black Sea, to Anatolia, to freedom, and to Orhan! With a last backward glance at the receding bulk of the yali, she turned to go.

Hassan stepped forward.

"My case," he said—"if I could have it?"

"Oh yes, naturally—do come down."

"I will fetch yours," he said. Downstairs, through the cabin door, they exchanged suitcases for the second time; Féridé left her own on the floor, she was too tired and too faint with hunger even to push it in under the bunk. She took off her çarşaf, threw her fur coat over the thin and rather smelly blankets, climbed up and lay down. And slept —for hours and hours.

In fact she did not really get up the whole of that day, nor did Nilüfer. The Black Sea was rough, as it often is in March, and both of them felt sea-sick and utterly wretched. Towards evening, before daylight had finally departed, Féridé crept to the porthole and looked out: their cabin was on the starboard side, but no land was visible, nothing but a grey tossing waste of waters. It seemed to have grown very cold. Shivering, she got some bromide, then climbed back into her bunk, and fell again into a heavy sleep.

When she woke, it was broad daylight—more, the sun was evidently shining, for a narrow gold ray was slanting in through the port-hole. Féridé climbed down, shook her dress—ugh, this sleeping in one's clothes!—washed her face and hands with Eau de Cologne and a handkerchief, and brushed and did up her hair. The long sleep had done her good; she felt eager, ready for this day on which the sun shone, and curious to know what was happening; she hastened up on deck.

To her dying day Féridé will never forget the sight that met her eyes then, as she stepped out from the dirty passage into the open air. The ship was only a few miles off-shore, and the land rose in a range of mountains covered with snow, shining white and golden in the morning sun, with blue troughs of shadow where the valleys ran up into them. Féridé had never seen snowcovered mountains before, and she gazed in astonishment and delight as she started to walk forward along the deck to get a better view. But what had happened to her fellow-passengers? Where were all those shabby seedy-looking unshaven men? The whole deck was now brilliant with uniforms—buttons and medals with bright ribbons flashed in the sun, gold braid shone on collars and epaulettes, polished boots gleamed, swords and spurs clanked; it was like a transformation scene on some stage. The girl fairly gaped—the ship seemed to be carrying an army. No, not a whole army; now she saw that the men were nearly all officers—officers or cadets from the Military Colleges. She spied Hassan in the distance, and wished that she could speak with him—she wanted to know where they were, and how soon they would land. It was glorious and inspiring, this scene, both aboard and ashore—but oh, she was so hungry, in the keen morning air!

Her gaze must have somehow penetrated Hassan's consciousness, as a look often does, for in a moment he turned, saw the black veiled figure, and came towards her.

"Is it Féridé Hanim?" he asked.

"Yes. Good-morning. How splendid all this is!"

"Is it not?" He waved his hand shoreward at the snowy ranges—"Anatolia! Freedom!" he said, then he gestured along the deck ahead of them—"And free men, at last!"

Féridé made an enthusiastic response, then—"Do you know where we are? And how soon we land?" she asked.

He pointed ahead—the ship was drawing near to the coast on a long slant.

"Do you see that town down on the shore, with a valley running up behind? That is Inebolu. We shall be there in about half an hour."

She glanced at her watch—it was 9 o'clock. "Then we had better get ready," she said, and went below to rouse Nilüfer, and pack; she also bethought her that without Osman they could not possibly convey their heavy suitcases up on deck. What should she do? Find a sailor and ask him? She recoiled a little from the idea—what did one say to strange sailors?—she had never spoken to one in her life. While Nilüfer was getting ready she went up on deck again and had recourse to Hassan Bey; he found a sailor, took him below, and between them the two men got the girls' gear up on deck.

The ship was by this time close in-shore, about half a mile from the land; the small white town with its pinkish-brown tiled roofs was plainly visible, spreading along the beach, climbing a low bluff on one side, and stretching up the valley inland. The snow on the mountains ceased a few hundred feet above sea-level, and the shore and the valley looked green and smiling. But there was no sign of a quay or jetty, just the grey line of the shingle along the shore below the houses. "Where do we land?" Féridé asked.

"On the beach, from boats." Indeed a number of roughlooking craft were already leaving the shore and rowing out towards them; and the next moment, with a metallic roar the anchor was let go, and the ship came to a standstill.

"He will come out in the boat, no?" Nilüfer asked of Féridé.

"You are being met, of course?" Hassan asked, hearing her question.

"Yes, we expect either my husband or my brother to come and meet us," Féridé replied. "Will they come out in one of these boats?"

"I expect so."

But when the shore boats, scudding like water-beetles, approached the ship, till their occupants were clearly recognisable, there was no sign of either Ahmet or Orhan. The two girls scanned every boat in turn: neither was there.

"He must be waiting for us at the hotel," said Féridé, with a cheerfulness she was far from feeling; for surely neither Orhan nor Ahmet would have failed to greet them at the first possible moment, nor left them to struggle with the business of getting ashore alone.

And that disembarkation at Inebolu was an awkward business. The moment the rowing-boats reached the ship, everything became wild confusion: from all sides luggage, cases of ammunition, shells and bundles of rifles were slung or flung overboard into them, as they bounced up and down alongside on the unpleasantly large waves; men shouted up from the boats, shouted down from the deck, yelled at one another *in* the boats—it was pandemonium. Hassan came across to where Nilüfer and Féridé stood, hesitating, beside their little heap of luggage.

"You have not seen them? No? Nor have I. But I will see if something cannot be arranged—you should get to the hotel, and have some food." He went off and presently returned with two sailors, who took up their luggage and his own, and led them to the ladder down the ship's side, where a boat waited at the foot, swinging up, swinging down, with the motion of each wave.

"This is for us—let us go," Hassan said.

The sailors ran nimbly down the ladder, which had an uneasy motion of its own, and flung their luggage into the shifting boat; Féridé and Nilüfer followed Hassan. He stood on the small platform at the foot, and as the boat swung up towards it on a wave, he sprang in; as the boat fell away again he toppled over, and collapsed on the luggage at the bottom—the boatman laughed.

"I cannot do that!" Nilüfer said, in a trembling voice.

"Oh yes, chérie, of course you can. Come on." Féridé drew her down onto the small platform, where she clung to the rope handrail, which was horribly unstable itself.

"No, I shall fall in!"

"Come, come! Jump!" the boatmen yelled. As the boat swung up again Féridé grasped the outstretched hand of one of them, and jumped; like Hassan she landed in a heap in the bottom of the boat.

"Now the other!" the men shouted—but Nilüfer, terrified, could not bring herself to jump. A boatman sprang up onto the platform, took her in his arms like a bundle, and on the next rise jumped with her. The passengers were stowed in the stern on a wet, salt-stained, rather dirty seat, and the men rowed towards the shore. The beach as they approached presented an aspect of feverish activity. As the boats, laden deep with ammunition, ran in among the breaking waves men rushed down to meet them, wading breast-high into the foaming water, seized them, and guided them up onto the beach, where stout hawsers were attached to the bows; they were then drawn up onto dry land by very primitive capstans, consisting of four small tree-trunks projecting from a wooden drum—a team of turbaned men, pushing the tree-trunks, wound each boat slowly up over the shingle to the rhythm of a loud monotonous song. The moment a boat was beyond reach of the waves a shout checked the capstan team; other men rushed to pull out the cargo, the hawser was cast off and the boat thrust down to the sea again, where her crew launched her, sprang on board, and made off as fast as they could towards the ship. There were five or six capstans at work, and though the whole business looked very crazy and rough-and-tumble, in fact the arms and ammunition were being got ashore at an astonishing speed—once out of the boats, yet other men carried them up and dumped them in piles on an open space above the beach.

Hassan was greatly impressed by this primitive but effectual organisation, but the young women were really only concerned with two things —whether the motley crowd concealed one or other of their husbands, and how they themselves were to get ashore through the tumbling surf. There were a number of uniforms to be seen, but they were mostly new arrivals from the ship; of Ahmet or Orhan they could see no sign. Meanwhile their boat ran in among the breaking crests, and several of those soaking figures plunged into the water and dragged the heavy craft to land; as the keel grated on the shingle and began to move up it two stalwart fellows, wading alongside, plucked Nilüfer and Féridé off their seat like bundles, threw them over their shoulders, and carried them unceremoniously up the beach, where they set them down. Féridé, startled and breathless, burst out laughing as she found her feet. "Well, that is one way of landing!" she said to Nilüfer, shaking herself like a cat, and pulling down her skirts. "And now, where are they, do you suppose?—or him, whichever it is?"

He, or they, did not appear to be anywhere. Hassan, who had also been carried ashore, paid the boatman and went off to make enquiries of a very tall man with a big, flattish, rather square face, pale blue eyes, and a short blunt nose, who seemed to be directing operations.

"They have not announced themselves down here," he said when he returned. "Let us go up to the hotel and eat, at least. We may get news there."

This was a blow. They set off, with two porters for the luggage, in a gloomy little procession—along the sandy space past piles of rifles, shells, and ammunition, up some steps, and along cobbled streets to Inebolu's one and only hotel.

In the year 1920 this hotel was not good. In the hall—which smelt strongly of sanitation, and was both cold and dirty—Hassan first of all booked a room for the two young women, ordered lunch to be served there as soon as possible, and then sought out the proprietor and asked if Ahmet Bey or Orhan Bey was staying there? No, they were not—and had not been.

"Oh, *what* do we do now?" Nilüfer whispered to Féridé.

"Wait!" Féridé said, taking her hand—"Listen!"

Hassan was pursuing his enquiries. Was there any letter, or message, for Féridé Hanim or Nilüfer Hanim?

The landlord thought not—and his attention was deflected at that moment by the arrival of a whole swarm of cadets and officers off the ship, who came surging into the hotel, clamouring for food.

"Come up to your room," Hassan said urgently to the two girls—he realised that unless they acted promptly rooms, food and all would soon be taken by others. He got the key, and they went upstairs, found the room. "I will see about the luggage," said Hassan, and limped away.

When he had gone Féridé went to the window and flung open the shutters, letting in a flood of light. Neither she nor Nilüfer had ever stayed in a Turkish provincial hotel before, and that bedroom looked almost as peculiar to them as it would have done to a European. Fringed embroidered draperies swathed the windows; below them, and round most of the walls ran very hard divans, covered with a thick woollen material; on the walls hung two or three rugs. There were three beds, with brass bedsteads and cheap quilts, a cheap modern dressing-table with a huge mirror, on which stood a china jug and basin; and between two of the beds a common wooden chair with an empty candlestick —and that was absolutely all. The room was very stuffy, with a mouldy unused smell, and dankly cold.

In their weary and half-starved state this was a moment, above all others, when a really comfortable room and a cheerful welcome would have meant a great deal—what they found was very discouraging. Féridé burst out laughing.

"What is funny?" Nilüfer asked, with quivering lips.

"This! All of it! It is so horrible that it is really funny." She paused, and looked round the room. "We must get warmth, somehow," she said; "I wonder where the bell is."

There was no bell visible but a cord with a dusty tassel, hanging down beside the door; when Féridé gave a tug at it it came away in her hand and fell, like a shabby snake, to the floor. Féridé, undaunted, went out in to the passage and called—a chambermaid appeared, dressed entirely in various shades of plummy pink, with a white veil with a border of tiny black flowers swathed all round her head, face, and shoulders. Féridé demanded a brazier; the woman, who was elderly and rather sour, at first said she was not sure if there was one to spare, but Féridé's firm insistent tone of command overcame her sulky inertia, and she went off to get it.

"I wish lunch would come," Féridé said then.

"What are we to eat it on? There is no table," said Nilüfer gloomily.

"We can eat it off the bed or off the floor, anything, if only it comes!" Féridé exclaimed.

It did not, however, come for some considerable time. When it did, they perched on the divans and took their first proper meal for four days. The food was nasty, ill-cooked and ill-served, but they ate hungrily. As they were finishing the brazier was brought in.

"Well, we are advancing," said Féridé—"we have at least eaten, and we have some warmth."

"But *where* can Ahmet be?" Nilüfer asked. "It is so strange."

"Hassan Bey will find out, I am sure. Do not fret, my dearest—there must be some confusion," Féridé said, with a confidence she was far from feeling. "Why do you not rest a little?"

Nilüfer thought she would, and selected one of the three beds. The sheets were dubious, the single pillow as hard as a bullet, laced elaborately down the back into a pillow-case covered with coloured embroidery, very scratchy to the face; Féridé put a scarf over this, pulled out a soft shawl from one of her cases and arranged it inside those dreadful sheets, and then made her sister-in-law creep into the sort of cocoon thus formed and lie down. When she had settled her in, she herself took out a little writing-case and wrote a brief note to Réfiyé Hanim, saying that they had arrived safely so far; she was careful to put no date, and to say nothing about the total absence of any husband, only stressed the great beauty of the snowy ranges above the sea, and mentioned that Hassan Bey "has helped us greatly on the voyage." She put the letter in her purse, hoping that Hassan would contrive to send it for her. Oh, how much easier everything was at home, where a maid gave the letters to Osman, and that was that! (Féridé had never bought a stamp in her life.)

She was just about to lie down and take a rest herself when there came a knock at the door—with a beating heart she ran to open it. It was only Hassan; he had a letter in his hand.

"I am sorry to have been so long," he said—"May perdition overtake this landlord! I went to the Post Office to enquire for the letter, then to the bureau of the Kaimakam, and there was nothing—when I return here, and ask again, he has it all the time!"

"I am sorry you have had all this trouble!" said Féridé. The letter was in Orhan's writing, and she longed to open it. "Have you eaten yet?" she asked.

"No, but that is unimportant. I should be glad to know if it contains any news." (Poor Hassan was beginning to feel the responsibility for his two fellow-travelers rather heavy.)

"Yes, of course. Wait—why not go and eat, quickly, and then return? We shall have read it then."

Hassan agreed. Féridé went back and opened the letter. There was an enclosure for Nilüfer from Ahmet, but as Nilüfer was now asleep she tossed it onto the divan beside her, and read her own.

Orhan wrote in considerable distress, to explain why neither he nor Ahmet could come and meet them. "Fresh operations are in prospect in the Taurus, and your brother is tremendously occupied, trying to equip and train reinforcements. Ah, if you knew what this shortage of everything means! I hope your boat has brought what it should bring." As for himself, it was totally impossible that he should leave just now— "There are certain difficulties in many districts with the population, who have been misled, and these get worse and worse; we have to take countermeasures, to make the people understand the truth of the situation, but this needs time and personnel—and we are so few! Ismet Bey has just arrived, and is a great support; but our Chief is working eighteen hours a day, and really I cannot leave him at such a moment! I know you will understand, Light of my Eyes, what it means to me not to meet you, and to leave you to make this journey alone; but there are sure to be many on the road who will assist you. Here is a note for the Kaimakam—if you send it to him, he will see that you get a carriage, with a good driver. I enclose some money. Oh, hasten!—and may God guard you every step of the way."

Féridé's heart did fail her a little when she read this, and realised that there was definitely no hope of either Ahmet or Orhan coming to escort them on their journey. Sitting on the hard divan by the window, look-ing out on the blue waters which dashed coldly on the rocks below, she let a few tears fall. She had only the vaguest idea of how far it was to Ankara, or how long the journey would take—in the hurry of their de-parture from the yali she had not consulted the map. However, she pulled herself together, washed in cold water on that hideous dressing-table, and got tidy; when a tap on the door again announced Hassan's advent she was ready, and went out to him. In the chilly passage she told him what Orhan had written, and gave him the letters for Réfiyé Ha-nim and the Kaimakam—"Could you, do you think, get someone to take it there? We ought to start as soon as possible."

"I will take it myself," the young man said—"It will be safer. There are so many travellers, and much confusion. Are you all right? Have you what you need?"

"Oh yes, for one night we can manage, thank you."

She watched him hobble away, then went in search of the chamber-maid, and demanded candles and more candlesticks, and told her to have a table and another chair sent. The woman grumbled, but did as she was told. Féridé was actually beginning to take a sort of queer pleas-ure in using her powers in this new and unfamiliar way. Fanny, she was sure, would do it all much better—Fanny who used to travel alone in the train to school when she was only fourteen! You could not im-agine Fanny being beaten by any difficulties, and she, Féridé, was not going to be beaten either.

When she had done all she could for the moment, she read Orhan's letter again. One sentence puzzled her very much—the reference to "difficulties with the population, who are being misled." What could that mean? Since Orhan's departure she had heard little or no talk of the political situation, except such major happenings as the occupation of the capital; she and her father studiously avoided the subject of pol-itics, and she saw no one else. So she was unaware of the new move-ment that had begun, and was becoming daily more menacing to the Nationalist cause. The Allies could not get at Mustafa Kemal up in Anatolia; but the Sultan and his government could, by using the Turks themselves against the man who was fighting for his country's in-dependence. Among a people wholly without political experience, and far more swayed by emotion than by anything else, reaction is always a factor to be reckoned with; and a reaction from the first great upsurge of patriotic feeling, which had launched the Nationalist movement a few months before, had begun to set in among this war-weary nation. By payments, promises, and skilful propaganda the Sultan's agents were fostering it with all their might, and wherever they could; anti-Nationalist bands were being formed, Mustafa Kemal's recruiting agents were being maltreated—and even tortured in some regions; in fact there were already the beginnings of civil war on a small scale.

Féridé, ignorant of all this, sat puzzling and worrying over her husband's letter in that dreary room in the hotel at Inebolu, while the heat from the small brazier grew less and less, and a chill began to creep into the room, along with the bluish shadows that dusk brings beside the sea. Presently Nilüfer roused up; Féride opened the picnic-basket and made tea.

It was almost quite dark before Hassan returned and tapped at the door—Féridé went and opened to him.

"Voyons, come in," she said—"This is in fact our salon! Let us not stand on ceremony; come and take a cup of tea." Gratefully the young man came in and sat down. "Mais comme vous êtes bien installées," he said holding out his hands to the dying brazier. Féridé let him drink his tea in peace; then—"Have you been able to arrange something with the Kaimakam?" she asked.

"Yes. A carriage will be here for you early tomorrow morning. The horses are quite good, and I have spoken personally with the driver; he seems a decent sensible fellow. He will take you the whole way to Ankara."

"Ah, that is excellent! How we thank you. And you?"

"I have hired a horse," Hassan said. "I cannot walk like all the rest."

Chapter Ten

THE long cross-country trek on which Féridé and Nilüfer set out a day later will doubtless go down to history by the name which Turks use for it today, in pride and affection—The Road of the Revolution. They started a day late because the carriage promised by the Kaimakam, characteristically, was only forthcoming then, and this applied equally to Hassan's horse; so all three endured another twenty-four hours of cold, discomfort, frustration and bad food in the hotel. But at last they started—and whatever the delays and discomforts endured, happy those who then took that road, for they carry a memory of one of the great national revivals of our time.

The conveyance into which the two girls stowed themselves, their luggage, and Hassan's suitcase was a sort of open victoria, very small, drawn by two sturdy little Anatolian horses—a cold sort of carriage to travel in for long. In their total ignorance of a journey of this sort neither of the young women had thought to bring a rug; this mistake Hassan remedied by cantering off to the market and returning with a hairy, rather smelly, goatshair blanket, which he folded round their knees before they bowled off through the narrow cobbled streets.

They were soon slowed down: it was market-day in Inebolu, and dense crowds brought the carriage to a foot's pace—crowds largely of women, dressed like the chambermaid in skirts and quilted jackets of a prevailing tone of plummy pink, with vivid aprons striped in indigo-blue and dull red. But it was their headdress which ravished the two girls. Instead of the dreary black çarşafs of Istanbul the heads, faces and shoulders of these Anatolian peasants were swathed in big white scarves bordered with a minute pattern of black, so that the narrow thronged streets seemed to be filled with clouds of enormous white butterflies—in the bright spring sunshine the effect was magical.

Once clear of the market and the town they made a good pace again. For some distance the road followed the river in the main valley; then it branched off to the left, crossed a bridge, and began to climb steeply through cultivated land, now dank and sodden after the winter's snow, but richly set along the edges of the fields with fig, chestnut, and mulberry-trees. Higher, these were replaced by immense cherry-trees, thirty feet or more high; higher still cultivation was left behind altogether, and they passed into the mountain woodlands, where through the beech-scrub spread a glossy dark undergrowth of that familiar English evergreen, *Rhododendron ponticum,* growing wild on its native heath. Patches of snow began to appear in the hollows and under the banks; the air grew cold, and the horses slowed to a walk on the steep, muddy, rutted road.

Nilüfer and Féridé took little interest in trees or shrubs, either culti- vated or wild; what arrested and held their attention, from the moment of crossing the bridge and beginning to climb the slopes above that side valley was the astonishing procession which was plodding up one side of the road. It was like a chain-gang, except that there were no chains —spaced about a metre and a half apart, in single file, walked an un- ending line of human beings, all bending forward under the weight of various burdens: bundles of rifles, boxes of ammunition, shells slung in loops of cord—all the things that Féridé had watched being transshipped so stealthily that last night off Istanbul. So this was how the cargo of their ship was being transported over the Kuré Dagh! Most astonish- ing of all, more than three-quarters of the carriers were women, some in the pink-skirted local dress, others in brightly-flowered cherry- coloured trousers; quite a number were carrying a baby in their arms as well as a shell bound on their backs, others were accompanied by two or three small children, who pattered beside them in the greasy mud. Up, up, up; steady, slow, unceasing; now and again one called to a straggling child, but for the most part they walked in silence, breathing heavily, with the weight of their loads and the steepness of the ascent. The road was getting very steep indeed, and soon they came altogether into the snow—dirty slushy stuff at first, but as they climbed even higher, the roadside banks and the slopes about them were pure un- tracked white, under which the broad-leaved rhododendrons dis- appeared as heaped shapeless masses, while above the slender bare twigs of the beech-scrub, too thin to hold the snow, stood out in a delicate dark tracery. And still, against this wintry background, that unending file of figures trudged on, monotonous and statuesque as figures on a frieze—only no one has ever yet sculptured a frieze of women with veiled heads carrying heavy loads, and children running like calves at foot beside them.

Féridé, of course, wanted to know all about this phenomenon, and since Hassan had disappeared she applied to Mehmet, their coachman, who sat silent and apparently rather sulky on the box, muffled up in a sheep-skin coat.

"Mehmet, why are these packages carried by women?"

"Because the men are at the war, Effendim," replied the driver, without turning his head.

"But why do they not use carts?"

"The road is too bad, Effendim—with such loads carts would sink in the mud."

"Heavens! Shall we too sink in the mud?" Nilüfer exclaimed.

"We may well do so, Effendim," said Mehmet fatalistically; "or we may stick fast in the snow. This often happens on this road."

Féridé was not interested in the matter of sinking in snow or mud. "Where do these women and their children sleep?"

"But by the side of the road, naturally," the coachman replied. "Next day, they rise and walk forward."

"How do they eat?"

"They get food in the villages, or at the hans, and eat it, and then go on. We shall soon come to the Solgan Han, the first one—we rest the horses there."

"How far do they go? All the way to Ankara?"

"No, Effendim—only to Seydiler. From there onwards the road is better, and the loads can be taken on carts."

"This is wonderful!" Féridé said to Nilüfer. "What endurance! They are the caryatides of our time!" she exclaimed, again leaning out to study the faces of the plodding women, some of which were indeed contorted with the strain.

"Yes—how strong they must be. But"—lowering her voice and speaking in French—"do you suppose that we shall really get stuck?"

"Oh no, I don't expect we shall. These seem to be very good horses, and we are not as heavy as shells!" said Féridé, laughing—the sun, the keen mountain air, and the snowy mountain landscape about them were filling her with a strange exhilaration, which was deepened by the sight of that silent line of figures on their right. "Look at that woman there—she is carrying *twins!*" she exclaimed. "Oh, really they are wonderful—" for indeed they were now passing a woman with two bundled babies, one in each arm, and a wooden box of ammunition strapped to her back; their light-footed little horses went just a trifle faster than the load-bearers, so that they kept seeing new ones all the time.

The road, which had been zigzagging to and fro up the northern side of the valley, now turned and flattened out on a sharp narrow ridge, overlooking both the slope up which they had come and the main gorge; on this razor-back stood a small wooden structure, about which a crowd of cadets and ammunition-carriers were halted, eating bread and drinking coffee. Mehmet drove up to the door, and for once turning in his seat said—"This is the han; here I rest the horses for a space. The ladies can descend and take coffee."

He set the ladies an example by descending himself, fastening the horses to a post, and stumping into the inn. The two young women sat in the carriage, hesitating; when the door opened to admit the coachman they caught a glimpse of a low room full of men, eating and drinking at long trestle tables. It was not at all the sort of place they had ever expected to enter.

"I think we should wait here, outside. I am not hungry—are you?" Féridé said.

"No!" Nilüfer spoke with a shudder—"Do not let us, on any account, go in there. How could we?"

So they stayed where they were. Féridé got out and walked about, peering over into the gulf of the valley to their right; but the snow was cold to her feet, and spectacular as the scenery was, she had just got into the carriage again and huddled down under Hassan's blanket when she saw the woman with twins coming up the road, and paused, to see what she would do. First she laid the two bundled babies down on the snow; then, unslinging the heavy wooden box off her back she sat on it, picked the two infants up, and unfastening the front of her dress, proceeded to give them the breast. As her companions came up with her, and likewise slung down their loads—"Bring me out some bread, presently," she called to them.

The others nodded, and went into the han; one shortly reappeared with a cup of coffee, which she held to the mother's lips—"Ah, that's good," the woman said. Another presently brought a hunk of bread and laid it in her lap, and when the babies had finished feeding she laid them across her knees, unconcernedly, and ate the bread, tearing it into large pieces and chewing them vigorously with her strong white teeth.

Féridé watched this from the carriage, fascinated; now, since there was still no sign of Mehmet she could not resist getting out again, and going over to speak to the woman.

"You do not get tired?" she asked.

"Not I, no—by Allah's goodness I am stout," said the woman, laughing; she had thrown back her scarf to eat, and sat there unveiled, regardless of the men coming and going to the han, to Féridé's amazement—the girl from the metropolis was not yet accustomed to the casualness of the Anatolian peasant-woman about the veil.

"Have you done this before?"

"Yes, six times; four before my children were born, and twice since."

"And do they not mind? I mean, do they thrive?" Féridé asked.

"Yes—I thrive, so they thrive," said the woman. "Let the Lady look at them"—and she unrolled the two bundles. Féridé peered cautiously at the tiny faces, which puckered up into howling images at this unexpected treatment. "Ah, be still! Can you not even do so much for your country?" the woman said, rolling them up again and giving each a cheerful slap on the back. She grinned up at Féridé. "The first words I shall teach them to say will be 'Mustafa Kemal,' " she said.

"And your husband?" Féridé asked.

"At the war. May Allah preserve him!"

At this point Mehmet re-appeared, and untied the horses; Féridé got in again, and they drove off.

"I wish now that we could have got something to eat," she said to Nilüfer, tucking the blanket round her feet; "seeing that woman with her bread has made me hungry. I wonder where Hassan has got to? He could have got us something."

They drove on, still climbing through woodland, though now less steeply; the snow grew deeper and deeper about them, and the air was very cold. As they approached the top of the pass, which lies at 1800 metres, the road presently ran between deep vertical banks of snow through which a passage had been cut; on these snowy walls were scratched inscriptions, and the girls, surprised, leant out to read them. "Ismir [Smyrna] shall always be ours!" some read; "O Edirné, to us thou shalt always belong," others; and "Not a foot of our soil shall be lost!" For several kilometres, as long as the snow was deep, these mute protestations kept them company all the way, clearly visible on one side, on the other partly obscured by that file of walking figures. The two sides of the road impressed Féridé deeply. This was how a nation was reborn, then—in this spirit, and with such a cheerful endurance of hardship as that woman with the twins had shown. She suddenly remembered what her father had said, on her wedding night, as reported to her by Fuad—"It seems that the women of Turkey must be heroic now, as well as the men." But what had she done, or could she do, compared with these peasants who trudged along, stooping under their loads, their raw goat-skin moccasins wet through with the snow, their ungloved hands red with the cold?—while she rode snugly in a carriage in a fur coat. Well, whatever she could do, she would, the girl resolved.

At the top of the pass Mehmet paused for a moment to breathe the horses, and Nilüfer and Féridé looked ahead eagerly to see what lay in front of them. The pass overlooked a deep valley, its sides clothed with beech forest clinging to the slopes; sheer grey limestone crags rose above, their faces too steep to hold the snow, and in the bottom ran a broad river, whose strong song came up to them where they sat. They could see the road at intervals winding away down the mountain-side through the leafless branches of the beech-trees, which threw a fine tracery of blue shadows on the gold-white of the sunlit snow—wherever they could see it, they saw also that ceaseless file of ammunition-carriers, and, here and there, groups of cadets, who were slithering and running downhill, singing and shouting as they went. After a few minutes' pause the driver cracked his whip, and they started down. This mountain road was much steeper than anything they had encountered as yet; the ground fell dizzily away below them, the road itself was narrow and full of hairpin bends, round which the small carriage rocked and swayed alarmingly.

"Could we not go more slowly?" Féridé called to the driver.

"Effendim, if we are to eat at Çuha Doğruğu, and sleep at the Ecevit Han, we must hasten," he replied, and whipped his horses up afresh.

"Oh well, he knows the road—and I shall be ready for lunch, I confess," Féridé said laughing and clutching Nilüfer as she was flung against her at a bend.

"I wonder what this han will be like, where he says we sleep," Nilüfer speculated. "I do hope it will be comfortable. I have never slept in a han."

"Nor have I. I believe Fanny used to sometimes, when she travelled with her Uncle," Féridé said. "However, think of these women sleeping by the roadside."

"We are not as they," said Nilüfer—which was incontrovertibly true.

Mehmet, who seemed to alternate between being almost deaf to commands at some points, and praeternaturally sharp of ear at others, now took a hand in the conversation, as usual without turning his head.

"At the Ecevit Han their Excellencies will find the perfection of comfort, have no fear. Ismail Agha, who owns it, is renowned—never had the keeper of a han such a name among travellers. What food!—chicken broth, chicken; pilau, salads."

"Well, that sounds excellent," said Féridé. "What about the place where we lunch, Mehmet?"

But Mehmet had turned deaf again, and made no reply. They lurched on down into the valley, passing groups of cadets who waved their walking-sticks at them in salute as they passed—Féridé waved back.

"In Istanbul one would certainly not do this," she said, "but here the circumstances are so peculiar, I do not think it matters, do you?"

"I suppose not. Certainly it is all *very* peculiar," said Nilüfer, with a small sigh.

"Courage, chérie—we shall manage. Are you cold?"

"I am, rather; but it does not matter."

They reached the valley bottom, crossed the river, and drove on up the southern bank through a narrow gorge into which no sun penetrated; but at this low level the snow was melting, and the road was full of a dirty slush which splashed up from their wheels onto that file, which never ceased, of ammunition-carriers—they turned, some of them, and laughed good-naturedly, shaking their skirts and waving at the occupants of the carriage. "How *nice* they are!" Féridé said, waving back, when this happened.

"Yes—but do please not ask me to emulate them!" Nilüfer said, with an unwonted flash of spirit. "I was not brought up to lead their life, and what is natural and easy to them would be, to me, quite impossible!"

Féridé laughed, and took her hand under the blanket.

"Dearest, I know it—and you are quite right. You must forgive my enthusiasm; Ahmet has always teased me about it."

"I know—but he admires it in you all the same! I often wish I had your courage and enterprise; but up to now, they have not seemed so important," said Nilüfer wistfully, her brief outburst of resistance dying down. "I am sure they come to you from Réfiyé Hanim—and also perhaps partly from seeing so much of little Fanny, with her independent English ways."

Féridé was astonished—her sister-in-law had never spoken like this before, of such things.

"Nilüfer darling, I had no thought of criticising you!" she said. "All this is rather troublesome and difficult, and really I know no more than you how to act in these new circumstances. Only—" she paused, and waved again to another four or five women whom they had splashed with muddy snow-water, whose only reaction was to wave gaily at the splashers—"this is so—so inspiring. I think we must leave our old ideas behind, now," the girl said seriously, "and live as best we can in quite a new world, at least till we get to Ankara, where Ahmet and Orhan will tell us what to do."

The road presently climbed out of the gorge and onto a shoulder of the hill—into the sun again, to their great relief—and soon entered Çuha Doğruğu, which was quite a sizeable place, houses with plastered walls, and a general air of prosperity. As they drove in, Féridé leant forward and tugged at the driver's coat.

"Mehmet, where is the han?"

"Just up the street, Effendim."

"Well, when we get there, go in and ask if there is a private room where we can be served with lunch. And when all is arranged, come out and tell us."

Mehmet grunted in what Féridé hoped was an affirmative manner —but when they drew up before the door of the han, among a crowd of officers and cadets gathered outside it smoking and talking in the sun stood Hassan.

"God be thanked!" Nilüfer said, as he hastened over to them.

"So, here you are! I came on ahead—I have a room kept for you, up-stairs, and lunch is ready; not good, but passable."

They went in through a downstairs room crowded with men eating, and up some wooden stairs into a small chilly bedroom with a table in it, where they were presently served with the "passable" lunch. They would not usually have called it so, but they were cold and hungry, and glad of anything at all. Mehmet came to summon them almost before they were finished, saying that they had another four hours' drive before them, and must hurry if they were to be in before nightfall, as the road was "bad—very bad." Hassan had gone on as soon as they arrived, promising to secure them a room at the Ecevit Han. "You have brought your bedding?" he asked.

Of course they hadn't—their bedding, as Féridé pointed out with an irrepressible giggle, consisted of the blanket he had bought them that morning at Inebolu.

"Oh well—I will see to it. Ismail Agha will arrange something, I am sure. Do not concern yourselves."

The Ecevit Han has become a legend in Turkey. It was the single place, on that long, rough, uncomfortable road from the Black Sea to Ankara where comfort, indeed by comparison with other hans something like luxury prevailed; there were travellers who had waited a week or more for a carriage amid the chilly rigours of the hotel at Inebolu who spent several days recuperating in Ismail Agha's care before resuming their journey. It lies just at the southern edge of the village of Ecevit, on a sunny grassy slope set with immense cherry trees, looking down over a valley bottom full of poplars and pollarded willows, which latter also line the road; the pines, austere and mountainous, have withdrawn to a certain distance from this sweet and gentle spot, and darken the hillsides above. The han is a long low wooden building, silvered to the usual tone of greyish beige, with a row of ten windows upstairs looking onto the village street, and another ten looking out over the be-poplared valley and the river; underneath is the vast stable, where the beasts were stalled among the stout wooden uprights supporting the floor above. Alas, now it stands desolate; Ismail Agha is dead, and motorists require no halting-place between Kastamonu and Inebolu, as travellers with horses did—but in some of the rooms inscriptions in its praise are still legible in the old Turkish characters on the plastered walls, signed with famous names.

Here Féridé and Nilüfer arrived as dusk was falling. Ecevit lies on the south slope of the coastal range, and there the snow had already melted in sun and southern winds—sweet smells of moist earth and growing things came to their nostrils as they approached across the shadowy slopes, a bird's song hung as it were poised above the song of the river coming up from below; the ten windows shone in a golden line. "How good it smells!" Féridé said. The road had indeed been very bad; they had had to get out several times while Mehmet, helped by some cadets, had hauled the carriage out of pot-holes; their feet were wet, they were chilled through, and exceedingly tired; but somehow the beauty of the place laid hold on them. Mehmet, when Féridé spoke, actually turned half-round in his seat—"Wait till the Hanim Effendi smells the odours that come from the kitchen!" he said, and whipped up his tired horses.

The sound of wheels brought Ismail Agha to the door, a comfortable middle-aged man with a cheerful face under his fez—Hassan followed close on his heels. "There you are! All is prepared. Come in, come up." They were unwrapped, helped out, led in (through delicious smells of cooking that fully justified Mehmet's prediction) up a flight of wooden stairs, along an immensely broad corridor walled with wood, and into their room. This was small but well-arranged; a raised sleeping-bench on one side, invitingly heaped with pillows and gay wadded cotton quilts, a table set for a meal, another with a mirror nailed to the whitewashed wall above it, holding a basin and ewer; two chairs; a lamp burned on a bracket, a cylindrical stove against the outer wall. It was all very simple, but homely, spotlessly clean, and piping hot. Ismail Agha's manners as mine host were perfect—he hoped Their Excellencies would be comfortable, how soon would they like their evening meal?—here was their luggage, here was his wife at their service. He and Hassan withdrew, the latter asking permission to return when they had eaten, and they were left to Madame Ismail's care. The tired girls were enchanted with all this. Féridé flung open the window and leant from it, hearing more of that bird-song above the deeper note of river-song, smelling the spring-like earthy smells, so delicious after the scentlessness of snow; Nilüfer meanwhile, escorted by the innkeeper's wife, was shown that astounding feature of the Ecevit Han, an indoor lavatory halfway up the stairs, and the upstairs kitchen from which meals were served to the private rooms. When they returned from this tour Féridé closed the window, and reluctantly coming back to the present from the spring-like thoughts of Orhan which bird-music in the twilight had roused in her, she asked Madame Ismail about the ammunition-carriers. "Do they sleep here?"

"Some of them, Hanim Effendi, yes."

"Where?"

"We have partitioned off a place in the stable, below,"—the woman pointed a thumb at the immense planks of beechwood, twenty inches broad, which floored the room. "They fetch their food from the kitchen downstairs, and eat it there, and sleep."

"And the drivers? Our driver?"

"They eat below, and there are sleeping-quarters for them a little way down the road. All is arranged"—she said with a benevolent smile.

The food, like the smells, was what Mehmet had foretold: there was chicken soup, pilau, boiled chicken, a vegetable—and all delicious. It was the first nice food that the two young women had met since they left the yali, nearly a week before, and they ate ravenously.

"Do you know," Nilüfer said, leaning back in her chair as they finished, "I really think we might do well to remain two days here, to rest ourselves—and the horses."

Féridé, after a moment's thought, demurred gently.

"It would be very nice," she said—"But do you not think we should push on? Our boat was three days late, remember; I think Ahmet and Orhan will be anxious, they will be wondering what has become of us."

They were still discussing this when a tap at the door announced Hassan, who came limping in, and with "You permit that I sit?" perched himself on one of the sleeping-benches.

"You have eaten well?" he asked.

"Splendidly!"

"This is a wonderful place," the young man said. "I wish all hans were like it. One could live here for weeks!"

"We were just considering whether we should not stay here a second night," Féridé said.

"What are the other hans like?" Nilüfer asked, before he could reply to Féridé.

"Mostly very indifferent—some *bad*," he said. "I came partly to speak of this. Tomorrow night—if you start tomorrow—you will sleep at Kastamonu, the chief town of the vilayet, where the han is quite tolerable, I am told; but while you are there you ought really to buy some bedding, for it is not normally supplied in hans, and you cannot be without. If I may suggest, it would be wiser to pass two nights in Kastamonu, and spend a day there in purchasing what you need for the rest of the journey; there is a good bazaar."

"What *do* we need?" Féridé asked.

"Oh, quilts, and light mattresses, and pillows—what you see here." He tapped what he was sitting on. "If you like, I could help you; I can delay for *one* day. But I ought not to be too long on the road; I am expected—by your husband!" he said to Nilüfer, smiling—"I shall be under his orders, I believe."

Féridé realised that Hassan wished to escort them all the way, though he kept up this polite appearance of its all being accidental, and a pleasure—and took her decision promptly, as usual.

"That is very kind, and will be the greatest help—will it not, chérie? We are not very expert shoppers! We will go on tomorrow. At what time should we start?"

"Moderately early—say at 9? It is about seven hours' drive to Kastamonu, but the road is better."

"Are there mountains?" Nilüfer asked, a little anxiously.

"No, no mountains!" Hassan said smiling—"an open road. Very well, I will arrange this with your Mehmet. Shall I order breakfast to be sent to you? At what time?"

"Really, I do not know how we should do without Hassan Bey," Féridé said when he had gone. "I hope you do not mind going on, dearest, but we cannot delay him too much, and it would be most uncomfortable to travel quite alone."

Nilüfer said, in a small voice, that she expected that Féridé was right—and they went to bed.

Their road next day was delightful—no snow, no chasms below, no savage rocks above; it rose gently over a shoulder of hill through pine-woods, and then emerged into open rolling country where the peasants were already at work in the fields. In one place, near a bridge over a river, the soil gave place to a vast outcrop of smooth grey-white rock, curiously lined—Hassan, who today rode near them, pointed out the striations, and explained that they were caused by ice in the glacial epoch. Not long after, they drove into the village of Seydiler Köy, where they lunched in a very simple han indeed, with a stove at one end of the room, racks for plates and glasses in an angle above a tiny sink, and trestle tables and benches—a small corner was capable of being curtained off for women travellers.

While their food was being prepared Féridé insisted on going out to look about her. Seydiler, as Mehmet had told them, was the terminus for the living chain of carriers, and for some time before they reached it they had noticed these on their return journey, now walking in groups, and gibing good-temperedly at the new arrivals still bent under their loads. The long street, here and there overhung by trees, was congested with this traffic; huge piles of war material were heaped up on both sides, leaving a narrow lane down the centre; more was coming in all the time, and being piled up as it left those burdened backs, while at the further end a group of cagnés, the small roughly-built Anatolian farm-carts, with solid wooden wheels, were being loaded up and moving slowly off, drawn by pairs of stolid oxen. Here and there along the street, wedged in between cases of ammunition and heaps of shells stood groups of the patient beasts waiting to be yoked, and meanwhile munching the stalks and leaves of maize or rather wiry-looking and indeterminate hay. An officer or two stood about, supervising the loading—one of them greeted Hassan, who was escorting Féridé. "Ah, so you've come! Was it all right, getting away?" As Hassan replied Féridé moved off out of earshot, with the usual Turkish feminine idea—quite a sound one, really—that men talking together do not want women about.

"Who is that?" the young officer then asked.

"Orhan Bey's wife. She and Nilüfer Hanim, the wife of Ahmet Bey, are coming up to Ankara to join their husbands."

The young man whistled. "To Ankara! Well, I wish them joy of it! Have they any idea of what they are in for?"

"Little, I should think. What are conditions really like, up there?"

"Oh, appalling. The cold!—you never knew anything like it. And no light, no water, no heating. It is a shocking place. I should think they will die!"

"Féridé Hanim I judge to be equal to anything," said Hassan slowly —"I am less sure of the other."

"Who travels with them? I saw both Orhan and Ahmet at Headquarters, only five or six days ago."

"I do," said Hassan, with rather a wry smile. "They expected a husband to meet and escort them, but he did not materialise."

"I should think not! My friend, you cannot imagine what difficulties are overwhelming us. May Allah's curse be on Vahdeddin and his friends!—it is practically a civil war that they have engineered." He went off into details, and Hassan listened with drawn brows—it was profoundly discouraging news.

"The people here seem all right," he said at length.

"Oh yes, splendid! Marvellous types! But you will see, in Ankara it is not so easy."

After the usual hour's halt for lunch they set off again towards Kastamonu. The country was still rolling and open, the road, for a Turkish road, tolerable; the spring sun was warm—even Nilüfer was cheered. Beside them now, instead of the chain-gangs, long files of cagnés crept along in convoys of thirty or forty, their wooden wheels creaking hideously on the un-oiled axles—but the teamsters were still nearly all women, who whipped, pulled, or prodded the lethargic oxen —here and there children ran in front or behind, and many loads of shells had a baby perched a-top. "Really," Hassan called out from his horse, "they are formidable, are they not?"

But what charmed Nilüfer was the flatter country. "So lovely, no mountains or precipices!" she said. However, the road presently climbed up through a shallow gorge of reddish earth pock-marked with dark bushes to a ridge; from the summit they looked out across a wide shallow trough of valley, spreading away for miles—and far beyond this, in the remote distance, blazing red and almost incandescent in the sunset light, a great range of mountains stood up, like the battlements of Heaven.

"How glorious! What is it?" Féridé exclaimed.

"Effendim, that is the Ilghaz Dagh," Mehmet replied.

"But we don't have to go *through* it?" Nilüfer asked, nervously.

"Effendim, we go *over* it," Mehmet replied, with gloomy relish. "The road is bad, very bad, terrible—and the hans are worse!"

"Can we not go round?" asked Féridé, who also thought this prospect sounded most unpleasant. She wished Hassan were there; she suspected Mehmet of taking a wicked pleasure in playing on their fears. But Hassan had cantered on ahead to arrange a room for them for the night.

"Effendim, that means going by Tosia, and there the road is far worse, indeed impassable at this season; besides being more than a day's drive out of our way."

So they drove rather gloomily down into Kastamonu, deriving more fear than pleasure from the sight of that great range ahead, from which the sunset splendours gradually died as they went, till they saw the lights shining along the embankments on either side of the Kara-Su, the Black River, and gleaming faintly from windows on the slopes above; and climbing a little through narrow streets drove at last through a great pointed-arched portico in a long brick façade into an immense courtyard, with two storeys of vaulted brick loggias surrounding it on all four sides, and a strange little wooden edifice in the centre—the principal han of the city.

Chapter Eleven

AT ABOUT the time that Féridé and Nilüfer were arriving at the han at Kastamonu the Pasha, down at the yali, went to pay his usual evening visit to his mother. Dil Feripé, who had been sitting with her, scuttled away when he came in; she seemed to have developed a habit of disappearing on his entrance, and though Asaf Pasha paid little attention to the comings and goings of the subordinate women of his household as a rule, he had begun to register this new phenomenon. However, it was not worth mentioning; and after kissing the old lady's hand with the customary greeting, he seated himself, stretched out his legs to the comforting warmth of the great brazier, and settled down for a chat.

"And when do our daughters return from Kandilli?" he asked presently. "They have been gone now nearly a week."

Réfiyé Hanim sat up rather straight on her divan, with concentrated eyebrows.

"My son, they are not returning," she said briefly.

He stared at her.

"Ané, what can you mean? Not returning from Kandilli?"

"Not returning at all. They have gone to Ankara, to join their husbands."

"But—" he was staggered. "You said they were going to Kandilli."

"I did. It was not true." Her old voice was astonishingly firm. "They have acted as faithful wives should, and are joining their husbands at their request."

The Pasha got up, and walked up and down the room, his long legs moving among the fragile green and white furniture like the blades of a pair of huge scissors; presently he came to a halt before his mother again. He was very angry.

"Ané, I am astounded. *You* to tell me an untruth! Should I not have been consulted, about my own daughter?"

"My son, I wished to avoid complications," said Réfiyé Hanim calmly.

"What complications?"

"Your opposition, which can now have no effect, and your anger, which falls on me alone." She looked at him steadily, but with a look of great beauty. "My dear son, I apologise for my untruth, but I could not do otherwise. Believe me that I was deeply distressed to lie to you."

He sank down in his chair again, with an almost bewildered expression. The world was all upside-down, and getting more so every day. Ané to tell him a falsehood—the girls to go off secretly to that barbarous place Ankara, remote from civilisation. It was all fantastic. And dangerous, too; there was opposition to this wild fellow Kemal and his rebellious followers: disturbances, down by Broussa even fighting. And at that thought anxiety mastered all other emotions.

"How did they go?" he asked.

"By steamer to a place called Inebolu; there Ahmet or Orhan was to meet them and take them up to Ankara."

"Who accompanied them to Inebolu?—besides their maids?"

At last the old lady showed signs of distress.

"No one—and they did not take their maids," she said unhappily.

"Not take their maids! Travel unaccompanied on a steamer! Ané, I do not understand, apart from deceiving me, how you could allow this!"

"Féridé refused to take anyone. It distressed me greatly that she would not, but she explained to me that their departure must be secret and unobtrusive, and that it was impossible to do otherwise!"

"You have always spoiled that child!" the Pasha said, in great vexation; "spoiled her, and given way to her. You could surely have insisted." But even as he spoke he remembered how Féridé had successfully opposed him, so gently, that day in her boudoir. No, one could no longer insist on things with Féridé—and his vexation altered its direction.

"It is all that husband of hers," he said irritably. "He is a fine fellow, but mad, quite mad; he has no sense of proportion." He paused, and lit another cigarette, for once without his customary "You permit?"

"And where are they to live, up there? I am told that there is nothing —no convenience, no comfort; a dreadful place."

"Ahmet and Orhan have taken furnished houses for them."

"And servants? maids? How can they find proper servants in such a place?"

This was a thing which had continued to worry Réfiyé Hanim, who did not altogether share Féridé's optimism on the point.

"One must suppose that their husbands will have arranged that," she said. "It would be natural."

"Bah! Ahmet, with his head in the clouds, and Orhan, reckless of the comfort of others! Much good they will be at such a task! They do not know what they will have to suffer, those poor children; they will live in undreamt-of conditions."

The old lady did not answer at once; she turned her head and looked out through the low window at the blue sky and blue water. At last—

"Perhaps undreamt-of things are coming to pass," she said slowly. "If so, they, the young ones, must bear their part in them."

    •   •   •   •   •   •

Kastamonu, where Féridé and Nilüfer spent that night, is a very ancient city—the Byzantine *Castamon,* in what had once been the kingdom of Paphlagonia, known as an important place during the middle ages, and eventually the seat of a Turkish vilayet. It lies astride a shallow bright river, climbing the slopes on either side; in the centre, startling as the castle at Foix, an abrupt iron-red rock, crowned with a bronze-coloured fortress, rises into the clear air. Except for the twin embankments along the river, flanked by beautiful old houses, plaster below and graceful silvery wood above, the whole town is on a tilt; narrow cobbled streets and passages lead up-and-down-hill between other houses, silvery grey, with carved super-pending balconies and strange little conceits of recessed arches, all alike enriched with the strange wooden harem-shutters, little lozenges of wood enclosing tiny lozenge-shaped openings, through which the inmates could see, yet not be seen.

This delightful town and the han itself, a noble square edifice of low brick, amused and pleased Nilüfer and Féridé; but they had little time to admire its beauties. A message from the Vali's bureau was sent to Hassan the night they arrived, telling him to proceed to Ankara as rapidly as possible—it was already three days old, owing to their steamer being delayed, and he came hobbling into their room to say that he thought they should start the following afternoon, and make a short stage to the han near the village of Bostan. "Then we can cross the Ilghaz Dagh next day, and get down to the han at Ilghaz itself. From there it is only four or five days' drive to Ankara."

"Another *four* days, after crossing these hideous mountains!" poor Nilüfer exclaimed. "But how vast this Anatolia must be!"

"Yes, it is rather large," said Hassan.

So they shopped quickly in the bazaar next morning, buying quilts and blankets in the small open-fronted booths. It had rained heavily in the night, but the sun was shining as they drove off after lunch, bringing out the strange metallic colours of the great rock crowned by its fortress, towering above the piled roofs of the town. The road left the valley in a series of steep bends till it was level with those menacing bronze walls, and then turned south over open downs, where the Ilghaz Dagh broke upon their view, plastered with new snow and glittering in the sun—Féridé exclaimed at its beauty, but Mehmet muttered gloomily about the road. At one point a very muddy track—one could hardly call it more—branched off to the left, near a small roadside cemetery full of tall narrow tombstones with stone turbans on top, leaning drunkenly at all angles; Mehmet pointed to it with his whip—"The Tosia road!"

"Well, it does not look good, I must say," Féridé observed.

Soon they were in among the foothills of the range; their road rejoined the river and kept beside it up a long valley, where thickets of buckthorn grew along the river-bed, their scraggy twigs, now set with silvery-green buds, rocking in the strong current. Then the hills raked back and the valley broadened out into a wide flat in which stood Bostan, a rather sordid village with a saw-mill; wood-cutters were coming home as they drove through it, and the last rays of the setting sun lit up a peak high above—the snow was only a little way from the road now, thin and patchy among the leafless beech-scrub; the air was damp and cold. And so they came to the Boston Han.

It was the most squalid place any of the three had ever seen. The downstairs room, as usual with a stove at one side, was filthy, the floor covered with refuse, the trestle tables greasy; there was a strong smell of rancid fat, combined with an even stronger smell of stables. A rickety staircase with a broken handrail led up inside the stable itself, which was deep in dung, to the upper floor, where the landlord showed them into a small bedroom with one table and one chair. The rusty stove had been newly lit—presumably with damp wood, for it was giving out abundant smoke but no heat—the sleeping-bench sagged down at one end, and the floor-boards were so ill-fitting that the stench from the dung and animals below was as potent as in the stable itself.

Here, after eating a miserable meal the two girls spent a wretched night, rolled up in their new bedding—cold, half-choked with smoke, and eaten alive by insects; neither slept much, but lay listening, after some time, to a steady downpour of rain on the roof. Would that mean more snow up above tomorrow, Féridé wondered; but though she knew Nilüfer was awake, she kept her speculations to herself. They rose early, and dressed at once; Féridé, going down in search of hot water, encountered Hassan in the nasty lower room.

"You are up—that is well," he said. "Shall I order breakfast at once? We ought to start as soon as possible." She thought he sounded anxious.

"It is the snow?" she asked.

"Yes—come and look."

He led her to the door. The mountain-sides a little way above the han were already white, and at a bend in the valley about a mile beyond, where the road turned above a bridge and began to mount, they could see a party of cadets trudging uphill, with the laborious gait of those who walk in snow. "We must lose no time at all if we are to get across tonight," the young man said, and now there was no doubt about his anxiety.

"I will go and hasten Nilüfer—please order breakfast. Is Mehmet ready?"

"Yes, he is harnessing the horses."

While Nilüfer packed Féridé, with her own unaccustomed hands, rolled up their bundles of bedding, corded them somehow, and then fetched Mehmet to take them down to the carriage. The man was full of gloom. "Terrible!" he said, waving his hand up the valley. "Certainly we shall stick fast!"

"Let us put our trust in Allah," said Féridé piously.

For the first two hours after they started it was not so bad. The road climbed steeply, winding in and out across the ravines that cut deep into the mountain-side; it was however very narrow, and the ground sank away below with horrible abruptness—moreover in many places the snow, sliding down off the bank above, had blocked the inner half, so that the carriage had to creep along the extreme outer edge; when this happened Nilüfer closed her eyes, and even Hassan, just ahead on his horse, cast an anxious eye backwards. The beech woods were left behind at last, and they were among the pines; no more snow fell, but a keen wind got up, whisking the fresh surface into small flurries, spilling the loads off the pine-boughs, and making the travellers very cold. The tracks of another carriage which had left the han before they did were always in front of them, as well as those of the cadets whom they had seen plodding up above the bridge, but their light vehicle had out-distanced all the cagnés—the few which had spent the night at the Bostan Han had not attempted to make a start in such weather. Féridé had in fact been surprised to find any there, and asked Hassan about it—"Surely they cannot have come with matériel de guerre off *our* steamer? They go so slowly."

"Oh no," the young man told her, "the stuff comes in all the time, in all sorts of boats, some quite small, sailing-boats, and they get it off as fast as the carriers return to Inebolu; then it leaves Seydiler as soon as cagnés come back from Ankara to take it. There are always some in motion on the road—so Ismail Agha told me."

Presently they overtook the cadets, who were sitting in a woodmen's shelter by the road-side, eating some food. Oh yes, they were going on, they told Hassan—"but it is a fatigue of perdition, walking in this snow!"

"So it is for my horses!" Mehmet muttered sourly. The snow grew deeper and deeper, and more and more slowly went the carriage, though the little horses strained to their task, their sides dark with sweat, with white lines of lather where the traces rubbed them. Half an hour later, rounding a bend where a bridge crossed a ravine, they heard a light jingling of horse-bells, and down the spur of hill beyond a carriage came in sight, descending towards them. "Hah!" said Hassan —"they come from Ilghaz. Good; the road must be in order."

But they did not come from Ilghaz. It was the carriage that had left the han before them, turned back; and as Mehmet pulled his horses in to the side of the road to let the other pass, a vigorous interchange took place between the two drivers. Hopeless, impossible, the other driver said—he was a Kastamonu man; the snow always deeper, worse and worse. "I will not risk myself and my horses—not I."

This had the worst possible effect on Mehmet, who was obviously not born an optimist, in any case. He was all for returning too. Hassan argued with him: he had *got* to go on, and he did not wish to leave the ladies; he offered the man a considerable extra sum to push on to Ilghaz. But Mehmet was sulky—no, he should turn back too; he would go on and find a turning-place, and then go back to the Bostan Han.

This was too much for Féridé's patience—sharply, to the immense astonishment of Hassan and Nilüfer, she intervened in the argument.

"So—like a man from Kastamonu you will let yourself be beaten!" she said. "This is strange! I thought the men of Inebolu were otherwise— equal at least to the *women* from there, who carry both shells and their infants together, for their country."

This appeal to local pride worked on Mehmet for the moment; grumbling and muttering, he nevertheless drove on—and drove past the next turning-place, and the next, and the next. At the fourth or fifth they saw the tracks in the snow where the other carriage had turned back, and both Hassan and Féridé silently feared the effect of this on him; however he drove past it, still muttering. But the snow became deeper still, till it was half-way up to the horses' knees; the slides from the banks above grew more and more frequent, and always more difficult and dangerous to pass—twice Féridé and Nilüfer got out while the little vehicle, tilted on a horrible slant, passed over the hump —Féridé to make the passage easier, Nilüfer because she was too frightened to remain in her seat. At last there came a point where the road, contouring a bold projecting spur of the mountain, swung out sensationally above an almost vertical drop, here bare of trees, into the valley below; and at this very point the wind had produced both a deep drift and a big slide. Mehmet drove forward till his horses were up to their knees, and the carriage wheels up to their axles, in snow;

then flung himself back in his seat with the single word "Yok!" (No.)

Hassan, who was ploughing along just ahead, heard him, halted, and turned his horse. "What is it, Mehmet?"

"It is that we cannot go further," the driver said. "The thing is impossible!"

Féridé, successful last time, was moved to put her oar in.

"Hassan Bey, will you not ride ahead and prospect? Perhaps round the bend the conditions are better."

"I go no further," Mehmet stated.

Hassan, ignoring this utterance, rode on—and returned presently to say that on the further side of the drift the snow was much less deep, in fact easy.

A long and unpleasant argument then took place between the two men. Hassan was at once determined to go forward himself, and unwilling to leave the two young women in the lurch. He offered a huge bribe over and above the contracted sum for the trip to Ankara—Mehmet appeared unmoved by this.

"Very well," Hassan said at last, angrily. "*I* will drive; you can walk—forward or backward, as you will! Féridé Hanim, could you lead my horse? Nilüfer Hanim, will you walk to lighten the carriage?" He dismounted, the girls got out; Féridé took his horse by the bridle, while he hoisted himself onto the box, displacing Mehmet. "You can lead your horses if you choose," he said, "but *we* go on to Ankara. "Zut!" he called to the exhausted little beasts, who once more strained forward gallantly.

This display of resolution disconcerted the driver. He went to his horses' heads, and dragged them forward; Féridé led Hassan's mount, Nilüfer stumbled through the snow. Pulling, whipping, shouting, the little procession moved forward; slowly, slowly, but always up and on. Now they were out of the long wind-piled drift, and the going was easier; but the horses were panting heavily, and Féridé insisted that she and Nilüfer should still walk, to ease them. "Soon, surely, we must reach the summit of the pass," she said. "Mehmet, you know the road—is it not soon?"

Oddly enough when one approaches the crest of the Ilghaz Dagh from the north the watershed is almost unnoticeable, whereas coming from the south it hits the eye, with a sharp descent and a wide view. The party from the Bostan Han only realised that they had really crossed the ridge when the road began, unmistakably, to go downhill—the horses stopped panting, and began to trot; whereupon Hassan pulled them up, relinquished the reins to Mehmet, and handed the two young women, who were soaked to their knees, into the carriage again. On this southern slope the sun had power: the snow grew less, then turned to slush, runnels of water ran musically in the roadside ditches; birds sang in the bushes about them, where tender leaves were budding on the boughs. Mehmet began to whistle to his horses, and cracked his whip—at a good round pace they rattled down into the valley of the Gok-Çai, where pretty houses, wooden-built like chalets above solid stone bases were grouped here and there, casting long shadows in the evening light. After some miles of this they quitted the main road, turned right over a shoulder of hill, and as the light was failing drove into the small town of Ilghaz. They were all in good spirits, in spite of being in the chilly state of drying-off after having been soaked through; even Mehmet seemed to share the general sense of triumph and achievement. The han, though modest, was clean and pleasant; a brazier was brought for warmth, and their clothes were dried. Untroubled by bugs, they slept like the dead—all but Nilüfer, who woke Féridé once or twice with a cry of nightmare, and mutterings about precipices.

The proper thing, as Hassan anyhow realised, would have been to spend two nights at Ilghaz to rest the horses, and he took counsel with the driver about this the first thing in the morning. Much to his surprise, Mehmet said that the next stage, to Çankiri, was an easy six-and-a-half hours, and the road, he had ascertained, good; he had attended properly to the horses last night, they were fine animals; if the Effendis wished to go on, it was quite possible to do so.

There is something rather soothing, but at the same time extremely monotonous about driving in a vehicle which can only do five or six miles an hour, for several days on end; and the monotony of the latter half of the drive from the Black Sea to Ankara is one of the things that seems to have impressed itself most on those who took the Road of the Revolution in the early days—that, and the stiffness and discomfort of sitting upright, hour after hour, in a carriage with poor springs or none, one's body made aware of every stone, rut or bump in the road as a series of jerks and jolts. Incidents to enliven the journey were few and far between: meeting a peasant on his donkey, overtaking a few cagnés, or, once or twice, encountering a horseman, riding fast, who appeared as a silhouette on the horizon in front, thudded by with a deep sound of hoofs on the unmetalled road, and disappeared over the horizon behind—couriers for Kastamonu or Inebolu, or distributors of the treasured newspaper, the *Hakimiyeti Milliyet*. The only other break in the monotony was the scenery, which changed, not swiftly as it does nowadays in a fast car, but very slowly and gradually.

All the same, the scenery was often remarkable. On the first day out from Ilghaz, after crossing the Devrez-Çai, the big valley which runs just south of the range they had crossed the day before, they climbed on the further side onto open downland sparsely covered by a low-growing oak-scrub, with stretches of wiry turf between. But this particular kind of oak—a variety of *Quercus Toza*—has the peculiarity that its first foliage is of a most extraordinary colour, shading from apple-blossom pink to carmine, overlaid with a sort of velvet of silver—Féridé and Nilüfer exclaimed at its beauty as they passed into it. For miles and miles they jogged slowly through this pink-and-silver world, with the great white-and-silver mass of the Ilghaz Dagh rising into the sky behind them, while to complete the enchantment flocks of silky-silver Angora goats, so strangely rectangular with their upright heads and tails, one at each end, were browsing all through the pink bushes, their newly-born kids so intensely white as to look almost luminous in the strong spring sunshine.

At lunch, which they ate in a very humble han on the further side of those fairy-tale downs, they learned something new. The han—like the village in which it stood—was built neither of stone, wood, nor plaster, but of rammed earth, and the room where they ate was filled with a strangely sour smoky smell which emanated, Féridé was told by Hassan, from the dried dung on which their food was cooked. For now they were up on the high, woodless central plateau of Asia Minor, where—since there are neither trees nor rocks—houses are built of clay, and dung is the only fuel.

"But what do they put on their fields?" the girl asked in surprise. "At the vine-house at Chamlidja the vines and the fields were always dressed with dung."

Ah, what indeed? Féridé had put her finger on one of the eternal problems of Anatolian agriculture—how to grow adequate crops without feeding the soil properly; in a land without wood, dung is the only fuel; but if you burn your dung you starve your soil. Hassan, a townsman, could not answer her question, and applied to the landlord; who, peasant as he was, was acutely aware of the problem.

"Ah, Effendim, what *can* we do? The dung of our beasts we must burn, or we should die of cold in winter, and moreover could not cook our food. We do what we can—in summer, when the streams are nearly dry, we dig up the mud from the stream-beds and spread that upon the land. There is feeding of a sort in it: from the leaves of the trees, and all that which is borne by the waters down a stream. But our crops are poor! However, Allah wills it so—we live in a harsh place!"

They saw for themselves that afternoon how harsh the place was; the landscape which they passed through was in the sharpest possible contrast to the fairy-tale, French-tapestry quality of that pink-and-white world of the morning—was indeed almost Dantesque in its strangeness and grimness. Bare gorges of pale soil, so deeply eroded by rainstorms that they and the hills above them resembled the hatching used to indicate mountains on a map, with, here and there, smears of a violent blue-green where the hidden chrome emerged on the surface. But not a tree, not a bush. And then, at sundown, they dropped into a big valley, that of the Akçi-Su, and followed it into the town of Çankiri, where they met the spring, suddenly, in full force—earth-walled gardens full of budding boughs and shoots of green things, and the poplars along the river hung with new leaves, bright as freshly-minted copper pennies. They turned up into the town, through the market, and drew up at the door of their inn.

This time it really was an inn. Around a long narrow courtyard open to the sky ran two tiers of wooden galleries; carriages and cagnés were standing about the courtyard, off which stables opened; men and women came and went, carrying water from the fountain in the centre, or bundles of fodder to their beasts. The party was led upstairs and along the lower gallery, off which bedrooms opened; the inn-keeper threw open door after door, disclosing in each room much the same thing—two or three brass bedsteads, divans upholstered in bright harsh woollen stuffs under the windows, elaborate fringed and embroidered valances above them, rugs hanging on the walls. It was all very neat, and fairly clean.

"What luxury!" Féridé said. "But could we not be on the floor above? We should get more air, and it would be quieter."

Yes, they could do that, and on the upper floor the two girls installed themselves. Féridé wandered about the gallery, leaning over the light wooden handrail to watch the activities in the courtyard below. She felt an extraordinary happiness and contentment filling her—so many difficulties overcome, the new life with Orhan so close ahead, this moment of peace now. Returning to their room, she leant from the window, where over the pink roofs of the town she could see the valley of the Akçi-Su stretching away to the west, all in a glory of sunset light, spangled with the metallic glitter of those young poplar-leaves, as far as the eye could see. "Come and look," she called to Nilüfer, without turning her head; "it is so beautiful."

Nilüfer came and joined her, and they leaned together, resting their elbows on the sill. "I wonder in which direction Ankara lies," Nilüfer mused.

"There—up the valley, where we are looking. It is to the west of us, I know," Féridé said, happily.

"And now how much longer is it till we get there?"

"Another day or two, I think—we will ask Hassan."

"It is a *very* long way," said Nilüfer, slowly. "This is our fifth day on the road, and we were two nights at Inebolu, and four on that dreadful boat! If it is really another two days, we shall have been travelling for nearly two weeks! Who could have imagined, when we set out, that it would take so long? And that we must do it alone?"

"Dearest, we are not altogether alone—we have had Hassan with us. Though how our two husbands expected us to manage such a journey with *no* escort, I do not know, I must say! But dji-djim, are you very tired?" she asked, suddenly struck by Nilüfer's pallor.

"Not very—yes, I am tired, a little. Yesterday was so wet and cold, and—oh, altogether dangerous and horrible! You do not mind these things—you are to be envied!"

"Well, now all is easy—and tonight you shall go to bed the moment after we have eaten," Féridé comforted her. "And soon we shall be at Ankara, in our own homes, and Ahmet will be with you, and all will be well."

The following day was not a very long stage either, and the drive was delightful to Féridé, whose glad mood of the previous evening was still on her. In any case that particular stretch of the road over the plateau has a strange and dramatic beauty, for all its barrenness—on either side of the valley rise cream-coloured hills, their flanks eroded into sharp gullies filled with blue shadows and capped, astonishingly, with a layer of red earth two or three hundred feet deep. It had rained in the night, and the rain had brought the carmine soil down into the river, so that the stream ran blood-red in its bed of white stones; thousands of the white goats were coming down to drink of the ensanguined waters, while overhead the great black-and-white Egyptian vultures, newly returned from the South, soared in vast circles in the blue. Just before sundown they came to Tönai, with its fields, gardens, and groves of poplars down by the river, and its little rocky hill, sparsely grown with black and stunted pine-trees, rising behind. Not even the news, given them by Hassan, that they had got to spend yet another night on the road, nor the discomforts of the poor han with its rammed-earth walls, wretched food, insects and general dirtiness, had power to dim Féridé's spirits. "What is one day?" she exclaimed when Nilüfer sighed about it—"Think of the days and days *and days* ahead of us, when we do get to Ankara."

All the same, the following day was disagreeable and trying. They had slept badly, woke early, and were longing to be off and away from the dirty infested place as soon as possible, but Mehmet insisted stubbornly on starting late—it was a short stage, only five hours, to Ravli, and his beasts could do with an extra spell of rest after all their exertions, he said. The monotony of the road was much more pronounced than on the previous two days—the red-and-white hills had been left behind, and the great bronze-coloured bulk of the Idris Dagh, looming up against a sullen sky ahead and to their left, was the only major feature except for the brownish villages, their houses walled and roofed with earth of the same colour as their unfenced fields, tucked away high in the hills on either side, far from the road. This peculiar arrangement aroused Féridé's interest, and as usual she asked Hassan about it—why were these villages not built nearer the highway? Hassan, also as usual, applied to Mehmet for the required information.

"But for the water," the driver replied. "The springs are in the hills, and the people must live close to the springs, naturally; for with such sun and such wind as they have here in summer, Effendim, the water dries away into the earth in what one could drive in a quarter of an hour—less! Look," he said, pointing with his whip to their right, where a stony track led up to a group of houses which seemed to cower in a cleft in the hillside—"See how there is a water-course, and no water." And indeed beside the track an obvious stream-bed, now stony and almost dry, descended towards the road. "Water—that is the problem here," said Mehmet oracularly; "water and fuel. No trees!" he said, and cracked his whip to clatter past a file of cagnés.

There were a lot of cagnés on the road that day. There had been a few convoys the day before, but not many—Mehmet, who habitually informed himself on all such matters, as leisurely users of the road have been wont to do for a couple of thousand years, stated that they carried the cargo of a boat that had put in to Inebolu three weeks earlier. Soon, too, the lack of water ceased to be apparent, for a violent rainstorm came on, blotting out the lowering outline of the Idris Dagh, and presently bringing foaming freshets coursing down those short dry stream-beds that ran out from the hills. "Mon Dieu, why do they not dam the streams?" Féridé said on seeing this, as she sat crouched with Nilüfer under the Inebolu blanket; "If they did that, they could preserve water, and have it at will. Mehmet!—why do they not dam up the streams?" But Mehmet, hunched up in his sheepskin coat, had turned deaf again and did not reply.

Presently both Féridé and Hassan noticed an extraordinary thing. They themselves, to get protection from the cold beating rain, were huddled—the girls under the blanket, Mehmet in his sheepskin, and Hassan in his military greatcoat; but the women of the plateau, who were driving the cagné-teams of slow-moving oxen, walked along unconcernedly beside the carts without their brown goats-hair cloaks, which they had spread over their loads; the cherry-colour of their flowered trousers and jackets becoming an even darker red as the rain soaked into them. "Goodness, why do they not *wear* their cloaks?"

Nilüfer exclaimed at last. "This is idiotic, what they do! Rain cannot harm the ammunition, can it, Hassan Bey?"

"No, certainly it cannot, packed as it is," the young man replied from his horse.

"Then do ask them why they do this," Féridé urged, impatiently. "Ask that one"—as they overhauled a woman dragging at the oxen which hauled a cart full of shells, whose swollen shapes were plainly visible through the sodden cloth which covered them. "Stop, Mehmet! —I wish to listen."

She never forgot what she heard when Hassan did as he was bid, and asked the woman why she did not wear her cloak, instead of spreading it over the insensate metal of the shells. A big fine creature, she stood still, drew herself up, and made this answer: "My body"—striking her breast—"is only my own; these"—and she gestured at the shells—"belong to *the Nation!*" And she turned away, to continue tugging her team along the miry road—to Féridé a figure of unforgettable splendour.

Soaked through, they ate some food in the han at Haleçik, and then drove on over a pass across an outlying spur of the Idris range, down into more fertile and cultivated land, where brown and twisted vines were showing knotty buds, and so came to Ravli, where they were to spend their last night on the road. Ravli boasted three hans, none of them good; Hassan chose what he thought was the best, and they did at least secure a brazier to dry their wet clothes. Nilüfer had caught cold, and was pale and silent; high time they did reach Ankara, Féridé thought, as she brewed tea, gave her sister-in-law aspirin, and tucked her up in most of the bedding—this journey had lasted long enough.

"She will be able to go on tomorrow, no?" Hassan enquired rather anxiously, when she went down to fetch some soup, all Nilüfer felt able to take. "It is only three-and-a-half hours on to Ankara."

"Oh yes, I think so, if we don't start too early. It has been hard for her, all this."

"Hard for you also, I think," the young man said, in a tone of undisguised admiration.

"Oh, I am hardy!" Féridé laughed, and tripped away with her bowl of broth.

A little later he came tapping at the door—"Féridé Hanim!"

"Yes," she said, slipping out—"What is it?"

"There is a messenger here on his way back to Ankara, one of those who carry the newspapers; he is riding straight on tonight. Would it not be well to send a note to your husband, to say that you are here, and arriving tomorrow?"

"Yes—indeed. I will write it at once. Will Orhan get it tonight?"

"Tonight, or very early tomorrow."

As she hurriedly scribbled a few lines, the girl thought how wonderful it was at last to be so near that what she wrote now, Orhan would receive in a few hours' time!—after their three months of separation and almost complete lack of letters, it seemed too good to be true. "Tomorrow! I shall see him tomorrow!" her heart sang ceaselessly until she fell asleep.

Chapter Twelve

"WHERE will they meet us, do you suppose?" Féridé asked of Hassan as they left next day. The rain had stopped, and in the morning sunlight Ravli was a pretty place enough, embowered in big poplars, with earth-walled gardens beside a small quiet river, where peach- and pear-trees showed signs of blossom.

"At the city's entrance, I imagine," replied Hassan, who really had no idea.

Mehmet, without turning round, put his oar in.

"Unless I am much mistaken, they will be waiting at the bridge; that is where travellers are met."

"What bridge, Mehmet?"

"But, the bridge over this river—the Çankiri Bridge, men call it, since it is on the Çankiri road."

Mehmet was right. After driving for a couple of hours along the valley, whose poplars and gardens were in sharp contrast to the desolation of the last three days, they came unexpectedly into a small range of low savage-looking hills; Nilüfer, whose cold was still heavy, gave a little moan—"Oh, not *more* precipices!" But the road wound through them easily, and rounding a last sharp bend came out at a bridge backed by a low bluff. That scene always remained imprinted on Féridé's memory— the grey double-arched bridge, the white-stemmed copper-leaved poplars rising in a group of Claude-like grace above the quiet slow-moving water, with two splendid horses tied to their branches; behind, above the road beyond the bridge, the steep bush-grown face of the bluff, so like the bluff that rose behind the yali, and two tall figures in uniform that at the sound of their horses' hoofs rose from beside a little fire, and hastened towards them with long swift strides—Ahmet and Orhan.

After eager and excited greetings the little cavalcade went on, up and over the rising ground—and there, across a wide stretch of cultivated land rose two low hump-backed hills, both covered with houses, one crowned with an irregular outline of fortified walls—Ankara! Calling from carriage to horses, from horses to carriage, they trotted towards the city, exchanging news; Ahmet was troubled by Nilüfer's pallor and obvious indisposition, but—"If you knew what we have been through!"

Hassan exclaimed. "Snowstorms, drifts, this appalling road over the Ilg-haz Dagh!—and rain yesterday; we were soaked through!"

"Do not forget the women," Féridé said—"The women who carry the ammunition and lead the cagnés; they are incredible!"

"And what about my horses, who pulled you all through the snow and over the mountains? Are they not also worthy of praise?" Mehmet asked. They all laughed, and praised his gallant team till the cross-grained old man was mollified.

It would be idle to pretend that the two young women's hearts did not sink when, having at last reached their journey's end, they were introduced into the abodes which their respective husbands—young, inexperienced and overworked—had prepared for them. Prepared is indeed hardly the word—the young men had looked at the houses, rented them, and that was that. Orhan's and Féridé's was within the citadel, tucked right in under the great wall and partly built out on top of it, commanding a tremendous view; Nilüfer's and Ahmet's was on the steep glacis just outside, and almost immediately below the other—actually from her upper windows Féridé could throw pebbles or flowers into Nilüfer's courtyard. On foot it was barely a hundred yards from one to the other—along a narrow alley, out through a great vaulted gateway, and down a steep passage and a flight of steps: but what a hundred yards! Rough cobbles, cruelly steep and cruelly hard to the feet, the channels between the stones grey with slops, and both the lane and the steps dirty and slippery with vegetable refuse, which tame sheep, tethered by a cord to their various doorposts, turned over and nibbled at with their sensitive muzzles. (Ankarians invariably keep a sheep as a household pet, like a cat.)

All this, of course, they did not realise on the day of their arrival. Externally, the houses had a certain charm; typical old Ankara buildings, half-timbered, with red tiles set slantwise in plaster between uprights of grey wood, and carved wooden harem-shutters shielding the windows. A door with a ring-shaped knocker in a high blank wall led into a small courtyard, with a well and a carved marble well-head—Greek, and covered with acanthus-leaves, in Féridé's case; there stood also a tree, slanting out over the paving-stones. But how the courtyard smelt! Various doors opened off it; Orhan led his wife up two steps to a large double pair, roughly but agreeably carved and panelled, threw them open, and led her in. She found herself in a long low room, half hall, half sitting-room, with four doors leading from it, and two windows at the further end; at one side a wooden staircase led up to the floor above. Chairs, a sofa and a table or two stood about; there were some rugs on the floor, which was again made of huge beechen planks, a cylindrical iron stove stood against one wall. Orhan flung open two of the doors—"Your room; my room," he said proudly. Peeping in, Féridé saw a strange mixture of furnishings, typical of the rooms in Ankara bourgeois houses, which are always used as bedrooms and sitting-rooms at once. There was a brass bedstead with a hideous quilt; the usual hard stuffed divans under the windows, with truly ghastly embroidered linen antimacassars fastened along their backs over the charming hand-woven upholstery of harsh brightly-coloured wool; an appalling sort of side-board with a mirror above it, a few chairs. What gave beauty and dignity to all the rooms were the big built-in cupboards with painted double doors, elegantly panelled, along one wall, and between them a sort of recessed niche with shell-shaped vaulting above and a shell-shaped basin below, over which depended a tiny metal spout—this however did not work; a door, in each case, led off into a stone-floored *cabinet de toilette* for washing.

Anything more different from the yali could hardly be imagined; but in these dwellings our two young women proceeded to settle down and build themselves homes as best they could. "Where there are houses, there must surely also be servants," Féridé had said airily to Réfiyé Hanim—but this proved to be by no means the case. Orhan and Ahmet each had his soldier-servant, or batman, who slept in one of the rooms off the courtyard and made himself as useful as he knew how—drawing water from the well and carrying it into the house, fetching charcoal for cooking, and cutting up wood into lengths suitable for the small iron stoves; he also learned in time to sweep out the downstairs rooms and to wait at table, and cleaned the yard after his fashion. But that was all. Dusting, bed-making, marketing—worst of all cooking—had all, it seemed, to be managed somehow by the youthful wives themselves— that, at any rate, appeared to be the husbands' notion.

Each set about solving her problems in her own way. Nilüfer in a very short time turned into an astonishingly good cook; this was a quiet unobtrusive occupation which she really enjoyed. Her "Française" had not been a scholar, like Mdlle Marthe, but given to the domestic arts, and she had taught her pupil to cut out, sew, iron, and even learn a little cooking; but Nilüfer could not bear going to the market to buy things—bargaining was a horror to her, and she was quite incapable of it. When she had come back once or twice with a basket of comestibles for which she had paid ridiculous prices, the wife of her landlord —a woolmerchant called Faik, with a shop down in the market filled with bales of silvery Angora wool and a strong goaty smell—took over the business of shopping for her. She lived two doors off, and took the liveliest interest in the doings of her young tenants. Her name was Güli, which means Rose, but she was by no means a rose without a thorn—a keen-tempered sharp-tongued woman, shrewd and masterful, she all the same soon developed a strong protective affection for the pretty creature who rented her house, and quickly routed out a peasant woman called Fatma to act as her servant. Between Fatma and the batman—who came from Thrace, and was called Demir—Nilüfer managed somehow.

Féridé, on the other hand, set about organising her household herself. Her landlord was a clerk in the bureau of the Vali of Ankara, called Ibrahim, with a fat round-faced merry little wife who bore, strangely enough, the same name as the old kalfa at the yali who had died four years before, Sitaré—for a long time, whenever Féridé addressed her it called up memories of that summer of 1914, Fanny's last summer with them!—when poor silly Sitaré had got into such trouble for showing Nilüfer Ahmet's photograph. So long ago, all that seemed now! On the very first morning Féridé went with Sitaré Hanim to the market, bought herself a basket, and then watched how to buy what was needed; she soon came to be a rare hand at a bargain, and thoroughly enjoyed it.

One only had to buy and bring home certain things, she found. Milk came to the door daily in chiselled pewter jars of beautiful shapes, and the man who brought the milk also brought eggs; another individual came round once or twice a week with chickens or turkeys—his cry resounded between the high walls of the alley, announcing his arrival. What one had to bargain for and carry home was meat—mutton, rather tough and stringy, a few vegetables, and salads. And oh how heavy the basket seemed, toiling up from the market outside the citadel, some considerable distance down the hill; how her feet ached from the cobble-stones, and her arms and back with the unwonted tasks of dusting, emptying things, making beds, and washing-up. Poor Féridé greatly envied Nilüfer her Fatma, stout ham-handed peasant that she was—but Sitaré Hanim seemed to have no ideas about procuring a servant for *her* tenants.

Help arrived at last in a very casual fashion. Féridé was just leaving the market one morning when she noticed—not for the first time—a rather pretty young woman, delightful in her flowered cherry-coloured trousers and bright jacket; as so often with Anatolian women, her veil only partly concealed her face. Something moved the girl to speak to her, and ask her what she did.

"Nothing. My husband is at the war; I have no children; I am alone."

On an impulse, Féridé asked her if she would like to come and be her servant? The woman agreed at once, and followed her home, carrying the market-basket; she was shown the house, a room off the courtyard was arranged for her, and next day she moved in. Kezban was her name, and at first it seemed to Féridé impossible that a grown woman should have so little idea of how to set about doing things in a house!— she herself, though she had never actually done them before, at least knew how they should be done from watching Ayshé and the other well-trained maids at the yali. However, mastering her natural impatience as well as she could, she taught and trained Kezban: to sweep before you dusted, to shake the rugs in the yard and not in the hall, to wash up cups and glasses before the greasy plates, not to throw slops all over the courtyard, but down the drain in the corner. Really they got on very well; Kezban, a peasant from the plateau, who had lived all her life in one of those rammed-earth houses, where conditions differed little from those in the animals' stalls next door, was at once amused by the fanciful notions of her young mistress, and full of admiration for her domestic skills—so the innocent creature regarded them—and for the beauties of her house. For Féridé quickly set about beautifying it. She was shocked by the absence of curtains, and when other things were more or less in train she went to the street in the market devoted to fabrics and bought thin woollen stuffs patterned in bright colours, stitched them into curtains, and made Temel, Orhan's Laz batman, stretch wires across the windows to hang them on, since curtain-rings were not to be had.

Kezban soon took over part of the marketing. The bread, rice and so forth she could fetch alone, though Féridé usually went down to choose the meat and vegetables. But the young mistress still had to do the cooking herself, in the curious archaic kitchen, opening off the courtyard, with the built-in earthen oven in which fowls and turkeys were roasted, and the charcoal brazier for grilling small pieces of meat on spits; boiling of vegetables was done either on a flat space above the oven, or over the brazier. It was all very uncouth and inconvenient; when charcoal ran out Féridé had to cook on dried dung, and the smoke got into the food and made it smell, to Orhan's great disgust— young as he was, he cared about his food.

Meanwhile outside Féridé's house and kitchen great things were happening. The first meeting of the National Assembly, which Mustafa Kemal had announced in March as a counterblast to the Allied closing of the Ottoman Parliament, was to take place in the still unfinished Assembly Building on April the 23rd, and for days beforehand Orhan, who was now a sort of political A.D.C. to Mustafa Kemal, was working early and late on the arrangements; when he came home in the evenings—having toiled up the hill on foot along the muddy roads—he could think and talk of nothing else. Seats and tables for the deputies had to be improvised somehow—Orhan was thrilled when someone hit on the device of collecting and using desks from the children's schools.

The semi-circular tribune for the President, up four or five steps, with a desk and chair, was ready, and the paraffin lamps to fit into the rather hideous chandeliers which depended from the ceiling in the big bare room, with its high galleries at each end.

The deputies themselves were rather a mixed bag. Some were members of the old Ottoman Parliament from Istanbul, who had escaped the fate of Fethi Bey and others of being captured by the Allies and interned in Malta, where they languished for nearly two years; some were provincial members, hurriedly elected—but with a very conscious and serious intention—in March for the new assembly to be held a month later. Among the former group was a fairly high proportion of men of the old school—stiffly religious, supporters of the Sultanate, who would never have attended a Parliament in Ankara if there had been any other for them to attend; they were to give a lot of trouble later on. But by no means all were present at the opening—they arrived bit by bit, in driblets. Meanwhile accommodation had to be found for those who had come, and these arrangements too formed one of Orhan's many tasks. Numbers were accommodated in a school just opposite the Assembly building, whence the scholars had been ejected and where—to their disgust—they had to sleep ten in a room. It was known, laughingly, as "the School for Deputies."

The great day came at last. Féridé and Nilüfer—of whose presence there could of course be no question—leaned from Féridé's upper windows above the citadel wall, and watched the assemblage gathering far below, between the school and the new building, on the dusty stretch of road leading from what there was of the lower town to the station. Troops held back the gaily-coloured crowd, and in the middle they could see the knot of deputies, darkly clad below their red fezzes, grouped outside the building; there they prayed, standing, and then moved in through iron gates into a sort of garden, up a flight of steps, and so into the council-chamber.

What happened after that was later recounted to Féridé by Orhan, who in view of his official position was able to slip in, and watch and listen from the gallery. Mustafa Kemal Pasha mounted the dais overlooking the sea of school-children's desks, and standing very upright, his hands clenched on the table in front of him—a mannerism that was to become a familiar feature of the Assembly for the next eighteen years—he gave a lucid and detailed exposition of the political situation, both internal and external. As his habit was, he started from first principles—Kemal Pasha was never a man to shrink from stating the obvious; on the contrary, he knew how to give it a touch of grandeur. So on this occasion—

"Life," he said, "is a series of struggles and combats, and success in life is only possible to the victorious; which means that one must rely on power and force." He emphasised, however, that the task of his hearers was to work for national happiness and prosperity within their own frontiers, and not to waste the nation's time in pursuing extravagant or external ends. But he was never one to pull his punches, and left the slightly astonished deputies under no illusions about the problems which faced them along their borders. Invaders must be repelled on not less than four fronts: the Allies at Istanbul, the Kurds and Armenians in the East, the French in the South, the Greeks in the West. Surely no man ever set out to try to build a new state under greater handicaps! Moreover there was the tricky and delicate internal situation to be managed somehow: a Sultan of the royal line still ruling, theoretically, in Istanbul, who was also the Khalif, the titular head of all who held the Moslem faith; but he was under the thumb of the Allied occupation forces, had no real power, and while still commanding the loyalty of many Turks, had condemned the country's real leader, Kemal Pasha himself, to death.

With a juggler's skill, amounting almost to genius, Mustafa Kemal dealt with all these complications. The Assembly, with every possible juridical formality, voted themselves into being the "Grand National Assembly of Turkey," in whom all power was vested, as the legal government of the country; the position of the Sultan-Khalif was taken care of by a masterly clause which stated that "once liberated from enemy constraint," his position would be determined according to the Assembly's ordinances—which put that problem on ice for the time being. An Executive Council chosen by the Assembly would promulgate and carry out new laws; and Mustafa Kemal himself was elected President both of Assembly and Council.

The effect of all this was electric, both within the Council chamber and through the country at large. There had come into being, in the brief space of four days, a new government with a new Head—not the decrepit and venal Ottoman institutions, but a living entity elected by the people. The civil war died away almost at once, for popular support for the Sultan was quickly withdrawn, and the nation rallied round their new leader. All the gloomy remarks of the young officer at Seydiler Köy to Hassan Bey were very promptly falsified.

But the new government had to function under most peculiar and trying conditions. In 1920 the great lack at Ankara was buildings of any sort, and the only one available for its departments was the Bureau of the Vali, a modest provincial headquarters. So the Department of Justice, for instance, consisted of exactly *one* room, into which as many tables, chairs, and officials as possible were crammed somehow—and all the others were the same. Never was the government of a nation carried on in more rag-time surroundings. Mustafa Kemal worked—like a fiend—under the same handicaps. He was at once President of the Assembly, Prime Minister, and Commander-in-Chief, and in each of these capacities had to use different premises. As President of the Assembly he had two rooms in the building itself; a largish one to the left of the entrance door, with—later—handsome curtains and pelmets draping the high windows, where he sat at a deal table and held discussions with the deputies who came to see him, seated on wooden chairs, like English kitchen chairs, ranged round the walls; for more intimate and important conversations there was a very small cubby-hole of a room just opposite, across the main corridor, with a screen round the door, another little cheap table, and more cheap common chairs. Both rooms were heated by plain cylindrical cast-iron stoves, such as the peasants used, burning wood, and lit by a single paraffin lamp. Compared with Downing Street or the White House, these were strange quarters for the activities of the Head of the State.

In his capacity as Prime Minister Mustafa Kemal Pasha had a room in the Vali's Bureau, only a short walk away, where the heads of the various Ministries came to him with their problems—which he solved with astonishing speed. He would listen, question, listen to the answers —his light blue eyes probing into those of the man he was talking to, as if to *see* the answer before he heard it, and to judge if it were true and valid; not with his head cocked sideways, as most people listen, but holding it straight on his square shoulders as he sat erect in his horrid cheap chair. Then, swiftly, he arrived at his decision, and gave it in clear concise terms. His decisions were not always immediately acceptable, but his Ministers in time came to know that they were nearly always right. Moreover, though not by nature a patient man at all, Mustafa Kemal had a quite peculiar gift for persuading people, and converting them, very fast indeed, to his own view—partly by his acute commonsense, partly by an extraordinary personal charm, partly by what one can only call magnetism. Everyone who worked with him has testified to this last; but it was nothing like the screaming paranoia of Hitler, it was the quintessence of spiritual and intellectual force, basing itself on an almost supernaturally sharp appreciation both of the point at issue, and of the man he was talking to.

As Commander-in-Chief he had to go further afield to work. The only building he had been able to lay hands on for his Headquarters was the old Agricultural School and model farm out at Kalaba, a large featureless white building on rising ground half-an-hour's ride from the city; from the bare uncurtained windows of the big room where he and Ismet Bey sat at a curious table with bulging legs—it is still there—he could, if he chose to turn from studying the military situation on the big maps tacked to the white-washed walls, see the two hump-backed house-strewn hills of the old city, and the yellow flat of the valley below, threaded by the silver line of railway, with the shed-like roof of the station, and hard by the gabled outline of the ugly modern villa where he usually slept—when he did sleep! A bathroom with a painted bath on short legs opened out of this gaunt apartment on one side, a bedroom with a camp bed, a dressing-table and a mirror on the other; if military affairs were desperately pressing he could sleep out at Kalaba, and often did.

All these different places to work in made things rather difficult for Orhan. He had to be with his master wherever that master was: whether at the Assembly Building, where he interviewed such deputies as Mustafa Kemal had not time to see personally; or at the Vali's Bureau, where Ministers, coming from their one-room departments, had to have time allocated to them for interviews—or, worst of all, out at Kalaba. Horses were in as short supply as everything else at Ankara, and when the Commander-in-Chief stopped being Prime Minister or President of the Assembly for a few hours, and rode out to his distant Headquarters, the wretched Orhan had to trudge after him on foot, unless he managed to borrow a horse, or unless Kemal Pasha—this often happened—said with brusque courtesy to some officer: "Please lend Orhan Bey your horse; he accompanies me. Mount, my son; quickly!"—and they would clatter off together. But it was quite a walk from Orhan's and Féridé's eyrie, perched up on the citadel wall, even down to the Vali's Bureau or the Assembly Building; and it was even worse when the young man had to plod through the deep dust or mud along the unmade road to that hideous villa by the station, where he frequently stayed, toiling with his chief over papers and reports, till the small hours—and then plodded home again, arriving all too often mud almost to the knees. "Do clean my trousers before the morning, Light of my Eyes," he would mutter, as he toppled, completely exhausted, into bed—and long after her husband slept poor Féridé's narrow hands would wrestle with the thick dirty material, washing out the trouser-legs, and then pressing them, instructed by Nilüfer, as best she could. She did manage to get an iron at last, smuggled up from Istanbul; but this was a job she could not trust to Kezban, so she did it herself, and it meant keeping the fire going in that courtyard kitchen half the night.

She had to be up early too, to see to her husband's breakfast of coffee, coarse bread, butter, and conserves. How they both longed for the French rolls of Istanbul—Ankara afforded nothing of the sort. But he was safe! Féridé often remembered those raids at night on the yali, and her terror then, and felt the hard work as a small thing in exchange for this new security.

Nilüfer really had an easier life than her sister-in-law; partly because she had this genius for cooking, partly because Fatma was a better maid than Kezban; but mainly because Ahmet was away a great deal—and as every woman knows, things are much simpler for the housewife with the man out of the house! Ahmet was absent from Ankara at least two-thirds of the time, employed on most congenial jobs. Sometimes he was far off in the provinces, getting hold of the many irregular bands who were fighting desultorily against the Kurds and Armenians, or the French, or the Greeks, and persuading them and their leaders to enrol in the new regular army; sometimes he was down at some port like Samsun or Inebolu, checking the identity of those who arrived by boat, and turning back undesirables—for spies, whether Allied or from the Ottoman Government, were always trying to make their way into the interior, and even to the new capital itself.

. . . . .

In Europe and America the creation of a rival Government up at Ankara was received with irritated incredulity. What was it all about, anyhow? It was ridiculous, and most upsetting and inconvenient. And on June the 20th, 1920, the Greeks were told by the Allies that since they had troops on the spot they could go to it, and force the Turks into submission. The Greeks lost no time. They moved forward quickly, and by July the 8th, after other successes, they occupied Broussa.

It was a curious political play and counter-play on all sides, at that time. In May the French, always realists, had concluded an armistice with Kemal Pasha's forces; this they broke in June by occupying another town. In June, also, the National Assembly passed a resolution declaring null and void any convention or treaty concluded by the Istanbul Government with any Power, since it was made under duress; but in July that same Government accepted the phantasmagorial clauses of the Treaty of Sèvres, and signed it the following month. From the outset that treaty was wholly unreal, and the only effect of the harsh and humiliating conditions to which the Sultan's Government set its hand—the Army to be disbanded, foreign Commissions to supervise the police force and to regulate taxes, customs, indeed every aspect of Turkish life—was to bring the waverers whole-heartedly into the Kemalist camp. The nation became defiant, and all through that autumn the "rebel" forces brought off a series of victories in the East over the Armenians, President Wilson's *protégés* and pets—victories marred, one must regretfully admit, by certain massacres. To add to the farcical element, a fortnight after the Ottoman Government had signed the Treaty of Sèvres the Ankara Government in its turn signed what was called "The Moscow Agreement" with the Soviet Union (against which the Allies were still fighting desultorily), thus securing peace on their eastern frontiers, apart from the Kurds and Armenians, who were being dealt with—according to Turkish ideas—very satisfactorily by old Kiazim Kara Bekir. This Russian agreement was Mustafa Kemal's first serious achievement in external diplomacy; but it also put an end to the last hope of the Armenians as a nation —and none of the Allied Great Powers, for all their pro-Armenian feeling, was in a position to prevent this small-scale but cruel catastrophe.

The play and counter-play received an even more fantastic twist during the autumn of 1920, when a male monkey took a hand in international affairs. The story of all the animals who have changed the course of history remains to be written. Everyone knows how the cackling of geese saved the Capitol of Rome from the barbarians; few know that Charles the Second's pet fox, leaping on his wife's bed, caused the miscarriage of her only male child, and by extinguishing the Stuart succession brought the House of Hanover to the English throne. But among these geese and foxes, the monkey of Tatoi must also take a worthy place. Winston Churchill said that a quarter of a million men died of that monkey's bite; and it is probably also true to say that the modern Turkish State owes its existence to the deplorable little animal.

The individual it actually bit, as he walked in his palace gardens on a bright October morning, was King Alexander of Greece, who had been set on the throne by the Allies after the removal of his father King Constantine; the latter, as the Kaiser's brother-in-law, had pursued an inconveniently and dangerously pro-German policy. But the young King's death from blood-poisoning threw the succession open again. Prince Paul, a younger brother, said that he would only accept the throne if the Greek people decided unmistakably against his father, the ex-King; an election had therefore to be held. Everyone fully expected that Venizelos and his party, who championed Prince Paul, would come in with a large majority; on the contrary, they were heavily defeated, and King Constantine's pro-German supporters returned to power.

One can hardly blame the Allies for what followed. A Venizelist, pro-Ally Greece they were prepared to support with money, munitions and diplomatic aid; to support a Greece led by King Constantine was tantamount to supporting the exiled Kaiser himself. In England all public sympathy for Greece died away, and with it all feeling of obligation to help her in her Turkish adventure. The French reaction was even more positive—it was shrewdly suspected that Kemal Pasha and his new government might really have come to stay, and French interests in the Levant would be best served, therefore, by peaceful relations with the new régime; there was no point in exacerbating the Kemalists by helping the Greeks any more. On December the 4th the Allies brusquely informed the Greek Government that if Constantine returned to the throne, Greece would receive no further financial assistance of any kind from them. However, he did return.

The pause in Greek pressure caused by all these events probably just saved the Kemalist régime, which that autumn, as well as waging war on three fronts, East, West, and South, was struggling with by far the most dangerous internal crisis which had yet threatened it. It was some time in August that Féridé and Nilüfer, over the evening meals which, because she cooked so well, they often ate in Nilüfer's house, began to hear talk on their husbands' lips of one Edhem the Circassian and his "Green Army." Edhem was the most successful and powerful of the leaders of those bands of irregulars which Ahmet was trying to bring into the new army—bands which had, so far, borne the brunt of the fighting, whether against the Sultan's troops, the French in the South, or the Kurds in the East. He hailed from what had been a Russian province, and was possibly infected with Communist ideas; and he was now showing himself haughty and truculent, and refusing to obey orders. Kemal Pasha had transferred him to the western front, hoping thus to diminish his influence; but this was not successful. As the hot summer evenings—when they sat sipping coffee on the divans under the windows to catch the last breeze—merged slowly into the cooler dusks of autumn, and the slopes of the long whale-backed ridge across the valley grew more and more golden in the rich evening light as the vines which clothed them turned colour, the tone of concern and dismay about Edhem's activities deepened in the young men's talk. The new regular army under Ismet Bey and Fevzi Pasha was growing fast, and becoming capable of absorbing all the irregular bands, but—

"So far from our getting their men into our forces, they are seducing our own men away from us!" Ahmet burst out bitterly one night.

Féridé, who was leaning her elbow on the window sill, looking out over the shadowy valley and the still glowing slopes above it, turned her head into the room, her brows drawn down over her grey eyes.

"But why, Ahmet? Why do they go to this Edhem rather than to you?—to our proper army?"

"Because we have *discipline!*" her brother replied, proudly and yet angrily. "*Our* men must obey orders, be tidy, and above all not loot! But Edhem allows his men to dress anyhow, and loot as they will, even from our own people!—and they like that, dastards that they are!" He was trembling with anger.

"But cannot *he* control this?" the girl asked. "Surely they listen to him?"

Orhan answered; answered Ahmet rather than her. Nine months of responsible work had given weight and substance to the wild willow-slim young man who a year ago had been raiding arms dumps and jumping out of windows to escape the police; he had been close to Kemal Pasha and had learned much.

"It is grave," he said. "There is support for Edhem even in the Assembly—I hear them, these deputies! Our people do not like discipline, and are too stupid and ignorant—what cattle!—to understand the need for it. They dislike a military government—which we *must* have, if we are to survive. Only today I heard two or three of them saying—'Mustafa Kemal makes us button up our tunics. Ah, we would rather wear the Green Uniform!' What can you do with people like that?"

"Sales types!" Ahmet exploded. "Did they really say that, Orhan?"

"Indeed they did. It is the new catch-word—'We won't button up our tunics.'"

"We will beat them, that is all," Ahmet said stubbornly. "May Allah's curse rest on Edhem and his brothers, and on all who support him."

Towards the end of that October—in fact a few days after the youthful Greek King succumbed in agony to the blood-poisoning which set in after the monkey's bite—Féridé, for the first time, was invited with Orhan to one of the little dinners which Kemal Pasha had begun giving to his intimates. Féridé drew her eyebrows together over this, her first invitation to a party in Ankara. "My husband, what shall I wear to this dinner?"

"But—some quiet afternoon dress; simple. And no peçé, remember—he does not like it."

"But I must wear *something* on my head!" the girl said, looking at him with large eyes.

"Halideh Edib does not," Orhan replied.

Féridé frowned a little: she had heard much about Halideh Edib, the intellectual, emancipated woman who dressed like a man, and galloped about the country rallying men and women to Mustafa Kemal's cause. (She was in fact a sort of La Passionaria of the War of Independence.) It was all very wonderful, but not quite in Féridé's line. In the end she hit on a compromise: she put on a high plain dress of sea-green silk—one of her trousseau dresses, so little worn!—and fastened some sea-green veiling that matched it over her dark hair with two diamond stars; the effect was charming.

"Yes, chérie—it is *very* pretty," observed Nilüfer, who had come up to help her dress, a task at which poor Kezban was not much good—"but what would Niné say?"

"That I must obey my husband!" Féridé retorted. "Niné is a realist, ma chère, above all things—if she were here, she would grasp at once that we are living in another world to hers."

"And what a strange world!" Nilüfer murmured, regretfully. "For me, I prefer the old."

Féridé was all muffled up in her çarşaf when Orhan came to fetch her with one of the little barrel-shaped Anatolian two-horse waggonettes, made of wicker, with bright pale flowers painted on the black wooden ends. He hurried in, made Temel brush his uniform while he changed his collar—all he could do in the way of dressing for dinner—and they clattered off down the steep cobbled street in the clear autumn dusk, big with the first stars; past the Assembly Building, and along the dusty road to the station. In the bare lobby of that ugly house Féridé took off her çarşaf—Orhan took in her head with a smile of approval. "Very discreet—very clever," he murmured; and then they walked into a room with a few people standing about in it, and Féridé for the first time came face to face with the being who for the last six years had been the idol of both her brother and her husband.

She saw a man not tall, but well-made; square-set, especially about the shoulders, and impeccably neat and trim in his civilian suit—*tiré à quatre épingles*, she told Nilüfer afterwards. She saw that strange bony face, all angles—an Epstein face as to structure, and a curious greyish pallor, and those pale light eyes under the fierce bushy eyebrows, which rested on her with a disconcertingly penetrating gaze for an instant; but she also noted with surprise an unexpected possibility of sweetness about the mouth. He made himself very charming—"Ah, so at last I meet Orhan Bey's wife! It was good of you to bring her, mon enfant"—with a hand on Orhan's shoulder. "And how does Ankara please you, Féridé Hanim?"

"Your Excellency, I like it very much. The air is wonderful." Young as she was, Féridé registered the quality of the charm clearly, and rather enjoyed playing up to it.

"You do not regret Istanbul?—the lights, the life?"

"Your Excellency, I regret only the servants down there—my cook and my maid, chiefly!"

He gave his sharp infrequent laugh, and turned to Orhan, while the other guests turned to stare at the young woman who made Mustafa Kemal Pasha laugh.

"Féridé Hanim has frankness—I like this!" he said, again with a hand on the young man's arm.

They went in to dinner, where the conversation was general. Halfway through the meal an officer came in and beckoned to Orhan; excusing himself, he rose and went out, while Mustafa Kemal continued to discuss military matters with the other men. In a few minutes Orhan returned, and leaning over his host's shoulder waited to speak to him—with polite excuses, Kemal turned to listen. At what he heard his face changed; the charm vanished, as if wiped off a slate by a sponge, so did all hint of sweetness anywhere; the tufted eyebrows came down over the ice-blue eyes, and a sudden anger flared out of the whole man, startling and terrifying. Féridé was really terrified for a second—what had Orhan said or done? But it was the news he brought, not Orhan himself, who caused the anger—which was quickly mastered. After a moment or two Kemal Pasha told the company, in calm tones, what had happened. Under Edhem's influence Ali Fuat, a commander on the western front, had made an attack on the Greeks without the authorisation of Ismet Bey, now the Commander-in-Chief, and had been soundly defeated. The dinner went on—when they rose from table Mustafa Kemal, with brief courteous excuses, left the room for a little while with Orhan; presently he returned, and pursued one of those long catechising conversations, in which he delighted, with the men present; they formed his main relaxation. The women sat and chatted in a group apart. European women would have found this tedious, probably, but Turkish ladies had a centuries-old habit of amusing themselves without male conversation. Indeed, that evening was the first time in her life, except once or twice with Hassan on their journey, that Féridé had sat and eaten, unveiled, in the presence of men who were not blood relations. She never forgot that night—partly for that reason, but chiefly because of the light it had thrown for her on the country's leader. As she and Orhan clattered slowly homewards up the steep hill in their little waggonette, she assessed this strange creature to her husband in French: "Il a énormément de charme, mais il peut être méchant, je pense." Orhan laughed. "You are right, my treasure; but he is only méchant to evil-doers. This affair is the end of Edhem—you will see."

It was the end of Edhem, as all Turkey soon saw. At considerable risk troops were called off the Greek front to deal with the Green Army—and dealt with it. Edhem and his brothers finally fled and took refuge with the Greek forces; the Green Army was incorporated in Ismet's new formations, and the danger—that danger—was over. But it was the monkey of Tatoi that had afforded the breathing-space that made it possible to repress Edhem—and the monkey must be held responsible for what followed.

One must really pity the Greeks at this juncture. Only in June the Allies had encouraged them to go in and finish Mustafa Kemal; by December, as a result of Constantine's return, France and England abandoned them. Venizelos was gone; the French were opening *pourparlers* with Ankara. In these circumstances the faintest prudence, the smallest degree of common sense would have indicated a withdrawal from the Anatolian adventure, which was employing 200,000 men, and costing the impoverished little country a quarter of a million sterling a week. But the new anti-Venizelist Greek Government was more wildly expansionist than the shrewd Cretan, with all his patriotic ambitions, had ever allowed his party to be; they pressed on in Anatolia, and at home raised the war-cry "To Constantinople!" They should have been warned by their minor defeat at the first battle of Inonü, in January of the new year, 1921. But they were not warned. They marched on their fate.

Chapter Thirteen

Long before the Battle of Inönü, which took place in January, winter marched in on Ankara. Winds from the east and north, Asiatic in their icy ferocity—the harsh bitter winds that blow across the greatest land-mass in the world, untempered by ocean moisture—swept over the bare plateau across which Féridé and Nilüfer had driven in the spring, to whistle through the aged window-joints and harem-shutters of the old houses up on the citadel, and chill the marrow of those who ventured abroad in the narrow draughty streets. All four—Ahmet, Orhan, and their two young wives—suffered cruelly from the unaccustomed cold. There was no fuel for the cylindrical iron stoves which stood in each room but wood—when wood was to be had; freshly stoked they blazed up furiously at first, making the room insufferably hot, but as the fire died down the insidious cold came creeping in again, round the windows and under the doors, till the two girls, even in their fur coats, shuddered with it. When the man with the cart of small tree-trunks, one of which he dropped off outside the door of each house every so often, was heard approaching, Fatma and Kezban would run out with loud cries of joy—and then run in again to inform their mistresses of the glad tidings. But the girls could not wield a saw, and unless Demir or Temel was about they had to shiver till the batmen returned. As the evenings drew in light became a problem too. One paraffin lamp was allotted to each household, which the girls carried from room to room: to their bed-rooms to wash and tidy, to the sitting-room to sew by—there always seemed to be so much mending to do! Féridé borrowed a tiny fairy-lamp affair from her landlady, Sitaré Hanim, for the kitchen, but really it did little more than cast huge shadows about the cavernous walls and ceiling; in the end she took to cooking all she could by daylight, and warming it up for the evening—which made Orhan grumble: "Light of my Eyes, is not this rice very dry?" [It was dry, of course.]

During that long harsh winter Féridé gained her first experience of the problems and troubles that sooner or later beset all young married women, whether western or Turkish. Her husband—young, brilliant, passionately absorbed in his official duties and grotesquely overworked—

was often unreasonable in his demands, and she saw this, and was troubled and vexed by it; it disturbed her conception of him as nearly perfect. Actually the Turkish tradition of obedience and subordination from wife to husband made things easier for her than our western ideas of equality could have done; the proper, the customary thing was to accept—and as the old copy-book saw says: "Custom Commonly Makes Things Easy." It was tiresome and sad that Orhan was unreasonable, but she had no *moral* sense of grievance, which is what really eats into one. All the same Féridé had a high spirit and temper, and the long months of that first winter were hard for her in every way; the endless unaccustomed household tasks, the bitter cold (she had chilblains all over her hands and feet), the lack of comforts, and the shortage of even the most necessary things, such as adequate light, and warm underclothes. Neither she nor Nilüfer had ever worn the thick woollens which cold climates demand in their lives, and naturally had never thought of bringing any. When the postal service between Ankara and Istanbul was reopened in the late summer of 1920, and letters began to pass between her and Réfiyé Hanim, she asked at first for such things as good tea, coffee, and caviare to be sent up, when anyone was coming; stockings and handkerchiefs for herself, and shirts, collars, and socks for Orhan. But by December her requests were for woollen stockings, and woollen vests and knickers for herself and Nilüfer—and old Mdlle Marthe, down in Istanbul, pattered out with Dil Fcripé to buy the things. The two girls laughed over them when they arrived, they were so coarse and ugly—but they wore them thankfully.

They also suffered a great deal from home-sickness, as the novelty of their new surroundings wore off, and the circumstances of their lives became steadily more unpleasant. Home-sickness for relations first and foremost, for someone to talk to; but also for Istanbul itself, with its extreme beauty and elegance, and the sense, so dear to all Turks, of living in a great capital city—for that nation tends to hate and despise provincial life. In Ankara Féridé and Nilüfer had no real confidantes but one another; they could chatter about the price of turkeys or meat to their uncouth maids or to Sitaré and Güli Hanim, but they missed the perpetual gay easy informal meetings with women friends, the books, the whole gracious happy flow of civilised life. "Really, we might be soldiers living in barracks!" Nilüfer often exclaimed to her sister-in-law. And above all Féridé, in particular, missed Réfiyé Hanim more than she could say.

Orhan shared the home-sickness for Istanbul, though his sense of isolation was less, since he was working all day with men he knew; but he too secretly loathed what he regarded as the uncouth provincialism of Ankara. It frequently happened that paraffin ran out, except for the official buildings; and then precisely two candles were allowed per household—one for the kitchen, one for the sitting-room. When Orhan had sat for an hour or so after supper, putting his eyes out over his work by the light of the solitary candle—"Oh!" he would exclaim, throwing his papers together, "I am blinded! Let us go to look at the station, and get some air." And muffling themselves up in coats they would go out into the narrow street, where the stars shone with a splintering cold glitter above the dark roofs, down through the great gateway, and out along the dusty track which led round outside the citadel walls, till they reached a point whence they could look down on the railway-station, with its six paraffin lamps backed by tin reflectors blazing along the platform, down in the valley. "Ah, there are the lights," Orhan would say, gazing at them hungrily. "But oh, my Soul, the lights of Istanbul! How beautiful they were!" And Féridé, holding his arm, would tell him, each time, of how she had last looked on those lights, as the ship on which she sailed for Inebolu gathered way and steamed up the Bosphorus. Then, faintly comforted by the sight of those six paraffin lamps bravely shining out in the empty Anatolian night, they would walk home again and go to bed. Foolish; pathetic; but for the first two years at Ankara those six lamps played an extraordinary part in the lives of the patriotic exiles.

If the Greeks had not learned anything from their defeat at the battle of Inönü in January 1921, the Allied Powers had; they decided at last to revise that monument of unreality, the Treaty of Sèvres, and called a conference for the end of February for that purpose. Orhan came bounding into the house one night, while Féridé sat shivering by the stove, cold and hungry, darning his socks with stiffened fingers by the light of her single candle. "Oh, my Life, such news!" he exclaimed; he was radiant.

"What is it?" she asked in wonder.

"They have asked us—us!—to this Conference in London! We are to send a delegation. Aha, they have had to recognise him at last!" He was fairly bursting with triumph.

"But this is wonderful!" she said, putting down her work. "Who goes? Does *he* go?"

"No, no—that would be impossible; he must stay here. The delegation is being chosen now—I shall know tomorrow."

"Why can he not go? I should have thought it well."

"My dearest, you do not understand. He is head of the State—such do not go on delegations at the summons of foreign powers! And besides, there is an infinity to do here, that only he can tackle."

"The deputies again?" Féridé was familiar by now with the difficulties perpetually created by the ignorant and recalcitrant deputies.

"Oh, they! Yes, they are always with us!" Orhan laughed. "No, but the Greeks are bound to try conclusions with us some time this year; they are set on it, we know that. At the moment they have had a knock on the nose, and have drawn back, but—" he paused.

"Should we not attack them now, then?" she interjected.

"Dji-djim, you talk like a deputy yourself! *No;* that is where Kemal Pasha is so wise, so patient. For the present he is letting the terrain and the weather fight his battles for him; the Greeks are becoming demoralised, they are sick, there is great attrition of their troops, they suffer from the cold. Brrr!—so do I!" he said, moving across to the log-basket—it was empty. He raised his voice. "Temel! Bring wood!" A distant voice answered "Swiftly, swiftly, my Captain." Orhan turned to Féridé again, and went on airing his views; he had got into the habit of doing this with his young wife, finding her still hands, her beautiful eyes raised to his, her air of calm concentration a stimulus and a relief.

"But whatever their difficulties, ours are greater. They have considerable superiority in men; in armaments great superiority. We must use every second of time that we have in preparation. We must get more men; that is Ahmet's job!—and train them, and arm them; and the arms must be got up behind the front, and supplies and ammunition too. There is *everything* to do—and only *he* can ensure that it is done. Do you know what slings our infantry-men are using for their rifles?"

"No."

"Lamp-wicks!" he said, with a kind of snort of finality—"rifle-slings of lamp-wicks!—belts of lamp-wicks! And this against an army equipped with everything of the best, by the accursed English and French."

There was in fact the most feverish activity in and around Ankara all through the spring and summer of that fateful year 1921. The existence of the nation was at stake, and the whole people knew it; the efforts they made were superhuman. After the Moscow Agreement the Russians had started shipping a little surplus war material to the Black Sea ports, Trebizond, Samsun and Inebolu; cagnés came in along the road over the plateau, and continued further westwards, towards Afion-Karahissar, Kütaya, and Eski-şehir, behind the temporarily static front. Ahmet was absent all the time, gathering in men, training them, equipping them, and sending them on; from Féridé's upper windows, on the citadel wall, she and Nilüfer used to watch the small contingents marching in and being drilled, and then marching out again towards the west—always towards the west! And as the two young women watched, they prayed; prayed for the safety of the men, for their country's preservation. Faith and piety are a natural and spontaneous growth among the Turks; in every house in Ankara—as in Féridé's and Nilüfer's—in at least one room a little velvet wallet, embroidered in silver thread with a holy text, hangs from a hook on the wall; it contains the Koran, the holy book.

Ahmet's perpetual absences from home became, by April, a source of anxiety to Féridé, for in March her sister-in-law started a baby, and, fragile creature that she was, Nilüfer's pregnancy took her hard. She was exceedingly sick; she was ailing, nervous, pale, and as the weeks passed became, Féridé thought, frighteningly unwell—she did not at all like leaving her sister-in-law alone in the house at night with only stout ignorant Fatma, even though that thorny rose, Güli Hanim, lived only two doors off. "Orhan, she must come to us, while Ahmet is away," said the nineteen-year-old wife seriously.

"My dearest, if you say so, she shall—but can you do more for her than Güli Hanim, out of your great experience?" he rallied her.

"I can give her comfort and support," said Féridé, more seriously still— "My husband, she should not be alone."

"Let her come, then. Perhaps she will be well enough to cook—she is a wonderful cook!" he said gaily.

But Nilüfer would not come, then. Ahmet never could—or at any rate never did—give notice of his occasional returns, and the young wife could not bear the thought of his coming home to an empty house. So she stayed where she was—which meant, for Féridé, a constant trapesing up and down over the steep dirty steps and cobbles between the two houses, and a constant fretting anxiety. Though inexperienced, Féridé had a good deal of practical common sense. "We should secure a mid-wife," she said. "Now, at once. November, is it? *When* in November?" Nilüfer said, about the 15th. "Very well—I will see to it. We must arrange for a doctor too."

But doctors and mid-wives were not so easily come by in Ankara then; they were mostly at the front, the latter acting as nurses. With much trouble, and running to and fro, Féridé secured the services of two who would, she hoped, be adequate. She had tried to persuade her sister-in-law to go down to Istanbul to the yali for her confinement; but Nilüfer would not hear of it. What!—leave her home, leave Ahmet? Impossible!

When she was not worrying over Nilüfer's affairs, Féridé's mind was wholly given over, housekeeping apart, to the political situation. Those little dinners with Mustafa Kemal Pasha continued; he was extremely fond of Orhan, and had taken rather a fancy to his Aide-de-Camp's tall, graceful, aristocratic wife, with her quick grasp of affairs and her lively uninhibited manner of speech. Kemal Pasha's paths had not lain much among the old Turkish aristocracy, in fact he rather despised them; he was amused and interested to find in a sprig of that aristocracy the qualities that he found in Féridé Hanim, as he always called her—he was a stickler for the formalities. Féridé too gradually shed both her awe of the great man and her embarrassment at appearing unveiled in mixed company, and talked away to the nation's leader with all her untutored native wit and liveliness. Kemal was enchanted; her husband was delighted. Those evenings were the only relaxation that Mustafa Kemal allowed himself, in days of stupendous effort. He was working sixteen or eighteen hours a day now—with a concentration, and at a speed, that left his colleagues and subordinates gasping; as for them, his furious energy and rapid methods drove them almost to a standstill. Even Orhan's young face was becoming drawn and haggard; his fair skin threw up the dark shadows under his eyes. His chief looked ghastly— for years he had suffered at intervals from kidney-trouble, and the strain and pace of his work had brought it on again. He should of course have dieted and avoided alcohol; but avoiding alcohol was the last thing Mustafa Kemal would ever do. Wine (to Féridé's infinite astonishment) flowed at his table; hesitantly, at his instance, she learned to drink a little of it. But there were occasions when Orhan dined with the head of the state and she did not; from these the young man came home at three or four in the morning, exhausted and hilarious. "I am late, my Life; forgive me," he would apologise, when hearing him come in she slipped into his room to see that he had all he needed.

"But Orhan, why are you so late? You must be up at eight!—you will get no rest."

"We were drinking," he would answer, with a momentary return of the boyish gaiety that had so charmed her when they were first married. "Oh, Kemal Pasha was so entertaining! How he talks!—and the stories he tells! You would never guess it, seeing him in society. My Soul, have you got some aspirin? Give me two or three."

Féridé began by attempting some gentle remonstrances with her husband over these drinking-bouts, but she soon gave it up. She knew that Orhan only drank with his chief—by his wish, and to keep him company; and her simple arguments about its being forbidden were met, invariably, with the over-riding one that this was a new dispensation, where the old rules and prohibitions no longer held good. "People drank wine in the days of Omar and Hafiz," he told her; "then illicitly, but you will see—presently they will do so again, and openly, and without trouble of conscience. Oh, not yet; he has great patience. But he knows the road our nation must travel, if it is to live in the world of today, and he will arrange it all, hodjas or no hodjas." Féridé, alarmed, asked him what he meant, but he would only say—"You will see. And in the meantime, do not speak of it."

By the end of May it was already becoming very hot, up there on the arid treeless plateau, where the naked rocks and the baked soil threw back the sun's heat with savage intensity; light airs moved at morning and evening up on the citadel hill, though even there the streets and houses were soaked in heat from noon till sundown—in the kitchen, off her enclosed courtyard, Féridé dripped with sweat as she stood over her primitive stove. But down in the valley, in the Vali's Bureau and in the Station House, the heat and airlessness became insupportable; there was no real coolness even at night, and Kemal Pasha, strained, overworked, anxious and ill, suffered greatly. But where else could he live?

The answer came unexpectedly. The wife of a member of his staff took a walk late one afternoon up through the vineyards towards the hills beyond the town, in the direction of the district called Çankaya; a little path, winding up a narrow valley beside a small stream, between bushes laden with yellow sweet-scented pea-like flowers tempted her on and on, far beyond her intention, till she came to a spot where under a group of immense poplars the spring itself, the source of the stream, bubbled out, singing, from among the rocks. And close by stood a largish, solidly-built stone house.

All Turks have a tremendous feeling for water—perhaps because for so many centuries the Prophet has forbidden them wine; they will, even today, drive as far to fill carboys and bottles with the water from a famous spring as Europeans will drive to bring home a case of Châteauneuf du Pape or Vouvray. This lady, then, looked about her—at the white-trunked poplars, their leaves talking softly in the evening air, at the bubbling spring, whose musical voice dominated the chattering leaves of the great trees; she went up and examined that low pleasant-looking house. And then she hastened back to the airlessness of Ankara, and told Kemal Pasha that she had found the perfect place for him. He went and looked at it, was enchanted, and bought it forthwith; he had shacks run up near by for Osman Agha and his troop of Lazes, who formed his personal body-guard, in their picturesque long Cossack coats and high boots; and in a very short time he entered into residence up at Çankaya. Thenceforward, there was a long uphill drive in the little Anatolian waggonettes for those who dined with the Head of the State —but they dined in coolness and beauty, now, to the music of water and whispering leaves. Mustafa Kemal never forgot the happy inspiration of that lady; long afterwards, when first the rather pretentious "Kiösk," in which he lived for so many years, and finally the big imposing Presidential dwelling had been built on the slopes near the bubbling spring, he would say to her—"It was *you* who brought me to Çankaya."

By early June it became as clear to the Allied Powers as it had long been to Kemal that the Greeks were about to try conclusions once more

with the Turks, in an attempt to realise their ambitions. Plans for mediation were mooted by the Allies, but before anything was done, the
Greek Army began to move forward, through difficult country, to attack the Turkish positions. They had an advantage of 3 to 2 in guns,
and of 8 to 3 in machine-guns, as well as a slight superiority in manpower; also they were in all respects better equipped and supplied.
Their two-fold object was to destroy the Turkish Army, and to occupy
Ankara—and to those who lived in that city their success seemed all too
probable. When the news of the Greek advance broke, the life of the
new capital became greatly disrupted. Ahmet, who had recently been
transferred to Ismet Pasha's staff, took a sad farewell of Nilüfer; she
clung to him, weeping. "Oh, may Allah preserve you, my very dear
husband!"

"Look to her," Ahmet said to his sister, hastening up to take farewell
of her too, in the house on the citadel wall.

"My brother, bid her come to me, here—then she will be under my
eyes, and I can look after her properly. This running to and fro is
impossible!" said poor Féridé, who had heard that morning from Orhan
that Temel, his batman, had been ordered to the front, leaving her
with only Kezban to help in the house. "You take Demir, I suppose?"

"But of course."

"Then she cannot stay there. Send her to me."

"I will—" And off he went.

Féridé had another caller a little later. There came a knock on the
great door that gave on the street; she was in her courtyard kitchen,
Kezban in the house, so she went and opened it. A soldier—ragged,
shabby, with the belt and rifle-sling of lamp-wick which Orhan had
described to her—stood on the threshold.

"Is the Gaiety of My House within?" he asked, humbly.

She was familiar with the charming paraphrase—Turks do not readily say "My wife."

"It is Kezban that you seek?" she asked, kindly.

"Yes, if it please you, Effendim."

"Come in—she is here. Kezban!" she called, and hurried back to the
kitchen to get some food for him; even in these straitened circumstances, so different from the spacious ways of keeping open house at
the yali, she clung to the Turkish tradition of hospitality. A little meal
was set out in the hall, and she left husband and wife together while
she went back to her cooking. But before he left the soldier came to
her too, and thanked her for her goodness to Kezban, who stood by,
weeping silently. When he had gone Féridé did her best to comfort the
good creature, and then sent her about her tasks, while she went on
cooking the beans, the aubergines and the shallots that, served cold with

oil, were to form part of Orhan's supper; opening the oven door now and then to baste the fowl that was roasting in it. Before long a loud clamour of weeping arose in the courtyard—Féridé went out to see what was the matter now. It was Sitaré Hanim, their landlady, her round merry face convulsed with crying. "They have taken my Osman, Féridé Hanim," she sobbed out—"only seventeen, and they have taken him!"

Osman was the only son of Ibrahim and Sitaré, and owing to Ibrahim's position as clerk in the Vali's Bureau, he had managed to get the boy a job as messenger in one of those one-room Government Departments. They had a girl too, called—like Féridé's own elder sister —Étamine, a pretty child of twelve with a round face like her mother's, who still ran about unveiled, in the bas-ortü, a long scarf of tinselled muslin which floated loose from her round dark head; but when strangers appeared, already with a swift gesture she would twitch it across her small face, so that only her immense black eyes peered out, as big as gooseberries, above the glittering folds.

Féridé—thinking all the while of what Orhan would probably say about his dinner that night, and wondering who would fetch the charcoal now that Temel was mobilised—gave her sympathy to poor Sitaré, of whom she had become very fond. Much comfort she could not give—there is no comfort for wives and mothers when a war is on; underneath all her practical preoccupation and worries she felt a steady nagging ache of anxiety about Ahmet, her adored brother. But she did what she could, and at last got rid of the good soul.

Late in the afternoon, having been down with Kezban to fetch the charcoal, and staggered up the hill again with one of the two sacks, Féridé slipped away to see Nilüfer. She was determined to get her sister-in-law into her own house as soon as she could, now that Ahmet was gone to the front. She found her sitting on one of those hard divans under the window, her feet on a chair, her elbow on the sill, gazing out towards the west, where Eski-şehir and Afion-Karahissar lay. Féridé usually walked straight into Ahmet's house, as Nilüfer did into hers; she had done so now. After a little talk she said gently—"Dji-djim, will you not now come up to us? We want you so much."

Nilüfer turned her splendid eyes, suddenly tragic, full onto her sister-in-law.

"Yes," she said, "I will—really, dearest, I must. Fatma has gone!"

"Fatma gone! Gone where?" Féridé asked in astonishment.

"But to the front; to carry munitions, water, food—que sais-je? Anyhow, she is gone—and oh Féridé, *he* is gone too, and I cannot be here all alone!" The eyes brimmed over with tears, and she hid her face on Féridé's shoulder.

So that evening ended with Nilüfer being escorted up to the house on the wall, with a small bag for the night. Féridé said that she would send Kezban—since they had no batman any more—down next day to bring up the rest of Nilüfer's things. But next morning Kezban came to her young mistress and announced, with gawky apologies, that she was going to the front too, that very day. And went.

"Well, really!" Féridé said to herself, standing alone in the empty courtyard, after the outer door had closed behind Kezban and her little bundle—"Now we must rely on ourselves alone!" She went to the carved marble well-head, drew up water, and filled the jars for the house, which in the excitement of departure Kezban had forgotten to do—hauling up the heavy bucket and tipping it out made her back and arms ache. She put fresh charcoal on the stove—which had also been one of Kezban's tasks—and began on another, that of washing and cutting up vegetables. Then she ran in to Nilüfer to tell her that she was going down to the market to fetch the meat. She took Étamine with her, and on the way home they collected some more of Nilüfer's belongings and brought them up; while her sister-in-law unpacked, she went back to the kitchen, and put on the rice for pilau.

The Greek Army began its advance on the 9th of July. Knowing that it was imminent, before that date Mustafa Kemal went down to the front to review the troops, and put heart into them; as at Gallipoli, as in the retreat from Palestine, he was always happiest when in touch with his soldiers, whom he knew, understood and loved. They marched past him in fine fighting style, in the shabby uniforms and bad boots, presenting arms smartly with their rifles. But alas, the rifles for the most part had no bayonets—there was no steel at Ankara with which to make them. Now the Turk is by nature a close fighter, and loves to use cold steel, as those who have ever fought against him know to their cost; and partly to encourage his own nation, partly to intimidate the Greeks, Mustafa Kemal sent off a long telegram to Zia Bey, the editor of "National Sovereignty," the Ankara paper, instructing him to describe the review, and to say how the Turkish army had marched past him with fixed bayonets, the bright steel glittering in the sun.

The battle begun on July the 9th lasted till the 20th. Far away in Ankara the dull mutter of the distant guns rumbled like thunder through the blazing merciless heat—and for some days that was all the news those who were left in the capital had; when the thunder grew louder, it could only mean that the battle was drawing nearer, and that spelt retreat. Actually very few were left; practically every man who could move, and nearly all the women, had gone to the front, the latter to do the work of draught-animals. Even Orhan had gone off on some mysterious mission; the two girls were now quite alone. Her elderly women neighbours began to cast nasty glances at Féridé, tall, active and lithe of movement, as she went to and from the market, and to mutter audible speculations as to why *she* was not gone to carry water and munitions to the troops. One day Sitaré Hanim actually came in to see her, and spoke of this. "Féridé Hanim, you are young and strong—are you not going to the front?"

"No," said Féridé, rather coldly—"Are you, Sitaré Hanim?"

"I, no—I have my husband and Étamine to care for. I cannot leave them."

"And I have my sister-in-law to care for, who is about to bear a child for the nation—I cannot leave her either; she is ill. You will oblige me, Sitaré Hanim, if you do not refer to this subject again," said Féridé, with a haughtiness which Réfiyé Hanim herself could not have surpassed. "But if you care to silence those muttering gossips outside, you may do so."

And Sitaré Hanim, cowed, retreated, and did in fact tell the gossips the state of the case.

The long hot days, filled with exhausting tasks, and still more the long hot nights, vibrating with the distant sound of the guns, combined with anxiety about her husband and brother, pressed heavily on Féridé—most intolerable of all was the absence of news. One night she felt that she could bear it no longer. The Red Crescent, the Turkish version of the Red Cross, had an office down in the lower town, at the foot of the citadel hill; and when she had put Nilüfer to bed she muffled herself in her çarşaf, and slipping out of the big courtyard door she sped away, out through the gateway, and down the hill by the Kara-oglan Çarsisi, the large street leading up to the citadel from the town below. Near the bottom stood a mosque, its dome and minarets black against the pale summer sky, the Zinçirli Kami; just beyond it a little street turned off to the right, the Zinçirli Kami Sokak. There, she knew, was the Red Crescent office—and if anyone had news, they would have it. But could she find the place? She stood in the narrow street, between the dilapidated wood-and-plaster houses; at the further end rose a tall building with arched and recessed balconies, rather like those she had admired at Kastamonu. Could that be it? She walked towards it, and then observed that light was coming from behind shutters in a very small building on her left—light, and the sound of voices. Féridé moved nearer; stood, and listened. At that moment a man came running up the street, and banged on the door; it was flung open, and through the stream of light that poured out she caught a glimpse of a very small room indeed, furnished like an office, with men sitting and standing about—in the light she saw, too, that the new arrival wore the brassard of the Red Crescent on his arm. He panted out an urgent enquiry—a train-load of wounded had just come in, he had run from the station, his Commandant wanted to know where they were to be put? Standing in the shadows, she could overhear also the discussion which followed, and the decisions come to: 560 men? then they could all be put in that big school half-way up the hill. Carts were ordered for transport, and one of the men walked off with the messenger to the station, while others were despatched to knock up the two or three doctors and nurses known still to be in Ankara. When only two men were left in the office, through the open door she heard one say to the other, "How, in Allah's name, are two women to nurse 560 men? And where are the dressings to come from? We have almost nothing left here—it all went to the front."

"Yes, and where are we to get mattresses and bedding for 560 men?" his colleague asked dismally, lighting a cigarette. "And who is to cook for them? I tell you, Eşref Effendi, this affair is not going to be so easy. No hospitals, no dressings to mention, no nursing staff, no hospital staff, and *three* doctors! And this is only the beginning."

Féridé now stole forward, and presented herself, rather timidly, at the open door.

"Eşref Effendi," she said, speaking to the man whom his companion had so addressed, "may I trouble you for a moment?"

Surprised, he got up and came to the door.

"Yes, what is it, Hanim Effendi? What do you want?"

"I came to ask for news," she said, a little nervously. "My brother is at the front, and my husband too, I believe."

He looked slightly annoyed. "And who may your husband be?"

"Orhan Bey. My brother is Ahmet Bey; he is on Ismet Pasha's staff."

The other man leant forward over the table at which he sat.

"Your husband is not Orhan Bey, who is in the Bureau privé of Mustafa Kemal Pasha?"

"The same, Effendim."

He got up. "And what news do you seek, Hanim Effendi?"

"But of the battle! We hear the guns, but we hear nothing else!" said Féridé, energetically. The two men laughed. "I should be so grateful to know—how does it go, well or ill?"

"Ill!" said the man called Eşref, dully. "Afion-Karahissar has fallen, Kütaya has fallen, Eski-şehir will fall at any moment."

"Oh." She paused for a moment, swallowing the evil tidings. "I thank you," she said then. She paused again. "I have a mattress or two to spare, and some blankets. I will see that they are got down to the school tomorrow morning."

"That is well—thank you," he said.

Féridé glided quickly away into the shadows again; but as she walked up the steep incline of the Kara-oglan Çarsisi towards the citadel, whose irregular outline, broken by crenellated towers, stood out black against the immensity of the summer night, full of stars, she thought over what she had just heard. It was fearful news. It meant that the whole Turkish line had gone, or was about to go, and with it the vital rail-way from Afion-Karahissar to Eski-şehir, of which Orhan had spoken so often; in his enthusiasm he had made diagrams for her of the fortified positions covering the precious line. If the army had to retreat from there, where would they stop? And what would happen to the wretched population of the surrendered towns?

Those were in fact almost precisely the questions that Kemal Pasha had been asking himself for the last twenty-four hours, ever since, on the heels of an urgent telegram from Ismet Pasha, the Commander-in-Chief, he had hurried to the front a second time. If he was to save his army, such as it was, he must withdraw, and withdraw rapidly, leaving the civil populations, his faithful people who trusted him, to the frightful brutalities—little suspected in the West—of the Greek soldiers. But his army was the only thing he had with which to face a hostile world —it was the one instrument of salvation for the Turkish people. Mustafa Kemal was, first and foremost, a professional soldier, and he took a professional soldier's decision. Eski-şehir was to be evacuated, and the troops withdrawn eastwards with all possible speed to behind the Sakarya River, some seventy kilometres distant. This would at once lengthen the Greek lines of communication, and, if the movement were executed swiftly enough, give a breathing-space in which to re-form and reorganise his weary and battered regiments.

The movement was carried out—in its ultimate results one of the most successful strategic retreats in history. The day after Féridé had crept down at night to seek news at the Red Crescent office in Ankara, King Constantine of Greece arrived at the front in person to direct operations. He found, really, no front. A brisk Turkish attack all along the line the following day covered the retreat of the main forces; the Greeks, counter-attacking, repulsed the enemy, but after that the enemy vanished. The Turkish Army, whose annihilation had been one of the two main Greek objectives, had retired practically intact; losses on both sides were roughly equal, between 7000 and 8000 men. But for the Greeks, though they were technically victorious, failure to inflict a decisive and ruinous blow on the enemy in fact spelled a defeat—and Kemal knew it. He sent out an Order of the Day to his weary troops, when they had finally reached and crossed the Sakarya River: "We have lost, now. But we shall reorganise, we shall win; and in the end, the Sakarya will be the tomb of the Greek Army."

Chapter Fourteen

When the news of the retreat became known in Ankara there was great consternation. Orders of the Day to the troops, to whom Kemal Pasha was both familiar and an idol, were one thing, but to persuade a frightened civilian population that it was all for the best to have the enemy two days' march from their doors was quite another. The evidences of defeat were there before their eyes: buildings choked with wounded, and the open spaces in the ramshackle lower town full of tents set up by the wretched refugees from Beylikoprü, Polatli, and Eski-şehir itself, who camped there in the open beside the cagnés and wagonettes in which they had fled from their homes, their disordered belongings piled about them, spreading their tales of misery to whoever would listen.

Fortunately, the people who had no time at all to spare to listen to horror-stories, however pitiful, were the house-wives of Ankara, who though shorthanded themselves—since all their domestic help had gone to the front—nevertheless now proceeded to shoulder the fantastic task of cooking, washing, and supplying necessaries for a hospital population of three or four thousand wounded men. Some doctors and a few nurses had come back with the wounded from the front; but the supply, of nurses in particular, was altogether inadequate. Now in Turkey, in those days, for a grown woman, veiled, to go and nurse men, wash their bodies and change their dressings was almost unthinkable—more unthinkable even than Florence Nightingale's activities at Scutari had been to Victorian England sixty years before. A handful of "advanced" women volunteered for the task, but the main work in those improvised wards of mattresses spread along the floors of schools was done by little girls of thirteen or less, who had not yet put on the çarşaf, working under the immediate direction of the doctors. One shudders to think of what they may have done—but Turkish girls are handy, resourceful, and above all obedient, and the Turkish soldier is a tough and hardy animal—a surprisingly high proportion of cases survived.

Étamine was one of these amateur nurses. Her bas-ortü flying out behind her, she scudded down every morning to the school to which Féridé had sent blankets and bedding, and there she helped the doctors to change dressings, made beds, emptied slops, and served to the wounded men the meals that her mother, Féridé, and hundreds like them had cooked. The food was not proper invalid food, it was whatever they could get in the market and cook on their primitive stoves; they carried it down and dumped it at the doors. For the worst cases and those with high fever there was soup—in saucepans, in big hammered pewter vessels, even in slop-pails; or yoghurt, the delicious sour milk, set firmer than a junket and so fresh and sharp on the tongue, in shallow vessels of every sort; for the less seriously wounded there was bulgur—wheat first boiled and then browned in butter, and kavurma, meat roasted in the fire-clay ovens, sliced, and packed into earthenware jars filled solidly with melted butter, as the French make *confit d'oie*: the bits of meat flavoured the browned wheat, or the rice. All these things Féridé and Sitaré Hanim and the rest prepared and took down, banging on the doors to notify their arrival—and the little Étamines would come out, smiling, and carry the great pots inside in their immature skinny little arms. But Féridé and Sitaré did not climb the hill again empty-handed—no, they swung between them great baskets of dirty bed-linen or soiled dressings, which they then proceeded to wash out at home; not in water flowing freely from a tap, it must be remembered, but every drop hauled up in buckets from the well-heads in their airless courtyards.

It was a gruelling job. The extraordinary thing was that though there was little or no real organisation—Turks don't organise, or did not then—it worked. The thousands of wounded were fed, tended, and washed for, by a miracle of improvisation and voluntary help—though at a cost in physical fatigue that can hardly be measured. Even Nilufer, sick, heavy with child and hardly able to stand, spent hours and hours every day in the stifling kitchen, standing at a table with the precious Istanbul flat-iron, pressing the sheets and bandages which Féridé had washed; and at night, after supper, the two sat by the windows in the sultry heat, looking out over the parched yellow plain, rolling the bandages up tight and neat, to be carried down next morning, tied up in a cloth, along with the soup and rice and all the rest. Every house had lent plates, cups, and bowls, of course, for there was hardly any hospital crockery available; the women even lent their stockings to cover the legs of the men restless with high fever.

If the deputies had displayed the same ready co-operation as the women, things would have been much easier then for Mustafa Kemal. But they did not. There were first murmurings in the Assembly, then open complaints against those responsible for the defeat; there ensued angry and embittered debates, coloured by ignorance and fear, as to what to do next. This was hopeless. Ignorant and frightened men always have poor judgement; the instrument which Mustafa Kemal had forged to express the national will seemed likely not only to cut the hand that forged it, but to destroy the nation itself.

One of his closest friends always said of Mustafa Kemal—"If he saw a fire, he did not send for a fire-engine; he went straight up to it, and stamped it out with his own feet." He did so now, in effect; but what he stamped on was the Assembly. He demanded outright to be made Commander-in-Chief himself, with extraordinary powers—complete power, that is, to control and organise every aspect of national defence. Cowed by that erect figure on the curved tribune, battered by that rasping voice pouring out a torrent of eloquent common sense, the deputies agreed, and voted him Commander-in-Chief, with all the special powers he asked for. Having gained his point, this astonishing man then turned round and himself presented a motion that he should only hold that office, and have those powers, for the space of three months, since he was merely "the faithful servant of the nation's sovereignty." This also was agreed to, and a week later, on August the 5th, the new Commander-in-Chief left to organise the new front.

He left amid a storm of popular acclamation and relief. Unlike the deputies, the common people understood well enough who, alone, was likely to be their saviour, and sent him on his way with cheers, prayers, and tears. Orhan went with him. His unexplained departure three weeks before had in fact been to the front—sent in advance, he had returned when his chief returned. He was still full of confidence and buoyant optimism. "Ah, you should have seen how everything changed, immediately, down there at Eski-şehir, when he arrived," he said to Féridé before he went. "Until then, all was discouragement, gloom; even Ismet Pasha was at his wits' end. Such a good man, and a fine soldier—but he is not Mustafa Kemal! But when he came, and walked among the men, and spoke with them, all were filled with a new spirit, were content, cheerful. Mind you, a soldier hates to retreat; you could not ask a harder thing of them than that—and leaving our people to these Greek devils! But even that, they have done for him with a good heart. Ahmet spoke so much of that—how he kindled, inspired the men."

Féridé listened to all this, her brows drawn down, thoughtful. She was less of an optimist than Orhan, and looked always to the practical side of things. "All the same, it is a fearful risk to take, this withdrawal," she said slowly. "I wish they could have stood on the old line. The Greeks are now only eighty kilometres away, I hear."

"Who told you that?" Orhan asked, sharply.

"Sitaré Hanim. Ibrahim, her husband, hears these things down at the Bureau."

"And tells them to his wife, to spread all through the town!" he exclaimed angrily.

"But Orhan, is it not true?"

The calm query sobered him.

"Yes, it *is* true," he said, rather reluctantly. "My Life, you are right—it is grave. I wish I need not leave you—and you look so exhausted! But—" his face was suddenly illuminated—"Trust *him!* He knows what is best," he said. "Trust him!" he repeated. He spoke as a man might speak of trust in God.

At the last she had clung to him. "Oh my dear love, may Allah preserve you! And Ahmet! Shall you see Ahmet?"

"Probably—I did, as you know, last time."

"Give him my love," she said.

Next day he went away—and she went down and stood humble and anonymous in her black çarşaf among the crowd that cheered their new Commander-in-Chief on his way; she saw her tall slender husband, gallant and trim in his uniform, his fair hair gleaming under the kalpak, the high brimless cap of black caracul, and prayed silently for his safety. When the procession had passed she turned away and climbed the hill again, perspiring under those muffling black folds, and at home told Nilüfer about that brave departure: the soldierly figure of Kemal Pasha, with his set resolute face, the praying, cheering, weeping crowds. Then she rolled up her sleeves and began to wash and wring out soiled and blood-stained sheets and shirts.

The Greek Army began to move forward from its positions near the Eski-şehir railway five days later, on August the 10th. Their movement was up the open marshy valley of the Porsuk, a tributary of the Sakarya; by the 23rd they had reached the Sakarya itself near Beylikoprü, while another group was approaching Haymana, slightly to the south-east. At dawn next day, under a tremendous artillery bombardment, they attacked, and for the next ten days the Greeks—too often derided as soldiers in modern times—fought with a heroism worthy of their classic exploits in the heroic age, at Thermopylae or Salamis. The conditions were gruelling beyond belief. No one who has not experienced an August in Anatolia can imagine them: the pitiless heat, a difference of 20 degrees Fahrenheit between sun and shade, most dangerous to the bodies of sweat-soaked men, the suffocating dust. In addition to all this Turkish bands, with devilish shrewdness and skill (inspired of course by Kemal Pasha, who had made himself familiar with every yard of the ground) constantly raided their lines of communication, slipping out from the narrow strip of wild hilly country lying between the Porsuk and the Sakarya, which run roughly parallel for many miles before they join near Beylikoprü, harrying the supply-trains, and slipping back into the hills again—so that the wretched Greek troops suffered from lack of food, of ammunition, and—most desperate of all—of water. Nevertheless, slowly, slowly, they succeeded in pressing the Turks—who were fighting with an equal savage courage—backwards for a distance of ten miles. Ten miles in ten days! And still they fought on, on both sides. The Turks were even worse supplied than the Greeks, who had managed in the interval between the Turkish retreat and the Battle of the Sakarya to amass lorries by the hundred and camels by the thousand; whereas Kemal's men had to rely on slow ox-drawn cagnés and on their women—their sisters, their wives, and their sweethearts, who did the work of machines and beasts, toiling forward in the heat under back-breaking loads of shells, ammunition, food, and water, their stifling veils flung back, strange men or no strange men, from their streaming faces. By September the 4th, both armies had fought themselves to a standstill, and still the issue hung in the balance: Ankara, the Greek objective, was only forty miles away, but it was not yet taken; the Greek Army was exhausted, but not defeated.

   .   .   .   .   .

Away in England, Dr. Pierce and Fanny learned the news with mounting anxiety. It was still strange to the Doctor to be in England in July and August—for twenty years his summers had all been spent in Turkey, and thither his thoughts always turned nostalgically at that time of the year. To escape the stuffiness of empty Oxford, choked with trippers, he had taken a little cottage in the Cotswolds, within reach of the libraries, but fresher and cooler, where Fanny, helped by a woman from the village, looked after him. His book on Turkish folklore had come out, and had had a great success—for once Dr. Pierce had made some money. Captain Grant, the Scottish officer whose general redness of aspect had so impressed the Pasha a year or more ago, was home on leave, and was making them a prolonged visit; technically, he and Fanny were still not engaged, but there was what the English so elastically call "an understanding" between them, and this gave him a sort of licenced position in the house.

Dr. Pierce of course read *The Times*, which got to the village from Moreton-in-the-Marsh at about 11. One day in the middle of July, sitting out in the garden, his eye was caught by a paragraph headed, in smallish type—"The Greek Offensive. Considerable Advance." It gave two communiqués from Athens, and the last sentence read: "The enemy has fallen back to strongly entrenched positions to the north-west of Eski-şehir and the southwest of Kutehia."

"Good God!" Dr. Pierce exclaimed—"Those wretched Greeks!"

"What about them?" Captain Grant asked, without much real interest—he was taking Fanny in later to lunch at the Mitre, and his thoughts were on whether he should propose or not.

"They're advancing—it looks as if they meant to have a try for Angora." (Ankara was still called Angora in England in those days.)

At that moment Fanny came out, and caught his last words.

"Who's going to have a try for Angora?" she asked.

"The Greeks. Look—" and he handed her the paper. As Fanny studied it a look of concern came over her face. Still small, her nose still slightly beaky, Fanny had nevertheless become quite pretty; her complexion was clear and pink, her blue eyes had an eager animated expression, her yellow hair was cleverly and becomingly arranged; she no longer tore her clothes, and her cool cotton frock was fresh and trim.

"*Oh!*" she said now, on a distressful note, "how horrible! I wonder where Féridé is, and what she is doing? I hope she isn't in Angora."

"I should think she was bound to be, by now," Captain Grant observed. "She told you in that letter that her husband had gone there."

"But Alec, she didn't say that *she* was going."

"Ah, but that was eighteen months ago, or going on for."

"Conditions in Angora must still be pretty primitive," Dr. Pierce observed—"hardly suitable for anyone brought up as Féridé has been. Those girls led extraordinarily sheltered lives."

"Goodness yes. The yali—what luxury!" Fanny said. "And the old Pasha was such a lamb."

"My dear, that is hardly the word I should have used for him," Dr. Pierce said mildly.

"No, Uncle darling, but you know what I mean. Alec, I *do* envy you, having been there. Isn't the yali a lovely place?"

"Seemed all right to me," said Captain Grant.

"Oh Alec—'all right!' It's one of the most exquisite houses in the world."

Captain Grant chewed a little on his small red moustache. "Well my dear Fanny, I know you have this passion for the Turks, but personally I don't quite get it. I thought a lot of their buildings awfully flimsy, as a matter of fact. Though mind you, I found the Pasha a perfectly decent old boy."

"I don't know why you're always so beastly about the Turks," said Fanny.

"Kut," Captain Grant responded briefly.

"Oh well—" Fanny could not defend the treatment meted out by the Turks to the surrendered garrison of Kut-el-Amara; no one could, she knew.

But Alec Grant had no desire to quarrel with her.

"As for this fellow Kemal," he went on, placatorily, "I will say he seems to be a first-class soldier. He did frightfully well at the Dardanelles, and he managed that retreat from Palestine superbly too, I heard. But I didn't gather that the old Pasha thought an awful lot of him."

"Did you talk to the Pasha about him?"

"Lord, yes. He seemed rather anti-him, if anything."

"He would be, necessarily," said Dr. Pierce, who was often rather troubled by the extreme Anglo-British simplicity of his probable nephew-in-law's views on all subjects relating to foreigners. "The Pasha supports the Sultan and the actual régime—men of his generation all do."

"Oh well, I don't know about all that," Alec Grant said, blithely dismissing the complexities of Turkish politics. "He was a very fine old boy, the Pasha, but he didn't think much of Kemal." He glanced at his left wrist, and turned to Fanny. "Now, what about this lunch? It's nearly twelve—do you want to change or anything?"

"Yes, of course."

"Well, hadn't you better get a move on?"

When Fanny came down ten minutes later into the little sitting-room where he was waiting, he glanced with a sort of hungry appreciation at her. "Darling, you look divine!" He went over to where she stood, minute, almost elegant, and oddly forcible for anything so small; she had put on a yellow silk dress which increased her resemblance to the familiar cage-bird. "That damned old Pasha said they called you 'The Canary,' " he muttered as he put an arm round her. "Oh darling, yes— just one!"

But he didn't propose to Fanny that day. Over the excellent lunch at the Mitre, which he had ordered in advance by telephone from the village post-office, rather to his annoyance Fanny persisted in her speculations about Féridé, and what might be happening to her in these new circumstances.

"Now look, Fanny," he protested at last, "I can't think why you go on and on about this girl. You haven't seen her for seven years, and you were both children then, after all."

"Yes, it *is* a long time," said Fanny thoughtfully; "but she was a wonderful person, Alec; one couldn't just forget about her."

"Oh darling, rubbish!—A child can't be a wonderful person—not really a person at all, you know."

"*She* was. And I was, too," Fanny added slowly. "I can't explain to you, Alec; you somehow don't seem to have *got* the Turks at all, although you've been there all those months. But they are wonderful people—not a bit like us, not efficient or anything, at least they weren't then; but they have a sort of quality."

"This Kemal fellow is efficient enough," the soldier in Alec Grant protested. "He's terrific at his job, by all accounts."

"Oh well, I don't know him, or anything about him," Fanny said calmly. She could not know, there in Oxford, how time was to rectify this statement.

During those summer days at the cottage Fanny and Dr. Pierce, among the roses and sweet peas in the little garden, under the tall English elms standing between the green English fields full of quiet grazing cattle, followed the course of that conflict away on the burning uplands of Anatolia. On the 20th of July they read that Kutaya had fallen, on the 22nd that the Greeks had captured Eski-şehir, on the 23rd the caption ran—"Greek Victory. Advance towards Angora"; and two days later "The Story of the Greek Victory. Turks Outmanoeuvred." But after that a note of caution, almost of doubt, crept into the communiqués. "Prospect of guerilla fighting," said one. "Fresh stand to be made," said another. And then *The Times* switched over, suddenly, from Anatolia's front to the ill-starred Greek attempt to form a Hellenic state on the southern shores of the Black Sea. Massacres of Pontine Greeks were reported. But on the main front there seemed to be a sort of pause.

In the middle of August, however, Turkey sprang into the headlines again with—"Greek Offensive Resumed," and next day Fanny and the Doctor read the words—to them so ominous—"New Advance on Angora. Turks Leaving." This communiqué for the first time mentioned the Sakarya River, and added—"There is no longer any doubt that the Nationalist Civil Government is removing to Kaisarieh"; it further stated that Mustafa Kemal was retiring, "as he appears to be unable or unwilling to make a stand."

"Oh Lord!" Dr. Pierce exclaimed with a groan, dropping the paper on the grass beside his garden chair. "This looks very bad. The Government going to Kayseri!—that's miles away. They must feel that the game is up."

Fanny was silent. She was thinking of Féridé, and of what all this must mean to her—the unknown, grown-up Féridé, whom she nevertheless felt that she knew so well. A few days later, on August the 20th, she and Dr. Pierce read that the Greeks were now only fifty miles from Angora. "Oh blast!" Fanny exclaimed—then, sitting safe and quiet in that English garden, in the tranquil misty sunshine of late summer, she threw up her yellow head defiantly.

"Whatever the Government does, I bet Féridé doesn't run away, if she *is* in Angora," she said.

Fanny was quite right; Féridé did not leave. She watched her neighbours, with agitated haste, climb into the little black wickerwork waggonettes with flowers painted on both ends, piled high with bundles and bedding, and clatter off down the street and out under the great gateway, bound for Amasia, the town inland from Samsun on the Black Sea where Kemal Pasha had had his first Anatolian Headquarters in 1919. Among them were Güli Hanim and Faik, Nilüfer's landlord; they came up to say goodbye, and eyed the two young women curiously. "You do not go?" "No, we do not go," Nilüfer replied. She and Féridé knew much better than their neighbours what that journey involved, and Nilüfer, whose baby was due in three months, was hardly fit to undertake it, in the conditions which a refugee exodus would certainly create. Besides neither of them wanted to leave the house to which their husbands would return—if they did return; nor had they been bidden by those same husbands to go.

Being in Ankara had one immense asset for Féridé, who was always avid for news; the Red Crescent, which was the single source of fairly reliable information, still functioned there. It had moved from its old and quite inadequate headquarters, that very small room in the Zinçirli Kami Sokak, to the Hadji Moussa quarter, where it occupied the lower part of a fair-sized house; just opposite, in a courtyard shaded by a tree which leaned out into the street a regular dispensary occupied a second house—the workers and a couple of doctors slept there. The Red Crescent, almost an embryo a few weeks before, was growing rapidly under the pressure of circumstances. The Hadji Moussa quarter was a good deal further away, but on the other hand M. Eşref by now knew her well enough to tell her the truth at once, without any perambulations.

She soon found yet another reason for staying where she was for as long as possible. As the fighting increased in intensity and the front drew slowly nearer to Ankara, the flow of wounded into the city became a flood. The old houses up in the citadel shook all day long with the vibrations of gunfire, now barely fifty miles away; at an extra loud explosion the storks, alarmed, rose from their nests on the chimneys and housetops, and soared slowly up into the blue, on black-and-white wings. And night after night little Étamine returned, tired out, with miserable accounts of men in the hospital calling for water, for food, for help in their pain, in those overcrowded wards. At last Féridé could bear it no longer, and took the resolution to go and nurse herself.

It was not altogether easy to her to do this. It is true that her family background had given her a certain independence of outlook and indifference to the opinion of other people; on the other hand her upbringing had been rigidly conventional, the Pasha being what he was.

To go and nurse strange soldiers with one's face unveiled (for obviously one could not nurse in a çarşaf) meant throwing aside the tradition of centuries—centuries during which the Turkish conception of personal modesty had become inextricably entwined with the idea of the veiled face. Even the hardy Anatolian peasant women went veiled in their villages, whatever they might do at work in the fields. Féridé had to work the thing out for herself, and by herself; it would have been no good discussing it with Nilüfer. She had disliked at first that aspect of the dinner-parties at Mustafa Kemal's; but if she had shown her face to strange men there, surely it was far more important, more right, to go and nurse the sick and wounded without a veil? In the middle of her secret arguments she remembered that Fanny had been a nurse during the War—and scrubbed floors! This idea brought a curious comfort; she made up her mind, told poor Nilüfer, was patient with her remonstrances, and went down with Étamine to nurse.

As August drew near its close the situation in Ankara became more alarming than ever. By day there was the bumping roar of artillery filling the hot air, rattling the windows, and disturbing the storks; at night, behind the ridge of hills to the west, the sky was red with the glare of burning villages, where the homes of harmless peasants were going up in flames—sitting by the open windows that looked out over the citadel wall, after supper, rolling bandages, the two girls watched the angry flares with dismay. More and more people left; the neighbours who remained observed the movements of the wives of Ahmet Bey and Orhan Bey closely and curiously—their husbands were important men, they should be well-informed; their actions might give a useful clue. Nilüfer and Féridé found this scrutiny very oppressive, but they hid their despair—Féridé, at any rate, was almost in despair—and put on a cheerful manner to go about their daily tasks. Rather to her surprise, Féridé found the nursing absorbingly interesting. Unlike Fanny she was never put to scrub floors—the palliasses on which the Turkish wounded lay were so close together that there was hardly room to walk between them, let alone to scrub; but all day she was lifting, washing, emptying, carrying, and very soon changing dressings and bandaging too. It opened an entirely new form of activity to her, and hard as the work was, she loved it, in spite of the heat, and the really overpowering smell. The medical side enthralled her, and quite overcame any dismay that she had felt at first at the sight of blood and pus; for the first time in her life she experienced, with a strange pleasure, the thrill of scientific knowledge.

.   .   .   .   .   .

On a day towards the end of the month Fanny read in England—"March on Angora. Greeks follow up Victory"; the communiqué ended with the words:—"No further resistance is expected. Angora will probably be occupied in a couple of days." She took the paper out to Dr. Pierce in the garden, and handed it to him in silence—then, completely miserable, she went indoors.

. . . .

Ankara, that same night, was full of rumours—the Greeks were advancing, the capital would soon be occupied. Féridé heard them in the hospital, which was a great centre for rumours, with fresh wounded coming in all the time, and the Red Crescent orderlies going to and fro. She went home to supper, sat and rolled bandages for a while, and then put Nilüfer to bed—one could almost undress now without lights by the glare in the sky from the burning villages away to the west. But when Nilüfer was tucked up, and she sat alone by the window watching that terrible red horizon, she felt suddenly that she must know the facts —the worst. And the only place where she could learn that was the Red Crescent. She put on her çarşaf and ran downstairs. In the courtyard she paused. She did not want to go out by her own door: it was early still, and her neighbours would be keeping up their ceaseless spying on her movements from behind their pierced shutters—they would notice a nocturnal sortie. But the fourth wall of the courtyard was formed by Sitaré Hanim's own house—all the windows on that side were open to let in air, and by placing a wooden box from the storeroom under one of the lower ones it would be easy to climb in. She did this, and tiptoed out of the room which she had entered like a burglar into a long passage, which led to the main entrance. By the door stood the row of wooden shelves on which the inmates left their indoor slippers when they went out into the street, their street shoes when they returned to the house; to wear the same footgear indoors and out was to Turks an inconceivable form of dirtiness. Slipping out, unnoticed, through Sitaré's front door, Féridé made her way down to the Hadji Moussa quarter, through lanes and alleys lit, like Nilüfer's bedroom, by that sinister glare in the western sky.

In the Red Crescent office M. Eşref, poor man, was still at his desk.

"How does it go?" Féridé asked.

"We are still holding," the weary official said, putting down his pen, "but for how long, Allah alone knows. It is truly frightful, Féridé Hanim; the losses are ghastly, theirs as well as ours. And they have such a superiority in ammunition."

In spite of her own anxiety, Féridé felt full of pity for the sad little man. "Eşref Effendi, we are bound to win!" she said with conviction. "The Greeks have no commander like Kemal Pasha."

"No, and no women like ours! As to water, I hear that they lack it far more than our troops; the prisoners say so. What our women are doing!—right up into the front line, under fire, bringing water to the men; water and cartridges."

When she returned to the citadel, Féridé again slipped in through Sitaré Hanim's door; as she passed along the broad central passage she heard a low murmur of voices coming from a room on her right—the door was ajar, and peeping round it she saw a strange sight. Seven or eight women, all closely veiled, sat round on the divans like black nuns, praying. Much moved, she drew back, and listened for a moment to the low intercessory murmur. They were praying to the One True God—for succour, for their threatened country, for the safety of their men. Tears in her eyes, Féridé went on along the passage, dropped out through the window into the courtyard again, removed the tell-tale box, and returned to her own house.

Down at the yali, the news from Anatolia was followed even more anxiously than in the Cotswolds. For the moment the Pasha had rather changed his tune about Mustafa Kemal. The Greeks were now the one enemy, and the man who might conceivably beat them deserved approval. The Pasha went into the Club every evening to hear the latest news; before that, he waited impatiently in his study for Osman with the afternoon paper. On his return from the Club he always went up to the salon, where Réfiyé Hanim sat in her corner beside the unshuttered windows, wide open to let in the evening breezes off the Bosphorus after the heat of the day, and usually with Mdlle Marthe. Loneliness and anxiety had drawn these three people, whose thoughts and love were mainly centred on the same two persons, Féridé and Ahmet, very close together; and though the Frenchwoman rose courteously at the entrance of the master of the house, she did not even go through the motions of taking her departure any more, as she had used in the past.

On the evening of August the 25th the Pasha came up in a state of high indignation. After greeting his Mother and enquiring after her health as usual—"Imagine," he said, "the impertinence of these foreign newspaper-men! They have gone so far as to suggest that we have sent agents to Europe to ask for mediation!"

"That is not true?" Réfiyé Hanim asked.

"Naturally it is not true. A *démenti* has been issued to say so."

"By whom, my son?"

The Pasha hemmed a little.

"Actually, by the Anatolian Agency, the news bureau in Ankara. But it is official, of course." He hemmed again. "I fear that Salih Pasha has been indiscreet; he is quoted as having asked for mediation."

"He is an envoy of the Sultan, is it not so?" Réfiyé Hanim asked, with a non-committal blankness of expression.

The Pasha hemmed once more.

"Yes—that is so. But—well, it is a little complicated, but the resistance to these unspeakable Greek infidels is, after all, being furnished from Ankara, and—in fact, no one but those in command there can sue for peace on our behalf."

Réfiyé Hanim slid over this awkward point.

"Did you learn at all how things are going up there?" she enquired.

The Pasha hesitated; the old woman watched his face anxiously. At last—

"There is talk of evacuating Ankara, Ané," he said, unhappily.

"The Government or the population?" (Neither she nor the Pasha appeared to notice her use of the word "government" for the rebel Kemalists.)

"It is said that the Cabinet is going, but nothing is known definitely. But of the civil population, large numbers have undoubtedly gone." He paused, and then said slowly—

"We must hope that our children have left—the Greeks are now only about 80 kilometres from Ankara."

"Juste ciel! But that is not much more than two days' march away!" exclaimed Mdlle Marthe, who remembered the German campaign in France in 1870.

Réfiyé Hanim sat silent; her fine old hands, the colour of old ivory and veined with blue, trembled slightly on her lap. Then, like Fanny a few days before, she lifted her head and said—"I do not believe that Féridé will leave."

"I could wish that she might," Féridé's father said.

"No, my son. Think of Nilüfer! She is in no state to undertake a journey. Remember what they endured on the way to Ankara—those hans! Did you learn any news of Ahmet, or of Orhan?" she pursued.

"No, nothing. Ahmet was on Ismet Pasha's Staff—now that Kemal Pasha is acting as Commander-in-Chief, presumably he is one of his staff officers, as he was before, you remember. As for Orhan, I see no reason for him to go to the front at all; he works in Kemal Pasha's private bureau, I understand, so presumably he will have remained in Ankara."

"In that case, we can be quite certain that Féridé will *not* leave," said Réfiyé Hanim with finality.

But that night when she went to bed in her beautiful spacious room, opening on the cool currents of the Bosphorus, she too prayed, as the women had done in that stifling enclosed apartment in the citadel at

Ankara, for her country's preservation, and for the safety of those she loved.

. . . .

In England, towards the end of that August, a certain impatience, tinged with disquiet, began to manifest itself. After that cheerful statement in *The Times* about the "March on Angora" everyone expected the capital to fall promptly. Well, the Greeks were all right, and Venizelos was a fine man, of whom Mr. Lloyd George thought very highly, it was said. But instead of Angora falling, a note of uncertainty again began to creep into the communiqués. "Another battle on Greek front," said that of August 27th; "Turks making a stand" two days later; and on the 30th—"Turks holding on." What did it mean? *How* were they holding on? The British public was thoroughly puzzled.

They held on another ten days; that saved them. The Greek army had shot its bolt; the exhausted troops could maintain a certain pressure, but could not make a fresh attack in sufficient strength to force an issue. Mustafa Kemal's withdrawal to the Sakarya, so alarming and unpopular at the time, paid an immense dividend: that extra 70 miles of Greek communications, perpetually raided from the hills, just tipped the scale. Few men would have taken the risk, for what he risked was his capital; but he won his gamble—a proper soldier's gamble, when all is said.

But even the most gallant gamblers endure acute anxiety, and Kemal was no exception. He had broken a rib in a fall from his horse some time before, and was in constant pain—a sympathetic nervous reaction affected one leg, and made him limp; in spite of this, for hours each day he was out and walking about, watching the course of the battle through field-glasses from the top of some rocky hillock, where the stones burned the incautious hand that touched them, or down among his men, chattering with them, cheering them on, greeting the women and girls who staggered up to the lines with water and ammunition. The nights he spent in his rough Headquarters in the village of Ala Geuz, but not in sleep. Except for a few hours before sunrise he passed them pacing restlessly up and down the room, studying maps, moving flags, bending over diagrams with his Commanders, listening to reports, giving orders, drinking endless cups of coffee, half-smoking and stubbing out innumerable cigarettes. The last nights, during the lull, were the most agonizing, for the Turks, too, could just hold on, but no more, and not indefinitely. Worriedly Orhan watched his chief's face grow greyer and greyer, noted his savage swearing at everyone and everything, always with him a sign of anxiety, of doubt. For this was a situation in which his penetration, his courage, his energy could not do it all—his personality and his dynamism were in fact holding his men to their positions day after day, but no amount of dynamism could hold them so for ever. If the Greeks used this lull to re-form and attack again, he was done, and his country with him.

And then, very early in the morning on September the 9th, in that chill hour before daybreak when human vitality is at its lowest ebb, word came in to the bare dirty room, full of smoke and littered with cigarette-ends, that the Greeks were not re-forming, but were preparing for a general retreat. Orhan heard the sort of snarling shout of triumph with which Kemal greeted the news, and the change which came over his face—its very colour seemed to alter. At once all uncertainty was gone; with his old rapidity of decision he gave his orders for an immediate counterattack. Then he shouted for coffee—and when it came, instead of swearing at the men who brought it, he laughed and clapped them on the back, with a coarse friendly joke.

The Greeks resisted stoutly for two days, but Kemal with his usual deadly penetration in tactics brought his chief pressure to bear at a point which threatened their line of retreat. It was a dangerous threat, and poor King Constantine was not a man to take great risks; he was neither the soldier nor the gambler that his adversary was—as that adversary with his sixth sense about people well realised. Commanders in the field often do seem to get a curious mental or psychological intimacy with their opponents, merely from fighting them, and watching their military actions and dispositions, and Kemal had sized Constantine up very correctly. On the evening of September the 11th the whole Greek army began to retire westwards from the Sakarya, down the open marshy valley of the Porsuk; they retired in good order, slowly followed by the weary Turkish troops, but it was a fearful place in which to be caught by bullets—wholly without cover. Greek bones still lie there, white under the sky. A few days later the two armies had settled down again beside the Eski-şehir railway, in practically the same positions which they had occupied just over a month before. Neither of the two Greek objectives, to capture Ankara and to destroy the Turkish army, had succeeded—and for the attacker, failure spelt defeat.

.   .   .   .

On the morning of September the 13th Fanny was upstairs in her little diamond-paned bedroom at the cottage, packing for their return to Oxford. Actually for once she was not thinking about Féridé and the struggle in Anatolia. During the last week the headlines had all seemed to point to a foregone conclusion: "Fierce fight for Angora," "Fate of Angora," "Struggle for Angora," "Before Angora" and she had rather given that up in despair—the Kemalists were obviously doomed, and Féridé would be involved in the wretchedness of their defeat; she could not bear to think about it, and tried to put it out of her mind. No, she was thinking about Alec, who had left yesterday to return to Istanbul —or rather about herself and Alec. Fanny was a person who tried very hard to be honest with herself, at a time when private honesty about one's feelings was not so fashionable as it has since become, and she was asking herself now, as she stuffed her stockings into corners and folded her dresses, just why she had refused Alec again two days ago. She did like him, *very* much; she trusted him, one would be safe with him— moreover he stirred her. And yet—somehow she could not bring herself to the point of agreeing to become his wife; some part of her was not satisfied. It was more than that—something in her seemed to protest against something in him, and she was trying to get clear as to what that was. Curiously, when she did so she found her mind coming back, again and again, to his attitude towards Turkey, and towards her friends there. He had called the yali, to her a lost paradise, "all right." But that seemed so silly, in a way; she was English, she would have to live in England—or at least in Scotland; why worry about what one's husband thought about people so far away, whom she would probably never see again? "No!" she said to herself then—"no, I must go back some time; I promised." And there are some things, she thought, that people who are married *must* see in the same way, see together—or nothing is any good.

She lifted three more dresses down from where they hung on the end of the old press—it was too low even for her short ones inside it—threw them on the bed, took out the hangers, and made a neat layer of the pretty stuffed things across her case. Taking up one of the frocks to fold it, she found herself humming the tune of the Falcon Song. And with a rush of memory there came back to her a recollection of the day she heard it first, in the salon at the yali, with Ahmet at the piano, Féridé hanging over the instrument, and Réfiyé Hanim in her corner under the wide window. The English girl stood suspended, the dress hanging limply from her hands; a strange chill stole round her heart. What had Réfiyé Hanim said then? Oh, she remembered it all too well —"the heart does not come back."

That was somehow rather frightening. With a little shiver, she forced herself into activity; folded the dress and laid it in the case. And then she heard Dr. Pierce's voice, uplifted below—"Fanny? Are you up there? Come down a minute, child."

Glad of the interruption, she ran down. Dr. Pierce stood in the tiny parlour, *The Times* in his hand. "Look at this!" he said; his face was all aglow. Fanny took the paper he held out, and read:

ANGORA BATTLE ENDED.
GREEKS WITHDRAW.
HEAVY CASUALTIES.

She stood silent for a moment, thinking of what this news would mean—at the yali to the Pasha and still more to Réfiyé Hanim; to Féridé, wherever she was.

"Splendid, isn't it?" said Dr. Pierce.

"Yes, it is. Thank you, Uncle. Goodness, what a mercy! Well, that's that." She paused. "Ahmet always did say that Mustafa Kemal was the goods," said Fanny, handing back the paper—and went upstairs to her packing again.

Chapter Fifteen

THE news reached Ankara first in the form of rumour. Going into her "ward" in the hospital one morning—late, because Nilüfer was unwell again, and she had to finish the ironing that her sister-in-law should have done—Féridé found all the men with loud red handkerchiefs on their heads. "But what is this?" she asked, cheerfully—some charitable merchant had sent a consignment of red handkerchiefs to the hospital for nose-blowing purposes, and she had doled them out herself, one per man, only the day before.

"For the victory!" the men chorused.

"What victory?"

"On the Sakarya. We have won—the Greeks are running away."

Féridé went on with her work at the time, but when she had a chance she asked the chief surgeon, with whom she was by now on good terms, if the news was true? As usual, he was impatient. "Féridé Hanim, how should *I* know? If it is, we shall have fewer cases, and for that I shall praise Allah! But victory or no victory, we must tend the ones we have." He turned away, and Féridé, heavily snubbed, went back to her bandanaed jolly men.

But on her way home she decided to go round by the Red Crescent, and try to find out if there was anything in the tale. It was some distance out of her way, she would be late, Nilüfer would be worrying—she was so nervous always now, quite unlike her old tranquil self—but she *must* know. She sped through the hot narrow lanes on the slope below the citadel, her çarşaf floating out behind with her haste; turned right downhill, turned left, and darted along the familiar street towards the spot where the tree in the dispensary garden showed green over the wall. As she approached she saw that the door of the office stood open— M. Eşref, at the top of the steps that led up to it, was talking eagerly to one or two of the doctors from the dispensary, standing in the street below. She ran up to them.

"Is it true?" she panted out.

"Yes, Féridé Hanim, it is true. The news has just come. But how did *you* hear?"

"In the hospital." She told about the red bandanas, and the men all laughed, with the ready laughter of overwhelming relief.

"They are really in retreat?" she pursued; "it is victory?"

"Their whole line is withdrawing, and our men are in pursuit," M. Eşref said.

"Oh, may Allah be praised!" the girl said fervently. "I thank you." She hurried home.

On that night and on the two or three succeeding ones the mutter of guns grew fainter and fainter, receding into the distance, till finally it died away altogether; sitting at the window, after supper, Féridé and Nilüfer heard instead the singing and shouting of the triumphant populace coming up from the streets below, and saw the sky behind the Etlik Bagh, the vine-clad ridge of hills beyond which lay Sakarya, no longer red with the glare of burning villages, but calm with stars. The burning was still going on—the Greeks left a trail of devastation behind them—but it was now far away, too far to light the sky.

.   .   .   .

When Kemal Pasha returned from the front Orhan came with him— and also, to Féridé's infinite relief, Temel, the batman, who at once resumed the heavier household tasks. Féridé was at the hospital when Orhan arrived, and Nilüfer, who had taken to bolting the great door of the courtyard when she was alone in the house, kept him waiting while she got up from resting on her bed, and dressed herself to go and open the door; by the time she reached it the impatient young man was in a fever of anxiety. When she apologised to him—"But why do *you* have to open the door?" he asked.

"Who else is there? Fatma and Kezban are both at the front," she said simply; and he realised at last on what terms his household had been carried on during his absence. He was rather aghast to learn that Féridé was nursing, and sent Temel to the hospital to fetch her home. That night when they were alone—"My Life, this has been hard for you," he said. "I did not realise *how* hard. You have equalled the labours of those women at the front! But I think you should cease this nursing. You are tired—you are *thin*," he said, looking at her with concern.

"I am in good health, my husband, by the goodness of God," Féridé said—and suddenly remembering her grandmother, on whose lips that phrase so often was, she most unwontedly burst into tears. "Oh, sometimes I do so wish for Niné!" she explained to Orhan, when with distracted tenderness he consoled her. "It is nothing—that is all. I am not really tired. Do not think of it." But she stopped nursing.

.   .   .   .

At the yali the news of the victory of Sakarya was received by the Pasha with unconcealed triumph. However loyal one might be to the Sultan, the Greeks were the Greeks, the ancient enemy, and Mustafa Kemal had beaten them. "He is a good general—this one must say of him," he told Réfiyé Hanim and Mdlle Marthe, sitting in the salon in his fez, his legs as usual stuck out in front of him.

"My son, in my opinion we may thank God for him," said the old lady solemnly. "But tell me—does this victory mean peace, real Peace? Could our children now come home?"

"Ah, I fear not that, Ané. The Greeks are thrown back, but they are still in the country; they hold Ismir. There can be no peace till they are gone, the last man of them!" he said with energy. "And the Entente forces from here, also," he added.

The old lady sighed. "I hope peace comes soon," she said, half to herself. It was eighteen months now since Féridé had gone away, and in all her nearly ninety years of life, never had any eighteen months seemed so long as these, without her treasure, her darling. Old Marthe glanced at her with sympathy; she could read her thoughts. Réfiyé Hanim desired above all things to see her grandchild once more before she closed her eyes on this world.

"Féridé, at least, might come down on a visit, I suppose," the French-woman said.

"Impossible!" the Pasha said brusquely. "The Greeks are still astride the railway near Eski-şehir—indeed, I believe they have torn up much of the line. And my good Mdlle Marthe, you would not wish my daughter to repeat this journey by Incbolu, I imagine? No, we must have patience. Peace will come in time." And he rose, bowed over his mother's hand, and stalked away to the selamlik on his long scissor-like legs. Did he, too, not wish to see Féridé again? he thought as he went. But one must not be unreasonable, as women so often were.

.　　.　　.　　.　　.　　.　　.

On September the 19th the Assembly met in Ankara, and the deputies, once more enthusiastic, conferred on Mustafa Kemal, by acclamation, the titles of Marshal and Ghazi—"the Victorious." The Turks like resounding names, and if anything could have added to the public rejoicing and excitement, it was this. "The Ghazi!"—so they call him still, and always with an exclamation-mark in the voice. Orhan of course was in the Chamber, and heard it all; in the evening he came rushing up to the citadel and described the scene to Féridé and Nilüfer—how the black cloth which had draped the Presidential desk on the curved tribune ever since the Greeks captured Broussa over a year before had been solemnly removed, and of the emotion visible, for once, even on the leader's stone-hewn face. Small wonder. The man whom the Sultan's Government had cashiered from the Army with ignominy two years before was now raised to the highest known military rank, that of Marshal.

"I must go and change a little—I dine with him," Orhan exclaimed at length. Féridé, unable to contain her excitement, ran out into the street, where people were greeting and embracing one another, and mouthing the new title:—"Ghazi! The Ghazi!" Ibrahim and Sitaré Hanim were there, laughing and weeping at once, along with all the neighbours; the rejoicings went on till late into the night—as for Orhan, day was breaking by the time he got home, after one of Kemal's rowdier and more prolonged parties.

But even before the rejoicings were over, Kemal settled down at once to the next task. Ankara and the Turkish army were saved—by the skin of their teeth—but the Greek forces were still more or less intact, Greeks held a large block of Turkish soil; there could be no security, no lasting peace till, as the Pasha had told Réfiyé Hanim, the last man of them was thrown out. Kemal's own army, crippled by their recent efforts, must be reorganised throughout; fresh supplies must be arranged, more men must be raised—above all, they must have more heavy guns, and those essential bayonets must be produced somehow. [This in a blockaded country, without any home steel production to mention.]

Here the well-known realism of the French came to his assistance. That shrewd nation was quick—quicker than any of the other Entente Powers—to read the lesson of the Sakarya. M. Franklin-Bouillon, a former Minister, plausible and skilful, promptly turned up in Ankara to negotiate a treaty with the newly-victorious régime, and signed it exactly a month after Kemal Pasha was made a Marshal. The state of war between France and Turkey was brought to an end—incidentally without a with-your-leave or a by-your-leave to the Sultan's Government at Istanbul—and the French undertook to evacuate Cilicia, down in the south, which released nearly 80,000 Turkish troops from the Syrian front for use against the Greeks; the French also handed over equipment for 40,000 men, and agreed to sell the Turks a few big guns and some aeroplanes. It was a signal diplomatic triumph—and not least because it represented the first breach in the united front of the Entente Powers against the rebellious and successful Kemalist Turkey. Orhan went about effervescing with glee for days. "Now we have only *one* front to concern ourselves with," he told Féridé triumphantly.

There, then, were the extra men, 80,000 of them. The problem of the heavy guns and the bayonets was solved by means so drastic as to be almost sublime. On their retreat from the Sakarya the Greeks had blown up, or torn up, a considerable stretch of line between Eski-şehir and An-kara. This was a section of the Taurus Railway from Istanbul, a con-tinuation of that blue line of rails which ran glittering along the valley, past the station at Ankara with its six paraffin lamps. If the Greeks could be dislodged from it and the damaged sections repaired, the principal life-line for supplies to the new capital would be open again. But no attempt was made to repair it. No—here, in those bent rails flung in all directions, was steel, good hard steel, quite suitable for forging and hammering into bayonets, and still more for making rammers for can-non. A fair number of pieces of artillery had been captured from the Greeks, others seized earlier in raids on the Allied arms dumps; but most had been temporarily put out of commission when their former owners either removed the breech-blocks or, more usually, carried off the rammers by means of which the shells were pushed home far enough to engage with the rifling and leave the correct space for the one, two, or three bags of lyddite or cordite which formed the charge. For in World War One fixed ammunition, shell and charge combined in one unit, hardly existed, even for the smaller calibres.

Where the breech-block had been removed there was nothing to be done; ordinary smiths were quite incapable of making new ones with sufficient precision. But steel rails were eminently suited to being cut into lengths, rounded to give a comfortable grip to the hands of a gun-crew, and having a flattened end hammered down to fit the diameter of a gun-chamber. So now the forges in Anatolia rang and resounded night and day, making the long rammers to bring the big guns into commission again, and forging wicked bright bayonets for the close fighting beloved of the Turks. The smiths laughed and shouted over their work—"*This* for a Greek, and *this* for a Greek," they cried, as they hammered away.

Kemal next flung himself into the task of military reorganization and supply, working like a demon, and driving his already over-driven peo-ple harder still. A week before the signature of the Franklin-Bouillon *Accord*, as it was called, the Treaty of Kars had been signed with the Russians, which finally settled all problems on the eastern frontiers; and now the Bolsheviks began shipping arms and ammunition to the Anatolian ports along the Black Sea in a big way. Once more those long files of women trudged over the Kuré Dagh, bending under their loads, to Seydiler Köy; once more the convoys of cagnés toiled slowly across the plateau to Ankara and beyond. Féridé had hoped that now Kezban and Fatma would return—for Nilüfer could do less and less, as her confinement approached, and Orhan's presence in the house made a lot of extra work. But not a bit of it; they and all the other able-bodied women were plying to and fro behind the front, bringing up supplies and ammunition, working almost as hard as during the battle of Sakarya itself.

In the great "Discourse," lasting six whole days, which Mustafa Kemal pronounced to his listening people in October 1927, he used these words about this particular phase of his country's struggle for independence:

"You understand perfectly well that whoever says 'War,' speaks of a struggle, not merely between two armies, but between two nations, who risk their whole existence and throw in all their resources, all their goods, all their material and moral strength. It was therefore my duty at that time to bring the entire Turkish nation into the war, physically and morally, just as much as the army at the front. Not only those who stood face to face with the enemy, but every individual—in the village, in the home, or tilling the fields—had to recognise himself as being invested with a mission equal in importance to that of the actual combatants, and to dedicate himself wholly to the struggle. . . . This was the aim which we worked to realise."

But this early demonstration of "Total War," though possible and even stimulating for the robust, was very hard on the fragile or sickly. "Woe unto them that are with child, and to them that give suck in those days." That time of stress bore hardly on Nilüfer. By the second half of October, when M. Franklin-Bouillon was signing his treaty, and Orhan was fizzing with jubilation, the cold was already beginning to creep into the old house again; the evenings drew in, the shortage of paraffin was worse than ever, and if Nilüfer—as she mostly did—felt too unwell and exhausted to remain in the draughty sitting-room after supper, she had to lie in bed in the dark, since her brother-in-law needed the one lamp or candle for his work; he fidgeted about impatiently while Féridé carried it off to put the poor creature to bed. Ahmet was away, training the regiments newly recalled from Syria, and amalgamating them with the seasoned troops who had fought in the battles of Inonü and Sakarya. Now and again he dashed home on two or three days' leave, and of course stayed in the house on the city wall; friends came in to see him, and Féridé had to cook more diligently than ever in her uncouth cavern of a kitchen—there was no longer any question of Nilüfer doing anything at all. Temel chopped the wood and drew the water—really life was very biblical in Ankara then—and fetched the charcoal and swept the yard and the downstairs rooms; when Orhan did not need him he also went with his young mistress to carry things home from the market, but if he was not available Féridé had to drag food for five people up the hill herself, unless she could get hold of Étamine, who had been released from her hospital work when more nurses and orderlies returned from the front.

Faik and Güli had returned from Amasya, a little shamefacedly; the thorny Rose, who had become possessively fond of her Nilüfer Hanim, wanted her to go back to her own house, but Féridé would not hear of it, and Ahmet, on one of his brief visits, put his foot down absolutely in the matter. This was as well, for Güli and Féridé could never really get on together, both had too much spirit and temper; and the younger woman, a stranger, had some trouble in resisting the wishes of the tough Ankarian house-wife. As for Nilüfer, she wished to stay with Féridé, but was too gentle and irresolute, in her enfeebled condition, to say so firmly to her kind masterful landlady. Orhan, absorbed in national affairs, and like everyone else round Kemal Pasha cruelly over-pressed, could not be bothered with such matters. "Oh, Light of my Eyes, send the woman to perdition!" he exclaimed, when Féridé sought his advice—a sentiment which thousands of husbands have expressed in their time, though perhaps less picturesquely. So Güli Hanim, sulky but resigned, at least made herself useful by coming sometimes to sit with Nilüfer when Féridé was in the kitchen or at the market.

Sometimes, but not always—and it so happened that on the day when she was most needed she was not there. Nor was Temel. Orhan had asked one or two friends in to dinner, and Féridé, who had secured a turkey from the man who came round with poultry, had gone down to the market to buy the best she could in the way of salads, vegetables, and fruit. The luscious honey-sweet little "pears of Ankara," with their thin brown skins, renowned throughout Turkey, were in season; but the fruit-seller who usually brought them to the door had only had indifferent ones, so she wanted to find better. And olives and late aubergines (to be roasted on charcoal till the burnt flavour penetrated through the skin into the pale greenish flesh, which was then scraped off and used as a foundation for the rest of the salad) and the last of the tomatoes. She climbed up the hill, a basket on each arm, pleased with her purchases, looking forward to cooking a dinner which would do Orhan credit in the eyes of his friends, and earn her his praise; putting her baskets down in the kitchen, as always she ran into the house to give a word and a kiss to her sister-in-law, calling "Nilüfer, chérie, ça va?" as she went.

To her surprise there was no reply. Nilüfer was not in her usual place, under the window in the sitting-room, nor in the hall. A little disturbed, Féridé ran upstairs to the bedroom; as she reached the top she heard moans coming through the half-open door. She went in—Nilüfer was lying on her bed, clutching one of the hard bolster-like cushions off the window-seat; as Féridé spoke to her a pain came on—she turned greenish, her face contorted itself, and sweat sprang out on her forehead. Féridé waited till the pain had passed, and she saw Nilüfer's hands relax and the agonised expression leave her face. "Dji-djim, can this be *it?*" she asked then, in surprise. "But it is only the seventh, and you said the fifteenth!"

"It must be it—never have I felt such pain!" Nilüfer said. "Oh, I thought you would never come!"

"Dearest, I did not know. But we must get the doctor and the mid-wife, quickly. Will you be all right for two instants, while I go to send Étamine for them?"

"Oh, here it is again!" was all Nilüfer's reply, as another pain came on, and she clutched the cushion to her as before.

Féridé was terrified, and for a minute stood undecided. She had no knowledge whatever of childbirth, and was afraid the baby might arrive at any moment; but if it did, she herself could be of no use. Oh, why was Temel not here, today of all days? With a last frightened glance at the bed, she turned and flew downstairs, and round to her landlady's.

"Sitaré Hanim, my sister is in labour! Is Étamine here? Could she go for the doctor and the mid-wife?"

Étamine was there, and after memorising the names and addresses aloud, she sped off on her errand.

"Oh, that is kind," Féridé said as the child departed. "But I wish we had some other messenger also. I must get word somehow to my husband —he was bringing friends to dinner, and he must put them off."

"As to that, I can cook your dinner, and serve it too, at a time like this," said Sitaré Hanim cheerfully. "Do not disturb Orhan Bey, Féridé Hanim—let his friends come, and enjoy their food! Maybe a man-child will be born while they eat—a child to serve his country!—and they will rejoice. Do you but show me now what is to be cooked, and I will prepare it." She snatched up an apron as she spoke. "For what hour?"

"Eight—he said eight," said Féridé distractedly. "But Sitaré Hanim, I cannot come to the kitchen now—I must return to be with Nilüfer Hanim—I cannot leave her. The child might be born!"

Sitaré, good creature, was putting on her çarşaf to pass the twenty yards through the street; as she did so—"When did the pains begin?" she asked practically.

"I do not know. She was all right when I left for the market, a little after two."

"Then all is well. Children are not born so fast! Come and show me your dinner; there is time enough. Children have been born before, you know!" said Sitaré blithely. "The first is the worst!—but it is all in the order of nature; there is no cause for alarm."

As they passed out through the street to reach Féridé's courtyard they encountered Güli, and never had the sight of her been so welcome.

"You come in a good hour, Güli Hanim—labour has just begun," said

Sitaré, who was in tremendous spirits over the whole affair, as primitive people are wont to be.

Güli had indeed come in a good hour, for when Étamine returned, after what seemed to Féridé an age, it was to say that the mid-wife had gone off some days before to a big hospital which had been opened in a school near Sivrihissar, behind the front—she had of course forgotten to mention the fact. So Güli took charge. In a rough-and-ready way she was really surprisingly efficient. She tied one of those long towels of Féridé's to the foot of the brass bedstead, and made her patient pull on it when the bearing-down pains came on, to help the birth—an immemorial practice, and a very good one; she made Féridé light the stove and hang the infant's first garments round it to warm, and set her to line the wooden cradle, which she herself had lent, with the soft shawls sent up by Réfiyé Hanim from Istanbul before the Greek advance closed the railway. She sent Étamine down to her own house for old linen—such things as rubber sheeting did not exist in Ankara then— and distracted Sitaré in her culinary operations by insisting on having pots of water kept hot on the stove. Étamine was next despatched to a neighbour for a metal tub in which to bathe the infant when it should emerge into the world. And all the while she kept up a ceaseless flow of exhortation and encouragement to the struggling girl—"Pull, my little love; pull hard! That's my brave one! There!"—wiping Nilüfer's streaming face with a damp cloth, and displaying a tenderness which astonished Féridé in that sharp-tongued, uncompromising person.

The labour was short and violent; there were barely thirty seconds between the recurring pains—which to Féridé, looking on in horrified helplessness, seemed like a series of earthquakes shaking Nilüfer's body. The doctor arrived precisely five minutes before the baby was born; he studied the patient's face, and then took her pulse with a slight air of anxiety, Féridé thought, as she stood a little apart, now and again putting another log into the stove, and turning the little garments that hung round it on chairs. It was dark now; Étamine had been sent off some time before to fetch the one lamp from her mother's house; it cast huge distorted shadows of the doctor's and Güli's forms on the ceiling, as they bent over the bed, doing mysterious things, while Nilüfer's unending moans rose, at last, to a crescendo of shrieks. Quite suddenly the shrieking ceased, and into the silence came the sound of vigorous slappings; after a moment or two a new voice was uplifted, in a loud sharp wail. Another human being had entered the world, and appeared to dislike it from the outset.

"That's my mannikin!" Güli exclaimed triumphantly. "Féridé Hanim, quickly fetch the hot water, I beg of you. Nilüfer Hanim, my darling, you have a son!—a splendid son, to follow his father and his grand-father."

Féridé hastened down to the kitchen for the big pewter pots of hot water; as she returned with them across the courtyard, Orhan and his guests came in by the street-door. Busy as she was, she had not troubled to put on her çarşaf—she carried her jars swiftly into the house, and then called from the door, softly and imperiously—"Orhan! One moment, if you please."

He hurried to her. "What is it, my Life? Is dinner ready?"

"It will be, soon; Sitaré Hanim is preparing it. A son has just been born to Ahmet and Nilüfer—you must excuse me, my husband; I must take these upstairs."

"Well, this is good news! I will tell our guests; they will understand. Is all well?"

"I hope so. Oh Orhan, it has been terrible for her!"

"Ahmet will be happy. What is better than having a son? It is worth some pain in travail. Congratulate our sister for me," Orhan replied airily.

Up in the bedroom, Féridé found the doctor holding Nilüfer's wrist with a worried expression. Güli wiped the baby hurriedly with warm water, bundled it up anyhow in the shawls, without troubling to dress it; then she dumped it in the cradle, and hastened to join him at the bedside. Nilüfer was lying with her eyes closed, her face waxy white. The doctor now made a brief examination—"Yes, it is a bleeding," he said to Güli. "Féridé Hanim, I must have some cold water—the coldest possible—and some cloths. Has your husband any brandy, by chance?"

Actually Orhan had that most unusual thing, a bottle of brandy; Mustafa Kemal had given it to him on their night of celebrations after the victory of Sakarya. "Yes, there is brandy," she said. "Which first, that or the water?"

"The brandy."

She ran to fetch it. It was kept in the dining-room, where Orhan and his friends were now beginning their dinner. Féridé had mislaid her çarşaf in all the hurry and confusion; she opened the door, behind which rose sounds of talk and loud laughter, a little way, and called through it urgently—"Orhan! One moment, I beseech you."

He rose and came to the door. "What is it?"

"I must have the brandy for Nilüfer."

"Is she ill?"

"I do not know—she looks ghastly. But the doctor asks for it."

Excusing himself to his guests, he fetched the bottle, uncorked it, and brought it to the door.

"And a glass, and a spoon," Féridé said, and darted upstairs again. As she entered the room she heard Güli exclaim—"Allah be merciful! She is going!"

"No," the doctor said. "Ah, you have it." He snatched the bottle, poured a little brandy into the spoon, and raising the girl with one hand, tipped the liquid into her mouth. Nilüfer gulped, gasped, coughed, and opened her eyes.

"That is better," the doctor said. "And the cold water?"

Féridé ran downstairs again. Out in the dark yard, where the air was icy under the immense glitter of the autumn stars, she dropped the bucket into the well, and started to haul it up again by the glow of light from the open kitchen door. Sitaré, hearing the echoing splash, came running out.

"What is it? What are you doing there, Féridé Hanim?"

"The doctor wants cold water—very cold," the girl replied.

"But, in Allah's name, then take it from the jars! It is freezing here above, and in the well it is warmer," the practical woman said, moving over to the group of great earthenware vessels, filled by Temel, which stood by the kitchen door, looking for all the world like something out of Ali Baba and the Forty Thieves. As she filled a pewter jug—"What is it? A bleeding?" she asked.

"Yes. Oh Sitaré Hanim, she looks so white and ill," said poor Féridé.

"Ah, she is weakly! Now, I will carry this up for you," said the good soul, who was longing for an excuse to get into the bedroom and see the baby. "The dinner was good, eh?" she chattered on as they went upstairs. "The turkey was *perfect*; a noble bird! And I made my special stuffing, of chestnuts with herbs. And the sauce!—and the salad! Ah, Ibrahim always says I am a witch with salads!"

In the sick-room she handed the can of water to Güli, and hurried to the cradle, where she unwrapped the baby to admire it. "Ah, the little man-child! Oh, what a boy! Listen to his voice!" For the baby, objecting violently to this disturbance, gave vent to a series of cries with lusty vigour.

While Sitaré crowed above the cradle with biblical joy, Féridé stood watching Nilüfer's face as Güli Hanim and the doctor wrung out cloths in the cold water, and applied them to her body She looked entirely peaceful, as if in another world already—but so white and bloodless. The doctor kept grumbling and muttering to himself as he worked: "She should be in hospital; she should have oxygen and strychnine. But we have no hospitals here, nor drugs; nothing!—we live like the animals in this place!" "She should never have had it here—she should have gone to Istanbul in time, and had it there. Ankara is no place for such as her." And the thorny Rose, catching his mutterings, answered angrily that Ankara was a splendid place!—but did not cease her energetic ministrations.

Between them they saved her, though the struggle lasted most of the night. Orhan came tip-toeing to the door several times for news, and Sitaré forced Féridé to go down to the kitchen and partake of some of the turkey and the notable salad. Güli would not think of leaving her patient, and one of Féridé's last tasks was to drag in a mattress and make up a bed on the floor for the faithful Rose.

Nilüfer lived, but she had little strength, and no milk. During the next thirty-six hours Güli again and again put the baby to the breast, where it sucked and tugged with energy, for it was a vigorous little thing—only to let go, after a time, with an angry wail of frustration. Search was made for a foster-mother, but fruitlessly; all the men had been at the war for so long that there were hardly any babies about, and in any case most of the young women were at the front. At last recourse was had to the bottle, in Ankara something almost unknown; the doctor produced a solitary and rather ancient teat through which goat's milk, diluted with water, was administered to the baby. This seemed to be successful. Nilüfer adored the little mite from the outset, and insisted on holding it in the crook of her arm and giving it the bottle herself, weak as she was; she was wretchedly ashamed at being unable to nurse it. Güli and Féridé tried to cheer her up, pointing out how ill she had been; but it was no good. "I am a useless creature," she kept saying; "I was never fit to be his wife."

But after about five weeks, when Nilüfer was at last beginning to get up, and the baby was sometimes brought down to the sitting-room to lie in its cradle near the stove, suddenly it got ill with some form of acute gastritis. Nilüfer, distracted, showed the green slimy motions to Güli Hanim, who said it was nothing, a small disorder—it would pass. But it did not pass. The doctor was sent for and pronounced it to be a form of diarrhoea—which indeed the women could have told him themselves; he ordered dill-water. This did no good; the tiny creature, obviously in pain, roared incessantly. The doctor came again—"Ah, it should have glucose," he said gloomily. But in all Ankara there was no glucose, nor any form of patent baby-food. Féridé felt almost a hatred of such a barbarous place as she watched the baby getting weaker and weaker, and the mother more and more distraught—the sense of utter helplessness was horrible. At her suggestion they tried sugar and boiled water, but nothing was of any use. Obviously the baby had picked up some germ, either from the goats' milk or from that appalling rubber teat. The poor little creature turned now, with a weary wail, from the bottle that had poisoned it; its angry roars of hunger diminished till they became faint whimpers. In a despair past imagining Nilüfer held the tiny thing in her arms night and day, talking to it, *willing* it to live, till Féridé wept to hear her. And then one evening, while the young mother still cradled it in her lap, Güli came in from cooking a meal for her neglected and long-suffering husband in the house below the wall, and went up as usual to peep at the child—after one glance she laid a hand on Nilüfer's shoulder.

"Nilüfer Hanim, my darling, give him to me. He is dead," she said gently.

"He is not! He is not! He is sleeping, that is all," Nilüfer almost shrieked, clutching the child. "Do not disturb him, Güli Hanim; sleep is good for him."

But nothing would ever disturb the baby again.

Chapter Sixteen

AHMET managed to come home on leave when he heard of the baby's death, and did everything he could to console his wife, comforting her with a gentle patience that astonished Féridé. His own grief at the death of his little son was very keen, though mostly he kept it to himself; secretly, almost shyly, he sought out his sister and questioned her endlessly about the child—how had he looked? Whom was he like? When—"Would he have been tall, do you think?" he asked one day, Féridé cried—she could not help it. "Oh, do not cry, my sister," he said, fondling her. "Please God, we shall have another son, when Nilüfer is stronger again. Take care of her—though I cannot thank you enough for what you have done for her already."

"I wish I could have done more," Féridé said, wiping her eyes. "But really, my brother, it is *not* easy in this place—one cannot even keep warm!" "Except here," she said, with a little laugh—they were talking in the kitchen, where Féridé spent most of her time; she was peeling vegetables, while the young man sat on the table, his uniform and shining boots and spurs looking very out of place among the pots and pans. He laughed too, and for a few minutes they chatted together in the ease and intimacy that is special to brothers and sisters. To Ahmet Féridé could confess what she would never have dreamed of admitting to Orhan, how wearisome she found the cold, the dark, the discomfort of that second winter, with all the charm of novelty long since worn off, and conditions harder than ever, without Kezban to help her.

"Orhan makes me anxious, also," she said. "He is so tired; often too tired even to eat properly! I wish you could persuade him to take a little more rest. Sometimes after supper he falls asleep at the table, over his papers—one night he upset the lamp! But if I speak to him, he only says that the work must be done."

Ahmet had noticed for himself Orhan's drawn expression and red-rimmed eyes, from constantly working in a bad light, his increased restlessness, and bursts of sharp impatience; and that night, when the women had gone to bed, he spoke to him about his health. "Could you not lessen the pressure at all? Or take short leave? I get the impression that you are really quite exhausted."

The young man stretched out his arms with a gigantic yawn.

"Oh Heaven yes!—you are right; there are days when I am almost finished. The worst is when I cannot sleep; that is often the case nowadays." He looked oddly, half-shyly at his brother-in-law for a moment, and then went on—"But here is an extra-ordinary thing: I may be quite worn out, extenuated, but if *he* comes and puts a hand on my shoulder, and says, 'Well done; that is well done!'—all my fatigue seems to leave me; strength returns, I can do anything! And do you know, that lasts for several days." Again he gave Ahmet that side-long look. "Does that sound foolish to you?"

"But, not at all! It has been the same with me, at the front," the young officer said. "And on the men his effect is something quite phenomenal—really it is as if an electric current were passed into them! I have seen them, not once but over and over again, hungry, parched with thirst, and so exhausted with marching that they could hardly lift a rifle to their shoulders: and he has but to come among them, and speak, and especially to turn his eyes on them, and they will hoist on their packs and pass to the attack, or march another twenty kilometres, *singing!*"

"Yes; well, that is how it is with me," Orhan said. "I have heard that it is so with the troops, but then to them he is a legend. He is not a legend to me," he said laughing; "I am practically his valet de chambre! But it is a most extraordinary circumstance. I hardly liked to tell you—I thought you might laugh at me," the young man said candidly. He had an enormous respect for this slightly older brother-in-law of his, with his directness, simplicity, and courage, though intellectually he was much the abler of the two.

"No, I should not think of laughing at you—we all recognise it in the Army, this power of Kemal Pasha's," Ahmet said. "But what it is, and *how* he does what he does to others is a mystery. It puzzles me," he added thoughtfully, "for he is not in the least a man of strict life. You know how he drinks; he swears with such profanity that the men themselves are sometimes shocked by his language; and he does associate sometimes with—well, with rather loose women," said Ahmet, with elegant understatement, and an air of distaste which made Orhan smile. "And you know he can be utterly remorseless, especially to those who oppose him. He is not really at all one's idea of a *good* man." He paused. "And yet we would all die for him," he ended abruptly.

"I know." In spite of his smile, Orhan answered in all seriousness. "He has these defects—I realise them even better than you do. People accuse him of being ambitious, too, and of vanity. Well, he has a sort of simple vanity—like a child's, really, about being well-dressed and so on." He paused, thinking.

"*Is* he ambitious?" Ahmet asked—"I often wonder."

"Personally ambitious, I do not believe he is in the least. For Turkey, for our country, he has ambitions—proper ones: she must be freed from the foreigner, and our people must be given the possibility of developing their energies and talents—an opportunity which has always been denied them up till now by the despotism under which we have lived." He paused again, still considering. "Naturally he sees clearly enough— for he sees everything!—that he can do for our nation what no one else can. Enfin, can you suggest someone to put in his place?" he asked.

"Of course not," Ahmet said. "He has no equal among us."

"Very well—there you are. Then it is not surprising that he sweeps out of his way, annihilates, those who oppose him, blind and ignorant as they usually are! He does that ruthlessly, actually without scruple, I admit. But he is never mean—I do not think he knows what meanness is, any more than he knows what fear is."

"Ah, that! Yes, his courage is fantastic—and of course that is a thing the soldiers worship."

"Yes, my friend—but there have been brave generals before him, who yet could not do what he can do: destroy fatigue, pour new life into an exhausted body, and send half-dead men singing into battle! And you see this happen on the battle-field, in the excitement of combat; but I see it—*feel* it—in cold blood, sitting at a desk, poring over papers! And I tell you that his touch then is like the touch of some heavenly power."

Ahmet stared at his brother-in-law at those words, which were spoken with a strange intensity. "You mean, then," he asked after a moment, "that he *is* really good, after all?"

Orhan shook himself impatiently.

"My dear Ahmet! Good—bad—what do we know of them? He leads a life, often, that men call bad; and he displays qualities, powers, that we associate with holy men—and not with so many of *them!* I cannot read the riddle for you! I know that he has absolute integrity, which is rare; I do not think power will ever go to his head—it has not done so yet, anyhow, and his power now is practically absolute. One cannot over-simplify about such a being. What I know, that I tell you—that when I am three-parts dead, his commendation raises me to life. I ask no more! This seems to me of greater import than keeping the letter of the Koran, or abstaining from alcohol, or pilgrimaging to Mecca! And I will tell you this: he has one sole aim—the welfare of the Turkish people, *our* people."

"I wish I could put things into words as you can," Ahmet said enviously.

"Oh, words! You do things, which is really better. Sometimes I come to hate words—especially on paper," he said, indicating the litter on the table. He swept them together, "Come on—let us go to bed."

. . . .

The long winter came to an end at last, and one evening towards the end of March, when even the keen air of the plateau held a hint of the softness of spring, Orhan came home with the news that the Entente Powers had made proposals for an armistice. Any sign from the outside world that the Ankara Government and Kemal Pasha were recognised as a force to be reckoned with filled all Turks with a triumphant pleasure, and Orhan was jubilant.

"And shall we accept?" Féridé asked.

"Ah, that depends on the terms! We shall see. The Ghazi will do whatever is wisest."

The meeting to discuss the terms took place in Paris; it ended in a deadlock. The Allies proposed that the Greeks should evacuate Asia Minor *after* the armistice. The Greeks, who were fully aware that they had really been abandoned both by America and the Entente Powers, and whose army and nation alike were suffering from the disabling effects of inactivity and suspense, agreed to an armistice, but were silent as to the terms; the Turks refused even to consider one till after the Greeks had left Anatolia. Mustafa Kemal knew as well as any Greek captain in the field what the sense of isolation, the lack of the small comforts like tea, sugar and tobacco—on which soldiers more than all men depend—and the incessant preying and prowling of his own guerillas were doing to the enemy's morale. He could afford to wait, and he waited, forcing his restless ignorant Assembly to wait too. In fact a sort of truce did obtain along the front itself; behind it, one must regretfully admit, the Turks spent the months of May and June in methodically exterminating such Greek settlements in Anatolia as were in reach.

In July the Greek Government made one last desperate attempt to retrieve their wretched situation. They withdrew two divisions from Asia and despatched them to Thrace, where they commanded the European approaches to Istanbul in overwhelming strength; thereupon they demanded from the Entente Powers permission to occupy the city. This astute move did thoroughly disconcert Mustafa Kemal; had it taken place it would probably have reduced his intransigeance and brought him to terms, as well as avoiding the horrors that lay ahead. But the Allies—divided by the French defection, and bored and irritated by everything to do with the Greece of King Constantine—abruptly refused permission, and actually ordered their own Occupation Forces to stand to arms to prevent a Greek entry into the capital. Once again, justice was indubitably a fugitive from the camp of the conquerors.

And now Kemal's long months of patient waiting came to an end. The diversion of the two divisions to Thrace had rendered his forces fully equal to those of the Greeks in Anatolia; thanks to the French and Russians, and to the labours of his smiths on the rails of the Taurus Line, he was better equipped than ever before; in the air, again thanks to the French, he even had a slight superiority. The moment to strike had come, and he struck.

Ankara society, such as it was, was all agog during that last fortnight in August over a big reception which the Ghazi, as they had begun to call him, was giving up at Çankaya on the 26th. It was the first entertainment of the kind to be given in the new capital, and there was much excitement and anticipation. All the deputies were invited, the diplomatic corps—so far represented only by the French and the Russians, who now had envoys of a sort in Ankara—and the journalists, of whom quite a number had already made their way to Anatolia. Very few of these last had actually seen the great Kemal Pasha face to face as yet, and they were gloating over the opportunity. Orhan was in a great fuss over all the arrangements—the drinks, the tables, the flowers; but Féridé thought she noticed a hint of sly amusement, a sparkle of suppressed excitement about him which puzzled her.

"Really, Orhan, will it not be rather dull, after all, this party?" she said. "Who comes? These not very interesting deputies, the men from newspapers, the Frenchmen and Bolsheviks! I cannot imagine why you are so excited over it."

He exploded with laughter.

"Oh, Light of my Eyes, perhaps you are right! Yes, indeed I think it may end by being a *very* dull party—really a flop." And he laughed again, leaving her more puzzled and suspicious than ever.

But on the day itself the party was suddenly put off. No explanation was given, save that owing to unforeseen circumstances the Ghazi was unavoidably prevented from being at Çankaya that day. This of course created a tremendous sensation—to announce a party on such a scale, and then to cancel it—what could it mean? Féridé guessed, when she woke that morning and found a note on her pillow—"My heart's love, I must leave you. Expect me only when you see me. Not a word, even to Nilüfer.—Orhan."

But by the time the public in general learned what it meant, the party had achieved its purpose—of securing an element of complete surprise for the stroke of the Turkish army; most important of all, those inquisitive people the journalists had been kept safely smoking and drinking in Ankara while the battle was set in train.

Mustafa Kemal had in fact gone off in deepest secrecy to the Army Headquarters at Akşehir on the 20th. From there he despatched a fair-sized force to threaten Broussa, so drawing some Greek troops away to the north; a cavalry sweep lured others to the south. Then, at 5:30 A.M., on the very morning of his party, he flung three Army Corps against the enemy's main positions on a fifteen-mile front from behind Eski-şehir southwards to Afion-Karahissar. His immediate staff, including Orhan, left Ankara before dawn in fast cars, and arrived at Headquarters in time to see the opening of the action.

For the first twenty-four hours the fighting was bitter. Behind a tremendous artillery bombardment the Turkish troops surged forward to the attack, over much the same ground as that across which they had been forced to retreat almost exactly a year before—in the same savage heat, the same choking dust, their water and ammunition brought up after them by the same undaunted sun-blackened women. But in other respects this year was very different. The extra guns made a real artillery preparation possible; ammunition was abundant, and numerically the Turks were equal to their foes. Above all, this time they had bayonets.

The Greeks, in their desperation, fought well; savagely even. The rumour had long run among their unhappy ranks that they would have to leave Anatolia anyhow, win or lose; but their age-long hatred for the Turk made them determined to sell their lives and their positions as dearly as possible; there were even some quite fierce small-scale counter-attacks. And in one of these Ahmet was involved.

He was on Ismet Pasha's Staff, and should not properly have been in the fighting-line at all; but about noon, from the rocky hill-top of Kocatepé, where Fevzi, Ismet, and Mustafa Kemal in his riding-breeches and high boots, a cigarette between his fingers, were directing operations, the three Commanders saw that one Turkish group was in danger of being overcome. The ground here was very broken, all hills and ridges, from which the Turks were emerging and pushing the Greeks back onto the rather lower and more level ground near the road; the threatened position was on a low crest near the entrance of a gully up which supplies from the rear were coming all the time by a side track. A Greek battery had got its range and was shelling it, while some Greek machine-gunners had worked their way into a situation on another crest from which they were pouring a stream of bullets onto the defenders; in front, in a dry stream-bed, a concentration of enemy infantry was evidently preparing to rush the position.

"You must get some more men up there," Kemal said brusquely to Fevzi Pasha. "We mustn't lose command of that gully. And put some guns onto that battery." He went on peering through his powerful field-glasses. "I don't see any officers; you had better send someone to take over—that will stiffen them. There's no time to lose."

Fevzi was already giving rapid orders about batteries and a shift of men; at this last command of his leader's he said, rather gloomily—"We have not so many officers to spare; I do not know where to lay my hand on one, at this moment."

"Send a Staff Officer," Kemal snapped. "They can fight too!"

Ahmet, who was standing close behind the three men—Kemal, Fevzi and Ismet—stepped forward and touched Ismet's arm. "Could I not go, Sir? Do you need me here?"

Before Ismet Pasha could answer, Kemal wheeled round.

"Ah, Ahmet! Yes, go my son—go quickly," he added, as he turned his field-glasses onto the small tepé again.

The prudent way to reach the threatened position would have been to come at it from behind, down the gully, where the files of ammunition-carriers were sheltered from everything but shells lobbed over from in front. But Ahmet was in a hurry—had not Kemal said "Go quickly"? He ran back downhill to where the horses belonging to the Headquarters Staff stood in a dismal group, their clever heads drooping in the heat, seized his own charger, a lively chestnut stallion, sprang on its back, and rode off at a gallop. The most direct way to the mouth of the gully lay on a slant across under the hilly ground from which the Turkish troops were pushing out, firing as they went; Greeks on the flatter ground below were firing back at them from their trenches, and when driven out of these, from such cover as they could get. It was the usual rather confused scene of a modern battle field—a haze of dust, puffs of acrid smoke and dark fountains of earth and stones where shells burst, and now and again little figures running, to disappear behind some rocks as one side or the other advanced or retreated, all in the blaze of the noonday light. Now along that rough open space, through the whine of shells and the clatter of machine-gun fire, a horse and rider appeared, galloping headlong.

"Allah's mercy! What is he doing?" Kemal ejaculated—then he turned and thumped Ismet on his frail back. "What a boy you have there! But why does he do such a crazy thing?"

"You told him to hurry, Sir," said Orhan, who was also standing close behind the three Commanders—"And he is going the quickest way." After his long months of working in close contact with Mustafa Kemal, and knowing himself much liked, the young man had given up all the customary Turkish flattery of the great—which in any case was contrary to his nature—and spoke his mind as he chose; he noticed the slight start of surprise which his words produced in Ismet and Fevzi. As for Kemal, he burst into laughter.

"Quite right, my son!—I did," he said, his glasses still to his eyes. "But I did not mean him to kill himself—he is too valuable." All four men stood watching this crazy ride. Miraculously, Ahmet got safely through;

they saw him dismount behind the crest, throw his reins to an ammunition-carrier, and run up to the summit. There he re-formed the disorganised men, and made a charge away to the right to rush the machine-gun posts which had been decimating them. It succeeded; the Greeks broke and fled as the bright bayonets flashed among them in the sun—but some of their machine-gunners fired to the last, and the watchers up on Kocatepé saw a score or more of Turks fall.

A messenger came up at this moment with a report from the commander towards the centre of the front, further north. The Greeks were showing signs of yielding there, in positions which had been strongly fortified for a whole year; could a little more artillery support be given, and a few reserves thrown in? If so, it might be possible to punch a hole in the middle of the enemy line.

This was a major operation, and Kemal bent his whole attention onto the pencilled message. But he lifted his head from the scrawled paper to say to Orhan—"My child, go and find out if Ahmet is all right." "And take a *reasonable* route to that tepé!" he added, with one of his grins which were like a grimace, as he turned to concentrate again on the tactical problem.

As Ahmet had done shortly before, Orhan ran down the rocky rearward slope of Kocatepé, seized his horse, and galloped off towards the scene of the small action in which his brother-in-law had been so unexpectedly engaged; but unlike Ahmet he made the rational detour through the broken ground behind the actual firing-line, and galloped down the gully from the rear. Upon the crest he encountered a sergeant, sweating, exhausted and wretched, who told him that "the Staff Officer" had been killed in the charge. "He led us all, Effendim," the man said; "he put life and soul into us, and we went forward again, when we thought we were beaten, with our officers gone, and this accursed shelling. But now he is killed."

Orhan told the man to send out a party to bring the body in. Yes, it was Ahmet all right—long and slender, he lay all limp on the hot soil, in the trim uniform which Nilüfer had so often brushed and pressed, the dark-lashed lids closed—a soldier had done that for him—over the grey eyes that were so like Féridé's; he might have been asleep, except that his mouth was wide open, like that of a man shouting in a loud voice. Bending over him, his throat contracted in distress, Orhan found himself wondering if that last shout had been of encouragement to the men, or of anguish when the machine-gun bullets entered his chest, drilling that close row of holes in the cloth, from which a dark spreading stain was oozing.

But his chief thought was of Féridé. "Oh my life, my darling, how are you going to endure this?" he muttered to himself. His mind turned

with deepest pity to Nilüfer—first her baby gone, and now her husband!
—and then to the poor old Pasha, his father-in-law, who was losing his
only son. "This will finish him!" he thought. But his mind passed
swiftly from Asaf Pasha to Réfiyé Hanim, with whom, from the outset,
he had always been linked in a sympathy that was curiously close. It
wouldn't finish *her*—nothing would finish her, marvellous old woman,
but Time's inevitable processes, but it would cruelly darken her last days.
Standing in the blistering heat of that Anatolian gully, with Ahmet's
body at his feet and the long file of the gaily-dressed ammunition-carriers passing him all the time in a ceaseless flow, the young man paused
for a long moment, lost in sad thoughts of the imminent sorrow of his
grandmother-in-law.

He was roused by the sergeant, who touched him on the arm to ask
what they should do with the officer's body? Should it remain there?
He would like to go forward—the men of his platoon were following
up the retreating Greeks, "and if there is no officer, I can lead them for
a time."

"Yes, go on—go and slaughter the machine-gunners!" Orhan exclaimed. "I will send for him." He went and got his horse, and taking
the bridle of Ahmet's chestnut over his arm he rode back to the knot of
Staff horses.

"Where is Ahmet Bey?" one of the soldier-grooms asked, as he dismounted.

"Dead," the young officer replied briefly. The man broke out into
loud lamentations.

Up on Kocatepé the small group of the General Staff was now watching the distant progress of the central thrust, Fevzi and Ismet mostly in
silence, Kemal now and again giving vent to a brief ejaculation of satisfaction. None of them noticed Orhan's arrival at first, but presently
Kemal, without taking his field-glasses from his eyes, said—"I wonder
where on earth Orhan Bey has got to? He should have been back
long since."

"Here I am, Sir," said Orhan, stepping forward and saluting.

"Then why in the Prophet's name don't you say so?" Kemal snapped,
looking round. "And where the devil is Ahmet?"

"He is killed, Sir."

Kemal Pasha let his field-glasses drop from his hand—they fell the
length of the strap by which they hung round his neck.

"So," he said, slowly, almost thoughtfully. "That is bad news—very
bad. Did you learn how it happened?"

"The sergeant said that he re-formed the men, and led the charge,"
said Orhan stiffly. "But their machine-gunners got him from their nests
—there are six holes in his tunic."

"I wish this had not happened," Kemal said, in that tone of complete sincerity and simplicity which was one of the things that made men glad to lay down their lives for him. "I wish I had not sent him. My dear Ahmet! But they shall pay!" he added, suddenly savage. "Yes?" he asked sharply, as another officer came up with a fresh report and some further query. "Wait!"—then to Orhan—"Have him brought in." Orhan saluted. "Now," Kemal said to the new arrival, and took over the direction of the battle again.

By nightfall the central thrust had completely broken the Greek front, and a general retirement began, which turned rapidly into a rout. Kemal displayed his usual generalship, and by swift moves of his cavalry and of the 4th and 6th Turkish Army Corps succeeded in cutting off and destroying a high proportion of the wretched Greek army near Çalkoi, north of Dumlupinar—six divisions were practically wiped out. Those who could, fled towards Smyrna, but retreat to the north was barred by the cavalry. Four days after the battle had begun Kemal issued this Order of the Day: "Armies! Your next objective is the Mediterranean! Forward!"—his weary troops cheered it to the echo.

Forward indeed they went, but the enemy fled with such speed that though the Turks covered a hundred miles in three days, they never caught up with the fleeing Greeks till they reached Smyrna on September the 9th; General Tricoupis, the Greek Commander-in-Chief, was captured with his entire staff on the 2nd. But swiftly as the Greeks fled, abandoning everything—tents, barbed wire, clothing, guns, stores of food, rifles—they found time to kill practically every Turk they encountered on their way, mostly old men, old women, and children, and to burn down every village, in a frenzy of wanton cruelty and destruction. Their pursuers, following hard on their heels, saw what they had done—the still-smoking ashes of ruined homesteads, the grey-haired faces turned up to the sky, the small crumpled bodies of children, with flies buzzing and settling on the darkened blood; and this explains, even if it cannot excuse, what happened to the Greek population of Smyrna when the Turkish army finally arrived there.

Some days before that Kemal, accompanied by Ismet, Fevzi, and several Staff officers, walked over the horrifying battle-field at Çalkor, where the Greek troops who had not succeeded in escaping had been destroyed wholesale. Under the hot sun— the great vultures circling in slow sweeps overhead casting ugly shadows—the air was full of the stench of putrefying corpses, lying everywhere in heaps, mixed up with abandoned ammunition and weapons of every description. This was one of Mustafa Kemal's great hours; his ceaseless work, his faith, and the sacrifices, courage and endurance of his people here had borne a visible, a most appalling fruit. With a cold silent pride, a sort of reserved triumph, he picked his way between the heaped bodies of his enemies, noting their numbers and the amount of war material that they had abandoned with a professional eye. And here he gave, suddenly, a curious example of his own peculiar brand of chivalry. At one point the party came on a Greek regimental standard, lying trampled in the dust; it caught Kemal's eye.

"Pick it up!" he said curtly to a Major on the Staff, who was walking with the three Commanders.

"Sir, it is only a Greek flag," the Major unwisely ventured to say. Kemal rounded on him furiously.

"It is the symbol of independence of a nation! I tell you to *pick it up!*" he stormed. The officer, abashed, obeyed, and continued to walk after his chief over the hideous field, carrying the enemy's flag.

But there was no chivalry in Kemal's behaviour at Smyrna, or rather in the behaviour of his troops there—which one must suppose that he permitted. An appalling massacre of the large Greek civilian population took place, and the greater part of the rich thriving mercantile city was burnt to ashes—what was left of the Greek army, from their transports lying just off the harbour, watched the town which they felt belonged to them going up in flames, and listened to the shrieks that travelled out over the water—above all to the hideous screaming of their transport mules, which they had left on the quays when they embarked; the Turkish soldiery, themselves desperately short of transport, in crazy wantonness butchered these useful animals in thousands, with the same savagery with which they were busily slaughtering innocent civilians.

Altogether, Smyrna was an ugly business. And the Turkish victory raised serious issues for Europe. It was obvious that Kemal would now turn his attention—his highly victorious attention—to Istanbul, which like Smyrna had a large Greek and Armenian population; and this might well ignite afresh that troublesome area the Balkans, whose very soil seems to be composed of dynamite. Churchill, summing up his account of the Turkish struggle, uses harsh and bitter words to point the moral of the whole episode—words worth remembering, for they have a permanent truth.

"Victory over Turkey, absolute and unchallenged, had been laid by the Armies upon the council table of the Peace Conference. Four years had passed, and the talkers had turned it into defeat. . . . All the fine pretensions of Europe and the United States, all the eloquence of their statesmen, all the hiving and burrowing committees and commissions, had led the erstwhile masters of overwhelming power to this bitter and ignominious finish."

"The talkers had turned it into defeat"—that is the essential phrase, the biting truth. The columnists, the politicians, the would-be statesmen pouring out platitudes, all the men of words almost inevitably do, in the end, turn the heroisms of the men of action into defeat.

· · · · · · ·

In Istanbul Kemal's threat to the capital created consternation. The news of the Smyrna massacres left the Turks themselves aghast; at the Club the Pasha heard details never printed, with profound dismay. The fear of armed conflict in and around the capital, still occupied by Entente troops and watched over by units of the Entente fleets carried his mind back to his anxieties in the summer of 1914. And then he heard the news of Ahmet's death.

The poor old man was stricken by this blow. Orhan had written him a long, respectful, and affectionate letter, giving full details of that gallant action, and stressing the military importance of its results—the Pasha read it aloud to Réfiyé Hanim, who listened in silence, the slow tears of old age stealing down her face. She was very much touched and moved by the tone in which Orhan wrote to his father-in-law, with whom he had seldom seen eye to eye about anything—and Asaf Pasha was, she saw, moved by this too. But curiously enough he was even more pleased by a brief note which arrived a day or so later from Mustafa Kemal himself, expressing courteous condolence; it ended with the words: "He was an officer whom all loved, and of whom the nation, in whose defence he died, can be proud."

"That is well said," the Pasha observed with some emotion to his mother, after reading it to her.

"Yes, he is clearly a person of sensibility," the old lady said, wiping her eyes with a cambric handkerchief. "My son, I should like Dil Feripé to hear those words, if you would most kindly leave the letter with me."

The Pasha rose and gave it to her. As he re-seated himself he said, clearing his throat with a slight elegant embarrassment—"Ané, do you perchance know this: is Nilüfer again with child?"

"Alas, my son, no," she replied at once. The young—and the middle-aged, even—have no idea of what it is like to be between sixty and seventy, with one's personal future so short, so short, and all expectation fixed on the next generations, one's children and one's grandchildren. But Réfiyé Hanim knew—she had passed through that age, and had been blessed in it with beautiful and devoted grandchildren; she understood very well what the hope of a grandson would have meant to her own aging son. But this hope was denied him, and she told him so without hesitation. She half feared that he would say something harsh

· 234 ·

about poor Nilüfer, but he simply bowed his head a little, so that the tassel of his fez drooped forward—and presently, bent, sad, and silent, he went away to his own quarters in the great house, so empty now. Réfiyé Hanim remained alone. Some time later Dil Feripé stole in, and she read her the letter from Mustafa Kemal; the faithful old creature wept afresh for Ahmet, her beloved nursling, and Réfiyé Hanim in her corner under the window wept with her.

Chapter Seventeen

THE news of Ahmet's death came to the house on the citadel in the middle of the frenzied rejoicings at Ankara over the victory at Dumlupinar—The Battle of the Commander-in-Chief, as the Turks still call it. Féridé's sorrow was almost speechless, while the only comfort for poor Nilüfer seemed to be to talk ceaselessly of Ahmet. But their sense of mutual obligation was very strong, and no strain or disharmony developed; they clung together, the one speaking, the other listening.

"He left no son—by my fault he left no son!" poor Nilüfer would reiterate; and Féridé, herself still childless, tried to comfort her—it had not been her fault, it was the circumstances, the goats' milk; and then, much against the grain, but with faithful patience, she led her sister-in-law on to talk of Ahmet himself till she was soothed and calm again.

All this listening took time, however, and it was an immense relief when first Kezban, then Fatma, came back from the front and took up their household tasks once more. When Orhan returned from Smyrna —at first rather silent and oppressed—he took steps to terminate the lease of Ahmet's house; it was an understood thing that when the railway was open again Nilüfer would return to her family, at the Eaux Douces or at Scutari. Orhan's presence was a greater solace to Féridé at that time than it had ever been before—it broke up the feminine atmosphere of helpless mourning which was so alien to her active resilient spirit.

However, the railway was not open yet, by any means. That broken stretch where the rails had been turned into rammers and bayonets had still to be re-laid, and there was considerable military activity further down the line, round Ismid. Kemal, having triumphantly thrown the Greeks out of Anatolia, Turkey-in-Asia, now wanted possession of Istanbul, with all the prestige which attached to the ancient capital; but he also wanted to repossess himself of Turkey-in-Europe—Eastern Thrace, which the Greeks still held. Thither he could send his troops easily enough if he could ship them across the narrow waters of the Dardanelles; but along the Asiatic shore of those waters, on both sides of the little town of Chanak, extended a thin line of English troops, and English men-of-war, with a fire-power which he could not possibly equal, patrolled the Narrows themselves. There had been French-held and Italian-held zones, too, along those flat shores; but on September the 18th the French, who for the past eleven months had maintained a curiously equivocal position—as one of the Entente Powers, but in diplomatic relations with Ankara, the enemy of those Powers—withdrew their troops. The Italians followed their example, and the thin line of English soldiers was stretched out to fill the gaps till it was thinner still; but three days before the French and Italian withdrawal the British Government telegraphed a request for reinforcements at Chanak to the Dominions—Australia, New Zealand, Canada—and the Dominions responded eagerly to the call. They would come and help the mother-country as before.

This response, which was widely publicised, gave Kemal pause. He himself had fought against the "Anzacs"—Australian and New Zealand Army Corps—on Gallipoli six or seven years before, and he knew what they were worth. Sir Charles Harington, the English Commander in Istanbul, an Irishman who combined British phlegm with Irish tact and gracefulness, informed the Ghazi that he had instructions to defend the neutral zone along the Narrows. Kemal ventured on a "try-on"—the Anzac troops could not arrive for some time, and he was well aware of the British weakness; by his order his famous cavalry, 1100 of them, entered the neutral zone. His bluff was called; the English General intimated that he would be obliged to fire on them if they failed to retire. They did retire—to return a few days later, now 2000 strong, and armed with machine-guns. But they did no more than remain, "grinning through the barbed wire," as Harington gaily reported to London—for behind the barbed wire, and not so far behind either, lay the Fleet with its great guns; shore artillery was on the way, and aircraft-carriers were joining the men-of-war almost daily. Kemal, so sensible, so practical, was not trying conclusions with the British Empire just then—through the barbed wire his troops continued to grin, but did no more.

There is a sort of natural affinity between the Turks and the English, or at least between Turkish soldiers and English troops—even in war they cannot help, for the most part, respecting and even liking one another. Alec Grant, who had been sent down to Chanak from Haidar Pasha to fill a gap among the officers of the Fifth Hussars, the regiment stationed there, wrote home to Fanny describing, in phrases as clipped as his little red moustache, the relations actually existing on the spot between the opposing forces at a time when European governments were cold with anxiety lest an "incident" should occur there, and make a fresh conflict inevitable. A rather senior Turkish officer, he reported, had come in one day under a white flag, with an interpreter, to ask—of all things—whether the English would lend him some rolls of their barbed wire? They seemed to have plenty, while he, for his part, was very short of it; and important people were coming down to make an inspection of his lines—if he could borrow some English wire he could put up a good show, and save a lot of trouble. He promised to return it when the inspection was over. The English commander had agreed, and Turkish details carried back an ample supply. A few days later, when the inspection had passed off satisfactorily (in fact Orhan was present at it) the Turkish officer returned according to promise, bringing back the rolls of wire. Over whiskies, in a most genial atmosphere, he made a further request. It was very tiresome, he explained, to have to dress oneself up as a peasant or a fig-seller in order to cross the lines and come into Chanak to take one's bath in the town hammam; it would save no end of trouble if the English would let him and his brother-officers through in uniform, without the bother of this disguise. "Of course we said Yes," Alec Grant wrote. "I will say this for the Turks, they do bathe like Christians. That hammam is top-hole —I go there all the time."

Since Irish tact, English calm, and the threat of Dominion troops—to say nothing of the British Fleet—were combining to bar the military way to Thrace, Kemal sought to gain his ends by diplomacy; in politics he never allowed himself to be swayed by either temper or pride, and was always ready to switch from one method to another, if the second appeared more likely to succeed. The Entente, towards the end of September, issued an invitation to the Kemalist Government to a Conference at Mudania, the port for Broussa, to discuss an armistice, and made it clear that they were prepared to offer a good deal, chiefly at the expense of the unhappy Greeks. Mustafa Kemal accepted, and the delegates met on October the 3rd. To Mudania also hastened the busy M. Franklin-Bouillon, where for forty-eight hours he spent his time persuading the Turkish delegation to ask for much more than the English would give; these efforts resulted in a deadlock. This appalled the French and Italians—they were ready to surrender anything and everything to avoid a further conflict. But the English held out, and started to prepare an ultimatum. Supple and wise as ever, Kemal resumed negotiations, and this time an armistice was concluded. He got most of what he wanted, and got it very cheaply: Eastern Thrace up to the Maritza immediately, and the removal of the Allied troops and fleets from Istanbul as soon as the permanent peace treaty should be signed. Turkey, in fact, had regained practically all the territory inside her actual ethnographic frontiers—those frontiers within which, as Kemal had told the deputies at the first Assembly two-and-a-half years before, they must work for the nation's happiness and well-being.

But it was quite clear to Mustafa Kemal that no very rapid progress could be made towards national well-being with two governments in the country, the Ottoman Government under the Sultan down at Istanbul, and the Nationalist Government up at Ankara. The Sultanate must be abolished; and if possible the Khalifate—the hereditary headship of the Musulman faith—too, and the way left clear to turn Turkey into a modern state. He began at once to feel his way towards these two ends. But what was clear to him was by no means always so clear to the National Assembly, and now that victory was won and the immediate danger over, the deputies became truculent. Among the more conservative elements there was fierce opposition to the abolition of the Sultanate—fiercer than he had reckoned on. Quietly, Kemal dropped all idea of touching the Khalifate for the moment; that could wait. He manoeuvred skilfully to get a decree passed separating the functions of the Sultan from those of the Khalif—hitherto the same person had automatically held both. Next a relation of the Sultan, Abdul Mejit, was appointed Khalif in his place, and on November the 1st, after some violent scenes, Kemal rammed through the Assembly, almost by armed force, a further decree abolishing the office of Sultan of Turkey altogether. Vahdeddin, the last ruler, slipped on board an English cruiser and was carried away into exile—after five centuries of conquest, corruption and misrule the Ottoman Empire had come to an end.

There had been considerable public feeling against Vahdeddin and his Ministers for their subservience to the Entente Powers, but to the more old-fashioned Turks the abolition of the Sultanate came as a terrible shock. One evening Orhan found Féridé more silent than usual, with a troubled expression; when he asked her what was the matter—"I have had a letter from my Father," she said.

"Is there bad news? Réfiyé Hanim is not ill?"

"No, no—it is about the Monarchy."

"Let me see it—if I may?" he said, abrupt but courteous.

"Orhan, really I would rather not show it to you. It—it is a terrible letter."

It was indeed, and had upset Féridé very much. The Pasha, for once abandoning his usual moderation, wrote angrily, almost violently, especially about Mustafa Kemal—he spoke of wickedness and impiety, and expressed horror at Féridé's being connected with anyone who had a hand in such things—"as I must reluctantly believe that your husband has." She had never imagined herself receiving such a letter from her own father, and was quite shaken.

Orhan had been half expecting this. He had listened to the debates in the Assembly and heard the private views of the more conservative Ministers and generals—he could imagine what Asaf Pasha's letter was like. But he hated Féridé to be distressed, and he wished in all things to carry her with him, to convince her that what was being done was right; so he sat down now and began, at first very calmly and gently, to explain the position, and why Kemal had felt it necessary to abolish the Sultanate. "Our enemies are conquered and our country is saved, thanks to him. But what will have been the good of saving it, of all our efforts and sacrifices, if we are to sink back into the weakness, the corruption and scandals of the old régime? Kemal Pasha sees what so many of the deputies do not see, what your Father does not see, that to live in the modern world we must be a modern nation—and to do that, we must learn to understand and share the ideas of the modern world."

"Yes—I see that this is right," she said, slowly and thoughtfully. "But could we not modernise ourselves *with* a Sultan? I should have thought that other things presented greater difficulties than he. We are not like western nations; we are Mahometans, and have our own ways, especially for us women. Why, Fanny told me in a letter that now women in England who are over thirty can vote for their deputies! Imagine such a thing! And always there, women have mixed with men, and spoken their opinions freely—and have been listened to! We are not like that," she said, rather stiffly.

Orhan surprised her by bursting into laughter.

"Oh my precious one, you looked so like Réfiyé Hanim, when you said that," he explained. "But you must—you *will*," he went on, now deeply in earnest. "You will leave off the veil, and live like European women; you will see, he will bring it about."

"Leave off the veil? Altogether?" She was incredulous.

"Yes; certainly. Do you not like the idea?" he asked curiously.

"In a way, yes." She spoke hesitatingly. "It would be strange—but the çarşaf is very hot! And those wives of the French diplomats have such pretty hats," she added irrelevantly.

He laughed again. "You too shall wear pretty hats, Light of my Eyes! Only wait—and we will go to Paris to buy them." She laughed too, a rather unwilling laugh. "After all, has it done you any harm to meet strangers unveiled, dining at Çankaya?"

"Harm? No, I suppose not—though I still find it difficult," she said, her brows drawn down. She paused. "The peasants here will not mind —they always do it in the fields. But there are many who will mind very much indeed."

"Who?"

"The bourgeoises—women like Madame Talaat and Madame Ali." (These were the wives of two deputies; Féridé had made the acquaintance of a good many of them by now, and knew what she was talking about.)

"Oh, the bourgeoises! They will have to put up with it, to learn.

What is the bourgeoisie, after all?—in all nations, the greatest pest and bore, so far as I know!" he exploded. "No, we must modernise, whether they like it or not. Our education too—and for that, of course, the Khalifate will have to go."

She stared at him aghast.

"Orhan, you cannot be serious! Abolish the Khalifate! It is incredible. For what conceivable reason?"

"Because of what I said—that we must share the ideas of the modern world; of Europe, that is to say. But how can we do that while so much of our education is based on the Koran, written centuries ago? In most of the medressés they teach little but the hadis" (the words of the Prophet) "and in Arabic at that! It is true that there are a few secondary schools, and places like the Galata-Serai but except in those, what are our people taught of mathematics, of modern science, of medicine? Nothing—because all is dominated by the Culte! Do you know that not long ago it was solemnly proposed in the Assembly to suppress our Minister of Public Instruction and to attach his functions to the Ministry of the Culte? And the reactionaries who proposed this, though they failed to carry it, actually succeeded for a time in forcing the Minister to limit all musical instruction to religious music!"

Orhan was rapidly talking himself into a state of exasperated excitement, as often happened. Actually he was opening up some quite new ideas to Féridé. She knew about the Galata-Serai, where most of the teaching was given in French, because Orhan had been educated there; and she and her friends all had their Mdlles Marthe, and met western thought and culture in the French books which they read all the time —oh the dreariness of these months and months at Ankara, with no new French novels or memoirs! But it had never occurred to her to wonder, still less to find out, what Turks in general were taught. Now she was learning, and her respect for knowledge was sufficient to make what she learned a shock. Meanwhile Orhan was going on—

"Why, in some of the medressés they do not even learn to read and write!—only to recite the Scriptures by heart; and all this because those schools are under the Culte. No—the Khalifate must go, and the Culte with it; we must have proper schools, where western learning is taught, and taught well, to our people. Not only science and medicine, I do not mean that: the classics, great literature, the whole European intellectual background—Homer, Aeschylus, Dante even. These things are the foundations of western civilisation—that is to say, of civilisation itself." He was really passionate; she had never heard him speak quite like this before. She considered it all, and then—

"But would you have us abandon the Faith?" she asked.

"No!" he almost shouted—"Of course not! Let us keep our religion, let us hold the Faith; but in Allah's name, let our children be educated as those of other nations are! Why should their minds be starved, denied all intellectual sustenance?" He got up, and walked about the room in his agitation.

Féridé was slow to answer; she was thinking it out. At last she said— "It is right, this. Yes, it should be so. Is it Kemal Pasha who has considered all this, and made these plans?"

"Yes, of course—who but he? Naturally some of these educational reforms were adumbrated by the Committee of Union and Progress, long ago—but the Culte has always stultified them, in effect. The Law and Justice, too—these must be freed from this tyranny. Why have we had to submit to the Capitulations, to foreign lawyers and Courts of Law in our midst? Because our own are all mixed up with religion, with archaic rules and dogmas. Law and education must be independent of these interests—Kemal Pasha understands that."

"It is really very remarkable," she said slowly. "I cannot conceive how he has found the time to be thinking of such matters, with all the other things that he has had to do—the war, organising our troops, and dealing with the Assembly." She sat, chin in hand, pensive. "He does really mean, I see it now, to open a new future for our people. Yes, it is *right*. He is greater than I thought."

Orhan listened to this with keen pleasure. He had a great respect for the opinion of his beautiful young wife, and he had often been aware that her enthusiasm for Mustafa Kemal lagged behind his—she was amused, interested, often charmed by the great man, but she preserved a certain detachment in her judgements of him.

"Ah, now you see what I see!" he said triumphantly. "That is well." "But do not speak of it," he added—as he so often did. "The matter of the Khalifate will not happen yet. Have patience, as *he* has patience."

Féridé was really in no great personal hurry for these drastic reforms, even if she approved of them in the abstract; her mind came back to her own private preoccupations, and her final word was a damping one.

"When it *does* happen, it will cause my Father infinite distress," she said. Orhan gave an impatient shrug of his shoulders.

"My Life, the nation's welfare cannot wait on Asaf Pasha's prejudices!" he said. She made no answer. He came over and caressed her. "You know that your distress distresses me," he said tenderly—"And I have the greatest respect for your Father—his learning, his uprightness. I am sorry for him. Calm him as best you can, over this. The other will not happen for some time."

The Pasha was in fact somewhat calmed by the opening, towards the end of November, of the Conference of Lausanne to discuss the final

Peace Treaty between the Entente Powers and Turkey. He found it rather hard to understand why the Japanese should be there—or even the Jugo-slavs—in which he was by no means alone. But Turkey was meeting her late conquerors on equal terms, at last, as a sovereign power; Ismet Pasha, respected by all, headed the Turkish delegation in his new capacity as Minister for Foreign Affairs, to which he had been appointed shortly after the Armistice of Mudania. One bitter thought was constantly with Asaf Pasha; if Ahmet had been alive, he would surely have gone to Lausanne with his chief; have taken a part in public affairs, as his father had done. The Pasha could not altogether avoid a slight feeling of jealous irritation at the increasing importance of his son-in-law, as one of Mustafa Kemal's right-hand men, but after he had incautiously let slip a remark on this subject to his mother, he was careful never to do so again; she was displeased, and for once allowed her disapproval to appear in a dignified silence.

Orhan's position brought certain practical advantages. Nilüfer was anxious to go home, and Féridé really did not think her fit to face the rigours of a third winter in Ankara; she had never properly recovered from her confinement, and after Ahmet's death she flagged more than ever. But though work was being done on the railway there was still a gap near Eski-şehir. So far only official cars existed at Ankara, and not many of those; Orhan however was able to arrange for one to take his sister-in-law down to a station whence she could complete the journey by train.

Féridé went with her. She was getting very anxious indeed to see Réfiyé Hanim again—Mdlle Marthe wrote rather alarming accounts of the old lady's health, and she wished to see her father too. Orhan drove with them as far as the rail-head; at one point the road passed by one of the battle-fields, and he began eagerly pointing out the places connected with this or that encounter. Actually they were many miles away from the scene of the action in which Ahmet had lost his life, but though she could not see Nilüfer's face, Féridé suddenly *felt* her distress—it was almost audible to her, as if all the strings of a violin had been harshly scraped inside the car itself. She twitched her husband's sleeve, and signed to him to be silent. He sulked a little, but did as she wished.

Once on the train, the whole journey was rapture to Féridé. She sat gazing out of the left-hand window, watching for familiar landmarks. Here was the Gulf of Ismid, so blue, so blue; the line coasted along it, to emerge at last onto the Marmara. Now she watched for the Princes' Islands, Büyük Ada and the rest—there they were, pine-crowned, their bronze and umber cliffs falling to the sea, and the gay white villas with their pink roofs, scene of so many summer excursions and holidays. As the train drew on towards Haidar Pasha she went out into the corridor to see the bare brown hills of Chamlidja, where they had so often picnicked at the house in the vine, with the black line of cypresses, like sable torches, which marks the great cemetery; then back into the carriage again, to look out over the water for the first sight of that wonderful profile of Istanbul—the domed mosques, the minarets, Seraglio Point, and Hagia Sofia towering above the rest. That city sky-line is to all travellers most beautiful, and to the majority also very strange—to Féridé it was deeply familiar, and the light of memory and affection lay over its beauty like an enchantment. Tears came into her eyes, she who so rarely cried, at the sight.

At Haidar Pasha Osman was waiting on the platform, his stolid brown face bright with joy. A brother was meeting Nilüfer, with a servant in attendance. The two girls clung together for a moment as they said goodbye. "You have been so good to me," Nilüfer whispered; "no one will ever know how good! What I shall do without you I do not know."

"Dji-djim, you will be with your family, safe, cared-for, comfortable," Féridé said.

"They will not know, not understand, as you do," Nilüfer said, with one of her rare bursts into reality; "we have been together through—everything! Oh, I shall miss you so much."

"Chérie, we shall see one another very soon; we are so close. Look —your brother wishes to leave, I think. À bientôt dearest."

Osman had the caïque waiting at the steps outside the station; for the Taurus Railway ends abruptly on a quay, with a stretch of tossing water between it and the city it serves—the water that separates Asia from Europe. Féridé looked in astonishment at the three men who formed the boat's crew, in their gay livery of full baggy trousers and brilliant embroidered Zouave jackets, sleeveless over their immaculate white shirts, and their tasselled caps; it was long since she had seen servants wearing livery. With a happy sigh she sank onto the cushioned seat at the stern—as the boat shot away to the rhythmic strokes of three pairs of oars she thought of Temel, in his stained shabby uniform, waiting on Orhan up at Ankara, and of Fatma and Kezban in their bright loud peasant trousers and quilted jackets, also faded and stained to a tenderness of hue which was less attractive in one's house than it was picturesque! But she soon forgot Kezban and Fatma—for the time forgot Ankara altogether. Here was Leander's Tower, squat and white, a lighthouse at night; there was Galata Bridge, with the ceaseless flow of traffic passing to and fro; above its southern end the slope of dark wooden houses, their windows like the whites of eyes, rose up to Péra, with the crenellated outline of the Fire Tower standing out boldly above them. The caïque's crew bent to the oar, pulling hard, as they turned up into the Bosphorus and met the current; Scutari with its exquisite mosque fell away behind; presently the battlements of Rumeli Hissar rose ahead, climbing from the water to the sky, mediaeval, pale, very noble. She remembered the last time she had looked on them—in the cold light of dawn at the start of her voyage to Inebolu. That brought her thoughts back to Nilüfer—and she was suddenly aware of a strange lightening of her spirit when she remembered that Nilüfer was now safe in the care of her own family. She had never thought of her sister-in-law as a burden during the last two-and-a-half years, but now that the responsibility for her—for her well-being, her happiness, her health—was placed on other shoulders, she felt as if a weight had been lifted off her own. This surprised her; she was rather shocked at herself.

Now, close ahead, she could see the yali, a long graceful complication of silvery baroque, and at the sight she forgot about Nilüfer as well as Ankara. Behind it the conifers of the koru stood out in dark masses—she thought she could even pick out the cedar in whose boughs Fanny had hidden, years and years ago; to the left of the garden, with its magnolias and Judas-trees, the low dark entrance to the caïque-hané gaped like an open mouth; beyond the house stood the great plane-trees, leafless now, under which her father and Dr. Pierce used to walk up and down, deep in talk, in those happy summers in the past. Now they were close inshore, and she could see a little group standing at the top of the short flight of marble steps which led up from the water—as the caïque drew in closer still she could pick out Zeynel, the gardener, old Mahmud, and a stumpy veiled figure which could only be Dil Feripé. There was a fourth, small and slight—"Osman, who is the youth on the terrace with the others?" she asked.

"Little Ali, Hanim Effendi—Mahmud's grandson. He works now under me—he has the makings of an excellent servant."

"Little Ali! He has shot up like a reed beside a lake! He used to be so tiny," Féridé said, remembering how Little Ali had crept like a mouse to her bedroom to warn Orhan of the arrival of the Ottoman police, only three years before.

"Ah, there is good living in our Pasha's house!" Osman said, complacently. "But we still call him Little Ali."

With a graceful sweep and a smooth skilful shipping of oars the long narrow boat drew up beside the steps—Little Ali ran down and held it as Osman stepped ashore and handed out Féridé. The next moment, with her old familiar pea-hen screech, Dil Feripé fell upon her, and hugged her as if she could never let go. "Oh, my little one!—my pet, my nursling—at last you return! Come in, come in—I wish to see your face."

"Dadi, it is good to be at home again," Féridé said, returning the hug.

"So I should think! What a terrible place, this Ankara! Greeks all about, and you, my poor lamb, with only these peasants, these Fatmas and Kezbans, to look after you. What a life for Our Master's daughter!"

Féridé had to laugh—Dil Feripé was exactly her old self. But now Zeynel came up, to bow low and greet her; and then it was Mahmud's turn. "Welcome, Kü-jük Hanim," the old man said, in his excitement using the word by which he had addressed her as a girl; his old face was working with emotion. "Allah is merciful," he said, and turned quickly away. Dil Feripé impatiently drew Féridé into the house; in the wide hall she pulled off the çarşaf and scrutinised her darling at length. "Thin!—much too thin," she pronounced. "Ah, we will put some flesh upon your bones here." Then she surprised her by asking—"And this Kemal Pasha, have you seen him, yourself? What kind of a man is he to look upon? Handsome? Ah, how I should like to see him! Is he tall?" It was clear that Mustafa Kemal had now become a hero even to dadis.

"He is not as tall as Orhan Bey," Féridé said, amused, as they started upstairs.

"Orhan Bey is a fine young man, we all know," the dadi said. "He is well? That is good. Very important, I hear he is now." Then her poor old face suddenly seemed to crumple up. "But oh, my Ahmet—my beautiful boy!" She wept.

Mdlle Marthe was waiting in the upper hall—too tactful to intrude on her pupil's meeting with Réfiyé Hanim, too excited to wait to see her till it was over.

"Alors, mon enfant, at last one sees you!" she said, embracing Féridé with much warmth. She too scrutinised her closely, and likewise said that she was very thin. Marthe herself had not altered in the least— the grey hair no greyer, the Victorian clothes no less Victorian, the old eyes as shrewd and watchful as ever. "Come in to your Grandmother," she said—"She has wearied for this moment."

"One second, dear Marthe; tell me how she is," Féridé asked eagerly.

"Better; much better, since she heard that you were coming. In truth, I think she has remained alive to see you! But she is fragile; the heart troubles her a good deal, especially at night. She gets little sleep. But come to her—she has been watching for the boat."

The Frenchwoman threw open the doors as she spoke—"Here is our

• 246 •

child, at last, Madame," she said, and went out, closing them gently behind her.

As Féridé crossed the wide spaces of the Savonnerie carpet, threading her way swiftly between the French furniture towards the familar figure by the window, silhouetted against the brilliant light outside, past and present together so flowed in upon her that she felt as if she were in a dream. Could it be real, the mixed beauty about her, the soft perfection under her feet? It bore no relation whatever to her life and surroundings for the last two-and-a-half years. But when Réfiyé Hanim rose at her approach, a thing she had never done in the past, and came towards her with small uncertain steps, everything else was blotted out in a bliss of profoundest affection and love. "Oh Niné, my dearest darling!—come back, sit down," she said, folding the old woman in her young arms. "There!" she set her on her sofa again, and knelt beside her. "Oh, why did you rise for me?"

"My child, I suppose I was impatient," the old lady said, fondling the crisp dark head beside her. "I saw the caïque come in—but of course there were many who wished to greet you, Mahmud and Zeynel and Dil Feripé. You cannot know how eagerly we have all waited for this moment! To us, you know," she said simply, "the time has seemed long, while you were absent. But let me look at you"—and she tilted up her grand-daughter's chin.

"Niné dearest, please do not tell me that I am thin!" Féridé said, with a little half-sobbing laugh—"I have had enough of that already!"

"Well, if it is true, and I fear it is, it becomes you," the old lady said. "You are very much en beauté, my darling. It is surprising, for it must have been hard for you, up there. Quelle vie!—no servants, all this work in the house and for the wounded. Ah well, it is another world, nowadays! Who could imagine you, doing the cooking!"

"Oh yes, Niné, I am become a very good cook!—though not as good as Nilüfer. But really, you know, in many ways Ankara is assomant—quite terrible! You have no conception"—she glanced round her—"how good it is to be here again."

"Je le suppose bien! Tell me, how is my dear Orhan? Also thin, also surmené?"

"Rather over-driven, yes. For the moment things are a little easier, since we are no longer in danger, and the Delegation has gone to Lausanne—he gets more rest. At one point I was really frightened about him—before the last battle." Her lips quivered, remembering that conversation about Orhan with Ahmet in her kitchen—it was the last time that she had had a really intimate talk with her brother. "Ahmet was worried about him too, then," she said with her usual outspokenness.

· 247 ·

The old lady's face changed at the mention of that name. "Ah, Ahmet!" she said, with indescribable sorrow in her voice. But at that moment the door from the dining-room opened, and the Pasha walked in. "We will speak of this later," Réfiyé Hanim murmured, as Féridé sprang up to greet her father.

The Pasha's appearance shocked her. He had aged very much. Orhan, standing with Ahmet's body at his feet in a gully on the battle-field of Dumlupinar, three months before, had said to himself that this would finish his father-in-law—and if it had not completely finished Asaf Pasha, it had certainly made an old man of him. His hair had turned grey, his thinness and his stoop were more pronounced than ever, all his taut firmness had somehow deserted him—only a sort of fragile elegance remained. He greeted his daughter with unusual warmth—"My child, it is very good to see you. I trust that you left your husband in health?"

"I thank you, my Father—by Allah's goodness, yes." But after her formal words she gave him one of her old impulsive hugs. "Oh Baba-djim, how I rejoice to be at home again!"

He was warmed and pleased, she could see, but all the same the conversation limped a little after he came in—it was very different from the complete spontaneity and ease of her intercourse with her grandmother. And so it remained throughout her visit, which lasted for over two months. Asaf Pasha was almost visibly restraining himself all the time from adverse comments on the abolition of the Sultanate; while Orhan's last words to Féridé, on the platform of the small station where they had boarded the train, seemed to be ringing perpetually in her ears when she was talking to her father: "Do not discuss politics with him; and above all, say nothing of the future. Kemal Pasha will choose his own time for the next move, of which I spoke to you." There was constraint on both sides, which really only vanished when they spoke of Ahmet. There Féridé could add more details to those given in Orhan's letter, and could describe her brother on his last visit to Ankara; and on this particular subject the Pasha could feel warmly, and speak warmly, about Mustafa Kemal and his courteous gracious letter, which had produced a tremendous effect on the old gentleman. He was proud, too, of the victory over the Greeks, and praised the Ghazi's military skill; but the horrors of the Smyrna massacres had tainted even this to some extent for him, with his old-fashioned correct uprightness. He fled as often as possible to happier and more neutral subjects of conversation with his daughter. "Do you ever see Ismet Pasha?"

"Oh yes, frequently, at Çankaya. He is a delightful person, so modest and gentle." She took pains to amuse and beguile her father with rapid verbal sketches of the new personalities up at Ankara, who, hitherto little known, now counted for so much; with her keen observation and gift for lively racy description she kept him happy and amused in this way for hours—when he drove off to the Club, he was able to regale the other old gentlemen there with all sorts of fresh titbits from the new capital, the *parvenu* political front.

To do this comforted her. Féridé was extremely fond of her father, and to see him stricken by Ahmet's death, aged by sorrow, and with his world as he knew it crumbling about him—with worse to come!—filled her with a profound pity. In her childhood's blue-and-white bedroom—she had refused absolutely to return to her own married apartments on this visit—she thought over, at night and in the early morning, fresh bits of gossip with which to entertain him; she put on the prettiest of the many pretty trousseau frocks for which there had been no room in the scanty luggage which she had taken to Inebolu, to please his eye —altogether, she exerted herself for his happiness and amusement with energy and skill. She was rewarded by his evident pleasure; his mind became more alert, even his walk and movements brisker under this treatment.

But with Niné all was ease, perfect ease and delight in the freest possible intercourse. Féridé had been starving for just this—to discuss, by the hour, all the new aspects of her own life, all her various and unwonted activities up at Ankara with her grandmother. She wanted to bring them, so to speak, before the tribunal of Réfiyé Hanim's wisdom and judgement—the tribunal before which, up till two-and-a-half years ago, her whole life had always been brought. She had said nothing in her letters about nursing in the hospital, fearing to cause the old lady distress; now, sitting quietly in the salon one morning, she told her grandmother all about it. "I wish you to know this, Niné," she said at the end. "I think I did right, but I should greatly like to hear your opinion. Oh," she broke off impetuously, "I must tell you one thing— so amusing, and so moving, too. One morning when I got to the hospital—it was during the Battle of Sakarya, at the very darkest moment of all—I found complete consternation. Thirty patients were missing—they had simply vanished during the night! They were all what are called 'walking cases,' men with wounds in the arms or head; and in time I learned from the men in my own ward what had happened—I was rather *bien* with them by then. They had quietly slipped out during the night, and set off to *walk* eighty kilometres, to rejoin their regiments and go on fighting!" She paused. "For such people, one would do anything! Is it not so?"

Réfiyé Hanim had listened very quietly to the recital of Féridé's doings, to her so extraordinary and unprecedented, making very little comment—now she spoke.

"My child, this is all very strange to me. But if men were suffering, perhaps dying, for lack of attention and help, certainly you did right to go and succour them. As for these dinners with strangers in Mustafa Kemal Pasha's house, that seems to me more doubtful. But since you tell me it was by your husband's wish, in fact at his direct command, I think that you could not do otherwise."

That satisfied Féridé. "I am very glad to hear you say this, Niné. I must confess that at first I found it very—difficult, trying; the dinners, I mean. Somehow nursing the soldiers was much easier; I suppose because it was a real, a human need, not just a social obligation. But Orhan attached so much importance to that—Kemal Pasha, you see, wishes to have everybody about him very modern, and in the European manner."

The old lady gave the tiniest sigh. But— "He is a great general; he has saved our nation," was all she said.

Féridé prolonged her visit to the yali from week to week. She found it very hard to leave her father and Réfiyé Hanim, to whom her presence was such an evident delight; and she was not in the least needed at home, since Orhan was away from Ankara, accompanying Mustafa Kemal on the first of his speechifying tours—"marrying his people," as Dr. Pierce called it afterwards. At Smyrna, at Ismit; to the journalists of Istanbul, who travelled westwards to meet him—the man was everywhere, explaining the future as he foresaw it, what he wished the Turkish nation to do and be, and how they should set about doing and being it. Féridé, remembering her talk with Orhan, was greatly struck by the speech which the Ghazi made at Smyrna on the status and the rights of women, in February. She was still at the yali, and as so often before Asaf Pasha brought the afternoon paper up to the salon, and sticking his feet out towards the great glowing brazier read excerpts from the speech aloud to his womenfolk. "If a society is content that only half the members who compose it should live in a manner appropriate to the ideas current in any given century, that society is weakened by half its potential. . . . Woman's principal duty is motherhood; but since mothers are those who give the most primary education of all, the importance of their role is evident. . . . It is on our mothers that we must depend, in great measure, to make adequate human beings of us. In the past they have done what they could, but now we need men of a new mentality, of a different sort of excellence." He read on a little further, and then threw down the paper with a snort.

"He has picked up these ideas from his 'advanced' women friends, who have thrown off the veil—and with it all modesty!—and gone abroad to get a so-called 'education'; and now they will be doctors, lawyers, and God knows what else!"

Réfiyé Hanim had listened in silence so far; now she said—
"It sounds strange to me, this, my son, as it does to you, but I am not
altogether sure that it is really so foolish. You noticed what he said
about motherhood being women's essential duty—that is true and wise.
Enfin, without women there would be no Turkish nation."

Féridé laughed out at that; the Pasha frowned at her.

"But I do not see," the old lady pursued slowly, "why wholly ignorant mothers should bring up better sons than women with at least some
education."

"Our daughters are well-educated, but so far they have not produced
many sons," the Pasha said, with a burst of uncontrollable bitterness.

Réfiyé Hanim frowned in her turn. "My son, in my opinion such
things are better left unsaid," she observed, in a tone of quiet severity.
It was the first and probably the only time, since he grew up, that she
had so spoken to her son.

Chapter Eighteen

THE negotiations at Lausanne dragged on till July, 1923—"It took as long to come to birth as a baby!" Orhan said laughing to Féridé, when at last the Treaty was signed. And it was another two months before the Entente forces finally left Istanbul; two days later the Turkish Army made their formal entry into the old capital.

This time Asaf Pasha went and watched everything, instead of keeping out of the way, as he had done five years before when the Allied troops, headed by Franchet d'Esperey, marched in. He was greatly impressed by the formal salute to the Turkish flag and the Turkish Army given by the English Commander, in his white uniform, on the open space below the mosque at Dolma-Batché before the embarkation; by the smartness and soldierly bearing of the troops who lined the square, and by the brisk music played by the military bands. "It was well done—very well done," he told Réfiyé Hanim on his return. "Enfin, the whole thing was extremely chic."

"My son, the English *are* chic—as my dear Father always said, they are 'gentlemen,'" she replied, using the English word. When the Nationalist troops marched in four days later, the old man was rather less impressed. The days of belts and rifle-slings made of lamp-wicks were over, and the smartest troops had been chosen for the formal parade of this entry—but their marching was a little ragged, their uniforms and above all the rather slovenly cut of their hair bore no comparison with the traditional "spit-and-polish" of the British Army. But they were fine tough-looking men, they had notable victories behind them, and above all they were Turkish. "They were stout fellows; really they looked very well," Asaf Pasha told his mother. "One cannot ask more of them, considering all our handicaps." "Now, I suppose," he added thoughtfully, "the Government will come to Istanbul. After all, this has always been our capital."

But in that the Pasha was mistaken, though he was by no means alone in his mistake—most Turks took it for granted that the seat of government would be transferred promptly from the remote and barbarous discomforts of Ankara to the more civilised surroundings of the old capital, with its lights, its shops, its beautiful buildings, all its metropolitan graces and elegances. That however was not in the least Mustafa Kemal's idea. He knew the old city too well—its age-long tradition of bribery, of the greased palm, and its large population of Armenians, Greeks and Levantines, whose methods no appeals to Turkish patriotism could ever touch or alter. The subject came under discussion one night when Féridé and Orhan were dining at Çankaya. Féridé was sitting beside the Ghazi; an elderly General on her other side leant forward and gave utterance to the popular opinion. "And when does the Assembly move down to Istanbul, Your Excellency?"

"Never, with my consent!" Kemal said curtly. He had already drunk a good deal. "Has this nation not suffered enough from bribery and corruption, and the soft easy life? Our new state must have its new capital—*here!*—where the air is clean." He whipped round on Féridé with one of his sharp questions: "What is your opinion, Féridé Hanim?"

She asked a question in reply, a thing few of his entourage ever ventured to do. "How will matters be managed with the Embassies and Legations? I should have thought it useful to have the Ministry of Foreign Affairs, at least, within reach of them. They all have their establishments at Péra and Therapia."

"They must come up here," he said. "If they wish to deal with us— and they do wish it, now," he added with a boyish grin—"they must do so in our capital. I will give them land to build on, free—the best sites, up here on the slopes. But come they must."

And very much under protest, bit by bit they came, grumbling at the climate and the lack of amenities—after the Assembly, for once docile, had voted a law proclaiming Ankara the capital of the Turkish State. Just over a fortnight afterwards another vote proclaimed Turkey a Republic; fourteen minutes later Mustafa Kemal was pronounced its first President.

. . . .

In the following February Féridé went down to the yali again. Mdlle Marthe had written more alarming accounts of Réfiyé Hanim's health, and she wanted to see her; Orhan was anyhow about to go off with Mustafa Kemal to assist at the Army manoeuvres at Smyrna. Orhan knew, but did not tell her, that one purpose of this journey was to sound out the extent of the Army's loyalty to his master —if it was sufficient, Kemal intended to abolish the Khalifate forthwith, and so free his hands for the prosecution of the educational reforms which lay so near his heart. But this would be touching the religion of a fanatically religious people; he recognised that he would meet with fierce opposition, which he could only risk arousing if he could count, in the last resort, on the Army.

Féridé found her grandmother much aged and weakened. She was now close on ninety, and had suffered from heart trouble for years; her mind was as acute as ever, her tranquil benevolence unimpaired, but the iron control which she had exercised over her body all her life had, at last, to be relaxed—she rose late, went to bed early, and there were little rests and naps during the day, and little nips of this or that restorative, brought in at all hours by Ayshé or Dil Feripé. These two faithful attendants were now themselves very old, so was Mdlle Marthe—Féridé was curiously oppressed by the sense of living in a household of old old people, so different from the ardour and vigour of Ankara. For the first time she felt that the Ghazi had probably been right not to transfer the seat of government to the old capital—a decision which had greatly disappointed her when it was taken.

On this visit she instituted what she had often wished for in the past, namely a daily paper for herself. It was Little Ali who now fetched the afternoon paper for Asaf Pasha, instead of Osman—who like the rest of the inhabitants of the yali was getting rather old—but in addition he brought a morning paper for her too. And before lunch on March the 4th, 1924, she read that the previous day the National Assembly had passed a decree abolishing the Khalifate, and the Ministry of the Culte as well.

"Tiens!" she exclaimed, laying down the paper—"Now I am in for trouble! I wish this had not happened just while I am here. I wonder if Orhan knew of it? Yes, he must have done. Really, he should have warned me!"

Orhan of course had not known of it for certain, since it depended on the attitude of the Army—during the manoeuvres Kemal's discussions with Fevzi, Ismet, Kazim Pasha and other officers had convinced him that he could take the risk; they were all agreed on the necessity for a better system of education, if only from the military point of view. Having come to a decision, as usual Kemal acted at once. But Féridé could not know all that, and she was still feeling rather indignant with her husband when she went to the salon. Réfiyé Hanim now only appeared at tea-time; after tea would be the danger-point, when the Pasha would come stalking in through the dining-room door, probably with the afternoon paper in his hand, and as she poured out a cup and handed it to her grandmother the young woman considered again, now that the trouble was imminent, whether she ought not to tell the old lady—a point which she had been debating with herself all the afternoon as she walked about the koru among the leafless bushes and under the dark conifers. She glanced at the old face, which now had a sort of transparent fragility about it. Darling Niné! —for the first time she saw her as rather helpless. Yes, she must not meet the Pasha's anger unwarned.

"Niné dearest," she said, taking another of the delicate Sèvres cups herself, and sitting down on a small chair—"something has occurred which will distress and infuriate Baba. I think I had better tell you now, for when he comes in, there will be a thunderstorm!"

"Is it some fresh performance of Kemal Pasha's?" the old lady asked. Féridé laughed.

"Yes, it is—naturally!" Then she became grave. "But this time it is really serious—you will mind, too," she said with concern.

"Tell me then, my child," the old lady said. She spoke calmly, and Féridé, not for the first time, blessed her grandmother in her heart for that priceless quality of calmness. It was something which the new generation at Ankara, for all their energy and vigour, were apt to lack.

"The Assembly has passed a decree abolishing the Khalifate," she said slowly, with a hesitation unusual to her.

The old lady received this in silence. After a moment or two— "Do you know why?" she asked. "There must be grave reasons for such a step, and I imagine that Orhan is acquainted with them—I understand that he is very much in Kemal Pasha's confidence." Réfiyé Hanim never spoke of "the Ghazi"; she was not a person given to new titles.

"Yes, there are reasons, Niné. It is the question of education, chiefly. So long as this is principally given in the medressés, our people are denied all knowledge of modern culture, modern science—why, in some of them they do not even learn to read or write!" she said energetically, quoting her husband. "In this century, to know the Koran by heart does not really suffice!"

The old lady mused, looking out across the Bosphorus to the outline of the Chamlidja hills; Féridé waited in a strange anxiety for what she would say.

"No—I suppose it does not suffice," Réfiyé Hanim said slowly at last. "We live now in a new world; and I think Kemal Pasha is perhaps wise in recognising this. I am very old, my darling," she said with a tiny sigh. "I am not skilful at assessing these modern needs, which nevertheless I recognise, old as I am. I wish they could have been met without a step which will affront the susceptibilities of simple people —for our people are very religious."

"Niné dearest, they could not!—really they could not. The Culte has exercised a positive strangle-hold over our intellectual life," Féridé said urgently.

Réfiyé Hanim sighed again.

"Perhaps—yes, possibly. I thought there had been reforms some time ago, under the Committee of Union and Progress. I suppose they were insufficient." She paused, with an air of fatigue. "Really, I do not know! I have a great admiration for Kemal Pasha—he has saved us from annihilation," the old woman said. "But this will trouble your Father very much."

"Do I not know it?" Féridé exclaimed. "That is why I wished to warn you in advance." She jumped slightly as the dining-room door opened, but it was only old Dil Feripé, who sidled in, as she always did —she looked very excited.

"Hanim Effendi, have you heard the news?" she cried. "Oh, the wickedness!—oh, the audacious profanity! They are going to kill the Khalif, God's Shadow on Earth! Ah, what disasters will fall upon us for this!"

"Nonsense, dadi," Réfiyé Hanim said brusquely. "Who talks of killing the Khalif?" But her eyes were anxious, Féridé saw.

"It is in the paper—Osman saw it when he brought it to Our Master."

"Dadi, this is all rubbish," Féridé said sharply. "There is no question of Abdul Mejit being killed. Osman should know better than to spread such tales."

"Ah, you are all mixed up in it, I don't doubt," the dadi retorted, with the privileged freedom of an old nurse to one of her children— "You and your husband! Orhan Bey is a fine young man, no one doubts it, and Kemal Pasha is a great general—but they should leave holy things alone!"

Before Féridé could answer the door from the dining-room opened again, and this time it really was the Pasha who entered. His brow was like thunder—at the sight of him Dil Feripé scuttled away through another door. Sure enough, he had the newspaper in his hand; he was greatly agitated; nevertheless he did not omit his formal greeting—"I trust, Ané, that your health is good?" And—"By the mercy of God, my son, I am very well," the old lady replied, as she had been doing for half a century and more.

"There is shocking news, terrible news," he said, sitting down. "I hardly like even to speak of it to you, Ané."

"My son, ill news is better spoken than hidden—in the light one may see its true colours more clearly," Réfiyé Hanim said.

He looked at her sharply, a little surprised at her speech.

"No amount of light can show these tidings as anything but black," he said bitterly. "The Khalifate has been abolished—by a decree of this upstart Assembly in Ankara! First the Sultanate, now the Khalifate! What do you say to that?"

Féridé listened eagerly for her grandmother's reply. She was a little frightened: in spite of his visible efforts to master it, the Pasha's anger was evident; it would certainly be directed against Mustafa Kemal, and therefore also against his trusted henchman, her husband, whom she was bound to support and defend—and yet she loved her father dearly. It was a cruel moment.

"This is very grave news, my son," Réfiyé Hanim said, seriously. "You are sure that it is true?"

"But perfectly sure—it is here!" He struck the paper with his hand. "Oh, it is too much, this! First he was shorn of his proper powers and pomps, and mulcted of his revenues; now he is turned out of the country, deported like any criminal—yes, put across the frontier at Chataldja, with a ticket for Switzerland! The Khalif!—the earthly deputy of the One True God! It is a fearful impiety."

Both women, the young one and the very old, had only one wish at that moment—to calm Asaf Pasha. Féridé was really afraid to speak— her father's state shocked her. His fez had come askew in the violence of his agitation; the tassel fell over his eyes; he brushed it aside angrily. Réfiyé Hanim took charge of the situation. "Tell me more, my son," she said quietly—it is always better to let an angry man talk till he runs down. The Pasha talked on; he ran down finally with the words— "Ah, this Kemal will have much to answer for!"

Féridé's natural impatience got the better of her, as often happened.

"For giving our country its rightful place among the nations again, he is answerable already," she said—gently, but with a sort of implacable firmness. The Pasha snorted—this was something he could not deny. "And you have not yet told Niné that the Ministry of the Culte is also abolished—which is really the root cause," she added unwisely.

"Ah, you are well-informed!" the old man exclaimed, with bitter sarcasm. "Doubtless your husband has had a hand in it all! So perhaps you can explain to me why this monstrous profanity has been considered expedient?"

"Yes, I can. It is to make it possible to liberate the minds of our people, and give them a true education, not the parrot-memorising of the hadis, which is all that they get in the medressés," Féridé retorted briskly. "Today, in the twentieth century, this is not enough."

"It has been enough for many centuries, when our nation was great," the old man said angrily.

"Our country has not been very great in *this* century, so far as I know," she returned energetically. "It was the Sultan's Government which signed the Armistice of Mudros and the Treaty of Sèvres, was it not? The terms of the Treaty of Lausanne are rather different, as I think you will agree—and for that, undoubtedly, Mustafa Kemal Pasha is answerable. Has he served his country so ill? Should we not trust him in other matters also?"

The Pasha almost choked. Féridé was a shrewd hitter, and it is always hard on the old when the young manifestly have the best of them in an argument. While he paused to think of a reply—and really there was no easy reply to her points—a small sound from the divan under the window made both the disputants, father and daughter, look round. Réfiyé Hanim had her hand to her breast; her breath was coming in little gasps. Féridé flew to her, while the Pasha moved across and rang a small silver hand-bell which stood on a table.

"Where are your drops? On your dressing-table?" Féridé asked.

"Yes—and fetch Marthe."

But the sound of the bell brought Mdlle Marthe hurrying in, followed by Ayshé, who had the drops and a medicine-glass in her hand. That small circumstance alarmed Féridé more than anything had yet done; evidently the little bell was often rung, and those within earshot knew what it signified. Miserable, penitent, anxious, she watched while the elderly maid and the elderly governess ministered to the old lady—presently they led her away to her room. The Pasha had withdrawn while all this went on; presumably to the dining-room, for when the door onto the upper hall closed after them he came back into the salon, where Féridé still stood, looking as troubled as she felt.

"We must avoid such arguments in your Grandmother's presence," he said, with a sort of stiff sadness. "She is not equal to them—she is rather delicate now."

Féridé went up and kissed him impulsively. "Oh my dear Father, yes! I am so sorry. What do all these things matter to us? Let us love one another in peace, as we always have."

The Pasha's stiffness relaxed. He kissed her in return, and stroked her hair. "You are my dear daughter still."

When Féridé went a few minutes later to Réfiyé Hanim's room she found the old lady propped up on a *chaise-longue* talking to Mdlle Marthe; she looked as bright as a button, and Marthe was actually smiling.

"Well, my child, did you make peace with your Father?" Réfiyé Hanim asked, before the girl had time to speak.

"Yes, I did. But are *you* better, Niné?" she asked anxiously.

"Much better, my child, I thank you; it was a light attack this time," she replied. Mdlle Marthe, a handkerchief to her mouth, made a sound like a discreet titter. The girl looked from one to the other.

"*Niné!* Oh, wicked one! You frightened me terribly," she said reproachfully.

"Better fear than anger and strife," said Réfiyé Hanim blandly.

.   .   .   .

Alec Grant had been sent to Cairo on a temporary Staff job when the Allied forces left Istanbul in October 1923, and rather more than a year later he returned to England again. He went down to Oxford for Christmas, and while he was there he laid siege energetically to Fanny. Even his Scottish deliberation and patience were nearly at an end; he was due to be made a major at any moment, and then they could marry—he had been dangling after Fanny for nearly six years, and now that he was likely to be at home for some time he wanted to clinch matters. His quiet determination—and more than a hint of passion—succeeded; in spite of a lingering uncertainty Fanny yielded at last, and their engagement was announced.

The next thing, of course, was for her to "meet his people," which she had never done, and early in the New Year they travelled up to Inverness and went to stay with his parents. Fanny liked the nice unpretentious uncompromising old house, with its plain well-kept garden; and she liked Alec's nice unpretentious uncompromising old parents even more—as for the Grants, they were charmed with Fanny's intelligence and good sense, even more than by her prettiness and easy lively manners. "She will make you a good wife, Alec—no man could wish for a better," Colonel Grant said to his son, with most unwonted expansiveness; and old Mrs. Grant said much the same, in her own fashion, and more words. They petted and made much of her—the whole atmosphere was charming and beguiling to a degree. It is always charming to be petted and approved of, especially as a daughter-in-law. But all the same panic seized on Fanny in that solid comfortable house in the North, with its crow-stepped gables and blazing fires, and kind faces round the fires. The harsh grey skies, the biting north-east winds, the mud—even the rich agricultural land, stark and gloomy in its winter emptiness; above all the evenings, closing in at four o'clock and confining one to the fireside, however pleasant, for the next seven hours. All these together filled her with a sort of fear, revulsion, even. Oh for sun!—sun and bright skies, heat on the skin and dry baking soil under one's feet, and dust in one's nostrils. Dressing for dinner one night in her cosy room, its pleasant chintzes glowing in the firelight, she asked herself in a sudden terror if she had made a mistake? And there and then she decided that however soon Alec got his majority, she would not marry him until she had gone back to Turkey, and seen all that again. She might be disillusioned; it might all be quite different now that Turkey was a Republic—and Kemal Pasha, whom poor Ahmet had idolised so, its President. (She had heard both from Alec and in one of Féridé's rare letters that Ahmet had been killed.) But whether it proved to be illusion or not, there was the place that had meant most to her in the world so far, and she would not embark on marriage, with Alec or anyone else—it was strange how that idea persisted—until she had seen it again, and seen Féridé again: Féridé, too, had meant more

to her than any other person so far except her uncle, and now, she supposed, Alec. And on her return to Oxford three weeks later—alone,
for Alec remained in the North with his parents—she persuaded Dr.
Pierce to let her write to Féridé and suggest a visit in the summer.

"Well, my dear, try it by all means," the Doctor said mildly. "I imagine they are still pretty anglophobe—after all it was we who beat them
in the first place, and then we stalled them at Chanak, when the others
ratted. Still, I gather from young Grant that this fellow Orhan Bey,
Féridé's husband, is pretty near the throne, as you might say; he will
know whether it's possible or not. I must say I should like to see old
Asaf Pasha again, very much. I wonder if the old lady is still alive?
She must be a great age by now if she is. Yes, my dear, write to Féridé,
and see what comes of it."

That letter reached the yali while Féridé was still there, and what
came of it was two warm invitations, one from the Pasha to Dr. Pierce,
inviting him and his niece to stay on the Bosphorus, and another from
Féridé pressing Fanny and her Uncle to visit her and Orhan at Ankara,
"and to stay with us for weeks and weeks!" "Oh, it is incredible to think
that we shall be together again," Féridé wrote. "Do you realise that it
will be *eleven* years this summer since I dragged Dil Feripé down to the
quay to say adieu? Oh my Two Eyes, I am already so full of impatience
and curiosity! As for my Father, he is joyful at the prospect of having
your Uncle's company again—and to Niné, I know, it will be the
greatest pleasure to see you."

But Réfiyé Hanim never did see Fanny again. She died in April,
just two months before the Pierces were due to arrive. She died very
quietly and peacefully, sitting as usual on her divan under the window;
in the middle of a conversation with the Pasha and Mdlle Marthe she
suddenly put a hand to her breast, saying—"Oh, what a curious pain."
The next moment she was dead.

Féridé hastened down to Istanbul when she received the news to be
with her father. Orhan followed later to attend the Mevlut, a sort of
memorial service which usually takes place forty days after the actual
death. It is given in a mosque, unless the house is large enough to ac-
commodate all the mourners—which the yali of course was—and is a
very beautiful and dignified ceremony. The Mevlut itself really con-
sists of a poem in very clear simple XIVth century Turkish describing
the birth, life and death of the Prophet Mohammed; when well chanted
it is extremely moving to listen to. On the day of the Mevlut for Réfiyé Hanim all the relations and friends of the family, summoned by a
formal invitation very like a French *faire part*, assembled in the great
stone-floored room with the fountain where Féridé's marriage had taken
place: the women, all veiled, were seated according to their age and

rank; the men, wearing their fezzes, stood. (In the old-style Turkey the wearing of the fez was a mark of respect; to be bare-headed especially in the presence of women, was a deep discourtesy.) When all the company were assembled the Hodja entered, in a black robe and an immaculate white turban, accompanied by six young Hafiz, or professional reciters of the Koran, chosen for the beauty of their voices, who proceeded to chant the lovely archaic words—a gold incense-burner, standing on a special table, filled the air with a sharp aromatic fragrance. The chant was followed by one or two hymns, in which the company joined; the name of the dead person was cited, and a prayer was said—on this occasion the names of Ahmet and his baby son were spoken also.

When the recitative, prayers, and hymns were over Dil Feripé came in, followed by Ayshé and two or three maids in rich dresses; their silk aprons were full of bonbons, Rahat Locoum (Turkish Delight) and other sweets, done up in cornucopias; they sprinkled rose-water from heavy wrought-silver bottles over the hands of the guests, and then handed to each a cornucopia of the traditional ceremonial sweet-meats. The maids were all weeping, of course; at such a moment it would have been almost an impiety not to shed tears, and in any case they had all loved and revered Réfiyé Hanim, and these were her final obsequies. Féridé, seated in her correct place among the ladies, glanced round the big low-ceilinged room—she could not help comparing this scene with the last time she had been in the sofa, on the occasion of her marriage. There had been weeping then too, but of joyful tears, and diamond brooches in dozens had been pinned by the givers on the bosom of her dress. It was very different today—Niné was dead, darling understanding supporting Niné; and she felt, quite truly, that with her grandmother a whole epoch had died.

She and Orhan stayed on at the yali for several days after the Mevlut, and during that time Asaf Pasha got on better with his son-in-law than he had ever done before. Orhan could no longer be considered as merely a brilliant and enthusiastic, but quite unimportant young man; he was now the trusted lieutenant of the President of the Republic and what he said counted. The old Pasha, with his strong political and social sense, fully realised this, and treated his son-in-law with quite a new respect—they met almost on an equality. Moreover in the campaigns against the Greeks they had an endless subject for conversation; and even more than Féridé Orhan could put the old gentleman *au fait* with the political scene in the new capital, give him, very discreetly, still more enthralling tit-bits to retail at the Cercle de l'Orient.

And of Ahmet they talked for hours on end. Turks love talking for hours on end anyhow—conversation there is still both a delightful occupation, and a recognised art: if it is *tête-à-tête,* so much the better. Painful as the subject was, Asaf Pasha could never hear enough of that action—of the layout, the terrain, the importance of the gully as a supply-line, and therefore of the small tepé which protected it; of Ahmet's ride along the space between the two firing-lines, and of the rout of the Greek machine-gunners. In the brilliantly-patterned, brilliantly-coloured study, where in 1914 Dr. Pierce had so admired the piece of Izzet's calligraphy—which had now joined many others on the walls—Orhan, on the very same table in the window, drew diagrams of the battlefield over which the old gentleman bent absorbed. "And Kemal Pasha said— 'Oh, my dear Ahmet!' And he really said—'I wish I had not sent him'?" —he would ask, over and over again, trying to console himself for the death of his only son by these words of the new leader; then he would go to his big European desk and get out the letter from Mustafa Kemal, and show it to his son-in-law—"See, here is what he wrote to me. Read it." He did that at least six times—grief and *désœuvrement* had made a very old man of the Pasha.

This was something which worried Féridé a good deal when she and Orhan had to return to Ankara in June—Kemal Pasha could spare his A.D.C. no longer, but it disturbed her to leave her father alone. It was a comforting thought that Fanny and Dr. Pierce would be at the yali in a fortnight; they would keep the old man company, and distract his thoughts. But—"Oh, how I should like to be *here* with Fanny!" she exclaimed on the last evening, as they sat in the salon, which seemed strangely empty without Réfiyé Hanim's figure in the corner under the window. "It would be so delightful to go over all the old places with her. What games we used to have, up in the koru, away from Dil Feripé."

"You were very wild children," Mdlle Marthe said.

"Yes, dear Marthe; I am sure we were perfect torments to you!" She smiled in recollection of the fun of being a torment. "I wonder so much what Fanny will be like now," she said then.

To her immense surprise the Pasha replied to this speculation. "I am sure you will find her a very sensible, well-mannered woman," he said with conviction.

"Baba! What makes *you* say that?" she exclaimed.

"Because she was a very sensible, well-mannered child—and as you bend the twig, so the bough grows," he replied.

Marthe put in her oar. "Ah yes, your dear Grandmother said the same. She often spoke of Fanny on the last weeks; she looked forward so much to seeing her again." She wiped her eyes.

"Did she really, dear Marthe?"

"To me also," the Pasha put in, "your Grandmother spoke much latterly of Fanny. She had a great affection for her, and went back often in recollection to that last summer when she stayed here with us. Ah"—he grunted—"Our last summer of peace and happiness, and the established order."

Chapter Nineteen

In the middle of July, 1925, Fanny and Dr. Pierce came up to stay with Féridé. Ankara was already a very different place from the city into which Féridé and Nilüfer had driven from Inebolu five years before. A big hotel, the Ankara Palace, had been run up near the Assembly Building on the way to the station—which was no longer alternately a sea of mud or dust, but quite a respectable road; streets and boulevards, planted with acacias, were being laid out along the valley below the citadel hill; the Government departments functioned in buildings of some sort, instead of each in a single room. A capital was gradually coming into being, albeit in a most bleak and uncompromising place; the foreign Embassies and Legations now kept one or more officials in Ankara to transact business—they lived mostly in the gaunt newly-built hotel, while their new Embassy buildings were going up on the sites which Mustafa Kemal had given them—as he had told Féridé he would, at dinner at Çankaya nearly two years before.

Orhan and Féridé had left their old picturesque but inconvenient quarters up in the citadel, and had taken a house among the vineyards on the slopes below Çankaya, not far from the Kiösk, where Kemal Pasha lived. It was an amusing and rather charming place, whitewashed, with a tiled roof and low cool rooms. Owing to the slope of the hill it was on two different levels—a track, along which a car could drive, led to the lower one, which was occupied by the owner of the house and vineyard; a flight of steps led up to a garden with a fountain, beyond which was the upper house, where Orhan and Féridé lived— long and low, with farm buildings opposite. The whole thing was a delightful mixture of summer villa and farm; the garden at the top of the steps was brilliant with flower-beds, Féridé's creation; on the other side of the house the rooms opened onto vine-wreathed balconies with a wide view across the valley to the twin hills, speckled with white houses and crowned with the battlements of the old citadel, while in the background rose the sharply-pointed summits of the Hussein Ghazi Dagh— all brilliantly clear in the dry glittering air. Life had become quite civilised, even in Ankara; Féridé had several servants now that the war was a thing of the past, including a tolerable cook and the faithful Fatma; Kezban, weeping loudly, had returned to her husband, to be the Gaiety of his House once more.

To this new home of her childhood's friend Fanny came driving in a smart official car on that hot July morning. Orhan had met them at the station, and came with them; she studied him with deep interest, this husband of Féridé's. Certainly he was very good to look at, so tall, so slight, with his eager intelligent face and his astonishing fairness. His exquisite French was less of a surprise—she expected Turks to talk good French, because Féridé, Ahmet, and Réfiyé Hanim had all done so; but Orhan's ebullient fluency in the foreign tongue was striking, all the same. In fact he was pleasing altogether: quick, enthusiastic, gay and friendly, with an expansiveness not very usual among Turks of the old régime. Féridé really seemed to have got a husband worthy of her, Fanny decided, as the car left the road to the Kiösk and began to lurch along the rutted dusty track which led off it to their destination. She was in a mood of heightened perceptiveness to everything that morning. From dawn onwards she had crouched at the window of her sleeper, gazing out at the Anatolian landscape—the bare rolling uplands with cream-coloured ranges of mountains rising out of them, mountains which took on unimaginably lovely tones of pink and violet as the sun rose, striking the peaks and casting shadows behind the ridges; at the valley-floors covered with short-stalked wheat, through which rivers wound in white stony beds, set here and there with noble groups of enormous old willows whose foliage, silvery as it was, yet detached itself with an effect of darkness against the prevailing pallor of tone of the whole landscape. How bare it was, how austere, how dignified! Yes, that was the word. And all the way, looking out on this scene, she had imagined Féridé travelling through it on her first journey to Ankara, in that little open victoria—had imagined that journey with an emotional intensity which surprised her herself. What a country through which to travel into the future, the unknown!

Ankara itself, the new, developing town, had given a jolt to this mood of the morning; the general rawness, the unfinished buildings bristling with scaffolding, the newly-laid roads planted with small wilting trees had no appeal at all. But as they bumped along the track between the vineyards, and the view across towards the citadel hills opened out, Fanny began to re-capture some of the charm which had held her at day-break, and when they pulled up beside the long house with its trellised vines shading the front, and climbed up the steps into Féridé's bright garden with its small tinkling fountain, the spell of Anatolia bound her again. A few steps along the upper courtyard, and there was Féridé herself at her open door.

For a couple of seconds the two friends stared at one another in silence, both trying to recognise the past in the present. Fanny saw a very beautiful young woman, poised, graceful, and still taller than her memory's picture, with a bright scarf twisted through her crisp dark hair; somehow strangely elegant, even in her simple summer frock, and even more strangely dignified, in some subtle way—but the grey eyes, the short nose—yes, it *was* Féridé! As for Féridé, she saw once again her little Canary, with her yellow head and decided mouth, her small sharp nose and fearless blue eyes, exactly the same as eleven years ago, save for the accomplished neatness of her dark silk travelling-dress and small close hat. After that moment's pause in suspension, she flew at her guest.

"La Canaria! Oh, you are just the same as always. Think of it—you are here!" She kissed her, and then turned swiftly to Dr. Pierce, very much the gracious hostess—"Dear Doctor, it is an unimaginable pleasure to see you again, and to receive you in my own house."

Dr. Pierce wrung her hand.

"Well, my dear Féridé Hanim—I must call you that now, I suppose! —it is most awfully good of you to have us here!" He too looked her over. "You've grown, do you know?" he said.

Féridé burst out laughing.

"Oh, dearest Dr. Pierce, I expect I have—one does grow, you know," she gurgled. "But how delightful this is! Come in, come in! It is not at all like the yali, you will find," she added, as she led them indoors.

It was not—but it was charming all the same. A broad passage ending in glass doors led straight through to the balcony; beyond its green leafy dimness the citadel and the hills, emptied of colour by the fierce sun, stood out pale against the pale sky. A dining-room opened out of the passage on the right, but Féridé took them into the salon opposite— a low room, fairly spacious and also with glass doors, closed now against the heat, with the usual divans round the walls, but some comfortable upholstered armchairs as well; it was full of beautiful things. On her recent journeys down to Istanbul Féridé had brought up many of her own possessions: fine rugs, embroidered hangings for the walls and sofas, cushions, even one or two of the little inlaid tables with their bulgy legs. Fanny pounced on one of these with a cry. "That came from the yali! It used to stand in the little room beyond the salon, near the window, surely, Féridé?"

"What a memory you have!—yes, it did."

Fanny moved to the window and stood looking out at the heated landscape, the sun-bleached slopes, the peasants still hoeing in the vineyards before the noon-day rest. "Oh Féridé, I like it up here; this is a lovely place," she said.

"You would not have thought it very lovely when we first came—at least, not our immediate surroundings," Féridé said with a smile. "It was terribly close and stuffy in the citadel—and oh how it smelt!"

"Can one see your house from here?" Fanny asked, her little beak still glued to the pane.

"No—one of the gateways hides it. I will take you to see it though, one day, if you like."

"I do like! I must see it. You must show me everything, every room! —and tell me all about it. Oh, how hard I tried to imagine what it was all like while the fighting was going on—you can't think! We didn't even know if you were in Ankara or not, at the time!"

Orhan, who had been seeing to the disposal of the luggage, now came in, followed by a servant with the inevitable tiny cups of coffee— modern, European as he might try to be, he addressed himself auto- matically to the male guest.

"Doctor, the whole house is at your disposal. We have no haremlik here," he said, with a certain complacency; "for one thing there is not room, and in any case those customs must die a natural death, now. But I have arranged a small room for you when you wish to work, or read, or be alone. I will show it to you"—and he led him away. Left alone with Féridé, Fanny turned to her and gave her a long examin- ing look.

"What is it, dji-djim? Are you trying to be sure that it is me?" Féridé asked gaily.

"Oh, it's you all right," the English girl said, slowly. "I was just try- ing to see what you'd turned into, with all these wars, and being mar- ried and everything. But you just *are* Féridé—thank goodness! It was fearfully important to me to know whether you would be still."

"Why, my Two Eyes?" Féridé realised that there was more in this than met the eye. "Come and sit down," she added, seating herself and touching another chair.

Rather slowly, Fanny sat down too.

"I don't suppose I shall be able to make you understand," she said. "It's just that my life in England, apart from Uncle, has always been pretty dull—nice, but dull. My school!—with all those little girls; and then North Oxford, and the women there, and the old old dons. And I always had in the back of my mind you, and the yali, this whole other world. But I was so small when I came away; and I've been won- dering ever since if it really was as wonderful as I'd thought it, or if it was just my imagination—idealising, because I was trying to escape from the dullness. I didn't think it was all imagination, but people" (people meant Alec, of course) "implied that it might be. So I had to come back and find out. I wanted to see *you* again, anyhow—but I wanted to find out as well if all the rest of it—well, if Turkey was true!—was what I'd thought."

"Yes?" Féridé said, with a delightful warmth and encouragement in her voice, watching the English girl.

"Well, it is true," Fanny said, getting up and going over to the window again. "It's glorious," she said, turning around. "Oh!—well, I'll tell you the rest another time," she ended awkwardly. She came back and gave Féridé another kiss. "Goodness, I am so glad I came! One doesn't want to lose the biggest thing in one's life," she said slowly, sitting down again. "But if one did find out that it wasn't true, one would have lost it."

This conversation intrigued Féridé considerably. She could take Fanny's point about her two worlds well enough, and understand her need to come back and test the reality of her childhood's paradise, for the yali had been a paradise to her too. But she had an intuition that there was more to it than that. However, she took no steps to find out just then—these things had a way of declaring themselves, sooner or later. Soon she took her guest upstairs to her room, also giving on a balcony smothered in vines, but with a different view—westwards, over the tiled roofs of the farm buildings beyond the upper courtyard to some nearer slopes covered with vineyards and tillage. Fanny of course went at once to the window—Féridé followed her. "Over there, to the left, do you see the tops of some big poplars? That is where the Kiösk stands —you can't see the house itself."

"What is the Kiösk?" Fanny asked; she could see the poplars.

"The Ghazi's house."

"The Ghazi?—oh, Kemal Pasha; yes, of course. Do you know him too, Féridé? What's he like?"

"I expect you would find him agreeable," Féridé said temperately— "people do, very often." (She, by "people," meant women.) "Of course for us he is simply the saviour of our country; we know him as that, and so to us he is wonderful," she ended quietly.

"Alec always says he is a wonderful general," Fanny incautiously slipped out.

"Alec? Who is Alec? *Fanny!*—Who?"

Fanny laughed.

"He's my fiancé, dji-djim. Yes, I'm engaged. I was going to tell you presently," she added, a little embarrassed.

"Is he a soldier? The red one—who came to the yali, and sent on my letter? But that was *ages* ago!" Féridé said, her eyes wide.

"Yes, that's the one. It did take rather a long time," Fanny said, a little shamefacedly. "But why do you call him the red one? Did you see him?"

"No, of course not!—how could I?" It was Féridé who was embarrassed now—her tongue had run away with her. "Baba saw him—he liked him. But is not his hair red?" She suppressed the lively picture which the Pasha had drawn for her at the time, of a red face, red hands, and red knees under the kilt.

"Well, yes, it is—absolutely couleur de carrottes!" Fanny said gaily. "But he is frightfully nice. I like red hair." She left Alec—she did not tell Féridé that she too would like her fiancé very much, because she felt morally certain that if they ever met they would have practically nothing to say to one another. She went back to Mustafa Kemal, who at that time aroused a sort of international curiosity, as certain individuals occasionally do. "Tell me more about the Ghazi," she said.

"Oh, do call him that to Orhan! How nicely you said it," Féridé exclaimed.

"All right, I will. But tell me about him. Is it true that he's married?"

"He was," Féridé said.

"Well, what happened? Did she die?"

"No. There was a divorce. It is rather a sad story," Féridé said thoughtfully. "Latifé Hanim was a splendid person, I thought—clever and quick, well-educated, and with advanced ideas. But"—she paused.

"But what?" Fanny was deeply interested.

"She was rather politically-minded," Féridé said thoughtfully.

"But doesn't he like women to be politically-minded? I thought I remembered reading that he was all for women's education, and the equality of the sexes, and all that. Didn't he make a speech about it?"

"Yes, he did. Yes, he is, really," Féridé said; "I mean in theory. Oh, and in practice too, I am sure—in time. But I suppose a man's wife can be a little too political, even in Europe—n'est-ce pas?" she said, with a fine little smile.

Fanny laughed.

"Oh, goodness yes! We have them in dozens! But certainly ultra-political wives must seem rather strange here." She paused. "I suppose everything is changing—bound to, probably. Oh Féridé, what a lot we shall have to talk about! Tell me, what time is lunch?"

In the pretty dining-room, over the delicious Turkish food—"I must say it is wonderful to eat a kébab again," Dr. Pierce said, wiping his moustache after demolishing a plateful of little noisettes of mutton, grilled on a spit and served on a basis of sour milk curd, and smothered in a rich sauce—Fanny was careful to slip in a remark about the Ghazi, as naturally as she had done upstairs, and Orhan turned to her with obvious pleasure, and with more attention than he had yet bestowed on her. He had agreed readily to his wife's eager desire to have the Pierces to stay, and had given himself quite a lot of trouble to arrange the visit, telling his chief what an important Turkish scholar Dr. Pierce was—really with an international reputation—and how turcophil; on these grounds the Embassy in London had been instructed, as an exceptional measure, to grant them visas, and Orhan had seen to it that the formalities on their arrival at Istanbul were not too tiresome. He had been genuinely curious to meet the Doctor; as to Fanny, his attitude to her had approximated fairly closely to Alec Grant's towards Féridé—a childish enthusiasm, idealised over the years, which could not really have any serious importance for his wife; but if she wanted her to come, come she should. With Dr. Pierce he was already delighted: he was learned, he was cultivated, employing very choice elegant Turkish turns of phrase—Orhan had a passion for elegance of phrase, written or spoken; and now that he turned his attention to Fanny, he began to be pleased with her too. It was an odd experience, whatever he might say about the desirability of the disappearance of the haremlik, to find himself sitting at table in his own house next to a foreign woman; and this particular foreign woman also talked astonishingly good Turkish. He asked her how that came about—"I should have thought you would have forgotten, in all these years."

"Oh, Fanny has kept it up—we've worked a good bit together, and she took a course in Persian and Turkish classical literature, after the war was over," Dr. Pierce answered for her.

"Persian, too? No, that is really astonishing!" Yes, she was quite a personality, this little Canary of Féridé's, as her sharp lively observations showed—and what an enthusiast for his country! "We shall show you everything!—Féridé, we must make many expeditions," he said.

"Before anything else, we must go up to the citadel, Féridé and I, and see your old house, and Sitaré Hanim," Fanny said.

"So!—you even know of Sitaré Hanim! But that was a terrible place," he said. "It would hardly interest you."

"On the contrary, it will interest me passionately," Fanny said briskly. "Not see the place where Féridé lived through the war?—what an idea! I must see that, and the Red Crescent building, and the hospital—everything!" And Orhan, half-pleased, half-startled at her decisiveness, had to laugh and agree.

They went a few days later. Orhan had to be at his bureau in the mornings, and for part of the afternoon too; Dr. Pierce had settled himself and his papers into the little room allotted to him, and worked there a good deal, but he also started going off for long walks alone, along the tracks between the vineyards and up over the stony hills beyond, covered with stiff sun-dried thorny plants, nearly all shining with glittering silver or gold seed-heads—he chatted with the older peasants he met, and usually came home very pleased, with several new proverbs or folk-tales. So the two girls, haremlik or no haremlik, had the salon to themselves, and talked away by the hour, covering bit by bit, patchily and discursively, the immense amount of ground left by their eleven years of separation, and re-learned one another as two people.

Sitaré and Ibrahim had moved back into their own larger house when their tenants left, and when Féridé lifted and let fall the big ring-shaped knocker on the familiar door, and stood waiting for it to be opened, she pointed out to Fanny the various features in the courtyard. "We pulled all our water up from that well, when we were washing for the wounded," she said.

"Goodness! But what a glorious well-head. It's Greek, surely?"

"Orhan thought it was," said Féridé carelessly—nothing Greek had any great merit for her. "And look—that is the kitchen, over there; we must wait for Sitaré Hanim to show it to us—it is a most extraordinary place!"

The door was now opened by Étamine, her lovely little face deliciously swathed in pale green muslin; gone were the careless days of the flying bas-ortü.

"Oh Féridé Hanim, it is you! Oh, what a pleasure! I will seek my Mother."

Sitaré, more roly-poly than ever, but still exceedingly pretty, was at the door in no time. "Ah, my dear dear Féridé Hanim! How seldom you visit me!—What an honour!" She checked at the sight of Fanny, an unveiled stranger in a hat, and with such yellow hair, plain for all to see! —a foreigner, obviously.

"This is my friend Fani Hanim, an Englishwoman," Féridé said, with due ceremony. "She wishes, Sitaré Hanim, to see the house where I lived so long, through the dark moment—if you permit?"

Sitaré babbled a startled acquiescence; she was astounded to be answered by the foreigner in fluent Turkish, with graceful thanks and all the correct expressions of politeness. In any visit to a purely Turkish house, however modest, there is always an immense amount of ceremonious formality, a sort of ritual of courtesy to be gone through. The two guests were led through the long hall into the "best" room at the further end, and made to sit on the best divan; Sitaré handed them sweets in a glass dish, Étamine hastened to bring cups of coffee, while various female relations, hearing of the exciting visitors, came in one after another, were introduced, and then seated themselves to listen silently to the main conversation. Several, to Fanny's great entertainment, brought their needlework in with them, and, their feet tucked up under them on the divans, continued either to do delicate embroidery on pieces of soft muslin, or to crochet narrow borders of silk lace along the edges of bas-örtüler or head-scarves; from these borders crochet roses, exceedingly close and fine in texture and an inch-and-a-half across dangled at intervals. These enchanted Fanny particularly, and she went over to a girl who was actually making one and asked to be shown how to do it, and what they were called? Oya, the girl said shyly. "A specialty of Ankara, Fani Hanim," Sitaré called across to her. Gradually the formal politeness gave way to a flood of eager chattering conversation, in which everybody joined; Fanny was struck with the immense gaiety and liveliness of these Ankarian women. Since embroidery clearly interested the English visitor, Sitaré Hanim, helped by Étamine, brought out her household treasures from the sandik, a splendid chest of inlaid wood, rather like an Italian *cassone*, which stood at one side of the room—embroidered muslins, nahlins, an embossed silver ewer; Ibrahim and Sitaré were substantial people, and had a great store of such things.

But one can have enough of other people's household treasures, and when they had been duly admired Féridé turned the conversation onto the war, which she knew was what most interested Fanny. At once a pandemonium of reminiscence broke out. The noise of the guns; how the houses shook and the windows rattled; Sitaré led Fanny to the window to show her where they had seen the red glare of burning villages in the sky—"There, over behind that long hill. So close!—we expected the Greeks at any moment. Many went away." They turned to their own immediate experiences—the washing, the cooking, the toiling up and down the hill laden with burdens. "Féridé Hanim did wonders— she who had no experience of such work—cooking, washing, nursing! Imagine!" Sitaré turned on Fanny—"Féridé Hanim nursed in the hospital, exactly like my Étamine, who was but a child, not yet wearing the çarşaf."

There was an interruption then. Someone brought in Güli Hanim —the news of Fanny's and Féridé's visit had spread through the quarter, and Güli had hastened up to get her share of the excitement. She like all the rest marvelled to see an Englishwoman, marvelled still more to hear her speaking Turkish; but being what she was, the Rose rather took charge of the conversation. "Did you know my dear Nilüfer Hanim?" "Yes, I met her once or twice," Fanny told her, and this led off onto a dramatic account of the confinement—"Ah, what a night! Never shall I forget it! And the fine little manlet, dying after all! And then his poor father killed too—so handsome, so brave!" That led them back to the war again; most of these cheerful chatting women had lost a husband, a brother, or a son. "Ah well, it was the will of Allah," they said. "They died for our country; they saved us." And then, quite spontaneously they began to speak of Kemal Pasha, with a simple fervour which astonished Fanny. "Ah, he was our leader! They gave in, those others down in Istanbul, but not he—not the Ghazi! He said we should be free, and free we are today." "And not sparing himself, look you—always in front, always among his men. My son told me—" the red-hot epic flowed on, till Fanny glowed. "How he used to shout, how he used to curse!—so my brother said." "And he made them laugh, and then they could fight again."

The visit, as often happens in Turkey, lasted for hours—visits are expected to last for hours in that timeless land, as timeless as Ireland. Fanny did at last succeed in seeing the rest of the house, including the kitchen, which really made her gasp, but not without some forcible tactfulness on Féridé's part. Before they left, a final little ritual of hospitality was gone through; Étamine, shy, lovely and smiling, brought out a bottle of rosewater, which she sprinkled over the hands of the guests—one of the prettiest forms of speeding the parting guest in the world. "Go with God," said the women; and "Remain with God" said Fanny and Féridé in reply.

In the car, driving back, Fanny turned enthusiastically to Féridé. "That was really wonderful—I wouldn't have missed it for anything. They talked so vividly—one might have been there oneself, during the Sakarya battles! What splendid people they are—and so friendly."

"Of course that you can talk to them made all the difference; they soon stopped being shy," Féridé said. "I doubt if any of them had ever spoken to a foreign woman before."

"No, I suppose not. Goodness, how they go on about Kemal Pasha, don't they? They fairly worship him," Fanny said. "He must be a terrific person."

"He is," Féridé said, without a smile.

"I should like to see him, I must say," Fanny said—"but I don't suppose he cares about the English much."

This time Féridé did smile.

"He is not a person to *garder rancune*," she said. "But he does not appear very much now, since Latifé Hanim left; he just sees his own intimates. You might meet him—you never know. I should wish that it might happen; you would be interested."

From which Fanny deduced, correctly, that her hostess did not feel it possible to take any steps to bring a meeting about. Oh well, why should she?—he was the Head of the State, after all, and who were they, the Pierces? But she could not help a slight feeling of disappointment—the way the women spoke of him had kindled her interest.

One afternoon a few days later she and Féridé were sitting in the salon after tea—Féridé did not feel well, so they were not taking their

usual evening walk up through the vineyards onto the open slopes above. Orhan and Dr. Pierce had gone riding. Actually Féridé was in the salon, with her feet up, but Fanny was out on the balcony as usual, watching the women on the flat terrace below making tarhara, small cakes or balls of yoghurt, barley, and flour which, dried in the sun, would keep for months, and be used for putting into the winter soup. Others were threading the fresh leaves of the vines onto strings till they looked like fat marabout boas; these would be sun-dried too, and used to wrap round small bits of meat when they were stewed or grilled. This was a different procedure from pickling the leaves in brine, which was the practice down at the house in the vine at Chamlidja, and Fanny was talking about it to Féridé, through the open door into the shaded room—"I suppose it's the dry air up here; probably they would get mouldy down there, so near the sea." Suddenly—
"Hullo, here's a man coming," she exclaimed.
"Probably to the farm," Féridé said languidly.
"I shouldn't think so—he looks frightfully urban," Fanny said, watching a square-set figure approaching along the lower track, wearing a kalpak above a very well-cut suit, a dog at his heels. "Besides, he's got a pointer with him. I think he's coming here," as she saw him turn to go up the steps into the garden. "He's got such a peculiar face," she said, coming back into the room—"all points and angles, and *furrows*. Who can it be?"
At her words about the dog Féridé had taken her feet down off the sofa, and was patting her hair hurriedly. Instead of answering Fanny's question—"Is it all right at the back?" she asked urgently.
"Yes—perfectly. But who is it?" As she spoke a servant threw open the door, and Mustafa Kemal Pasha walked into the room.
It was a thing he often did. He loved to stroll about the countryside alone, pausing at those flat-roofed dwellings of rammed earth which seemed to be squatting among the vineyards, and chatting with the inmates—he particularly liked talking to the old women, delighting in their broad cheerful earthy humour, their salty shrewdness. Occasionally they knew who he was, much more often not—the rash of busts and photographs of the national hero had not yet covered the face of Turkey as it does now. But when he had had enough of playing Haroun-al-Raschid, he had a habit of dropping in unannounced at the houses of his friends, to get a little informal conversation—it was another form of escape from official life.
When he came in Fanny guessed from Féridé's manner who it was, even before she was introduced and heard the great man's name. Like the women in the citadel he stared in surprise when she spoke. He did vaguely remember about the English Professor who was such a famous

Turkish scholar, and had even thought he would like to take a look at him some time; but if he had ever heard of a niece, or daughter or whatever she was, he had forgotten all about it, and he was immensely surprised to find a little yellow-headed Englishwoman, talking Turkish like a native, in Orhan Bey's drawing-room. He put one of his brusque questions to his hostess—"But how comes it that your friend speaks Turkish like this? *She* is not a professor?"

"No, no," Féridé laughed; "but she was much in Turkey as a child, and often at our house—she even stayed with us. She can write Turkish also," she added, a little mischievously.

"The script?"

"Yes, the script."

He stared at Fanny with his ice-blue eyes under the bushy eye-brows —she met his gaze steadily, a thing few people could do with any comfort for long together.

"How came you to do that, Mademoiselle?"

"Oh, I picked it up from my Uncle, and then it was useful for helping him with his transcriptions." As he merely stared harder—"Féridé Hanim and her family were so good to me," she said easily. "The happiest days of my life were those spent in Turkey."

"She was my favourite companion," Féridé put in.

"Yes, but the dadi did not approve of me, because I made you do such wild things!" said Fanny gaily, with a side-smile at their visitor.

"For example?" he asked, only relaxing his rigid scrutiny a very little.

"Oh, climbing trees, and tearing and losing her çarşaf," Fanny rattled on. "I may tell you, Your Excellency, that as a small girl Féridé Hanim had a great detestation of the çarşaf!" She had heard a good deal already about the Ghazi's views on the veil, and spoke with a half-mischievous intent.

"She has my sympathy," he said. "And you, Mademoiselle, what do you think of it?"

"Oh, enormously dignified and picturesque, of course, but madly unpractical. I should hate to have to wear it myself," said Fanny frankly.

"Some of our ladies are, I hope, learning to share your views," he said.

At this point coffee arrived, and immediately afterwards Orhan and the Doctor came in from their ride—they had heard from the servants who was there, and came straight to the salon. After the introductions Orhan promptly steered the conversation onto folk-lore and Dr. Pierce's book; he knew that mere chit-chat was apt to bore his chief. Kemal Pasha at once began his characteristic catechising—it was one of his chief ways of conducting a conversation, by which he amused himself and studied the person he was talking to at the same time. Intent, brusque, and yet not unfriendly, he rapped out questions. "Your book was well received?"

"Quite well," Dr. Pierce said tranquilly. "It sold over 9,000 copies. That is rather a lot, you know, with us, for such a specialised type of book."

Since a book which sells 3,000 copies in Turkey has had practically a *succès fou,* Kemal Pasha was impressed. But he did not show it—he never did. He went on to the next question.

"You study the folk-lore of all nations?"

"To some extent—for purposes of comparison. Of European countries, I mean; I know very little about the African and South American stuff," said Dr. Pierce, with his quiet scholarly comprehensiveness.

"Well, let us confine ourselves to Europe," said Kemal Pasha, on whom this carefulness of expression was not lost—here was obviouly a man who knew enough to impose limitations on himself, and recognising limitations was his own strong suit. "Do you find in Turkish folk-lore any special features, different to those of other countries?"

Dr. Pierce considered this.

"Not many," he said at length; "not beyond what one would expect. All folk-lores reflect the mode of life of the people who have created them."

"Do they not also reflect a people's attitude to life, a national character?" Kemal Pasha asked rather sharply.

"To some extent. It varies." Dr. Pierce was not going to distort facts for any man. "The folk-songs here show rather marked differences," he pursued calmly—"they are quite distinctive."

Mustafa Kemal pounced.

"For example?"

"Allusiveness; the indirect approach; and a sort of quality of reverie," said Dr. Pierce. "North European folk-songs, especially, are often just long stories full of incidents, ballads really, however dramatic—like the *Twa Sisters o' Binnorie* or the *Berkshire Tragedy.* I believe that has something like twenty verses, hasn't it, Fanny?" She nodded. "Whereas the Turkish songs," he went on, "frequently express a single situation, or not even that—just a frame of mind, an emotion, rounded into a brief lyric, and so full of allusions to the whole body of the people's thought and history that a person unfamiliar with those can't pick up the point at all. I think that does throw a light on the national character—the pensiveness, the sense of nostalgia of the people."

Kemal Pasha had been listening with close attention; when Dr. Pierce ceased speaking he leaned forward and asked—"Can you give any instances?"

Dr. Pierce considered a moment, and then turned to Fanny. "That song you got from young Ahmet, our last summer at Bebek— that was a good example. Can you remember how it went?"

"Yes, of course."

"Well, let His Excellency hear that."

"Shall I say it or sing it?" Fanny asked, turning to Féridé.

"Sing it," Féridé said, with a glance at her guest—he nodded.

Fanny was no shyer now than she had been as a child. She stood up, and launched without hesitation into the Falcon Song, in her clear strong voice—the evocative words and haunting melody filled the low room, in which shadows were already gathering, though outside, beyond the foliage of the balcony, the bare heights were taking on a glow of pale gold. Orhan watched his chief's face while Fanny sang— half in reflected light, half in shadow, all the rugosities of its strange structure were brought out and intensified as he sat listening. When the song ended—"There, you see—" Dr. Pierce began; but Kemal Pasha held up his hand.

"Once again," he commanded curtly.

Fanny, with a half-glance of amusement at Féridé, sang the song once more. Even through her close singer's concentration on the sounds, the articulated syllables, the emotional content of what she sang —one of the most elaborately complex forms of consciousness that exists —she was just aware of the thought—How strange to be singing this again, in Turkey—and for Turkey's ruler, Mustafa Kemal!

When Fanny's voice fell on the last notes for the second time, Kemal Pasha turned to the Doctor.

"Yes, an excellent example of what you say—and a beautiful song." He wheeled round on Fanny—"Sung by an admirable singer! You have completely caught the spirit of it. My felicitations, Mademoiselle." From then on he gave rather more of his attention to Fanny; he was evidently pleased by this foreign singer of his country's songs, praised her voice, and asked if she had had it trained?

"Oh, Fani Hanim could always sing," Féridé put in; "when she was little we called her la Canaria."

He smiled, courteously, slightly, with a half-glance at that yellow head. "Yes, a true Canary—a genuine song-bird."

Fanny asked Féridé if she still had the setting which Orhan had made for the song.

"Oh yes—it is among my things."

"I should like to hear it again," Fanny said, "and be sure that I have got it right." She turned to Kemal Pasha—"Eleven years is a long time to carry a melody in one's head, Your Excellency."

"It is eleven years since you heard it? More remarkable still! But I too should like to hear this setting made by Orhan. I did not know you composed, mon enfant."

"There has not been much time, Sir, for composing music these last few years," Orhan said gaily—he was delighted with Fanny's little success.

"Quite right, quite right! Nor will there be in the next few years —we shall see to that!" Kemal said laughing. He rose, and slapped his A.D.C. on the back. "Plenty of work for the good workers, who can do it!" Then he turned to his hostess. "But, now, Féridé Hanim, I must hear this early *opus* of Orhan's, and I must hear your Canary—or nightingale, perhaps"—glancing in Fanny's direction with a little bow— "sing again. You must all come and dine at the Kiösk, when I shall also hope to talk more with you, Professor. Would tomorrow suit you?"

"Tomorrow Fethi Bey and half the Cabinet are dining with you, Sir," Orhan reminded him.

"Are they, my son? I am sure you know! Well, my social conscience, tell me when it can be?"

And Orhan told him that it could be three days hence.

Chapter Twenty

THREE evenings later, accordingly, they went to dine at the Kiösk. As they left the car Fanny paused and looked about her: at the great poplars standing round the spring, their leaves, in the evening breeze, whispering to the murmuring water; at the half-seen view down the glen of the valley and the hills beyond, brilliant in the late light. "What a beautiful place!" she murmured to Féridé.

But no one could call the Kiösk very beautiful inside. Either Latifé Hanim or Kemal Pasha himself had shown little taste in interior decoration—which indeed is not the Turkish strong suit, according to western ideas. Turks still halt undecided between their own carved woodwork, screens and tables, their passion for inlay, mother-of-pearl, and embroideries, and the European furniture of which, having little experience, they are poor judges—for the most part their taste is quite at sea among these alien objects, and they live cheerfully with pseudo-Jacobean horrors, or Victorian mahogany, or just plain Tottenham Court Road. To Fanny's eyes the interior of the Kiösk was mostly hideous. They entered by a hall with a fountain in the middle, a piano in one corner, and miscellaneous chairs and tables scattered about; the dining-room was furnished with rather heavy richness—the food however was good, and the wine admirable. The prettiest place was the drawing-room, with pale colours and curtains, and a general effect of light and spaciousness; but they did not spend long in it, for soon after they rose from the table their host ordained an adjournment to the hall in order to try out Orhan's accompaniment to the Falcon Song. He sat down at the piano and strummed it over a couple of times—he played easily and agreeably—and then summoned Fanny to his side and played for her while she sang.

"Charming, Orhan—very pretty," he said at the end. "Do you know any other Turkish songs, Fani Hanim?"

Fanny did know one or two, and he vamped an accompaniment to them, not unskilfully—playing the piano was a thing he enjoyed. Dr. Pierce looked on with interest. This tranquil parlour scene threw quite a new light on the brilliant soldier, the harsh politician, the ruthless creator of a new state out of the ruins of an old one.

Next Kemal Pasha asked Fanny if she knew any English songs?—folk songs?

"Oh, many!" she told him.

"Then sing me one—what about this one with twenty verses, of which your Uncle spoke?"

Fanny had no intention whatever of inflicting *The Berkshire Tragedy* on an audience which understood no English, and declared roundly that she could not remember it. "But there is one—oddly enough it is more Turkish in feeling, for it is just one situation, one mood—a young woman who wishes to cross a river to meet her lover, and asks her maid to find her a boatman."

"Sing it, then," Kemal Pasha said, his fingers straying softly over the keys—and Fanny sang *The Water of Tyne*.

> *"I cannot get to my love, if I should dee,*
> *The water of Tyne flows betwixt him and me,*
> *And here I must stand, with the tear in my ee*
> *Both sighing, and sickly, my sweetheart to see.*
>
> *Oh where is the boatman, my bonny hinny?*
> *Oh where is the boatman?—bring him to me*
> *To ferry me over the Tyne to my honey,*
> *And I will remember the boatman and thee.*
>
> *Oh bring me a boatman—I'll give any money,*
> *And you for your trouble rewarded shall be—*
> *To carry me over the Tyne to my honey,*
> *Or row him across that rough water to me."*

The Water of Tyne has a singularly beautiful air, pensive in spite of the urgency of the words, which Fanny conveyed very well; there should be, and she gave, a slight *rallentando* on the last four syllables, all on the same note—her little audience remained silent for a moment at the close. Then, to her great surprise, Orhan burst out laughing.

"But this is not romantic at all!" he exploded—"Sir, it is all about baksheesh! This young lady offers bribes to the boatman, bribes to her maid to find him!"

"And does this never happen in Turkey, Orhan Bey?" Fanny asked, rather nettled. Before he could answer—"Do you know English then, Orhan?" Dr. Pierce enquired with surprise.

"A little—enough!" Orhan said, still bubbling with mirth.

His host spoke rather repressively. "All the same, it is a beautiful song. I thank you for it, Fani Hanim."

Fanny bowed slightly. She was still rather cross with Orhan for spoiling her effect.

"Is it not a little close?" she said. "Could we not sit outside, Your Excellency, and listen to the water and the sound of the trees?"

"Certainly we can," Kemal Pasha said. He summoned a servant, and chairs were carried out onto the driveway in front of the house, where they could indeed hear the gentle voice of the spring and the now almost inaudible murmur of the poplar-leaves high overhead; the stars, huge and splendid, burned in the indigo sky and sparkled through the pale whispering foliage; faint scents of sun-dried aromatic herbage came to them on the small movements of air which stirred the warm night. Fanny, and Féridé too, would have been well content to sit quiet and surrender to the spell of the hour and the place, but Kemal Pasha was never one for sitting quiet—a rather un-Turkish trait in him. Tables promptly followed the chairs, and trays with Scotch whisky and soda the tables, out onto the gravel by the great trees; drinks were poured out. But for the moment the Ghazi had had enough of music and feminine talk, and turned his attention to Dr. Pierce. He sounded him out, in his cross-examining way, on national characteristics in general, and on the Turkish ones in particular—each nation, he insisted, had its particular genius, which must be respected, freed from whatever cramped it, and fostered. He explained exactly how the old system of education had cramped the mind of Turkey, and how he proposed to make the people free of the riches of western ideas by new schools, new methods. "To be modern, to be European, electric light and sanitation are not enough—that is the mistake which the Shah of Persia and the Amir of Afghanistan have both made. I shall not make it! If a people is to be modernised, Europeanised, they must think and feel as Europeans do; and for that they must share in the mental background of Europeans."

"You mean, give them access to European literature? All along the line, from Sophocles to Dickens?" Dr. Pierce asked.

"Certainly."

"That's a tall order. Even when you've had the translations made, it's going to cost hundreds of thousands to get text-books printed for your schools; your script is so infernally expensive to set up in type," Dr. Pierce said.

"You are right! 75 per cent more costly than roman type. But we shall not use our script!" Kemal Pasha said triumphantly.

"You mean you're going to romanise the alphabet?"

"Just that. Then, when boys and girls from the higher schools learn French or English, they will be able to read French and English books. That will give them a key which opens the doors of undreamed-of-treasuries!"

"Well, that's practical," Dr. Pierce said with approval. He thought for a moment. "They won't learn the old script at all?" Kemal Pasha shook his head.

"Well, you see what that also means," the Doctor said. "The key that unlocks one door will lock another—you will close the past to them."

"My dear Doctor, I wish to lock the door of the past! It is dead—of what use is it to them today?"

"It has beauty and dignity," the Doctor said mildly.

"Well, scholars can use it!—the old books will be there for them. But —you are a practical man, and I ask you this: has our youth *time* both to imbibe modern ideas and western culture, and also to mouth over archaic texts? And if they cannot do both, which will serve them best in the world of today?"

"Ah well, I'm a bit of a traditionalist, myself," Dr. Pierce said, "From the practical point of view no doubt you're right. The script is certainly an obstacle. But don't forget that you yourself recognize the importance of *respecting* the national genius of a people. You'll make a mistake, I fancy, if you try to go too fast."

Mustafa Kemal Pasha was not accustomed to having it suggested to him that he might make a mistake. The combination of practicality and sympathy which the Doctor showed for his schemes, together with that hint of caution, caused him to launch into one of his famous orations, this time on the future of Turkish culture and the Turkish people, as he envisaged it. It was very much what Orhan had outlined to Féridé long before, but immensely amplified—the man who, two years later, was to make a speech lasting for six days now held forth to his guests for over two hours. Féridé, to whom these discourses were no novelty, and who secretly longed to be in bed, glanced anxiously at her friends; but Dr. Pierce was listening with attention, now and again trying—and failing—to slip in a remark, while Fanny sat frankly spell-bound.

They only left at 2 A.M. when their host, like a clock, had at last run down. Driving home in the starlight Dr. Pierce, stifling a vast yawn, gave his comment. "Really quite sound, a lot of what he said. He's got it thought out, you can see—though whether he will be able to put it through is another matter. Your nation is pretty conservative, Féridé Hanim—it's a strength, in one way." He stifled another yawn. "But my goodness, what energy! The man's a perfect dynamo! I suppose he was working all day, wasn't he, Orhan, my boy?" And Orhan replied, with detail and emphasis, that his chief had been at work since 9 A.M.

· · · · · · · ·

The hot, hot days of the blazing Anatolian summer flowed by—gently, lazily, as time does flow in Turkey; with long spells of conversation, in the salon or on the embowered balcony, with walks, with strolls—

rather early or rather late, when the sun was endurable. They made some of the expeditions that Orhan had promised: to the Kary-aghdi-Dagh—the "It Snowed" Mountains, a low range about two hours' drive from Ankara, full of small steep glens, clothed with a thick natural growth of pines; to the Tschubuk Brook, a rather muddy stream not far from Kalaba, famous as the site of one of the battles of Tamburlaine the Great, the Scythian warrior immortalised by Marlowe.

"Is it not brave to be a King, Teychelles?
Usumcané and Theridamas?
Is it not passing brave to be a King,
And ride in triumph through Persepolis?

—Fanny spoke the resounding words to Kemal Pasha, who for once was with them, as they sat under the silvery willows on the low bank, and then made a rapid *ad hoc* translation of them into Turkish. He asked who the poet was, and she told him of Marlowe the Elizabethan, and his tremendous drama of Tamburlaine. He appeared struck by this, and made a curious comment—"In Elizabethan days the English seem to have understood our outlook better than they do now."

"That is perfectly true," Dr. Pierce said. "For one thing everyone was familiar with Turkish battles and Turkish exploits then, because we and the Venetians and so on were always fighting them. And the Elizabethan Englishman was quite untroubled by washy nineteenth-century humanitarianism—he was a natural man, as your people are still." At which the Ghazi laughed loudly.

Besides the picnics, there were rides. Orhan had horses at his command, and he and Dr. Pierce had ridden from the outset of the Pierces' visit; but after a few days Kemal Pasha offered Fanny the use of one of his own horses, and a beautiful mare, Nazli, was put at her disposal. Féridé did not ride; she had confessed happily to Fanny in the course of the first few days that she was at last pregnant.

Fanny was delighted. "My Two Eyes, this is wonderful! I am so glad. How I wish Réfiyé Hanim could have known! But what a joy for your Father. It was so terribly tragic, Ahmet's poor little baby dying like that."

But though Féridé could not accompany them, the rides were an extreme delight to Fanny. During those summers in the Cotswolds a local resident with a large stable who had taken a fancy to the Oxford don and his lively niece had lent her first a pony, then a staid cob, then a well-mannered and reliable hunter—and on this succession of mounts she had become a fairly competent and a very ardent horsewoman. She was quite fearless, and delighted in the swift movement and the feel of a horse under her. At home she could not afford to ride, and one of her unconfessed disappointments about Alec's home had been that his parents kept no horses—except in the Borders the Scotch do not, on the whole, ride. But at Ankara, evening after evening a groom brought the nervous beautiful mare to the foot of the steps—sometimes with the message that the Effendis should first pass by the Kiösk, where the Ghazi would join them; then she and Orhan and Dr. Pierce would ride off along the sandy track and draw rein under the poplars beside the spring, where four or five horses waited in the shade—Kemal Pasha would come out, trim as ever in riding-dress, followed by several A.D.C.s, and the whole company would clatter off, laughing and talking: up onto the Dikmen Hills, where the tracks are rough and stony, and through their shallow arid valleys, or away to the south, always over open rocky country with wide pale views on all sides. Kemal Pasha and Fanny occasionally rode together a little ahead, the grooms and A.D.C.s keeping a respectful distance; once or twice he dismounted beside a cabin and took her in with him to talk to the people inside, and roared with laughter at their amazement at the yellow-haired unveiled foreign girl, who talked Turkish like one of themselves. Altogether Fanny was extraordinarily happy during those summer days. She was back in Turkey, and it was all that she had dreamed it through years of absence; she was with Féridé again, and found the "wonderful person" of her childish memories a beautiful, distinguished, and charming woman, with a clear intelligence and great sincerity and integrity. She thought quite honestly that these things were the principal source of her happiness; her occasional meetings with the national hero, the Head of the State, were just delightful extras, the cream on the pudding, so to speak. There were social doings too, though not very many—pleasant afternoon visits to the houses of various members of the new Government with whom Orhan and Féridé were on intimate terms, who like the peasants were startled and pleased to meet an English Professor and a pretty girl who spoke perfect Turkish, and made no calls on their careful French; and now and again a little dinner at Çankaya, at which the host always made Fanny sing Turkish songs to his guests, accompanying her himself with a slight, rather satisfied air of showmanship—Look what a pretty clever creature I have got here!

His attentions to Fanny, slight and formal as they were, began at last to disquiet Féridé a little. She knew his charm for women, though she herself had never actually suffered from it, and she knew too his curious irresponsibility where women were concerned. But she only began to worry seriously after the ball.

Late that summer Mustafa Kemal Pasha gave a ball at the Ankara Palace. He had caused the hotel to be built partly, at least, for the express purpose of having a place in which to do large-scale entertaining, impossible at the Kiösk. The invitations came out, and caused a buzz of excitement. It was to be one of the biggest entertainments so far given; all the foreign diplomats were to be there, and all the Turkish wives were invited, as well as their husbands. A day or so after the cards had been sent Kemal Pasha dropped in one afternoon at Féridé's house, in his casual fashion—sitting in the salon, over coffee and cigarettes, he made a formal request to his young hostess that she would appear at the ball *en grande toilette,* if possible with a *décolletage,* and without even a scrap of tulle on her head. (Féridé still clung to her discreet habit of wearing a graceful arrangement of pale-coloured French veiling, pinned with diamond stars over her dark hair, at the dinners at Çankaya.) "This is my personal request to you," he said, with urgent persuasiveness. "You will have the support of your young friend" —glancing at Fanny; "she, I am sure, has never veiled her head! And it is important that the foreign diplomats who will be present should see that there are at least some Turkish women who are up-to-date, and liberated from outworn customs."

Féridé, with a reluctance which she did not allow to appear, agreed —she could hardly do anything else. But when he had gone—"This is going to be exceedingly disagreeable!" she exclaimed to Fanny. "With the diplomats it is all very well. They know how to behave. But there will be many among our own people who will disapprove furiously, and will make themselves unpleasant, you will see. I wish he had asked anything but that! It is quite another thing for you—you are accustomed to going bare-headed, and wearing low-necked dresses."

"Yes, but I haven't got one here," Fanny said briskly—"I never thought I should need it. I've only got that black one I showed you, with the transparent lace top and sleeves, that you liked so much. Will that do?"

"If it is all you have, it must do. How I wish I had something as discreet! In Istanbul I should mind less; people are more advanced down there. But here!"

Fanny thought for a moment.

"Have you got a black dinner-dress?" she asked.

"Yes—why?"

"We could take out the sleeves and cut a décolletage to fit my lace top, and you could put in my lace, and I could go lowneck, and you 'discreet,' as you call it. You're no bigger around than I, only taller."

"Fanny, this is brilliant! Would you do it? Do you not mind?"

"Goodness no—I don't care tuppence about going low-neck, naturally. You can lend me some white lace to dress up the neckline, can't you?— I expect you've got masses."

Féridé had masses, and the alterations to the dresses were put in hand at once. The two girls were both actually engaged one morning on gathering some old fine duchesse flouncing to make a bertha for Fanny's frock when Madame T., the wife of a young Government official who was rather friendly with Féridé, was announced. Mme T. was a pretty lively young woman, who always dressed well; she had already met Fanny, and after the usual flow of graceful politenesses had been gone through she had no hesitation in embarking on her errand in front of the foreigner, though she made some courteous apologies for doing so. To her also, it seemed—but through her husband—it had been suggested that the Ghazi would like her to appear in evening dress— "et sans tulle!" "Oh Féridé-djim, do give me your advice! What are you going to wear?" she said urgently. "I have no low-neck dress, naturally. I must say I wish the Ghazi had not quite so many of these European ideas! Fani Hanim, I mean no discourtesy; to you all this must seem folly, for I suppose you appear constantly with your shoulders bare," she said with a disarming smile—" but to us it is a difficult thing, you understand."

Fanny knew enough to understand very well how difficult it was, and said so. At her suggestion they went to Féridé's room and showed Mme T. the dress with the newly-arranged black lace top and sleeves; this compromise commended itself, and the young woman went away somewhat comforted, to organise a similar transparency for herself. "Mon Dieu," Féridé said to Fanny when she had gone, with a rather rueful laugh, "we shall see some curious toilettes at this party, I wager you!"

When the day came, they did. Orhan being in attendance they had to be there early, and stood and watched the big garish rooms filling up. Many of the Turkish men had by now risen to tail coats and white ties, but a large number wore their fezzes as well, which produced a very odd effect. Men predominated; the more old-fashioned and stubborn of the deputies had left their wives at home, invited or not, and stood staring sourly at those who had come. One thing struck Fanny particularly—as these married couples passed through the entrance of the big room where the company was assembling, several of the wives stood politely aside to let their husbands pass in first, as a man would do in Europe; and she saw that Féridé noticed this too. Most of these ladies had made no attempt at formal evening dress, indeed Mustafa Kemal had only suggested it to a few of the younger, more enterprising and more elegant women in Ankara, and especially to those who, like Féridé, were sufficiently well-born to be less likely to suffer from the inhibitions of the bourgeoisie. So the room became fuller and fuller of high necks and long sleeves, of every colour and kind; the wives of the foreign diplomats, in their French dresses, jewels, and long white gloves looked like birds of Paradise among a flock of hen pheasants in this curious throng. Féridé knew several of them, and after introducing Fanny took her place near them, sheltering in their company till the President of the Republic should arrive; from this coign of vantage she looked round curiously to observe how many of her countrywomen had carried out the Ghazi's behest. Only about a dozen, so far as she could see. Mme T. had made quite a success of her transformation, having (not too obviously) converted the lace sleeves of her silver dress into a transparent neck, leaving short ruffles at the shoulders. Féridé glanced with envy at the tiaras worn by one or two of the foreigners. "How I wish I had a diadème also!" she murmured to Fanny—"My head feels so strange. That one there is like a hat, it is so big!"

"Get one made; you have diamonds enough for six!" Fanny returned merrily.

When Kemal Pasha eventually arrived, "looking absolutely smashing in full fig," as Fanny incautiously phrased it afterwards in a letter to Alec—and indeed he did, with stars and orders glittering on his faultless dress clothes—there was a certain amount of ceremonious presenting, arranged largely by Orhan, and then the dancing began.

Dr. Pierce leant against the wall and looked on. To him it was a very strange spectacle indeed, this mixed gathering of men and women— in Turkey, and in public. He thought of the past with something very like regret; the past had been so dignified, the people so content with the ordering of their lives by custom and tradition. As he watched these Turkish women dancing modern dances, body to body with foreign men (for the diplomats were doing their duty) it occurred to him to wonder, first, whether the western way of life was really so superior to the oriental, and then whether it could be right to do such violence to national tradition, national feeling? Kemal himself had said, at their first dinner at Çankaya, barely a month before, that the peculiar genius of a nation must be respected, fostered. Was the national genius being fostered here, at this moment, let alone respected? Close by him, also propping up the wall, were several old Generals and reactionary elderly deputies—and as Féridé, Mme T., and the other heroines of the occasion spun past, with uncovered hair and shoulders visible, even if through lace, he heard their hissed comments: the Turkish equivalent of "brazen hussy!" The women heard—the old men saw to that— and Dr. Pierce saw their embarrassment, their distress, and wondered again if all this was really for the good of the nation which he loved. But then he was a traditionalist, and therefore perhaps something of a reactionary himself.

Fanny also noticed it all—little was ever lost on her. As she was twirled round the great room under the glaring lights in the arms of Orhan, of young diplomats, or of various Turks she too heard the hissed comments, and noted the discomfort of the women whose uncovered hair and shoulders called them forth. "How very ill-bred those old men are!" she made a point of saying, very audibly, to her Turkish partners; she too might regret the past, but the present made her angry. "So ignorant, also," she would add, and was delighted to see the angry looks which greeted her shafts as they reached the grumblers ranged along the walls.

But the *décolletées* ladies had a much doughtier champion than Fanny, as the whole room presently saw. Very little was ever lost on Mustafa Kemal Pasha either, and he had been expecting this particular development, and was on the watch for it. Poor Mme T. was really beginning to falter, at last, under the public unpleasantness of this adverse comment, which grew bolder all the time, and after she had just passed a trio of old men whose remarks were especially opprobrious she turned to her partner and murmured that she was tired, and would like to sit down. She had hardly taken her seat when she found Kemal Pasha himself standing before her.

"You are tired, Madame? Would you like some champagne to restore you? No? An ice, then? One moment"—and he stepped across the floor, the dancers making way for him, to the three elderly deputies. "Come, Mehmet Effendi, Talaat Effendi—I have a little task for you. Follow me, please"—and he led them over to Mme T.

"Madame, allow me to present Mehmet Effendi to you—he will fetch you an ice. And this is Talaat Effendi—he will bring you a glass of water. Hasten, my friends; see that Madame T. is served well." He remained at her side, talking to her with the most deferential politeness till the outraged old men returned, and under the eyes of the whole company were obliged to wait on her. Then he sought out the third, and made him do the same to another woman in a low-necked dress; and so he continued to do throughout the evening —quite easily, apparently quite casually, but with a look in his eye that all who knew him understood. None of the unmannerly elders were spared: deputies, Generals, Valis, all were pressed into the service of the low-necked ladies, and no one dared to disobey. In a way it was a scene of high comedy, besides its wider significance.

This also Fanny saw, and her combative little spirit glowed with approval. She was dancing with a boy from the British Embassy called Fisher when Mme T. and the next woman were singled out for Kemal Pasha's protective attentions, and to her countryman she was not afraid to say what she felt. "Isn't he *magnificent?*" she exclaimed.

"I must say I like to see those old toads of deputies being done down,"

Mr. Fisher said temperately. "I couldn't understand what they were saying, but they looked like the Elders accusing Susanna."

"They were being *exactly* that," Fanny returned.

"Awful shame," said Mr. Fisher—"I call it exceedingly plucky of those girls to turn out in evening dress—or at least to have a shot at it! I wonder how the Ghazi got them to. Such a pretty girl, that one in silver; I wish I knew her."

"Oh, that's Mme T. I can introduce you to her—I know her," Fanny said.

"Oh, good. Of course you know all these people, don't you? You're staying with Orhan Bey, aren't you? I wish you'd introduce me to Madame Orhan—she looks an absolute stunner. That's a very pretty frock she's wearing—and what diamonds!"

"I will," said Fanny obligingly.

"Oh, splendid. I see Orhan Bey occasionally—he's an awfully able fellow, and so amusing, too. How do you come to know them so well?"

"She and I played together as children, as a matter of fact."

"What, out here?"

"Yes—I used to come with my Uncle every summer. Oh look," she said gleefully—"there he goes again!"

"What, the President? Oh, so he is," said Mr. Fisher, steering his partner skilfully in the direction of another group consisting of a lady in a low dress, the Ghazi, and two rather ancient Generals who under an appearance of civility both looked as if they had just swallowed an emetic.

"I do think he's superb," Fanny said as they danced away again. "It's so frightfully *kind*, for one thing. But then he is awfully kind."

"That's about the last thing one usually hears said of him," said Mr. Fisher, in surprise.

"Oh, because people don't know him, that's all. He's so considerate, and frightfully amusing—and yet without ever losing that sort of special dignity he has. And if ever there was a man who loved his country, and worked himself to the bone for it, it's he!" she said eagerly. "He half-killed himself during the war, Orhan Bey says, and even now he simply slaves away, night and day, to get things better for them. I think he's absolutely wonderful. He's so sweet with the country-people, too"; she went on—"he goes in and sits down in those little houses, and hobnobs with the old crones, and rags them, and lets them rag him back—a little crudely," the girl said frankly, "but that's what they like, of course."

Mr. Fisher fairly stared.

"But you haven't *seen* him doing that?"

"Oh goodness yes—several times. He takes me in with him when we're out riding," said Fanny simply. "I think he thinks it's good for them to see an Englishwoman, and especially bareheaded!"

Mr. Fisher's surprise was by now such that it almost robbed him of speech. That a fellow-countrywoman of his own should go for rides with the remote and inaccessible Head of the State, who only received Ambassadors at the most formal interviews, fairly took his breath away. "Let's go and have a drink," he said. "I must say he does one quite well in the matter of champagne—and that is a form of kindness which I personally appreciate very much."

Fanny laughed. At the buffet Mr. Fisher imbibed the champagne for some time in silence; he was thinking. At last—"It's coming back to me," he said. "Don't you know Alec Grant?"

"Yes."

"That's it. I knew he had a friend who had Turkish friends, when he was at Constant. Somewhere down on the Bosphorus, wasn't it? A Pasha or something?"

Fanny smiled. "Yes. Orhan Bey's wife is the Pasha's daughter. But how do you come to know Alec?"

"Oh, we were at school together. 'The Fiery Cross' we used to call him, he used to get into such terrific rages if anything upset him! And we've always kept up. I'm very fond of old Alec. Do you still see much of him?" he asked casually.

"I'm engaged to him," said Fanny, with a pretty sparkle of mirth.

"Oh, Good Lord!" Mr. Fisher began. "I say, you must—" But his aghast apologies were interrupted by a slight movement among the crowd about them, as Mustafa Kemal Pasha himself came up.

"Fani Hanim, will you do me the honour of dancing with me?" he said, with a formal bow. As she moved away on his arm Mr. Fisher turned to the buffet and secured himself another glass of champagne. He was still thinking; his duties in the ballroom could wait. So this was Alec's girl! He'd seen that he was engaged, but it was some months back, and he'd forgotten the name. Well, for a fiancée she seemed pretty much taken up with the Ghazi; his eyebrows went up as he recalled some of her remarks. But Mr. Fisher was a very conscientious young man, and the business-like thought also occurred to him that The Old Man (so popular Ambassadors are frequently referred to by their staffs) ought to know about this, and what friendly terms these Pierces seemed to be on with the Head of the State. It was the devil and all, dealing with Turks; they were so oriental, kept you so elegantly at arms' length, never showed their hand—and none of them more so than Kemal Pasha. Still meditative, he strolled back into the ballroom, where Fanny and her eminent partner were dancing with energy; he was laughing, and Fanny's face, bright with animation—or was it admiration?—was turned up to his.

As a matter of fact Mr. Fisher, who was young, and without much experience of human psychology, had been wrong in his deductions about Fanny's attitude to Mustafa Kemal Pasha; an older person would have realised from the very openness with which she spoke of him that her feelings were enthusiastic and admiring, but little more. It was only that night that they changed a little—and it was the dance that changed them. Kemal Pasha danced beautifully, with expert mastery of step and rhythm—and with another sort of mastery too; and Fanny, full to the brim anyhow with her innocent ardours of passionate admiration, could not remain unaware of this. When at last he relinquished her, to dance with Féridé—he had worked his way through the diplomatic and official ladies by this time—there was that about her face and her whole demeanour which was hardly to be accounted for merely by her having danced with the national hero.

However, she remembered to keep her promises, and introduced Mr. Fisher to pretty Mme T., with whom he at once danced; later when Féridé's dance with the Ghazi was over she introduced him to her too. "Only think—he knows Alec!" she said gaily, and—"Tiens!" said Féridé, as the young man led her away to perform a fox-trot. At 5 A.M. Kemal Pasha went off to play poker with his cronies in a private room down a corridor near the entrance, and his guests were free to drive home in the dawn.

Since English visitors were still rare in Ankara, and Dr. Pierce of a certain eminence, he and Fanny would probably have been the objects sooner or later of some form of Embassy entertaining, even without the conversation which Mr. Fisher contrived to have next day with "The Old Man." The Ambassador had come up to Ankara for the ball, as in duty bound, leaving the cool spacious comfort of the vast Embassy in Istanbul for the relative rigours of the Ankara Palace—the new Embassy in Ankara was not yet habitable. He listened quietly to what Mr. Fisher had to say (in his youthful inexperience that worthy even mentioned that Miss Pierce was engaged to an old friend of his) and at the end he said—"Yes, all right. They'd better be asked to lunch at Carpic's. This Dr. Pierce is her uncle, you say? I know his name, of course. I think you should keep up the contact, Billy. You'd better call, as you've met Mme Orhan. Orhan Bey is quite important; these anonymous fellows with no obvious position often are. Far more so," he added meditatively, "than the lay figures they put into the Ministries, in most countries. All right."

"All right," is often a dismissal, and Mr. Fisher took his departure. Two days later, after making some complicated enquiries as to where

Orhan Bey lived, he walked up to the villa among the vineyards to pay the indicated call. And so it came about that he was sitting in Féridé's salon, chatting in French with Fanny and his hostess, at the very moment when the tesbih which Kemal Pasha sent to Fanny arrived.

A tesbih looks more like a rosary than anything else: a looped string of beads arranged in groups, with a short pendant at the junction, only instead of a crucifix a small ornament like a finial dangles from this. They have a definite religious significance, connected with prayer, and elderly Turks can still be seen running the beads through their fingers. Sometimes of ivory, sometimes of turquoise, sometimes of coral, they are often to be found in the bazaars, and can be very beautiful things, with the fine delicate silken cord between the polished beads; a pretty tesbih is quite a normal and non-committal form of present. But the tesbih which Fanny, excited as a child by the parcel done up in white paper, opened in front of Mr. Fisher was of amber on golden cord—obviously an old one, and valuable.

"How lovely! Who can it be from?" she exclaimed in delight.

"Here's a card," said the young man, picking it up as he spoke from the floor where it had fallen from the wrappings—as he handed it to her he saw the name. Fanny saw it too, and even in the dim light in that green-shadowed room the blush that spread over her fair skin was unmistakable. She recovered herself quickly—"Oh, how very kind," she said coolly—"Look, Féridé, isn't it pretty?"

But Féridé had seen the blush, and in conjunction with the valuable present it troubled her; and Mr. Fisher, Alec Grant's friend—who had also so needlessly seen both—was troubled too.

Chapter Twenty-one

THE luncheon at Carpic's duly took place about a week later; "the Orhans" as Fisher called them were too important—potentially, any-how—to be asked at shorter notice; the Ambassador however did not feel called upon to stay in Ankara for it, so it was given by the Counsellor. To take a meal by day, in a restaurant, was yet another step in Féridé's progress towards westernisation—she had never done such a thing in her life. She had to have a hat for the occasion; Fanny's two or three were tried on, but none of them would satisfy her—in the end she confectioned herself a ravishing little toque of tulle, and ostrich-feathers from an old fan, to Fanny's immense admiration. "How you can be so clever at making a thing you never wear I can't imagine!" she said.

"I gave it much thought," Féridé answered simply. And in that reply probably lies the key to the astonishing elegance of Turkish women, at least those in public positions, today. Working in a new medium, as it were, they have applied their whole intelligence to mastering the technique of western dress—no running into a shop to buy a little frock or a little hat because it has "caught their eye," or is cheap, for them. As a result, their chic is amazing.

When it came to the point Féridé enjoyed the lunch very much. The Pierces apart, she had hardly met any English people, and Réfiyé Hanim's frequent praise of the English had left her with a strong curiosity about the race. The Counsellor was a good talker and an amiable host, and had been too wise to overload this party with dull people whom he wished to "work off"; he had merely added a witty and amusing French couple. The food and wine were excellent; Carpic himself, the White Russian proprietor, hovered beside the round table with his sloping shoulders and drooping eyelids, his immense dignity and solicitude "practically hypnotising one into finding everything delicious," as the Frenchman said—"though all of it *is* delicious." Orhan was in tremendous form, and kept the party alert and laughing in a way which made Féridé suspect that he had something up his sleeve. She was right; as they drove away—Orhan had come straight to the restaurant from his bureau—he said to Dr. Pierce: "What would you say to a trip to Kastamonu, the week after next?"

"Oh, that would be very pleasant," the Doctor said. "As I remember it it is a charming place."

"Orhan, why Kastamonu?" Féridé asked, almost sharply; she was always a little suspicious of her husband in these moods.

"I have to go. The Ghazi is going, and I thought we might all go also. It will give Fani Hanim a sight of Anatolia, which she would not otherwise get; and would you not like to return to some of the scenes of your journey here?" he said, looking mischievous.

"Not in the least! Our journey was horrible," Féridé began with energy, when Fanny broke in.

"Oh dji-djim, do let us go! I have wanted so much to see the way by which you came here. Orhan Bey, should we go by the same road?"

"Precisely the same—only we need not stay in all these terrible hans, because in a car one does it in one day. My Life, it is really an easy journey nowadays," he said, turning round to his wife—he was sitting by the chauffeur.

"And why does the Ghazi want to visit Kastamonu?" Féridé asked, still suspicious.

Orhan chuckled. "Ah, that I cannot tell you now. You will learn when you get there!"

"He can't be going to oust another Sultan or another Khalif," said Dr. Pierce calmly, "because there aren't any left. It cannot be anything very much, Féridé Hanim."

Orhan shouted with laughter.

"He will still find something to oust, Professor," he said. "You will see."

He was as pleased as a child over his secret, but as it was obviously an official one they let him alone about it. But Féridé, to Fanny's surprise and rather to her annoyance, raised a number of objections to the plan. It would still be fearfully hot; they had no conception of what the dust on the roads would be like; the han at Kastamonu would be sure to be over-crowded if the Ghazi was going. Everyone realised that she did not like the idea, but to none of them, not even to Orhan, did she care to give her real reason for opposing it. Both he and Fanny asked her privately if she thought the trip would be too much for her in her condition, and were told, quite brusquely, "not in the least—that does not enter into it." So she was overborne, and rooms were telegraphed for.

Her real reason was her faint anxiety about Fanny and Mustafa Kemal Pasha. She, like Mr. Fisher, had noticed Fanny's face at the ball, both during her dance with the President and after it; she had seen the brief expression of incredulous rapture which had accompanied the blush when the girl saw his card and realised that the tesbih was from him. That was before Fanny had collected herself and made that cool appraising remark about the splendid gift; but Féridé was much better at human psychology than Mr. Fisher—to her that cool remark was the biggest give-away of all. Forty-eight hours earlier Fanny would have gone on enthusing about the tesbih as candidly as she had continually enthused about the Ghazi himself; since the ball she rarely mentioned him. It was too unlucky that that wretched young man should just have happened to be there at that moment; diplomats were fearful gossips—"I suppose because they have nothing else to do," Féridé said to herself, unjustly. She feared that gossip might be beginning, and she did not want her dear friend *affichée* with Kemal Pasha, as she well might be if they practically accompanied him to Kastamonu. Actually they were going a day ahead, but the effect would be the same. But much deeper than this was her concern for Fanny herself, her happiness and her peace of mind. Féridé had now been married for seven years, and had lived in Ankara for five of them—since Orhan was one of Kemal Pasha's closest associates, and she herself a respected and favourite companion, she could not escape knowing him rather well. His charm for women was prodigious—she had seen respectable married ladies being bowled over by it like ninepins. As for Kemal Pasha himself, where his amusement or pleasure with women was concerned he had always been irresponsible, and since his divorce from Latifé Hanim— the one woman he had ever really cared for, however difficult and ultra-political she might have been—he was more reckless than ever. She had seen nothing so far to lead her to suppose that he was really attracted by Fanny—the gift of the tesbih might be no more than a gracious action to a friendly foreigner; but she knew what he was like, and nothing could have pleased her better at this juncture than that he should go off on one of his trips, expounding to the people in town and village his ideas for their improvement—whatever this latest notion might be—while Fanny remained quietly at Ankara; it would have made a break, and given the girl's enthusiasm a chance to die down.

It might have seemed an obvious thing to tell Orhan all this, and enlist his support; but Féridé felt a very natural disinclination to give Fanny away, and she could not be sure that her husband would not brush the whole thing aside as wholly unimportant. Orhan might pride himself on having no haremlik in his house, but in fact he was very far as yet from holding, let alone putting into practice, the commonly accepted western ideas on how to treat women—which are based, ultimately, on chivalry and Christianity. So she gave way, and the last week in August the four of them set off in a big car for Kastamonu.

Féridé could generally accept the inevitable with a good grace, and as this trip was inevitable she very sensibly gave herself up to enjoying it. Since her arrival in Ankara she had never been further afield along her old route than the Çankiri Bridge where she and Nilüfer had been met by Ahmet and Orhan—she pointed it out to Fanny as they passed—and it was a strange experience to bowl in a fast car over the road along which they had crept in their little carriage five years before. As for Fanny, she could not be shown enough of the scenes, or hear enough of the episodes of that journey; her interest and happiness were so vivid that Féridé began to think that really it would have been a shame for her to miss the expedition. When they lunched at Çankiri Fanny insisted on being taken up to the top floor of the inn to see the room where Féridé had looked from her window towards Ankara—"If I had known then what I was going to, I should have looked the other way, I can tell you!" Féridé said gaily. They went on, up over the rolling downs where the silver goats enchanted Fanny, down into the Devrez-Çai, whose chess-board of rice-fields along the valley floor was turning a rusty brown as the grain ripened, and up again into the forests of the Ilghaz Dagh. Orhan and Dr. Pierce were talking practically about soil and climate, agriculture and afforestation, and Kemal Pasha's plans for these two last; but as the road climbed higher and its surface grew worse, and the drop below more startling, the Doctor began to listen to Féridé, who was describing the snow-drifts—"It was here that the driver would not go on; I am sure it was here!—and Hassan Bey made us get out and walk, and took the reins himself, and drove, and I led his horse."

"Well, upon my soul!" commented the Doctor, "I shouldn't care to cross this road in winter."

"The hans were worse than the road, I assure you! I will show you the Bostan Han when we come to it"—and when the road dropped down through the beechwoods to the bridge over the Kara-Su she stopped the car and led the others into the han, which was still as dirty and degraded as ever; modern improvements had not yet reached Bostan. When she took them up the broken wooden stairs into the bedroom with the gaping floorboards, full of the smell of dung, even Orhan was aghast. "I had no idea it was as bad as this," he said, looking round him with dismay.

"Please imagine it all a foot deep in snow, piercing cold, and with a stove that smoked, also!" Féridé adjured him. As they went out into the clean air again Dr. Pierce turned to her with—"Well really, my dear Féridé Hanim, I think you ought to receive a decoration! Orhan, when is the Ghazi going to start an Order for Women?"

As they swung down the great loops of road into Kastamonu and saw the citadel on its vertical rock, glowing like bronze in the late light above the faint haze which hung over the old city, Fanny exclaimed with delight—"Oh, what a beautiful place!" The houses along the river with their silvery woodwork enchanted her still more; so did the great han, when at last they drew up before its low noble line of brick-work. One of Féridé's minor worries, and indeed a major preoccupa-tion of Orhan's, had been how Fanny would stand a night in a han, in spite of the elaborate instructions which had been telegraphed in ad-vance. Bedding of a sort had been provided, though naturally no beds; the bedding rested, as always, on a raised wooden platform. But neither Orhan nor Féridé need have worried—Dr. Pierce had slept in such places a hundred times, and Fanny took to it all like a duck to water: the room—a cubicle, really—which she shared with Féridé was charm-ing, the great loggias with their pointed arches round the central court were too superb (that was true), the food was delicious. In fact she stood up to it all far better than Nilüfer and Féridé, nurtured in lux-ury, had done, as Féridé admitted to Orhan. That young man was greatly impressed. "She might *be* a Turk," he said—and wondered why his wife frowned, her dark brows drawn down, at his words.

The next day they strolled about the old town, admiring the peculiar and rather specialised beauty of its architecture; loggias and balconies of silvery carved wood above pale plaster, recessed, or projecting star-tlingly across the steep narrow streets; the buildings of Kastamonu have a great reputation all over Turkey, and rightly so. In the market Fanny bought bright cottons and scarves. Orhan had to go and pay an official call on the Vali, and came back to lunch in high mirth. Everyone knew by now that this journey of the Ghazi's meant something, some new project to be launched, and the Vali had demanded eagerly to be told what it was. "If I do not know, how can I prepare?" he kept say-ing distressfully. "I told him to wait—so few hours to wait, and then he would see," Orhan said laughing.

"Well, in a few hours we shall all see," said Dr. Pierce tranquilly. "Fanny, do you want to come up and look at the citadel? He won't be here before five, will he, Orhan? Féridé Hanim, I shouldn't come if I were you—it's a bit of a climb."

But Orhan said that there would not be time for the citadel—they ought to leave soon after three, to drive out along the road a little way to meet the President.

"But we only got in at six," Fanny said.

"He will have left early," Orhan said. (In fact he left Ankara at 5.30 A.M. in order not to be seen off by anyone.)

They drove through streets thronged with people in holiday dress: many of the men in blue or white baggy trousers, with goat-skin moc-assins and high white socks, the women in loud gay jackets and trousers, and still gayer aprons, with white or coloured scarves over their heads. There was a general outward flow of this throng along the highway leading to Ankara—the car followed it too, moving slowly through the crowds, and after climbing the first two or three loops pulled off the road at a projecting curve. From here they commanded a view both of the road above and the town below, where the river seemed to be flowing between two vast flower-beds, so dense and so brilliant were the crowds filling the embankments which flanked it on either side. They got out of the car and sat on some rocks to see better; the crowd, still moving slowly upwards above and below them was in holiday mood as well as holiday attire, laughing and talking—but there was a curious sense of tension, of expectancy, and the most diverse theories were being put forward as to what "the Ghazi" would do, or tell them, or show them, when he came. "Ah, whatever it is, it is to *us* that he will tell it, not those blokes in Ankara!" Fanny heard more than once. "He comes to us and tells us himself what he would have us do—it is not like in the old days, when we had to take our orders from men like ourselves." The girl listened with a curious emotion. This was the opposite end, so to speak, of that two-hours' discourse to which she had listened under the poplars at Çankaya; here, among Kemal Pasha's own people, was where those far-reaching plans made their impact on the people themselves, whose lives they would affect—and she was here to see that impact taking place. Fanny was full of the liveliest curiosity as to what the new development would be, but she was quite unable to guess. Chancing to glance round now, she saw Orhan returning from the car carrying a square parcel done up in brown paper, which had been a good deal in evidence during the previous day's drive—it had always been getting under someone's feet, and Orhan had shown a tender solicitude for its safety.

"Orhan, what on earth have you got in that?" she asked now. He gave her his side-long smile—"Wouldn't you like to know, Fani Hanim?"

A burst of shouting and cheering from further up the hill made them look in that direction. Down the road, at a foot's pace, a small procession of cars was coming—in the leading one, standing up, rode Mustafa Kemal Pasha; but instead of the familiar high shape of the kalpak the astonished onlookers saw that he was wearing a Panama hat! —his entourage in the following cars were also seen to be wearing felt hats, except for one or two officers in flat Staff caps. As the crowd surged round his car, shouting, laughing and pointing, the Ghazi repeatedly pulled off his Panama and waved it at them, pointing to it with his left hand.

So the secret was out—hats for Turks! Dr. Pierce looked on regretfully; he liked the old ways, he liked the fez—and he realised that he was attending its funeral. Fanny, feeling ever so slightly deflated, glanced round at Orhan—taken by surprise, he was wrestling with the strings on his parcel; a moment later, triumphantly, he produced a neat trilby and clapped it on his head. Fanny turned away to conceal her amusement—the young man looked so odd in the unwonted headgear, and his air of triumph was so naïve that it quite upset her gravity. But Féridé was clapping her hands in sincere delight—she realised now why Orhan had insisted that she should put on the toque made for the Counsellor's luncheon. This was another step towards modernity, towards western ways, another move away from being a peculiar people. First the fez to go, then the veil—yes, that was the right order; and with the veil gone, a freer, fuller life, such as Fanny had always lived, would open for her and her countrywomen. As she watched her friend's face, ardent and yet grave, Fanny no longer felt like laughing; she realised a little of the meaning of what she was seeing.

She realised it still more that evening when they all went to the house of an acquaintance of Orhan's, across the river from the one where Kemal Pasha was staying, to watch the torchlight procession which the good folk of Kastamonu had organised in honour of the occasion. The streets were still full of those rejoicing throngs of people in their gay outlandish dress, the dress that he hoped to abolish; though many of the men had already abandoned their fezzes, and having nothing else to wear, went bare-headed. Whether the immense enthusiasm was really at the prospect of wearing Panamas and trilbys instead of the fez, or for the Ghazi himself, Fanny could not know, and dared not ask, for Orhan was in a state of blazing excitement over the new, the wonderful move; so she simply leant from the window and watched. Presently an orange glare away to their left heralded the advent of the procession—as it passed along the further embankment, the torches streaming in the air with the movement, a band drumming out a rather monotonous tune to a stirring rhythm, while the innumerable flames were reflected in the darkly-gleaming water, the thrill of the popular excitement ran like needles along her nerves, and she cheered as vigorously as the multi-coloured crowd in the roadway below. The procession halted outside the Ghazi's house, and after a moment or so he came out, bare-headed himself, and stood at the top of the steps, smiling down at his people, and raising his hand in greeting. While the crowd yelled with joy, pressing and surging round, Fanny watched his face, strongly lit up in that primitive orange glare—the extraordinary breadth and height of the forehead, the prominent cheekbones, the blunt jutting nose, the wide mouth above the solidity of the heavy chin; all now illuminated, not only by the flaring torches but by affection and even tenderness—the tenderness a hint of which had so surprised Féridé the first time she met him. Ah, no wonder they loved him, Fanny thought; no wonder anyone loved him. Now he was talking to the people, colloquially, jollily, they could see, though his words were drowned in the shouts and laughter of the crowd; presently he waved to them again in farewell and went indoors, and the procession moved on. Orhan, his face vivid with enthusiasm, swung round on Dr. Pierce.

"*Now* do you believe that he can do anything he wants with this people?" he demanded.

"*He* can," said Dr. Pierce.

Next day there was a tremendous reception in the Town Hall, attended by delegations from all the organisations in the city itself, and from the various prefectures throughout the vilayet—Orhan's party was of course present. Now for the first time Kemal Pasha was to speak his mind about the hat and the fez, and Dr. Pierce listened with the deepest interest to see how he would deal with the subject; the Ghazi's relations with his people were beginning to fascinate him, whether he would or no.

Kemal Pasha dealt with it with his usual practical simplicity. He asked if there was a tailor present, and a little man was pushed up onto the platform. Kemal showed him his suit. "Is this a good, cheap suit?" Yes. "Is it an international form of dress, such as civilised men wear everywhere?" The tailor, fingering it, agreed that it was—he spoke up stoutly, in a voice that all could hear, and other working men in the crowd averred audibly that it was indeed a good civilised sort of suit.

"Right. Well, you see what a simple suit it is, easy to make; and all the materials are manufactured here, in our own country. Now, you could make caps out of this cloth, caps with peaks, such as other nations wear." He beckoned to another man in the crowd, who was still wearing the national head-gear—"Come up here, my friend." Rather abashed, the man mounted the platform—Kemal clapped him on the back with cheerful friendliness. "Will you give me your fez for a moment?" he said. More abashed than ever, the man took it off, revealing a cotton skull-cap such as the poorer Turks, who had but one fez, habitually wore to keep it clean, and handed it to the Ghazi; the fez itself had a piece of embroidered linen twisted turban-wise round it, in the country fashion.

"Thank you," Kemal said nicely to the man—then he held up the turbaned fez for the whole gathering to see.

"Now, look what we have here: first a cap, then a fez, then an embroidered turban. How complicated!—and much of their cost goes out of the country, to foreigners. When I say this," he said, glancing at the owner of the despised objects with great kindness, "it is because I wish to emphasise one thing of great importance, this: we have got to become a civilised people, in all respects. We have suffered many evils—and for this reason, that we have never known or understood the outside world. Now it is time that our ideas and our mentality should become, from beginning to end, those of civilised peoples; and we will not listen to what this one or that one says about it! Look at the whole of Turkey, of the Islamic nations; think of the evils that they are suffering, even today, because they will not change their ideas and their way of life, and conform to the general advance of civilisation. That is why we were rolled in the mud during our recent disasters—and if we managed to save ourselves from utter ruin in the last five or six years, it is thanks to the change which we were able to achieve in our system of government." He was speaking now with an immense controlled emotion, and Dr. Pierce recognised the vibrant response of his audience, though they remained perfectly silent.

"Now," Kemal Pasha went on—and his voice rang out—"we cannot stop! We must go forward; we are forced to it. The nation must clearly understand this fact—civilisation and progress are a burning fire, which consumes those who stand aside from them, are indifferent to them. Our next task is to occupy worthily, nay, to raise still higher the place which we already hold in the family of nations—of *civilised* nations. In doing that, and believe me, only in doing that lies our prosperity, our happiness, and an existence worthy of the dignity of human beings."

He stopped—and when it was seen that he was not going on, tumultuous applause broke out, lasting for minutes. Dr. Pierce studied the faces of the audience. He had known Turkey well for over thirty years, and he was quite familiar with the rather moderate degree of enthusiasm or expression habitual to the race—this outburst of emotion was unlike anything he had ever seen, or ever thought to see. From the alive and ardent faces of the crowd in the hot hall his glance travelled to that of the man who had stirred up these depths of feeling in a normally impassive people. Kemal Pasha stood very quiet, not smiling now, with a sort of tenseness of expression, as if he were holding the people in front of him to their new resolution—it occurred to Dr. Pierce that that was precisely what he was doing; for he put up a handkerchief and wiped his forehead, and for the first time the Doctor noticed how far back his almost colourless hair had receded from it, and the greyish pallor of his face. It must be an exhausting job, he thought, first to create a nation out of the ruins of a decrepit empire, then to galvanise it into waging a successful war for freedom against impossible odds, and finally to start dragging it, primitive, stubborn and conservative as it was, along the road of progress and modernisation. He regarded Kemal Pasha with more sympathy than he had felt for him as yet.

Later that day he spoke of the speech to Orhan. "He did it most awfully well—so simply, and yet it couldn't have been more clearly, more tellingly said. The tailor was planted, I suppose?"

Orhan laughed, a little unwillingly.

"Well yes—he had to be. The one preparation I was able to tell the Vali to make yesterday, was to have some tailors in the hall. That puzzled him very much!"

"That phrase about the advance of material progress—I'm not sure that I should call it civilisation, myself—burning up the laggards is quite true, too," the Doctor pursued; "but he put it very originally. My goodness, what magnetism he has!"

"Ah, you felt that too? Yes, indeed." Orhan was pleased.

"It must take it out of him no end, doing that to a crowd, all the same. It suddenly struck me this afternoon that he's getting a little bald—he can't be a young man any more. How old *is* he?"

Orhan was vague. "Really, do you know, I am not sure."

"He is forty-five," said Féridé promptly. She was rather glad to have the leader's age and baldness brought out. But Fanny's reaction to this pleased her a good deal less.

"People like him have no age," the girl said decisively. Orhan however was delighted by this sentiment.

Mustafa Kemal Pasha spent a second night at Kastamonu, and then drove on to Inebolu; Orhan had to accompany him this time, and there was a suggestion that the rest might go too. But Féridé was really getting tired; there had been a lot of going about and social activity, and though Fanny was wild to go on and see the Black Sea coast and the port where Féridé had landed, and all that further stretch of the Road of the Revolution, on this occasion her hostess frankly pleaded exhaustion. So she and the Pierces returned to Ankara, speeding over that interminable plateau across which she and Nilüfer had crawled only five years before; travelling in the same direction, the contrast struck her even more forcibly than it had on the outward journey.

Back in the comfort of the villa among the vineyards they read—at least Fanny did, avidly—of the Ghazi's further activities on his tour. The young men of Inebolu, gathered to meet him, had greeted him with the cry—"Ask of us what you will! We will do it." In reply, with the same directness that he had used at Kastamonu, Kemal Pasha told them—"I speak to you as a brother, a comrade, or a father. The Turkish nation, which claims to be a civilised people, must demonstrate to the world that it is really civilised, by its outlook, its mentality, its way of life—and especially its family life." There followed a good deal more about clothes and head-gear: the fez was really of Greek origin, the soutane worn by the Imams was the dress of the Jewish rabbis; finally—"Nations which attempt to achieve progress encumbered with a mediaeval outlook and primitive superstitions are doomed to extinction, or at least to slavery and humiliation," he thundered—and the youth of Inebolu thundered their applause in reply. Back at Kastamonu, encouraged by the reception which his revolutionary ideas about dress had received, he showed his hand more clearly, and proceeded to an open attack on the religious orders, the monasteries full of dervishes and novices who encouraged the people in superstition. He made a neat pun on the word *tarikat,* which has the double meaning of a religious order, and a road or way—"The only rational tarikat is the tarikat of civilisation." And again the young applauded, but the older people went away shaking their heads and murmuring dissent. And so, pausing at many towns on the way to explain his views to fresh audiences of humble people, who at least listened to whatever he said because he had saved them and he loved them, and they loved him, he slowly made his way homewards.

Turkey is a great country for gossip, and even if Féridé was a little unjust to diplomats in general, they certainly do hear a lot of it—after all it is part of their business to do exactly that. So Mr. Fisher soon learned that Dr. and Miss Pierce had gone to Kastamonu for the hat announcement. Fisher had his full share of that odd loyalty to men who have been at the same school as themselves which is one of the most peculiar characteristics of Englishmen; it often persists into middle life, even in the case of a man they have hardly seen in the interval. But Fisher had "kept up," as he had told Fanny, with Alec Grant, and was very fond of him; and all this gossip, coming on top of the tesbih and what he had seen at the ball, vexed and worried him on his friend's behalf. Everyone knew what Kemal Pasha was like where women were concerned, after all. "If this goes on, that girl is going to make a fool of herself," he thought. And after twenty-four hours of angry cogitation he wrote what he considered to be a tactful letter to a mutual friend, who had also been at Wellington, telling him what was going on. "I can't make up my mind whether old Alec ought to be told or not," he ended uncomfortably. This letter went off by bag the day after Féridé and the Pierces returned to Ankara.

Two or three days later Kemal Pasha returned; and Orhan with him, enthusiastic over the success of the tour. Fanny could not hear enough about the latter part, which she had missed, and the two of them talked away about it, and the Ghazi, and Turkey's future, endlessly. Three weeks before this would have delighted Féridé; now her eyebrows drew together as she listened. The rides continued—and one evening when they got in Fanny, instead of coming to the salon as she always did, went straight up to her room—Féridé heard her light step on the old wooden stairs. For some reason this trivial thing made the young woman nervously alarmed—presently, unable to control her anxiety, she went up and tapped on Fanny's door. Fanny was changing, but bid her come in; she found her friend distraite, deep-eyed, with a sort of radiance about her that confirmed her suspicions. She asked about the ride—Fanny, pulling clothes out of drawers, chattered away in reply, elaborately casual. At last it emerged that—oh such fun —Nazli had been frightened by something and had bolted, "and the others all got left behind. We ended up in a little valley with a spring in it, all among the bushes, so pretty." That was all Féridé could get out of her, but at dinner and throughout the evening the girl had an absent look, with a silvery hint of bliss about it; when spoken to she would look up as if she were coming back a long way from some distant secret place. It was a look Féridé recognised—she felt certain that there must have been some passage between the two, and she worried more than ever.

The very next day they were to dine at the Kiösk, an informal supper with no other guests but a couple of Aides-de-Camp. All the same Fanny put on one of her prettiest frocks, Féridé noticed, and had obviously taken a lot of trouble with her hair. When they arrived Féridé watched the greeting that passed between her guest and her host closely. It all sounded natural enough—"Well, and how goes it after your adventure of yesterday? I am not sure if you must ride Nazli again; it seems that your presence makes her lose her head!" The talk at dinner was of the tour—it was the first time they had all been together since their return, and Kemal Pasha wanted to hear their impressions. Fanny made a lively tale of the remarks they had overheard in the crowd while they waited for his arrival, and he laughed out when she reproduced, with a strong country accent, the words about "those blokes in Ankara"; her enthusiasm pleased him. After dinner he went as usual to the piano—"Now, will you sing for us?"—and to Féridé's anxious ears there seemed to be an almost caressing note in his voice.

The A.D.C.s had disappeared when the meal was over, but as Féridé rose to leave Kemal rang the bell and told a servant to fetch Murad Bey; when the young man appeared, "Listen, Tjojukum," (my son) he said pleasantly, "go please to my study, and bring a small package which you will find on my desk." The young man hurried away and returned with a small flat white parcel. As they went out to the car and Goodnights were being said Kemal handed it to Fanny—"A little token of esteem for a good friend of my country, which I ask you to accept, Fani Hanim." Fanny took it a little consciously, but said the correct words of thanks.

"Well, what has he given you?" Dr. Pierce asked cheerfully as they drove away.

"It's no good undoing it in the car—it's too dark to see," Fanny temporised.

"Here is the light!" said Orhan, switching it on.

"I bet you know what it is, anyhow, Orhan my boy," Dr. Pierce said.

"Indeed I do not! This is something he has done quite by himself," Orhan said—a little indignantly, the Doctor thought; perhaps Kemal Pasha's social conscience felt that he ought to have been consulted. Meanwhile Fanny still sat with the package in her lap, making no move to undo it, a rather mutinous look on her little face. How tiresome of Uncle, how tactless and *stupid* of Orhan, switching on the light! It was *her* present—what business was it of theirs? Then Féridé spoke from her corner.

"We should all like to see the present that the Ghazi has made to the friend of his country, Fanny," she said. Fanny almost jumped, it was so like Réfiyé Hanim speaking—the voice, the tone, and the implied command behind the courteous words. Forcing herself to smile, she undid the little parcel, and drew out a thin gold cigarette-case, beautifully made, with her monogram in one corner.

"Well, I call that very civil indeed," said Dr. Pierce.

"Charming—it is quite charming!" said Orhan. "He has excellent taste." He snapped off the light again. Neither Fanny nor Féridé said anything at all.

Chapter Twenty-two

THE gift of the cigarette-case, coming on top of the episode (whatever it was) which she was convinced had taken place during the ride when Nazli bolted decided Féridé that she ought to talk to Fanny. She felt the greatest distaste for the task. Her pregnancy was beginning to trouble her; she slept badly, found it hard to eat, and felt irritable and nervous much of the time. To be nervous herself was a thing she had never known, and she was aware of a new compassion for poor Nilüfer, always so nervous, and what she must have suffered during those long hard days up in the citadel. But not to carry through a thing she had decided on was not in Féridé's nature, and as she lay shifting uncomfortably on her bed after their return from the Kiösk she determined to do it next day. *Poor* little Fanny!

But it could not be done in the morning, for she had to go down to the town to do some shopping; she left Fanny, who never wanted to go into the new Ankara unless she had to, on the balcony with a book of Persian poetry which Dr. Pierce had recently acquired. The days were getting cooler now, and the glass doors could be left open—Fanny sat under the yellowing vine-leaves, looking out over the slopes of the vineyards near at hand to the pallid distant gold of the hills. Now she read, now she put down the book and dreamed; once Féridé was safely out of the way, she ran up to her room and fetched the cigarette-case, to have in her lap, to touch with her fingers. Of course he had had to make that formal speech about being a friend of Turkey in front of them all—but it was for *her*, for her herself! That was not how he had spoken, how it had been in the little sun-filled glen by the spring. Oh, better not think too much of that, she told herself, with a little shiver— and turned to the book again. The Persian poet wrote of love in the rain—

And most on a wet day—oh, wet days are pleasant indeed—
'Neath a propped leathern tent, with a girl, to beguile the slow hours.

Féridé did her shopping now by car, with a servant to carry her parcels. She noticed with interest that morning that there was a fair sprinkling of hats and caps about the streets. Waiting outside Carpic's restaurant, while the servant was inside getting caviare, she was accosted by Mme T., who had recognised her car; she got in and sat with Féridé for a few minutes. In French, so that the chauffeur should not hear, Mme T. told her friend that some gossip was going round about the Ghazi and this pretty Miss Pierce, especially since the trip to Kastamonu—"and I hear he has given her a wonderful mare."

"The mare was *lent*," Féridé said; and they had all gone to Kastamonu twenty-four hours ahead of the President.

"Ah well,"—Mme T. was sure that there was no indiscretion on Mdlle Pierce's side, but—"enfin, ma chère, one knows what *he* is!" She did it so nicely that Féridé could not be very annoyed with her, tiresome as it all was, but she decided to talk not only to Fanny but also to Orhan, and when he came in before lunch she took him aside into his study.

"Orhan, have you mentioned Fanny's cigarette-case to anyone?"

"No—*he* asked if she liked it, and I said yes. Why?"

"Then please do not speak of it."

"But my Life, why a secret? He makes these presents to scores of women."

"Not usually to unmarried English girls. No, listen, Orhan—people are talking." She told him of the gossip that was circulating—about Nazli the mare, and about Kastamonu.

"What nonsense!" he said with irritation—but he frowned all the same. "Was this why you opposed our trip?"

"Yes."

"My Life, how often you are right when I am wrong. And you never tell me so!" He took her hand and kissed it. "But I do not think it is so serious," he went on, "there is always gossip about him with one woman or another. He is quite indifferent to it."

Féridé drew down her brows.

"All the same, we do not want any dedikodu with the Embassy. The English have different ideas on such matters."

He stared. "The Embassy? How does the Embassy come into it?"

"This tiresome Fisher was here when the tesbih arrived, and saw it."

"The devil he was! I did not know that." He frowned again, thoughtful. "So what now?"

"I shall talk to her, and urge discretion." This, in Féridé's opinion, was quite enough for Orhan. "But you see that it is better not to advertise the cigarette-case."

"Yes—you are right."

After lunch, when Orhan had returned to his bureau, and the Doctor gone off for one of his solitary walks, Féridé braced herself to her task. She had spent a lot of time, driving about the town that morning, considering the best line of approach, rehearsing circumlocutory

• 307 •

phrases which would spare them both the discomfort of open speech, if Fanny would take the hint; that was how she would have dealt with such a matter with a Turkish friend. But as she sat now opposite the English girl, looking at her resolute mouth and candid eyes, and remembering her habitual open and decided speech, she was not so sure that that was the right way with her—perhaps a directness that matched her own would serve better. Fanny would probably force her to speak openly in the end—the English were so fanatically, almost crudely outspoken. How difficult it was to decide!

While she thus cogitated Fanny, who was trying to crochet an oya, one of the silken roses which had so taken her fancy at Sitaré Hanim's, looked up and saw her friend's eyes on her. "You're very quiet today, Féridé," she said—usually their afternoons passed in a burble of tranquil chatter.

"I am thinking," Féridé said.

"Goodness, what an exercise!" Fanny gibed affectionately. "May one know what about?"

Féridé took the opening.

"About *you*," she said. She saw a slightly startled expression come into the girl's eyes; her face seemed to close up, as if shutters were drawn across a window.

"Do I need to be thought about?" she asked, still lightly and mockingly—but some of the warmth had gone out of her voice.

"I think so—yes," Féridé said slowly. "Dearest Fanny, with you at least—my best friend, my first friend—I would not beat about the bush. I am concerned about you."

Fanny was moved by that, she saw; but she was also put on the defensive. When she answered—after a pause—her voice was kind again, but she spoke lightly.

"Féridé, dearest, there is no cause for you to worry about me, I assure you."

Féridé plunged. "Fanny, is that true? I have the impression that you are perhaps becoming—well, interested in Mustafa Kemal Pasha."

This, which from a Turk amounted to extreme bluntness, took Fanny by surprise. She bristled up at once.

"And if I were, what of it?" she asked. "Would it concern anyone but myself?"

Féridé looked straight at her.

"Your unhappiness would cause me great concern," she said—"More almost than that of anyone but my husband—now." Fanny knew that she thought of Ahmet. "And if this were so, it could only bring you unhappiness."

"Why?" Fanny asked, looking obstinate.

"Because there would be nothing in it for you that you value—no reality. You want reality always; I know that. Listen to me, dearest," she said pleadingly, as she saw Fanny's small fingers fiddling impatiently with the silken thread. "I have no idea what has happened, or indeed if anything has. But Kemal Pasha has these engouements, these fantasies, for one woman after another, and they never last; they mean nothing to him. Latifé Hanim, it is true, made him marry her; she would not be his without marriage—but what came of that? A divorce. And yet she is the only woman he ever cared two little pins for!"

The thread in Fanny's fingers snapped—but she said nothing.

"See, I am showing you the reverse of the medal," Féridé went on earnestly. "This is his particular idiosyncrasy, his relations with women. They do not affect his greatness, his grandeur in other matters; indeed they do not affect him at all—that is the trouble."

"I'm not sure that that is really so," Fanny said at last, without raising her eyes.

"Oh dear one, it is true, indeed it is! I know him so well. Do not be deluded."

"He likes me," said Fanny, stubbornly.

"Naturally! As he has liked hundreds of women! And you are something fresh; English, clever, fearless, instruite; quite different from the ones he is accustomed to. Of course he is taken with you—a new toy, that sings, even! But all the same it means nothing to him, nothing serious. Oh Fanny, do reassure me—tell me that it means nothing to you either."

To her dismay Fanny burst into tears.

"But it *does* mean something to me," she sobbed out.

"Oh dji-djim, no! Not him—do not say it."

"I do say it. Of course it does; it can't help it," Fanny said confusedly, still crying. "He, and knowing him like—like this—is all part of it all."

"Part of what?"

"You, Turkey, everything! I told you how I felt I had to come back and see if all that was what I'd thought it, was real," said Fanny, wiping her eyes and speaking more rationally. "And before I came I was afraid that he and all he'd been doing—making it a Republic, and all these new laws and so on—would have spoilt it all. But he hasn't—he's added to it, because he's doing it so wonderfully, and—well, because he's so magnificent himself!" she ended, on a note, positively, of triumph.

Féridé was silent. In the face of that declaration, and Fanny's shining eyes as she made it—eyes shining through her still-wet lashes—for the moment she could think of nothing to say.

"You'd better understand," Fanny went on. "It's not just—carelessness, lightness, if you like—in me, falling in love with him; yes, I have—of course I have! At least I suppose you'd call it that. All these years that Alec's been asking me to marry him, I kept on saying No, not because I didn't like him enough, then, but because of this business of not being sure if the most important thing in my life so far was real or not; and if it were real, if he could take it! Oh, I don't see how you *can* understand!" the girl exclaimed, pushing back her hair with a gesture of desperation. "You weren't at my school, you don't know North Oxford! And it was all so long ago, Bebek and the yali, and you. But when I did promise to marry him, I felt I must come out again first, and see whether all that was really what I'd dreamed it to be, for such years; and if so, whether I could still marry him. You see Alec's real, too; and I wanted to see if my two realities were—were compatible," Fanny said, twisting her fingers together. "You'll think that mad, but I couldn't marry him without doing that."

"And *were* they compatible?" Féridé asked, seizing on the clearest point.

"Yes, at first. I realised, when I'd seen you again, and got to know you as you are now, that you and Alec would never have much to say to one another; but they were compatible *in me,* and that was the important thing. As far as that went, I could still have got married to Alec all right."

"But," Féridé began—and then paused, held up by the words "I could have," the fatal sound of the past conditional tense. "But you are still engaged?" she amended, trying to conceal her dismay.

"Yes—I mean, I've done nothing about it. I suppose I must break it off, now. The fact is, I haven't been thinking much about it!" said Fanny frankly, with a rueful little smile at her friend.

"Do not! Oh, do not do such a thing!" Féridé exclaimed.

"But dji-djim, I must. It wouldn't be fair not to. I can't marry Alec now."

"Oh yes, you can. You must! Go away, quickly—yes, I who love you tell you to do this. Go away, and forget, and marry your Alec and be happy."

"Féridé, I know that that's not possible," Fanny said slowly.

"Why not? Fanny, do you not believe what I have been telling you about Kemal Pasha? There is *nothing* here for you!"

"Yes, I do believe it in a way—though I think he may like me more than you think. But even if what you say about him and other women is all true, and I am just one of a crowd, what I've got with him is something bigger, more valuable than anything I've ever had, or ever could have with anyone else, just because he is so much bigger and more important. Goodness, do I have to come and tell *you* that he is one of the great men of all time?" Fanny burst out passionately. "And here and now, at any rate, I know something of what his love can be, although to him it may be only a fantasy, as you call it. Well, I don't call that a disaster, even if it does prevent me from making an ordinary humdrum marriage. I think I am enormously lucky. There!"

This declaration moved Féridé, but it exasperated her too, and exasperation got the upper hand.

"Really, you talk like a Turkish woman!" she exclaimed.

"Oh Féridé, don't be too vexed with me," Fanny pleaded. "I know it sounds awful, and you think me crazy, but I can't feel otherwise about it. It has just happened, that's all."

"It can pass. It will pass, if only you will be reasonable, be right-minded," Féridé said more gently, but still urgently.

"No, it won't pass," Fanny said. "I don't want it to, either. Why should I throw away the biggest thing that has ever come into my life—into almost any woman's life? What happens to me over it all is my affair—breaking off my engagement and all that; but at this moment this thing is mine, and I mean to hold onto it."

Féridé sat looking at her with an expression on her face that Fanny had never seen, and at first could not fathom.

"Are you serious?" she asked at last.

"Perfectly serious."

"So. I too am serious, and I say that you cannot do this." She rose as she spoke, slowly—there seemed to be no end to that long upward movement; when at last her friend stood looking down at her Fanny could no longer be in any doubt as to what that unfamiliar expression betokened. It was more than disapproval, it was a contained condemnation. Fanny was quite unprepared for this; it wounded her. Her temper began to rise.

"And why can I not?"

"Because it is not wise, and moreover it is not seemly. For your own sake it is unwise, and also wrong—you are betrothed. If you go now, as I tell you, it will pass; indeed it will pass in any case—all such things pass in the end," Féridé said, a momentary sadness dimming the sword-like edge of resolution in her face. "But it cannot go on; it must end, at once," she continued, her face again determined.

"Why?" Fanny asked again, coldly.

"Because there is gossip."

"I do not mind gossip," Fanny said, more coldly still.

"Possibly not, but I do. I will not have gossip going on about the Ghazi and a member of my household. It is unseemly," Féridé repeated.

"In that case we can go to the hotel," said Fanny, now in a cold fury —the word "unseemly," so reiterated, stung her intolerably. She too rose at last and stood confronting her hostess. "It is late today, and my Uncle is out, but we will go to the hotel tomorrow. I do not wish to leave Ankara at present."

Féridé looked at her a long moment, with down-drawn brows. There was pain in her face—this quarrel with Fanny was hideous—but there was also an implacable resolve and immense strength. All that she had become, all that had been forged in her to a fine temper by the events of the past few years shone from her now with an intensity that was like a clear flame.

"Fanny, you *will* leave Ankara, dear as you are to me, and whether you wish it or not," she said steadily. "You say that it is your wish to remain, but my country is more important than your wishes, more important even than our friendship. I will not have you, for the sake of your personal feelings, spoiling and undoing my work among the women here—which is also *his* work, his wish. See!" she said, throwing out her long narrow hands—"You come among us as a western woman, free, independent, what we aspire to be, what we are struggling to become. At the ball you gave us courage to appear in western dress; you wore it yourself, and we all envied you for the naturalness with which you did it, and your indifference to adverse comment." She paused for a moment, as if gathering her forces to say the necessary, the intolerable thing. "Do you remember those comments? 'Brazen hussies, loose women'? But if you, English, now behave before us all as a loose woman would behave, what can we think of western manners, western freedoms? What becomes of our aspirations?"

She paused again; but before that tremendous indictment Fanny was silent. Féridé watched her face, rebellious and wretched, in which the colour came and went for a few moments, and then went on.

"Do you not see, you of all people, that our women must be serious-minded, irreproachable, in their approach to European manners? I have been trying, I mean to try to do more to make them understand this. True, we begin with externals like dress, but behaviour is more than dress, and honour and seemliness are more than details of behavior, like passing first through a door! Freedom has its responsibilities— must I tell *you* that?" she asked, throwing the question in Fanny's face as Fanny had thrown her question about the Ghazi's greatness at Féridé herself a few moments before. Still the girl was silent, staring in stubborn anger at her friend. "Oh, you must see this," Féridé exclaimed. "You cannot be so blind! You must see that you must go."

"No, I don't see it, and I won't go!" Fanny burst out at last, furiously. "I will leave this house, but I won't leave Ankara. You—you've got it all wrong; you don't understand. I never thought you could be so cruel!" she exclaimed, half-sobbing in her anger and distress. "Oh!—"

Whatever else she might have said was cut short by the sound in the passage outside of the Doctor's voice, making a pleasant remark to the servant as the front door opened and closed. The two girls stood listening. His step was heard approaching—then another door closed. He had gone into his study. Without another word, but now sobbing undisguisedly, Fanny fled from the room and ran upstairs.

For both the young women the evening passed wretchedly—Fanny white and silent, Féridé conscientiously leading the conversation into channels congenial to her husband and the Doctor; when the two men, neither of whom was habitually very observant of the aspect of womenfolk about them, engaged in a prolonged discussion she lapsed thankfully into silence. Now and again she glanced warily at Fanny, but both at table and in the salon afterwards the girl avoided her eyes. They parted for the night upstairs, still in silence, and without their usual embrace. Nor did Féridé say anything to Orhan of what had passed; she waited on events. She had spoken; the next move was Fanny's. But she passed a wakeful and miserable night, thinking, thinking, thinking—of her friend, and of her quarrel with her friend. Oh, it was all wrong, this line that Fanny was taking about the whole thing, and besides it was all unreal. She was deluding herself doubly, Féridé was sure—as to Kemal Pasha's feeling for her, and as to her own feeling for him. "It is Turkey that she really loves," the young woman thought, just before at last, as dawn was breaking, she fell asleep.

The same discomfort prevailed the next morning, when Orhan had gone to his bureau and Dr. Pierce retired to his little room. There was no family breakfast at the villa; coffee and rolls were served in the guests' rooms, though Orhan usually took his on the balcony, and Féridé, in a wrapper, sat with him. This morning she remained there for a long while, waiting, listening for Fanny's movements, usually so audible in the fragile old house, and trying to decide what course to pursue. If she explained matters to Dr. Pierce he would, she was sure, see the necessity for their departure, but the very idea of doing so was deeply repugnant to her. If only she could make Fanny see it, and do the thing herself, naturally and gracefully. To Féridé, brought up as she had been under Réfiyé Hanim's calm and dignified sway, any roughness and ugliness in personal relationships was horrible, and this breach with her dear Fanny unspeakably so. At all costs that must be healed; they could not part in anger and bitterness. She got up and moved into the room, intending to send for Fatma and ask Fanny to come to her—but the recollection of yesterday's wretched scene, when she found herself standing in the actual surroundings where it had taken place, suddenly made her feel so ill that she sank into the nearest chair: her heart was beating uncomfortably, a light sweat sprang out on her forehead. Oh, could she really tackle Fanny again? Yes, she must; without giving way on the main point, somehow she must make their peace. In a moment, she thought; I must have a moment first— and folding her hands over the arm of the chair she rested her forehead on them.

It was in that position that Fanny, also moved by acute unhappiness and a restless desire for a reconciliation, found her. She too had spent a miserable night, and though in theory she was still determined to get her own way, the practical difficulties, as she had stared at them through the hours of darkness, had begun to daunt her a little. But whatever happened—before she spoke to her uncle, or did anything—she must get right with Féridé again somehow. Perhaps she could make her understand. The door of the salon was ajar, and moving noiselessly in her white tennis-shoes she came in without being heard. At the sight of her friend in that strangely broken attitude, she ran to her with a little cry.

"Féridé, dji-djim, what is it? Aren't you well? Oh, what is the matter?"

Féridé raised her head.

"It is nothing. I felt a little faint, or sick, or something—I am better now. I slept ill," she said apologetically. "But how are you, dear Fanny? You look pale. Did you sleep?"

"No! How could I sleep when you and I had quarrelled, and were angry with one another?" Fanny exclaimed impulsively. "Of course I did not sleep a wink."

Féridé began to laugh weakly. She put her arms round her friend and drew her close; childishly, Fanny knelt and snuggled her head into Féridé's bosom. (She had never had a mother to do that to since she was nine years old.) Féridé stroked the yellow hair as a mother might, in silence. This was an unexpected help. Oh what a boon affection was, the solvent for so many difficulties!—without affection everything was impossible. There darted into her mind, unbidden, a recollection of the day at the yali when Niné had feigned a heart attack in order to check a quarrel between herself and the Pasha—and involuntarily she gave another tiny laugh.

"What is amusing?" Fanny asked, lifting her face from Féridé's wrapper and smiling too, but rather uncertainly.

"Something Niné once did. But I shall not tell you!—it has no importance." She went on stroking Fanny's lifted head, almost mechanically, while she looked into the girl's face; the motion of her hand was something Fanny needed, was glad of—she realised that. But the point at issue had still to be dealt with, and she felt so weak, so completely unequal to it.

"Are we friends again?" she asked, as a preliminary.

"Oh dji-djim *yes!*—I do hope so. How can you and I be at odds? It has made me so miserable."

"Me too. But dearest one, all the same you must listen to me, whether either you or I like what I have to say or not." She felt Fanny stiffening in resistance within the arm which held her as she said that, but she forced herself to go on. Féridé's instincts were feminine and sure, based on a natural wisdom unclouded by modern notions of rights or economic independence or any psychopathic theories of "self-expression" for women; it was unaccountable to her that Fanny should not see what she saw so clearly: that gossip about an affair between the Head of the State and a foreign woman was a breach of taste, a breach of style, which was altogether impossible, inadmissible.

"Darling, have you reflected on what I said yesterday?—perhaps with too much heat, though it was true."

"Yes, I have," Fanny said, rising as she spoke; doing this, she released herself from the influence of that long hand which had been stroking her head so soothingly. "I really don't know what to say! I see your point, in a way, about the women here, though I don't quite see why my going on seeing him in—well actually in quite a proper way, as I've been doing—should matter so tremendously."

"He would not let it continue in a proper way for very long!—that is not his fashion, ma chère! And in any case no one would believe that it was an innocent relationship. That is an Anglo-Saxon conception which it will take us several centuries to arrive at—if we ever do!" She said that with a candid little grin, quite unlike her usual fine smile of irony, and Fanny made a rueful little grimace in return. "No, I am not so ambitious as that," Féridé pursued. "I want Turkish women to learn the alphabet of freedom, of life and behaviour outside the haremlik, before they start studying complicated English romances!"

Fanny smiled rather unwillingly.

"And I am to be sacrificed to their A B C?—I and my opportunity, my happiness?" she asked a little bitterly.

"Yes! I should say yes even if there were any opportunity of real happiness for you with Mustafa Kemal Pasha. But there is not—there is none! Oh, how I wish you would believe me when I tell you that."

"No, I don't quite believe you, because I've been made so incredibly happy by the little I have had from him. He's so rich!—he has only to give one a few odd pieces, crumbs, to make one feel like a millionaire," the girl said slowly. Féridé was moved, almost shaken by the soft tone of recollected rapture with which Fanny uttered those words.

"Oh my dearest, but that is all illusion! It is just him—it is his charm. It will pass, assuredly it will pass," she said urgently, as she had said the day before.

A photograph of Réfiyé Hanim stood on a table at the further side of the room. Fanny went over to it.

"No, it won't pass," she said, staring at the picture. "Réfiyé Hanim was quite right." She turned back to Féridé. "Do you remember what she said, the very first time that Ahmet sang the Falcon Song, down at the yali?—'The heart does not come back.'"

This time it was Féridé who burst into tears. Memories of Niné, memories of Ahmet came over her in a flood; and memories of Fanny too, the little merry Canary of long ago, who now spoke those fatal words with such fatalistic calmness. "Oh, don't cry, dearest," the girl said, going over to her. "Don't cry for me. No, stop," she said, as Féridé's sobs became more violent, putting her arms round her and holding her close—"Remember the baby; it will be bad for him if you get so upset."

But Féridé was now quite overwrought. The strain of having had to broach the subject again, the moral effort which, so vainly, she had put out to persuade Fanny against this infatuation, and now seeing the imminent wreck of her friend's happiness was too much for her self-control. Fanny, alarmed, went on trying to soothe her. Distracted as they both were, neither had heard nor heeded the sound of a car drawing up outside the house on the track below. Fanny was really worried—Féridé, so poised, so calm as a rule was not only sobbing, but murmuring broken phrases:—"Oh, it is cruel! Why must this happen to you, whom I love so much?" And then with a fresh access of sobbing—"And what will *he* say to this, your fiancé, your poor Alec?"

Before Fanny could answer a servant threw open the door, and Alec Grant walked into the room.

It so happened that precisely when Mr. Fisher's letter reached his friend Alec was in London for a regimental dinner, and they encountered one another at the club. Over a drink the friend remarked that he had heard from Fisher. "Did he say anything about Fanny? She mentioned that she'd seen him," Alec said cheerfully.

"Yes—yes, he said he'd met her," the friend replied, with some constraint; he was a good deal embarrassed. "At a ball," he added needlessly.

"Oh yes—Fanny wrote about the ball," Alec said, still cheerfully. "It sounded a pretty queer show."

"Did she say anything about Mustafa Kemal?" the friend asked, rather nervously.

"Yes—she said he beat up the old Turks who were being rude about the ladies in low-neck dresses," Alec replied readily. "I must say the Turks are a queer lot."

"Ah," said the friend—and nothing more. Alec at last noticed that there was something odd about his manner.

"I say, what's up with you?" he asked briskly. The friend said— "Nothing, nothing"—with such an obvious air of guilt and discomfort that Alec became suspicious, and rounded on him.

"Look here, what *is* all this? Is it something about Fanny? Isn't she well?"

The friend floundered. "Oh, she's *well* enough," he said.

"Then what is it?"

"Well, Billy's worried—he wasn't sure if you ought to be told or not," the friend stammered.

"Told *what*?"

"Well, Billy thinks that—that perhaps—"

"Oh, cough it up, man, for God's sake," Alec interrupted impatiently, as the friend showed signs of bogging down again.

"Well, he said he thought she seemed to be getting rather interested in this man Kemal," the friend said uncomfortably—Alec was beginning to look remarkably like the Fiery Cross.

"Have you got his letter on you?" Alec asked, with a sort of cold sharpness. "Yes, I see you have"—as the friend reddened and leant back in his chair. "Let me see it, please."

"Oh I say! Really, I'm not sure—" the wretched friend protested.

"Hand it over," Alec said implacably, quietly stretching out one of those hands whose redness had so impressed the Pasha—and the friend, cowed, drew out his pocket-book and did as he was told.

Alec, sitting in a deep armchair in the comfortable club room, read the letter through without the smallest change of expression. Mr. Fisher, though he had written in anger at what he regarded as Fanny's "goings-on," had not exaggerated; the temperateness of expression which is instilled from the outset into English diplomatists already coloured even his private correspondence. But he did report that Fanny had danced with the Ghazi, about which, carelessly, she had said nothing to her fiancé; and he mentioned the gift of the tesbih, as to which she had also kept silent. "It was a wonderful thing—the finest I've ever seen," wrote Mr. Fisher, who was becoming an amateur of Turkish objects of virtue; "and when she saw his card she blushed."

Alec Grant folded up the letter, slipped it back into its envelope, and returned it, still impassive, to his friend. "Thank you," he said coldly. "If you will excuse me, I'll go now. I have an engagement." And he stalked away. The poor friend thought that Alec seemed to take his girl's flirtations with another man uncommonly quietly. But Captain

Grant made his way at once, by taxi, to his Colonel, who was also in London for the dinner, and asked for twelve days' leave—to go to Turkey, he said, in reply to a question; on urgent business.

"But will twelve days be enough?" his startled C.O. asked.

"Yes, Sir, thank you. Five days to go, five days to come back, two days to do my business."

The leave was granted, and Alec went off to the Foreign Office, where he had a friend, to arrange about his visas, and then cabled Mr. Fisher to get him a room in Ankara. And all through the four days and nights in the Simplon Orient Express, staring out of the window by day, turning over in the narrow bed at night, the poor Fiery Cross, shooting like a meteor across Europe, cursed all Turks in his heart, and three of them especially—Mustafa Kemal Pasha, this Orhan Bey, and above all his wife Féridé, who had put some sort of an enchantment on Fanny when she was too little to know any better, from which she had never been able to free herself.

.   .   .   .   .

When Captain Grant walked into the salon and saw his fiancée kneeling beside a woman who was in floods of tears, he came to a halt just inside the door. Fanny sprang up. "Alec! What on earth! Oh, come outside a minute," she said, going over to him and taking his arm; she led him across the passage and into the empty dining-room. "Wait just a second—I can't leave her now; she's all upset, and she's going to have a baby," she said hurriedly, and ran out again.

In the salon Féridé had pulled herself together, and was blowing her nose and dabbing at her eyes.

"C'est lui?" she asked.

"Yes, it's him all right," Fanny said rather grimly.

"But why has he come?"

"I don't know. I'll go to him in a minute and find out—if you're all right?"

"It will be this Fisher!" Féridé pronounced.

"Probably, as they're friends," Fanny said. She was collected and calm to a degree which astonished Féridé.

"Oh, my poor one! How frightful this is for you!" she exclaimed.

"Perhaps it's just as well to get it over quickly," said Fanny. "But look, I must go to him."

"Bring him in here—I go upstairs," said Féridé. "Where is he?"

"I put him in the dining-room; the coast is quite clear," said Fanny with a tiny grin.

When Féridé had gone she went across to the dining-room again.

"She's all right—she's gone upstairs. Come to the salon—the chairs are better," she said.

But in the salon, where Alec stared about him for a moment in surprise at the many strange objects and furnishings, they did not at once use the chairs. Fanny stood in front of him and looked up straight in his face.

"Alec, I don't know what you've heard, though I can guess why you've come, but I'd better tell you at once. I'm going to break it off, my dear. I must."

"Will you please tell me why?" he asked—the sight of Fanny, and the rush of feeling that it brought, for some reason made him very angry.

"Yes, you're entitled to know that. I've fallen in love with somebody else—anyhow enough in love to make it impossible for me to marry you." Fanny had determined if possible to keep Turkey out of it—Turkey, and her previous doubts and hesitations because of Turkey.

"Is it this Kemal Pasha?"

"Yes, it is."

"And are you going to marry him?"

"Good heavens, no! There's no question of that," she said decidedly.

"Then what *do* you mean to do?"

"Just not get married at all."

"But that's simply senseless!" he said. "If you're not going to marry him, I can't see why you won't marry me." Then she saw the cloud of a horrible suspicion come into his eyes, but he didn't utter it directly. "Do you mean to stay out here?" he asked, very coldly.

"No—we shall be coming home fairly soon, I expect; term's begun, but Uncle arranged to be a bit late if he wanted. I haven't settled anything with him yet—he doesn't know about this; but now you've come, I suppose he'll have to," said Fanny rather bitterly.

"Did you expect me to stay quietly at home and hope for the best, when I heard that another man was making love to you and giving you presents?" Alec Grant asked angrily.

"I think you might have written to me, and told me what gossip you'd heard, and asked if there was anything in it. You know you'd have got an honest answer," said Fanny stoutly.

"I should have thought that in the circumstances you might have written to me," he retorted.

"I was going to, today," she said disconcertingly.

"Why today? Why not before?"

"You mean when this owl Fisher wrote off and told you all the tattle of the town?" she asked, angry in her turn. "Yes, I don't doubt there *was* tattle, because I'm English, and talked good Turkish—I was 'news,' and he's always news! But there wasn't anything to write to you then—it's only just blown up, really, in the last day or two."

"Why has it blown up now, then, if there was nothing in it before?"

"Because I suddenly realised what it meant to me," said Fanny slowly. "I suppose it had been growing in me before, without my knowing, like it does; but I honestly only realised it these last two days. Oh Alec," she said, suddenly noticing his stricken face, "don't look like that!" She made a movement as if to put her hand on his arm, and then drew back. "I am so frightfully sorry," she said. "It's hideous for you, and impossible of me! You can't say anything worse to me than I think of myself, when I think of you."

But Alec Grant was not the man to lose his bride without a struggle —he had not raced across Europe to hear, and quietly accept, her decision not to marry him. He saw that little impulsive movement of penitence and affection, and he stepped forward and took her in his arms. "This is all the bloodiest nonsense I ever listened to," he said, between ferocious kisses. "You're going to come home and marry me, and forget this chap. Why, you haven't known him two months, and I've loved you, and well you know it, for six years." He went on kissing her.

Fanny didn't struggle or resist, and presently her passivity disturbed him. He let her go.

"Won't you?" he asked, now pleadingly, looking in her face.

"Alec, I can't. It's impossible. I'm sorry; frightfully, desperately sorry, but you must believe me when I tell you I can't."

The bitter argument went on, Alec hurt, angry, and pleading by turns, Fanny penitent but implacable. "I can't understand *why*," he said at last, striding across the room and back. "You're bewitched, that's what it is—these people have got hold of you somehow. You always were bewitched by that—" He broke off as the door opened, and Féridé came in.

Chapter Twenty-three

FÉRIDÉ, while bathing her eyes upstairs, doing her hair and putting on a dress, had nevertheless made some necessary dispositions. First she sent a message by Fatma to the servants to prevent them from irrupting ceaselessly into the salon with cups of coffee; then, while she attended to her face, she thought rapidly. No, Fanny wasn't going to give way, whatever she said, or whatever her Alec said—she was sure of that. Wretched as it was, the fact had to be faced. So she despatched a note by the chauffeur to Orhan, telling him to arrange a small dinner that night at Carpic's for himself, Dr. Pierce, Captain Grant, "and this creature Fisher, if you can get him. Tell Dr. Pierce that the Cook has had a seizure! Captain Grant is the fiancé, but there is an éclaircissement going on—I will explain later, but I cannot have you all sitting round the table staring at a broken betrothal!" Féridé wrote hurriedly. Orhan gave one of his shouts of laughter when he read this in his office, before he sent the chauffeur off to book a table at the White Russian restaurant, and to take a note of invitation to Mr. Fisher.

Féridé also kept an eye on the time—this must be being horrible for Fanny. How unbecoming, how distressing, to have to arrange, and still worse to disarrange one's *fiançailles* for oneself! How much wiser and nicer to have a marriage carefully prepared for one by experienced and loving elders, who looked into disposition and character as well as resources and status, and produced a thoroughly suitable husband, to last a life-time—with whom, by the normal processes of marriage, one usually fell in love. She herself had had rather more latitude than most of her friends, thanks to Dil Feripé, and had been to some extent in love with Orhan before her marriage; but, she thought, glancing at the little French clock by her bed, in this particular she doubted if western ways were really as good as Turkish—English ways, rather, for old Marthe had often explained to her that in France too marriages were arranged. She looked at the clock again; they had had nearly an hour. Quite enough for that poor child! She went downstairs.

When she walked in and saw Fanny's face, pale and strained, and the face of the English officer, strained too, but flushed and angry, she felt that she was not too soon; they looked exhausted as well as utterly miserable, and she felt unspeakably sorry for them both. Someone had obviously got to take the situation in hand, and when Fanny had presented Captain Grant, "You had better go and rest a little, ma chère," she said. Fanny went, thankfully. Coffee was brought in as she went out, and Féridé, taking her cup, explained courteously—she had been a little unwell that day, Fanny had been waiting on her, she must be tired. Alec, listening to the beautiful French—his own was quite good—studied this evil genius of Fanny's, now that he was at last confronted with her, with a sort of angry fascination. An elegant woman, undoubtedly a lady, but clever as the devil, he should say, and probably as worldly as her appearance. But soldiers instinctively recognise the power of command in others, and he recognised it, grudgingly, in this tall well-bred girl with the quiet voice and the beautiful manners. No doubt that was how she had somehow put it across Fanny—look how she had just sent her upstairs, like a child! Her husband was Kemal Pasha's principal running-dog, so Fisher said—no doubt she had helped the thing along! Though he could not help noticing what honest-looking eyes she had—and queer that they were grey, too.

Féridé now dismissed the waiting servant with a nod, and then turned again to Alec Grant and gave him the greatest surprise of his life.

"Captain Grant, this thing has happened while Fanny was under my roof, and I cannot tell you how much I deplore it. You must pardon me for not greeting you when you arrived, but I had just been reasoning with Fanny about it; it was a painful conversation, and I was a little upset."

He stared at her, recalling the sounds of sobbing that he had heard as the salon door opened on his arrival, and the tear-stained face which he had seen over Fanny's shoulder as he came in—*un peu enervée* was putting it rather mildly.

"But—you weren't crying about this?—about Fanny and me?" he stammered, incredulously.

"Certainly I was—about what else? It is such a pity, such a misery!" He continued to stare, and she guessed shrewdly enough at his thoughts —his astonishment was so plain, in his honest red face and greenish eyes. "Is not this a thing to weep for, for her?" she said with great gentleness. "Did you expect her friends not to mind?"

Alec Grant's mind always moved rather deliberately, and at that moment his ideas were undergoing a complete revolution. For six years he had nourished a jealous dislike of these Turkish friends of Fanny's, and for the past few days he had suspected them of complicity in hateful things; now he was being given to understand, quite clearly, that the woman before him felt exactly as he did himself about Fanny and Kemal Pasha. He would almost have been glad to be able to think that she was putting it on; but he had seen her tears himself—and anyhow, face to face she didn't look like a liar. He was silent for quite a long time. At last he said—

"Madame Orhan, I owe you an apology. I didn't know," he paused, "that you were on my side," he ended rather awkwardly.

She skimmed over the awkwardness, left it aside. But she had got to help Fanny all she could, and it was no good giving him encouragement which would, she knew, be quite baseless, and would only involve Fanny in more wretchedness and arguments.

"Yes, I am. I should wish to see Fanny happily married to you. But I realise that that cannot be, now—I am miserable about it, but I accept the fact."

"Well, can you tell me why?" Alec Grant demanded, breathing heavily. "She will only go on and on saying that it's impossible. But people get over these things, don't they? Mightn't it come all right in time, if we wait a bit?" It did not occur to him to think how strange it was that he should be asking this sort of advice from a total stranger; and one whom he had disliked, without knowing her, for so long.

Féridé answered him with the same compassionate decision with which Réfiyé Hanim had answered the Pasha's question about whether Nilüfer might be going to bear a posthumous child to Ahmet.

"No, I am convinced there is very little hope of that," she said.

"It seems so impossible that a thing like that should happen in the time!" he burst out. "Only a few weeks, after all. I simply *can't* understand it!"

"No, it is not an easy thing to understand," she said thoughtfully. He looked at the down-drawn eyebrows that gave her such a peculiar expression of concentration.

"Do you?" he asked.

"Understand it? Yes, I think so. What she is really in love with is Turkey, and she has been in love with that for fifteen years! That is what gives her feeling for Kemal Pasha its strength."

Again he stared at her.

"Could you explain a little more? I'm not sure that I follow. How can one be in love with a country?" But even as he asked the question he remembered how often he had been irritated by Fanny's passionate absorption in Turkey and Turkish affairs.

"Fanny came here as quite a little girl," Féridé said—"from a most uninteresting school, and from a home where there was no normal family life. Istanbul and the Bosphorus are very beautiful, and Fanny was always impressionable; and she came and saw them year after year. And in our house she did find family life, the lonely little creature; she simply basked in it, and that became linked in her mind with all the beauty about her. She adored my Grandmother, even my Father was very fond of her. I remember her telling me one day how lucky I was to live in such a beautiful place, among such lovable people." Involuntarily a tiny smile crept round her mouth as she remembered that occasion, and Fanny stuck in the cedar-tree. "And that unusual childhood made, I am sure, an indelible impression on her," she went on, "and has given her an outlook that is not at all common." With his earnest faithful eyes—like the eyes of Kemal's English dog, she thought —fixed on her face she was aware of a strong desire to give him what comfort she could.

"Yes—go on, please."

"So you see, all this, the life here, the people, I and my home, everything to do with Turkey became for her through those years of the war and after it a sort of home for her spirit and her imagination—a place she went and hid in from dull and tiresome things. But she was intelligent enough to realise, as time went on, that it might all be an illusion, because she had been so young at the time. That was why she wished to return and see it with grown-up eyes. And when she came she found it no illusion; and the—it is hard to express it clearly—the longing that she had felt for this country for so long gave her a sort of famished appetite for it, made her love Turkey more than ever. Can you understand that at all?" she asked, a little anxiously—for now they were at the crucial point.

"You make it all sound much more reasonable," he said carefully— "I think you put it very well." He was silent for a moment, remembering how he and Fanny had argued in the cottage at the time of the Battle of the Sakarya as to whether a child could be a person or not, and how she had said that Féridé *was* a person, and a remarkable one. Fanny had probably been right. Then distress and impatience overcame him again. "But does one break off an engagement just for a thing like that?—for all that you've been saying?"

"No, not for that alone. Fanny is breaking off her engagement to you because she has come to care deeply for Kemal Pasha, who is a very remarkable person, it is generally conceded. He admires and likes her very much," she said steadily. "and has made his admiration plain by seeking her society, and by making her such presents as are customary here." She felt that it was important to stress the normality of the relationship, which she was sure that miserable Fisher had distorted and exaggerated, as Mme T. had done—it would perhaps lessen this poor Captain Grant's mortification now, and help his peace of mind later. "And he is, after all, the Head of the State," she went on—"I imagine most young women would find admiration from a man in his position flattering in a very subtle way."

"Couldn't you have stopped it, when you saw what was happening?" he broke in.

"No. I tried to, when I began to guess what might happen, but I failed," she said promptly. "Fanny is not a child; she has directed her own life for years, more so even than most English girls—and she can be very headstrong, as you probably know." She said this without any disarming smile, just calmly stating the fact—he nodded heavily.

"But what I should like to make clear to you, if I can," Féridé pursued, "is this—perhaps it is rather complicated, but I believe it to be true"—she stopped, seeking for words.

"Go on," he said. "I believe you really understand her better than I have ever done."

She could have wept at this unexpected tribute. "Oh, you are kind! It is only because we were children together—like sisters, and that is something different to anything else." She gathered her forces for the explanation, while he sat staring, vacantly, she thought, in the direction of the photograph of Réfiyé Hanim, which was opposite his chair.

"I want you to understand why her feeling for him is what it is," Féridé said. "He typifies what she has loved so long—Turkey! He is the visible emblem of the dream—the dream that has obsessed her for so many years. We think of him as the saviour of our country—and I believe the world recognises him as that, also; in any case, she thinks as we think. And she has seen him among his people! I tried to prevent that, but I could not," she said, with curious urgency. "So you see, this is it," she went on; "If she were a jeune personne who had just come out here and lost her head about him, I should say that she would get over it. But as it is, I ought not to tell you that I think she will, for I do not—though I wish with all my heart that she would, for as I was telling her, there is *nothing* in this for her!"

"You mean—it's really rather a one-sided affair?" he asked, to her surprise, after a moment.

"In the long run, yes."

He got up and walked about the room.

"Thank you very much," he said at last. "It's very good of you to have taken so much trouble—for both of us. And you don't advise my trying again?"

"Certainly not!—at least not now," she said with decision. "I should say goodbye, and go home, in your place."

She could not bear his face when she said that—no doubt he was thinking of the very different homeward journey for which he had hoped when he came out.

"They will be leaving soon, also," she added. "Captain Grant, I am so very sorry." There was nothing more to say.

He picked up his hat. "I think I'd better be going," he said. He paused by the picture of Réfiyé Hanim. "Do you mind telling me who that is?" he asked suddenly.

"My Grandmother, who died this year," she answered in surprise.

"It's extraordinarily like you," he said, still looking at it. "I should like to have known her." He turned and held out his hand. "Goodbye."

"I forgot to tell you that you are dining tonight with my husband and Dr. Pierce and Mr. Fisher at the restaurant," she said hurriedly. "You will forgive what looks like a lack of hospitality, but I thought it would be easier for everyone." He nodded. She thought of everything, this Féridé. "My husband will be here at any moment," she went on—"unless you would rather go now?"

"Yes, I think I'd better."

"Then I will find Fanny—she will wish to bid you adieu." She held out her hand, saying again—"I am so very sorry."

"I know you are," he said, as he wrung her hand. "Goodbye."

Whatever Fanny might have thought, in fact Féridé and Alec Grant had found quite a lot to say to one another.

·   ·   ·   ·   ·   ·

As Féridé passed through the hall on her way upstairs she encountered Dr. Pierce. She told a servant to send Fatma to tell Fani Hanim that she was wanted in the salon at once; and then with a hand on his arm shepherded Dr. Pierce into Orhan's study.

"Someone to see Fanny?" the Doctor asked.

"Yes—Captain Grant."

"Alec? Good God, what is he doing out here?"

Féridé sat down in the chair in front of the writing-table and fell into slightly hysterical laughter; the Doctor waited with his usual calm patience.

"Forgive me," she said at last—"It has all been *so* awful that it is almost comical! I believe that this miserable Fisher must have written and told Captain Grant that the Ghazi was—paying attentions to Fanny; he was here, you know—by the worst mischance—when her tesbih arrived from Kemal Pasha."

"Oh, did he send her a tesbih?" the Doctor asked with mild interest. "I didn't know. Was it a good one?"

"Yes, exquisite!" Féridé began to laugh again—she adored Dr. Pierce and his attitude to the events of life. But this time she checked herself quickly.

"It is very sad, really," she said—"Fanny has broken off her engagement."

"Oh, has she? Do you know why? I suppose she's upset at Alec's coming rushing out like this," the Doctor said. "Really, I don't altogether wonder. He's a rather insular person, Alec." Again Féridé was tempted to laugh, but restrained herself.

"Perhaps that is it. Anyhow he is in the salon, waiting to say goodbye to her." This was being unexpectedly easy, she thought—Dr. Pierce was taking it all so very calmly. But the Doctor, as an exceptional measure, was at last quietly turning his attention away from literature and folk-lore to his niece and her affairs.

"Féridé Hanim, my dear, do you think Fanny has fallen in love with Kemal Pasha?" he asked presently.

"Dear Dr. Pierce, I am afraid that she has, to some extent."

"Oh well, that is all folly," the Doctor said benignly. "He's a man of great charm, you know—one understands it well enough. But it won't do. If that's the way it is we'd better go home as soon as we can. We've paid you a tremendous visitation, anyhow, my dear."

"Dearest Dr. Pierce, we have enjoyed every hour of every day of your visit!" Féridé exclaimed warmly. "But I fear you are right—for her, it would be better to leave."

She spoke apologetically, as she felt, but no explanations were necessary with the Doctor; he took in all the implications of the situation, once it really came within the focus of his attention.

"Better all round," he said. "One can't have talk going on, especially about a foreigner. All wrong—particularly just now." Actually the expression he used for "talk" was *dedikodu*, the untranslatable Turkish word for something a shade more regrettable than gossip, which Féridé had employed when she spoke to Orhan about the cigarette-case. "I expect this Master Fisher may be able to hurry up our getting sleepers on the Orient Express—the Embassy people usually can."

"Yes, this at least he might do!" Féridé said tartly. The Doctor laughed.

"He's not a bad boy," he said. "He's a bit young."

"Oh, by the way, you are all dining together tonight—you and Orhan, and he, and this poor Grant. I thought it would be simpler than a dinner here," Féridé said.

"Oh yes, much better. Where?"

"Carpic's—it is the only place."

"Ah yes. Well, I'd better go and wash before lunch." But he didn't go—he lingered, looking thoughtfully at a framed piece of Izzet's calligraphy on the wall, which the Pasha had given to Orhan. Close by it was another, the gold paint in which the characters were inscribed very clear and bright, and the Doctor turned to this.

"That's Kemal Pasha's, isn't it? Beautifully done. Funny he should want to abolish the old script, when he's such a master at it himself. He's an astonishing man. Hmm. Poor Alec!" He was musing aloud. "Féridé, my dear, I hope all this hasn't been too much of a worry to *you*," he said, turning round on her suddenly.

"Oh no—only these last few days—and that I am so sorry about Fanny."

"Ah yes. Poor Fanny. Well, people have to go through these things, I suppose." He looked shrewdly at her. "I'm not sure that she'd have been very happy with young Grant," he said. "He's really very insular."

At that moment they heard the sounds of Captain Grant's departure in the passage outside. "He's sure not to have tipped your man," the Doctor said, listening. "I don't think he's the sort of fellow who ever learns the right thing to do anywhere." Féridé smiled.

"Perhaps. But he is really very nice—he is so sincere. And good," she added. She thought, but could not say, that if only Fanny had more of her lover's simple goodness and rectitude she would not be making this mess of her life.

"Well, I really must go," said Dr. Pierce. "You keep a man idling beside you, my dear! Your Mother, they said, used to be just the same."

When he had gone Féridé sat on where she was. She felt extraordinarily tired, and there was nothing more to do. She heard Fanny go upstairs, her usually light footfall slow on the treads. A few moments later she heard her husband come in, and called very softly—"Orhan."

He came into the study.

"You are here, my Life? Quel drame! Is it still going on? Where are they all?"

"No, it is over. Captain Grant has gone—I imagine he is staying with Fisher; Fanny is upstairs, and the Doctor is getting ready for lunch."

"Then why are you here?"

"I was too lazy to go back to the salon," she said, smiling up at him.

"Too tired is what you mean," he said, stooping to kiss her. "My poor treasure, what an affair! Does the Doctor know?"

"Yes, I told him. It is final, Orhan."

"And what did he say?"

"That he thought she would never have been happy with Captain Grant," said Féridé, beginning to laugh a very little.

"Why is this amusing?" he asked, stroking her head.

"It is not—it is sad. It is just the way he spoke of it, and of the whole affair. He loves Fanny, and is sorry for her, but he takes everything so calmly, because he looks always at the facts."

"He is a man quite of the first order," Orhan said. "But what happens now?"

"Oh, they leave. They must—the Doctor sees that clearly. They go as soon as sleepers can be arranged."

"Tiens! Well, I shall miss him. But now listen, Light of my Eyes; I have a piece of news for you—that is why I am late."

"What, then?"

"I am offered the post of Counsellor in Paris."

"In *Paris?*"

"Yes. The suggestion comes from the Minister of Foreign Affairs, but Ismet Pasha also approves of the idea."

"And what does *he* say?"

Orhan looked a little rueful.

"At first he was indignant, and shouted—the Minister made the proposal in a conversation with him, of course; he could not have done otherwise."

"Well, and then?"

"Enfin, after asking the Minister why he wanted to cut off his right hand," Orhan said, grinning rather happily, "he calmed down and told me that he did not wish to stand in the way of my career, and that I should decide."

"So did you accept?"

"Not immediately, no. I asked for time for consideration. That pleased the Ghazi, I could see. But," the young man said, with one of his rather rare bursts of simplicity and humility, "I wished for your opinion."

"Mine?"

"Yes, yours. Ah, if Niné were alive, we would consult her—she had such great wisdom. But I think she has left you some of it," he said, smiling at his wife. Féridé was silent—she was thinking of Captain Grant standing in front of Réfiyé Hanim's photograph. How strange that the stranger had felt that great old lady's power, merely from her lifeless picture.

Orhan could not interpret her silence—and when he was at a loss he invariably turned to words to fill the vacuum.

"Think of it!" he said—"Paris! The theatres, the music, the society— la ville lumière! And we could buy you such dresses, such hats!" Still she was silent—words were no *open sesame* to his wife's mind, as Orhan really knew by now. "I wish to do the thing that *you* would like," he said at last quite humbly, kissing her hand.

Her brows were drawn down. "I will reflect on it," she said.

Alec Grant left next day, and Fanny and Dr. Pierce as soon as they had succeeded in getting sleepers—with the ready assistance of Mr. Fisher, who was in rather a chastened frame of mind, this was arranged in three or four days. On the last afternoon—the train to Istanbul left in the evening—Fanny, tired with packing, went down into the salon where Féridé sat sewing by the open doors onto the balcony.

"Have you finished?" Féridé asked, as the girl sank wearily into a chair beside her. "What a disagreeable task packing is!"

"Yes, it is—loathsome," Fanny said. "Especially when one's going away from what one cares about." She leant her head back against the chair—then, changing her mind, leaned forward to look out. The leaves that framed the balcony were now a deep yellow, speckled with black, and the light that came into the room was no longer green and dim but warm and golden: pouring through the golden leaves, thrown up from the yellowing vineyards that sloped gently away below the house; further down the hill poplars and the scrub of acacias which filled the upper end of the valley were brilliant as daffodils in the afternoon sunshine. Autumn is the one season of the year when Ankara bursts into undeniable beauty, with this explosion of yellow and gold on every side. As if drawn by a magnet Fanny got up from her chair and went out onto the balcony, the better to see it all. Along the track to her right, dusty and white between the thick yellow pattern of the vine-leaves, Mustafa Kemal, followed by his dog, had come walking into her life. She gave a tiny sigh. "Lovely lovely place," she murmured to herself. Then she turned back to her friend.

"Féridé, do you think I shall ever see you again?"

"Yes, certainly," Féridé said, with calm decision.

"How? Where?"

"The world is large," Féridé said smiling. "But actually, there is a possibility that might bring me very near to you."

"*Is* there? Oh, what?"

"It is still not settled, so you will not speak of it, but Orhan may be going to Paris."

"Good Heavens! How exciting. When shall you know for certain?"

"When we have decided—the offer has been made, and Kemal Pasha will not oppose it if Orhan desires to go. I rather wished to talk to you about it," Féridé said; "I should like to hear what you think."

"What *I* think? But Féridé, what earthly use could my views be on Orhan's career?" Fanny said, her hand still on the rail of the balcony. "He wouldn't give half a piastre for them!"

"I am not sure even of that; but in any case, I am being consulted," said Féridé gaily, "and I wish to hear them very much."

"Darling, all right—only I can't imagine why." Fanny came in again and sat down, thinking how often she and Féridé had talked through the door onto the narrow balcony, and how often she had come in when a conversation began to get interesting. This was the last time. "Go on," she said: "I'm longing to hear all about it."

"The question is this," Féridé said, soberly now; "at least for me especially it is the question—Where can we be of most use to our country? I do not worry about Orhan's career; that is secure in any case, I think," she said calmly, and Fanny nodded emphatic assent. "I believe he would make a good diplomat; I know he is of great value to the Ghazi here. But I guess also that our Government is anxious at present to send diplomats abroad whose wives can représenter properly—not women who either refuse to appear at all, or who turn up at State functions, where everyone else is en grande toilette, wearing a long feradjé and with their heads swathed, so that they look like Imams!" Féridé said, with such vehemence that Fanny laughed.

"Dji-djim, I am sure you are right," she said. "If they looked like the deputies' wives at the ball they would certainly create a very odd impression in London or Paris!"

"Exactly. But our women here at home need encouragement and teaching—they require to be given a lead," Féridé pursued with great earnestness. "I am sure the Ghazi is right in what he desires for our nation, but these things do not happen by themselves!—someone has to work at them. You saw what it was like, at the ball, for yourself: how the foreigners looked at those women who stood aside to let their husbands pass first through the doorway." She spoke a little hesitantly when she referred to the ball, remembering with embarrassment the last time that they had spoken of it—Fanny remembered too, and the colour came into her face. "But if we do not learn to behave like the women of the western nations here at home," Féridé hurried on, "where shall we be in the modern world? The women of family can pick it up for themselves—really, they know it already—but not the rest."

"Yes, I see," Fanny said. "Really it comes to this, that what you do in this, in either job, is practically as important as Orhan's work."

"No, not so important; but not without importance. That is why I want your opinion. You have been here, now; you know the situation, and what is aimed at—and you have seen our women today and how far they are still from the goal. Also," Féridé said, with a dry little smile, "you know better than any of us what the goal is really like when one gets there, because you are at it!—you *are* a European."

Fanny blushed again, at that, but all she said was "Yes, I see," once more. She was thinking of what Féridé had become—poised and skilful, firm and wise; quite obviously a source of strength and inspiration to her husband, for all his own brilliance, and a counterpoise to his volatile temperament. And besides all this, she was now fitted to be a leader of women anywhere. She remembered what Alec had found time to say, even in those wretched moments of farewell—"She's a wonderful woman, your Mme Orhan; I'd no idea she was like that.

Now that I've met her, I see that you were right about her all along."
So astonishing, from him!

"Let me think," she said now, and sat twiddling the stalk of a vine-leaf in her fingers. Féridé waited quietly.

"No," Fanny said at last, decidedly. "I shouldn't go. I should stay here. I believe you can do far more at home, pulling these poor half-fledged creatures along, and showing them how to live the European life. You've got a tremendous influence over them; I can see that. I think you could do a magnificent job here, good as you'd be abroad, and heavenly as it would be to have you in Paris."

Féridé looked at her, glowing.

"Do you say so? I am so very glad. That was my own thought, too. But if I can, if I succeed, I shall really owe it so much to you," she said, looking earnestly at Fanny.

"Why on earth?"

"But do you not see? Think what it has meant to me, through all those years of my childhood, when a person's attitude to life is shaping itself, to have had your companionship, to learn your outlook—the outlook of an English girl! At that age one takes in ideas as a sponge sucks in water, without knowing that one does it. Marthe used to say that you made me wild, but it was only the wildness of freedom, of an independence such as our girls do not have. We are spoiled, choyées, yes —but we have not been independent, hitherto."

"I don't think I was so *very* wild," Fanny protested; she was rather startled by this outburst.

"No, you were not; you were very well-mannered—Marthe was saying so only this spring, and Baba also. But it was the independence—you went your own way, whatever anyone said."

"I'm afraid I still do." Fanny threw a half-guilty look at her friend.

"Enfin, yes, my Two Eyes! But I am thinking of the past. Do you remember when Dr. Pierce went to Trebizond, and intended to leave you alone in that terrible pension?"

"Yes, rather—and I should have been quite all right," said Fanny: "Mme Kaftanoglu wasn't a bad old thing."

"But do you not see?—that it was conceivable that you should remain *alone* there, a girl of fourteen! I realise now that Niné was really appalled by that, though she said nothing. And I remember how astonished Baba was when Dr. Pierce told him that you were helping to make the translations for his folk-lore book—he spoke of it to Niné and me. You were learned!" Féridé said, her grey eyes very wide. "Learned at fourteen! Our girls are not so."

"Well, yes, it was a bit unusual, my knowing Turkish," Fanny agreed.

"But that was just Uncle, and coming here all the time."

"Yes, ma chère—but what I have been saying is true all the same," Féridé returned. "All my life you have opened windows for me on new worlds. I think I should not have ventured to do that nursing if I had not known that you were nursing too. So if I am capable, now, of helping our women here to learn a new way of life, much of it I owe to my having known you."

She spoke with emotion as well as with conviction, and Fanny was touched. Féridé was being kind, of course, and she knew why, but probably there was some truth in it, too.

"Dji-djim, I am *very* glad to hear you say that," she said. "It's as if I had somehow been able to pay back a little, in return for all the happiness you and your family—and Turkey—have given me." She paused. "And it will make me feel as if, through you, I'm helping one of *his* things along," she said, colouring again. "Because I do think what he's trying to do for his country is so splendid."

"But now, when you go home, what shall you do?" Féridé asked.

"Oh, what I've been doing—look after Uncle. He needs someone, really; and I can help him in his work. But I was thinking—later on, if they want translations made of European books for the schools here— Kemal Pasha was talking about that—that would be a thing I could do. You *must* let me know if there were a chance of my doing that. You will, won't you? Promise?"

"Yes, I promise," Féridé said. She smiled. "I will keep it, too—as you kept your promise to me on the quay—do you remember?—that you would come back."

For some reason the tears came into Fanny's eyes, at that—the happy past was brought back so sharply by the memory of that parting in the crowd beside the steamer. "*You* were independent that day!" she said, with a little unsteady laugh.

"Yes, and *you* got the blame for it!" Féridé said.

"Well, I'm glad I came back, in spite of—everything. Oh, tremendously glad. I found *you* again," Fanny said, the tears now standing openly in her eyes—"and to you, I know that I am not just a fantasy!" The tears spilled over.

"You are not! Oh my dear one, indeed you are not to me. Nor to Orhan—he has formed such a high opinion of you. And this does not always happen, that a husband thinks highly of his wife's friends," said Féridé with an attempt at gaiety, though there were tears in her eyes as well.

"Dear Orhan—he is really an angel," Fanny said. "Oh; I am so glad about you, altogether. It does not always happen, you know, either, that a wife's friends think so highly of her husband!—at least not with us. You will have to learn to be critical of people's husbands, dji-djim, if you are to be truly European!"

Féridé laughed.

"But I wish I had seen Réfiyé Hanim again," Fanny went on wistfully. "It's all very well to talk about European women, you know, Féridé—but if ever there was a wise woman and a great lady, it was she. I think really you owe much more to her than you do to me."

Féridé did not answer for a moment. She was thinking that in those matters of intuitive good taste and right feeling, where Fanny had certainly failed, Réfiyé Hanim's feminine instinct would indeed have been unerring.

"I owe her very much," she said at last. "I believe that wisdom like hers is something international, and also outside Time. But I owe a great deal to you, Fanny, all the same."

Orhan saw the Pierces off that night. Féridé and Fanny said their Goodbyes in the salon. "I don't promise to come back this time," the girl whispered—"but I shall see you some time, somehow. Anyhow I shall never forget."

"Nor I," Féridé murmured back.

When Orhan returned from the station his wife was sitting in her place under the lamp sewing at a small garment. "So! Now we are alone again," he said, looking round him contentedly, as he sat down. "But it has been interesting, this visit. Almost *too* interesting, perhaps!" She nodded in silence.

"But now, have you reflected on this matter of Paris?" he asked. "These last days have been so full, I have hardly seen you alone."

"Yes, I have," she said, raising her eyes from her work. "I think we should not go."

"So!" he said. He looked surprised, and a little disappointed. "Why not, my Life?"

"For several reasons. First, I think that the Ghazi needs you; he is tired, he is not well, and every day he starts some fresh piece of work. There is this whole business of the property of the Tekkés to be cleared up" (the Tekkés were all the monasteries of various types, which Kemal had closed abruptly the very day after his return from Kastamonu). "There is the law abolishing the fez to be drafted, there is the opening of the Law School—it has no end!"

"He has said that he is willing to release me," Orhan objected.

"I know—but should you take advantage of that? You told me that he spoke of his right hand being cut off, when the Minister first proposed it."

"True, he did. And your other reasons?"

"For myself, I would rather remain here for the present, within reach of my Father," she said. "He is old now, and very lonely. From Paris I could at most return once a year—here I can slip down to see him at any time."

"Yes, that is so. But should one put such private considerations before one's duty?"

"No, certainly not," she said decidedly. "And if you are quite certain that it is your duty to go, and that no private considerations, such as Paris being a more amusing place than Ankara, enter into it, I have no more to say."

He laughed a little shamefacedly.

"My Life, you are too astute, and too incorruptible! I think that has weighed with me; and I thought that you would like Paris, too. But there is also this to consider," he went on—"It is important that our diplomats' wives now should be women who can hold their own in the society of foreign capitals. You could do so, and I have reason to believe that the Minister has taken this into consideration."

"I have taken it into consideration too," she said. "It is an obvious point. But on those grounds too, I think that perhaps we should remain."

"Do you? Why so?" he asked, puzzled.

"I think there is even more to be done among the women here," she said, "and that I might help to do it. We do not want many repetitions of a scene like that ball!"

"But what could you do, exactly?" he asked. "Certainly they need alteration, Allah knows!—but I do not see how you would set about it."

"I cannot préciser too much now," she said calmly. "If we stay you will see what I mean. But if the veil is to follow the fez, there will be much to be done first, to prepare our women and give them courage. And that is a sort of work that only women can do, really. Kemal Pasha can dragoon the deputies in public, and so perhaps teach them manners, however embarrassingly; but there are certain things that women can only learn from women."

"I believe you are right," he said thoughtfully—then he smiled. "Fani Hanim could have helped in this," he said rather slyly.

"Yes—a little; not so much as a Turkish woman, as I and Mme T., for example. From foreigners they would not take it; it would not occur to them to imitate a foreigner, as it is already occurring to some of them to imitate me," Féridé said smiling, thinking of the requests for advice on dress that she had received from various deputies' wives since the ball.

"I wonder what she would have thought about this, all the same. She is very intelligent, and she is a good friend to Turkey, as the Ghazi himself said."

"She was of my opinion," said Féridé.

"You asked her? But my Life, this should not have been spoken of; it is confidential still."

"I spoke of it to her four hours before she left," said Féridé. "And Fani does not need to be told what to repeat and what not—she has lived among men and affairs all her life."

"Tiens, you are becoming quite western yourself!" he said. "Arguing in this way with your husband! But Fani Hanim was of opinion that it would be better for us to stay?"

"Very definitely, from the point of view of our women; naturally for herself she would have liked us to be in Paris, within easy reach. And Orhan, I do not see why you should not take a post abroad later—it is these next few years that will be so critical. I think myself that the society of foreign capitals will be much more lenient to the wives of our diplomats now, when we are a new and young State, than they will be five years hence, so that we should use the present to educate ourselves in social matters."

Orhan got up from his chair to kiss her.

"Light of my Eyes, have you by any chance some Greek blood?" he asked—"for you are talking like an oracle!"

"No, but I have had a European friend," she said, returning his kiss.

The following morning Orhan told Kemal Pasha of his decision to refuse the Paris post and to stay in Turkey. Kemal turned his keen icy eyes onto him, from under his bushy eyebrows.

"Oglum, for myself I am delighted—I have no desire whatever to lose you. But is this really what you wish? I would not stand in your way."

"It is my wife's decision, Sir," said Orhan merrily.

"Féridé Hanim's?" Kemal said, his eyes and eyebrows now incredulous.

"Yes, Sir. She has become quite modern, practically American, and now directs the affairs of the family! This, I take it, has your approval?"

Kemal laughed loudly. "Orhan, my son, you are very impertinent. Is this the effect of your foreign visitors?"

"Partly, Sir, I think it is."

"And did Féridé Hanim vouchsafe to give you her reasons?"

"Yes, Sir. In the first place, she did not wish me to leave you during these next years," Orhan said, serious now. "She thinks the work will be tremendous, and flatters me by imagining that I could be of some small use."

"She has a very clear head," Kemal said, also no longer joking. "I shall be immensely glad to keep you by me. She has my gratitude. And in the second place?"

"She is concerned about the social education of the women here; she thinks that both more important and more urgent than an elegant diplomatic representation abroad, at the moment."

"And how are you to effect this?"

"*I* am not—she is to do that," Orhan said, smiling again. "I believe her idea is that she and a few other young women might form a sort of feminine corps d'élite here in Ankara, and by example and encouragement teach the wives of officials and deputies how to dress, how to behave in mixed gatherings—in effect, how to live as western women live. And she has the audacity to say, Sir, that though you may be able to teach the men, only women can educate women!"

Kemal's mouth smiled his peculiarly charming smile, but his eyebrows above his light eyes were as concentrated as Féridé's own.

"Really, she is formidable, Féridé Hanim! She is quite right. This task is more important than the other, and I fancy she is also right in thinking that in this particular affair she can do more for our country than I can." He spoke thoughtfully, and a sudden look of fatigue came over the whole man as he did so. "It is not an easy job, to turn a primitive oriental nation into a *twentieth* century one," he muttered. Then he seemed to give himself a shake, like a dog coming out of the water, and brisked up again.

"But with helpers like you, Oglum—and like her—it can be done. Now look, my son"—he pulled a file towards him as he spoke—"Here is this matter of the properties of the Tekkés in the Eastern Provinces which we must settle." And Master and man bent together over the desk, loaded with papers, and began to deal with the immediate problems confronting the new Turkey.

m.a.